GW01159472

Snowbound Horizons

Adeline Hart

Published by Adeline Hart, 2024.

SNOWBOUND HORIZONS

First edition. October 2, 2024.

Copyright © 2024 Adeline Hart.

ISBN: 979-8224037773

Written by Adeline Hart.

Chapter 1: A New Horizon

The mountain loomed above me, a titan dressed in white, its jagged peaks contrasting sharply with the brilliant blue sky. I could almost feel the pulse of the world beneath my feet, a rhythm that resonated with every beat of my heart. Cascade Mountain, with its slopes beckoning like a siren, whispered promises of transformation. I tucked a loose strand of hair behind my ear, my fingers brushing against the fabric of my jacket, the fabric soft yet cold, just like my resolve. This was it. This was my moment.

I took a deep breath, the air stinging my lungs, invigorating and pure, yet tinged with the scent of pine and frost. A sharp gust of wind swirled around me, sending a cascade of snowflakes swirling into a whirlpool of white. I shivered, both from the cold and the anticipation gnawing at my insides. Back home, the air had felt heavy with expectations and heartbreak; here, it was light, filled with promise, as if the mountain itself was inviting me to shed my past and embrace the exhilaration of the unknown.

The training lodge stood sturdy against the backdrop of the snowy expanse, a rustic structure with warm wooden beams and large windows framing the breathtaking view. Inside, the scent of freshly brewed coffee mingled with the crispness of winter, creating an inviting warmth. I stepped through the door, the warmth enveloping me like a familiar blanket. The chatter of fellow trainees buzzed in the air, a mixture of nervous laughter and enthusiastic chatter that ignited a flicker of excitement within me.

I spotted a group gathered around a large table, their faces glowing with youthful enthusiasm. They were all vibrant, alive with energy, and it struck me how different they were from the solemn faces I'd grown accustomed to back home. A sense of camaraderie surrounded them, a shared dream reflected in their eager eyes. I could feel my heart quicken as I took a step toward them, but then

I hesitated, suddenly aware of my own insecurities creeping in like unwelcome shadows.

"Hey, are you joining us?" A voice broke through my thoughts, bright and inviting. I turned to see a girl with tousled hair, her cheeks flushed from the cold, standing next to a tall guy with an infectious smile. He waved me over, the warmth in his demeanor making me feel less like an outsider and more like a part of something greater.

"Yeah, I—" My voice faltered, swallowed by the room's warmth and laughter. "I'm new here. Just started the training program." I flashed a tentative smile, hoping it looked more confident than I felt.

"Awesome! I'm Emma, and this is Ryan," she said, gesturing between them. "We're just going over the schedule for the week. You're going to love it here! The mountains are absolutely breathtaking." She looked out the window, her eyes shining with the thrill of possibility.

"I'm sure they are," I replied, allowing myself to be swept up in her enthusiasm. "I've never really skied before, though."

"Perfect! You're in the right place then. It's all about learning," Ryan chimed in, his voice smooth and encouraging. "You'll find it's like anything else—terrifying at first, but once you get the hang of it, it's pure joy. There's nothing like flying down a slope, the wind rushing past you. It's freedom."

I nodded, imagining the sensation of gliding through the snow, the adrenaline surging through my veins. The thought was intoxicating, stirring something deep inside me that had long been dormant. I felt a flicker of hope, something I hadn't allowed myself to feel in what seemed like ages. Perhaps I could be free again.

As we continued to chat, a spark of connection flickered between us, a small but significant thread woven into the fabric of my new life. They shared stories of their past ski experiences, moments filled with spills and triumphs, laughter echoing around the table. I listened, enraptured, the warmth of their camaraderie wrapping around me like a well-worn quilt. It felt almost surreal, like a scene from a movie where the protagonist discovers her place among a group of spirited adventurers.

Yet, despite the warmth blossoming in my chest, doubt crept in silently. What if I couldn't keep up? What if my clumsy attempts at skiing became fodder for their jokes? But as I glanced around, I noticed something in Emma's laughter—genuine, free, and unburdened. It resonated with my desire to belong, to shed the weight of my past, and to embrace this fresh start.

"Let's hit the slopes after lunch!" Ryan suggested, his eyes sparkling with excitement. "It's a great way to break the ice—and hopefully not break anything else," he added, eliciting a round of laughter that filled the lodge.

As the group erupted in playful banter, I felt the warmth of acceptance wrap around me. For the first time in a long time, I felt a flicker of hope igniting within me, a promise of new beginnings. Perhaps this mountain would not just be a backdrop to my journey, but a catalyst for the change I so desperately sought.

With my heart racing in anticipation, I realized that standing at the base of Cascade Mountain was more than just a geographical location; it was the beginning of a path leading to self-discovery, friendship, and the thrill of carving my own way through the unknown. In that moment, I took a deep breath, filling my lungs with the crisp air, ready to step into this new horizon, eager to embrace whatever awaited me beyond the slopes.

The sun crested the mountain, casting a golden glow over the snowy landscape, transforming the world into a glimmering wonderland. I stood at the edge of the slope, my heart pounding with a mix of excitement and dread. The swirling clouds of snow from earlier had settled into a tranquil blanket that begged to be disturbed. I could hear the distant sound of skis carving through the

powder, a melodic rhythm that pulled me closer, drawing me into the
fray.

As I strapped on my ski boots, the weight of my previous life felt
heavier than the gear I was struggling to adjust. The boots were tight,
biting into my ankles, yet each adjustment felt like a step further
away from my past. Emma and Ryan stood nearby, their laughter
ringing out like bells, mingling with the cool breeze. It was
infectious, washing over me like a wave, pulling me out of my own
thoughts and into the moment.

"Are you ready?" Emma called out, her voice bright against the
backdrop of the serene mountain. She looked like a vision, hair
pulled back and cheeks flushed from the cold, exuding an effortless
charm.

I took a deep breath, the cool air filling my lungs as I forced
a smile onto my face. "As ready as I'll ever be!" I replied, trying to
sound confident despite the knot of nerves twisting in my stomach.
I glanced down the slope, where the smooth expanse of white sloped
down like a promise of adventure. The idea of plunging down that
pristine surface was as terrifying as it was thrilling.

"Just remember, it's all about balance," Ryan chimed in, leaning
on his poles, his expression a mix of seriousness and mischief. "And
if you fall, just make sure to fall gracefully. Style points count for
something!"

The laughter that erupted from the group wrapped around me
like a warm embrace. It was the kind of laughter that echoed with the
shared understanding of facing fears, an unspoken pact to support
one another through the slips and slides of our newfound passion.

With a final flicker of hesitation, I pushed off, my skis gliding
forward, the thrill of movement rushing through me. The initial
descent was a chaotic whirlwind of flailing limbs and startled gasps,
my body unsure of what to do. I leaned into the slope, and suddenly,
the panic melted away as the rhythm of the mountain took hold. I

found myself moving, carving through the snow with a grace I didn't know I possessed.

The world around me blurred into a cascade of white and blue, the cold air rushing past my face, stinging but exhilarating. My laughter mingled with the wind, and I could feel a sense of liberation pulsing through me. Each turn became a dance, each twist a celebration of my newfound freedom. It was intoxicating, addictive, and I couldn't help but smile, the sheer joy of it washing over me like sunlight breaking through clouds.

But then, like a comet shooting across the sky, I lost my footing, my skis crossing in a way that sent me tumbling forward into the soft, welcoming embrace of the snow. The impact was jarring, yet the powder cushioned my fall, and I lay there for a moment, staring up at the brilliant blue sky above. Laughter erupted around me, and I could see Emma and Ryan skidding to a halt, their faces lit with delight.

"Nice landing!" Ryan called, a cheeky grin plastered on his face.

I couldn't help but chuckle as I pushed myself up, brushing the snow off my jacket, feeling a spark of camaraderie. "Well, I didn't expect to be a snow angel this early in the day," I quipped, my heart still racing from the thrill of the fall.

"Hey, it's all part of the experience," Emma said, her eyes dancing with amusement. "You just need to embrace the falls! They make the best stories."

With their encouragement echoing in my ears, I found my footing once more, ready to embrace whatever the mountain had in store for me. Each run brought new challenges, and though I stumbled more than I cared to admit, I also found moments of grace, each one filling me with a heady rush of accomplishment.

As the day wore on, the sun dipped lower in the sky, casting long shadows over the snow. With every run, I grew more confident, more alive, each moment pulling me further from the remnants of my old life. I was surrounded by laughter and light, a stark contrast to the muted tones of the days I had spent in my small town, where every glance seemed weighed down by unfulfilled expectations and the ache of memories.

Finally, as the sun began to sink behind the mountains, painting the sky in hues of pink and gold, I found myself at the lodge once more, a steaming cup of hot cocoa warming my hands. I sat outside on the deck, the air now crisp and cool against my cheeks. Emma and Ryan joined me, their breath mingling with the steam rising from our mugs, forming clouds that mirrored the snowflakes from earlier.

"I think you've got a natural talent for this," Emma said, her voice filled with sincerity. "It's like you were born to be on the slopes."

"Maybe I was just born to fall spectacularly," I replied, laughing as I took a sip of the rich chocolate, feeling the warmth spread through me. It was sweet and comforting, a perfect ending to an exhilarating day.

"Every great skier has to learn how to fall," Ryan added with a wink. "It's how you get back up that counts. Just look at you!"

The warmth of their friendship enveloped me, easing the lingering shadows of doubt that had clung to my heart. I realized that this place, these people, had already begun to shape me into something new. I felt lighter, freer, as though the mountain had helped me shed the layers of my old self, exposing a core that was eager to embrace this new horizon.

With the sun setting behind the peaks, casting long shadows over the snow, I watched the sky change colors, my heart swelling with a sense of belonging that I had long thought was lost. I was here, I was present, and for the first time in a long time, I felt like I could truly start anew.

The sun dipped lower, casting the mountains in a soft amber glow that shimmered like the lingering warmth of a bonfire. I sat at a rustic wooden table on the lodge's deck, surrounded by the melodic chatter of fellow trainees, all animated and giddy from a day filled with exhilarating chaos. Each person was a bright thread in the vibrant tapestry of this snowy enclave, woven together by laughter, shared triumphs, and the occasional tumble.

Emma leaned over the table, her cheeks still pink from the cold, excitement radiating from her. "Tomorrow, we'll start early! The fresh powder is supposed to be incredible!" Her eyes sparkled with the thrill of what lay ahead, and I couldn't help but catch her enthusiasm, the warmth of her spirit igniting a flicker of my own.

"I can't believe I actually managed to ski without completely wiping out!" I said, half-laughing, half-incredulous. The memory of my earlier runs flashed through my mind—some graceful, some not so much. But the most memorable moments were the ones shared with them, the laughter that echoed through the cold, creating a warmth that chased away the chills of my past.

Ryan raised his mug in a mock toast. "To surviving the slopes and to the inevitable falls that will only make our stories better!"

"Cheers!" we all echoed, clinking our mugs together, a small ritual that felt significant, marking the camaraderie we were building amidst the snow and sun. As I sipped the cocoa, the rich flavor enveloped me, sweet and warm, grounding me in this new reality that was slowly unfurling.

The night settled around us, blanketing the mountains in a serene quietude. The stars appeared one by one, piercing the darkening sky like scattered diamonds, each twinkling light a reminder of the vastness of possibility that stretched before me. I leaned back in my chair, letting my gaze drift upward, allowing the enormity of the universe to sink in. Here, I was just one small soul in a big, beautiful world, a world I was eager to explore.

As the evening wound down, we shared stories—some humorous, some heartfelt. Emma recounted her first ski trip as a child, how she had donned oversized gear that made her look like a marshmallow on legs, while Ryan shared tales of his wild adventures with friends on the slopes, moments filled with mischief and laughter that still brought a blush to his cheeks. Each story layered into the shared experience, binding us tighter with every chuckle and gasp of disbelief.

The warmth of the lodge and the company around me infused a sense of hope, an inkling that I might finally be stitching together the frayed edges of my heart. I realized how much I longed for this—connection, laughter, adventure—things I had put on hold for too long, stifled by fear and sorrow.

The next morning dawned bright and clear, the air sharp and invigorating as I pulled on my gear, my heart fluttering with a mix of excitement and nerves. Today was about more than just skiing; it felt like a leap into the unknown, a commitment to embracing whatever this new chapter had to offer.

We gathered at the foot of the slope, our collective energy palpable as we awaited the day's challenges. Emma bounded ahead, her eagerness contagious, while Ryan offered tips and encouragement that settled over us like a blanket of comfort. I felt anchored in this newfound kinship, buoyed by their belief in me.

"Today, we conquer the blue runs!" Ryan declared, his voice booming with enthusiasm.

"Blue runs?" I echoed, glancing at the steepness of the slope, my stomach dropping. "What happened to taking it easy?"

"Nothing ventured, nothing gained!" Emma replied, her grin wide and inviting. "Besides, you've already proven you can handle yourself. You'll be great!"

So, with a deep breath, I followed them up the mountain, the ascent stirring a sense of determination within me. As we reached the crest, I marveled at the breathtaking vista that spread before us—an endless expanse of snow-capped peaks bathed in sunlight, a postcard-perfect scene that felt like a dream.

"Are you ready?" Emma asked, her eyes sparkling with challenge. I looked down the slope, feeling a rush of adrenaline. This was the moment I had been waiting for—a chance to embrace the thrill, to let go of the past and carve out my future. "Ready or not, here I come!" I shouted, pushing off and gliding down the slope, the wind whipping through my hair, my heart racing as I maneuvered through the turns.

For the first time, I felt an exhilarating sense of freedom, each curve and twist exhilarating, like I was dancing with the mountain itself. I carved through the snow, feeling alive in a way I hadn't in what felt like eons. I could hear the laughter of my friends trailing behind me, their cheers of encouragement spurring me on.

But then, as I turned sharply to avoid a small mound of snow, my skis tangled, and I went tumbling down, landing in a heap, laughter erupting from my lips even as the cold enveloped me.

"Beautiful dismount!" Ryan called, his voice echoing from a distance as he skied to my side, concern etched in his features.

"Just practicing my snow angel technique," I grinned, brushing the powder off my cheeks, feeling exhilarated by the thrill of the fall. I had landed softly, and that was all that mattered.

With their support and laughter echoing in my ears, I found my footing again, rising like a phoenix from the snow, invigorated by every fall, every challenge. We continued down the mountain, the day unfolding with laughter and camaraderie, a tapestry woven of shared experiences and blossoming friendships.

As the sun began to set, casting a warm golden light over the peaks, I felt a profound sense of gratitude wash over me. This journey was more than just about learning to ski; it was about reclaiming a part of myself I thought I had lost forever. Each run was a testament to my resilience, each fall a reminder that even in moments of chaos, I could rise again.

Later that night, as we sat around the fire, the crackling flames casting flickering shadows on the walls, I realized that I had found more than just a new skill; I had discovered a sense of belonging. The past felt lighter, the future brighter, and in that moment, surrounded by laughter and warmth, I embraced the horizon that lay ahead, ready to carve my own path, one exhilarating run at a time.

Chapter 2: The Winter Warriors

The crisp air enveloped me like an icy embrace, the kind that snaps you awake and demands your attention. Each morning, the world unfurled beneath a thin layer of frost, delicate and shimmering under the first light of dawn. I felt as if I had stepped into a snow globe, the kind you'd shake to watch the flakes dance and twirl, settling like whispers on the ground. Here in Aspen, where the air was rich with the scent of pine and adventure, I was determined to prove myself in this grueling training program, each day a test of my resolve, my limits, and the very fabric of who I was.

The ritual began before the sun peeked over the jagged mountains. I could hear the murmurs of my fellow trainees echoing through the early morning hush, our breath visible in the frosty air, mingling with the promise of the day. The crunch of snow beneath our boots echoed like a metronome, setting the rhythm for our daily battles. We pushed each other, driven by an unspoken pact to conquer the slopes that loomed above us, their icy faces daring us to stumble and fall. Each morning was a reminder that while the beauty of the mountains was undeniable, the path to mastering them was fraught with challenges that demanded every ounce of grit I possessed.

Jessa was my anchor in this chaos. Her laughter rang out like a beacon, cutting through the tension that often hung in the air. We would share knowing glances as we lined up for drills, the corners of our mouths lifting in unison, ready to tackle whatever absurdity was thrown our way. With her wild curls bouncing in rhythm to her every step, she radiated an infectious energy that had a way of lighting up even the darkest, coldest mornings. I often found myself marveling at her ability to find joy in the simplest things—a fleeting snowflake caught on her glove, the way the sun seemed to ignite the mountain peaks, or the satisfying crunch of snow underfoot as we raced down the slopes.

Then there was Theo. The enigmatic ski instructor whose presence felt electric. With an effortless grace, he glided through the snow, his movements smooth and fluid, as if he were part of the mountain itself. The first time I watched him carve through the powder, I was struck by a blend of admiration and something more—a fluttering in my chest that made it hard to focus on the instructions he shouted over the wind. He had this way of making you feel both terrified and exhilarated, as if he saw the potential hidden beneath my uncertainty and was determined to coax it out into the light. Each time he caught my gaze, a spark ignited between us, something unspoken that hung in the air like the promise of an impending storm.

Every fall on the slope was a lesson etched into my bones. I learned to embrace the cold bite of disappointment, to rise again with a fierce determination. The first time I tumbled into a bank of powder, the snow enveloped me, cold and soft, cradling my body in a way that felt both humiliating and oddly comforting. As I lay there, breathless and laughing, Jessa's voice echoed nearby, her encouragement like a warm blanket against the chill. "Get up, warrior!" she'd holler, and I would scramble to my feet, a newfound resilience coursing through my veins.

As days turned into weeks, I began to understand that this was more than a training program. It was a crucible, forging bonds of camaraderie that would last long after the last ski run was completed. Our little group—Jessa, Theo, and a few others—found solace in shared moments of triumph and defeat. We would gather around the fire at the lodge after a long day, sipping hot cocoa and recounting our most ridiculous falls with exaggerated gestures, each retelling drawing us closer. Laughter echoed off the wooden beams, drowning out the cold that nipped at the windows, creating an oasis of warmth in our shared experiences.

Evenings in Aspen held their own magic. The sunset painted the sky in hues of orange and pink, the mountains silhouetted against the fading light like ancient sentinels watching over us. I often found myself gazing out at the view, contemplating how far I had come from the timid girl who had first arrived, overwhelmed by the daunting slopes and the weight of my own insecurities. With every run, I was shedding layers of doubt, each carve in the snow a declaration of my growing strength. I could feel the shift within me, a gradual awakening of the girl I had forgotten existed.

The physical exhaustion from the day's training melted away in the warmth of our conversations, the flickering fire casting playful shadows that danced across our faces. Theo would sometimes share snippets of his life—stories from his adventures across the globe, tales that shimmered with possibility and a hint of danger. His words painted vivid images in my mind, each one enticing me to step beyond my comfort zone. I could see the way Jessa would hang on his every word, her eyes sparkling with wonder, and it sparked something in me. What was it about him that made even the most mundane stories feel extraordinary?

As the weeks wore on and the snow continued to fall, I began to realize that my heart was becoming entangled in this place, in the thrill of the slopes, in the warmth of my newfound friends, and in the uncharted territory of my own feelings. I was no longer just a girl trying to conquer the mountains; I was a warrior in the making, carving out my path on these frosted trails, learning that true strength comes not just from the victories but from the falls and the unwavering will to rise again.

Each morning, the sun broke through the mountains with a slow, almost reluctant grace, casting long shadows across the training grounds. The frost that had once clung so desperately to the trees now shimmered like diamonds in the soft light, glistening with the promise of another day filled with challenges. The air was electric, charged with potential and the heady scent of pine that filled my lungs and wrapped around my heart like a comforting embrace. I could feel it—the thrill of what lay ahead, a mix of anticipation and fear that kept my adrenaline pumping as I laced up my boots, ready to face whatever awaited me on the slopes.

As I stood at the edge of the training area, I took a moment to glance around at my fellow warriors. Jessa was perched on a nearby rail, her bright red ski jacket popping against the pristine white of the snow. She was animatedly recounting her latest misadventure on the slopes, her hands gesturing wildly as she punctuated her story with bursts of laughter. Even the grizzled veterans training with us couldn't help but crack a smile at her enthusiasm. There was something about her spirit that lit a fire in all of us, a reminder that this journey, as brutal as it was, could also be filled with joy.

Theo, on the other hand, stood a little apart from the group, his eyes scanning the mountain as if he could see every hidden hazard before it revealed itself. I caught sight of him, the way the sun highlighted the angles of his face, transforming him into a living silhouette against the backdrop of white and blue. His smile, when it appeared, was like the sunrise—warm, inviting, and full of promise. Whenever he looked my way, I felt a jolt of warmth spread through me, igniting an eager flutter deep in my stomach that I had long since buried beneath layers of self-doubt.

Today's drill was daunting, a series of timed runs that would test our speed, precision, and perhaps most importantly, our ability to handle the unexpected. As I positioned myself at the starting line, my heart pounded in rhythm with the ticking seconds. I glanced at Jessa, who shot me an encouraging thumbs-up, her eyes bright with mischief. We exchanged a knowing glance, a silent pact that whatever happened out there, we would face it together.

With a sudden rush, I pushed off, the snow exploding beneath my skis. The world around me transformed into a blur of white and blue as I navigated the slopes. Each turn was a dance with gravity, every bump a challenge to my balance. I could feel the chill of the air slicing against my cheeks, a refreshing reminder that I was alive and racing against the day. It was exhilarating, a freedom I hadn't experienced in years, and I thrived on it, channeling every ounce of energy into each movement.

But then came the first twist of fate. Just as I approached a steep incline, my ski caught an edge, and I was thrown off balance. Time slowed as I felt myself tumble, the world flipping upside down. In those heart-stopping moments, I couldn't help but let out a breathless laugh, a sound that mingled with the rush of wind as I crashed into the soft powder below. For a second, I lay there, limbs sprawled, staring up at the wide expanse of sky above. The snow encased me, cool and forgiving, and as I gathered my bearings, I felt a surge of determination rise within me.

Jessa's laughter echoed nearby as she skied down, her graceful form gliding effortlessly over the powder. "You okay?" she called out, her voice like a lifeline. I nodded, a grin stretching across my face as I pushed myself up. "You know me, just testing the depth of the snow!" I shouted back, feeling the thrill of being part of something bigger, a team that thrived on the same reckless spirit.

As we continued through the drills, the rhythm of our movements became almost instinctual, a dance that flowed with the landscape. The camaraderie grew stronger, our shared falls and victories forging bonds that felt unbreakable. Between runs, Theo would call out tips, his voice calm and steady, guiding us through our mistakes with a patience that inspired confidence. He had an uncanny ability to identify our weaknesses and challenge us to push past them, igniting a spark in each of us that made every fall feel like a step closer to mastery.

In one particularly exhilarating moment, I felt emboldened by his encouragement. I decided to take a more difficult route, a narrow path that wound through a grove of trees, its allure both thrilling and intimidating. My heart raced as I navigated the twists and turns, the branches reaching out like arms eager to catch me if I faltered. Each successful turn felt like a small victory, and with each heartbeat, I could feel a new layer of confidence emerging. When I reached the bottom, breathless and flushed with exhilaration, I glanced back up the slope, where Theo stood watching, a proud smile gracing his lips. In that instant, I felt a connection beyond the training—a shared understanding of risk and reward, the beauty of pushing boundaries.

As the day drew to a close, we regrouped at the lodge, our bodies exhausted yet buoyed by the thrill of accomplishment. The fire crackled in the hearth, casting a warm glow that chased away the chill of the day. Jessa and I claimed our usual spot by the fire, our cheeks flushed, recounting our most memorable falls with exaggerated gestures that had the others in stitches. Laughter filled the air, a joyous chorus that felt like home.

But even amidst the laughter, I could feel Theo's gaze lingering on me. There was something magnetic about the way he watched, as if he were waiting for me to say something, to bridge the gap between us. The thought sent a thrill down my spine, a warmth spreading through my chest that I couldn't ignore. I wondered if he felt the same spark, the electric energy that crackled when our eyes met, the unspoken words hanging in the air between us.

As the evening wore on, I couldn't shake the feeling that this was more than just a training program. It was a journey of self-discovery, a chance to uncover the pieces of myself that had been buried beneath fear and doubt for far too long. In the embrace of the mountains, surrounded by friends who believed in me, I was beginning to realize that I was not just a participant in this adventure—I was becoming a warrior, ready to conquer whatever challenges lay ahead.

The following days unfolded like a well-choreographed ballet of snow and sweat, the routines becoming more demanding as we acclimated to the challenges of the slopes. Each dawn, the air crackled with the promise of new experiences, the ground beneath my skis a canvas waiting to be painted with my progress and failures. I relished the taste of adrenaline on my tongue as I skied down runs that once seemed impossibly steep, the thrill coursing through me like electricity. It was in these moments that I felt most alive, every muscle engaged in a symphony of movement that defied gravity and logic.

Jessa became my confidante, the sister I never had. After training sessions, we often found ourselves retreating to the lodge's common area, a warm sanctuary adorned with rustic wooden beams and the sweet scent of cinnamon wafting from the kitchen. The walls were lined with photographs of skiers from years past, their smiles frozen in time as they reveled in their victories. We would settle into a plush sofa, the crackling fire casting flickering shadows around us, and talk for hours, sharing our dreams and fears, our hopes for the future intertwined with laughter that echoed through the room.

One evening, as we huddled under a shared blanket, the world outside blanketed in soft white, Jessa's expression shifted from mirth to contemplation. "You know," she said, her eyes glinting with curiosity, "I've never seen you look at anything the way you look at Theo."

I felt a rush of warmth creep up my cheeks. "What do you mean?" I replied, feigning innocence, though the flutter in my stomach betrayed me.

"Oh, please! The way your eyes light up when he walks by, like you've seen a unicorn. It's adorable," she teased, nudging me playfully.

I rolled my eyes but couldn't suppress a smile. "He's just... inspiring, you know? He challenges me to push past my limits." My voice trailed off, the truth of my feelings hanging between us like a fragile thread.

Jessa laughed softly. "Inspiring? Maybe. But you're also totally smitten."

Before I could retort, the door swung open, and the chill from outside rushed in, carrying Theo with it. He was clad in his signature black ski gear, a stark contrast to the bright atmosphere of the lodge. As he shook off the snow from his hair, I felt the warmth in the room spike, the collective breath of our small group hitching in a mix of excitement and nervous energy.

"Ready for another round of training tomorrow?" he asked, his voice smooth and deep, cutting through the haze of the cozy room. I nodded, my heart racing as I met his gaze, the flicker of something unspoken lingering in the air.

Later that night, I lay in my bunk, the sounds of laughter and chatter from the lodge filtering through the walls. I stared at the ceiling, replaying the day's events in my mind, savoring the moments of connection—the shared laughter with Jessa, the thrill of racing down the slopes, and the unguarded glances with Theo. I thought of how he had pushed me to tackle my fears, coaxing me to take on steeper hills and sharper turns. Each run down the mountain felt like a metaphor for my life, a reminder that I was capable of more than I had ever believed.

But beneath the exhilaration lay a gnawing doubt. What if this journey was only a temporary escape from the realities I had left behind? The question hung heavy in my mind, a shadow over the growing light in my heart.

As the next day dawned, I stepped outside into the crisp air, the world transformed into a winter wonderland, shimmering beneath a blanket of fresh snow. The morning light cast a golden hue over everything, illuminating the icy landscape in a breathtaking display. I could feel the energy buzzing around me as my fellow trainees gathered, their enthusiasm palpable.

Theo led us through warm-up exercises, his voice a steady anchor amidst the chaos. "Today, we're focusing on advanced techniques," he announced, a spark of excitement in his eyes. "I want you to find your flow on the slopes, to let go of your fears and embrace the thrill of the ride."

His words resonated deep within me, igniting a flame of determination. As we began our drills, the world around me faded, and all that existed was the rhythm of my breath, the sound of skis slicing through snow, and the exhilarating rush of adrenaline. I felt the weight of my doubts begin to lift, replaced by an exhilarating sense of freedom.

After several exhilarating runs, we broke for lunch, gathering outside the lodge where the air was filled with the rich aroma of freshly prepared chili. We sat in a circle, exchanging stories and laughter, the camaraderie growing deeper with each shared moment. It felt like a family—an eclectic mix of personalities bound together by our love for the mountains and the thrill of the challenge.

As the sun dipped lower in the sky, casting long shadows over the slopes, Theo called for everyone's attention. "Tonight, we're having a small celebration," he announced, his smile infectious. "You've all pushed yourselves harder than I could have imagined. We'll have a little bonfire outside, hot chocolate, and a chance to unwind together."

Cheers erupted around us, a chorus of excitement and gratitude. The thought of gathering around a crackling fire, sharing stories and laughter, filled me with warmth. As the sun set, painting the sky in deep purples and fiery oranges, I felt a sense of belonging wash over me. It was a feeling I had longed for, a reassurance that I was not just surviving but truly living.

As night fell, we settled around the bonfire, the flames dancing in the cool evening air. Jessa and I nestled close, the warmth of the fire wrapping around us like a blanket. The night was alive with chatter, the sound of laughter mingling with the crackle of wood burning. Theo moved gracefully through the group, his presence magnetic, and as he shared stories of his own adventures, I felt my heart flutter with every glance our way.

"Tell us about the time you skied off the edge of a cliff!" Jessa called out, her eyes sparkling with mischief.

The laughter that erupted was infectious, and I felt my spirits soar as Theo recounted the tale, weaving it with humor and self-deprecation. Each story revealed more of his character, layers peeling away like the bark of the trees surrounding us. He was passionate, daring, and undeniably charming, and the way he interacted with the group made me feel as though we were all part of something extraordinary.

As the fire crackled and the stars twinkled overhead, I caught Theo's gaze. In that fleeting moment, everything felt right—like we were suspended in time, wrapped in the warmth of shared dreams and newfound friendships. There was an understanding between us, a connection that whispered promises of adventure and possibility.

The night wore on, filled with laughter, camaraderie, and the sweet taste of hot chocolate. With each sip, I felt more at home, more alive. I knew then that this training program had become so much more than a mere challenge; it was a transformative journey that would redefine my perception of strength, friendship, and love. I was no longer just a girl on a mountain; I was a warrior ready to embrace the unknown, to carve my path through the snow, and to forge bonds that would withstand the test of time.

In the heart of winter, surrounded by kindred spirits and the vast, beautiful world, I felt a sense of belonging that was both exhilarating and terrifying—a reminder that sometimes, in the pursuit of adventure, we uncover the very essence of who we are meant to be.

Chapter 3: The Slippery Slope of Attraction

The crisp mountain air wrapped around me like a delicate scarf, each breath filling my lungs with the invigorating scent of pine and freshly fallen snow. As I stood at the edge of the slope, the world unfurled beneath me, a breathtaking panorama of undulating white hills and shimmering trees, all kissed by the soft glow of a waning afternoon sun. The distant laughter of fellow skiers drifted through the stillness, a symphony of joy and adventure that somehow amplified my sense of isolation. It was a Saturday like no other, the kind that promised exhilarating runs and the thrill of pushing limits. Yet, on this day, my heart was tethered to thoughts that had little to do with the mountains.

Theo arrived with a confident stride, his silhouette outlined against the brilliant blue sky. There was an ease about him, a natural charisma that pulled attention like gravity. He grinned, a flash of warmth that was disarmingly infectious. My stomach fluttered at the sight of him, the way his eyes sparkled with mischief as he surveyed the slope before us. I had spent the last few weeks trying to brush off my attraction, convinced it was a mere distraction in this adrenaline-soaked landscape. But today, as he approached, I felt my resolve wobble like a novice on a snowboard.

"Ready to master the snowplow?" he teased, a glint of challenge dancing in his gaze. His voice was rich and smooth, and I found myself nodding, suddenly unsure of whether I was prepared for the lesson or for the man himself. The warmth of his presence enveloped me, the subtle hint of cedar and something uniquely him igniting a flutter of anticipation.

As we began our session, I watched him demonstrate the technique, his body fluidly navigating the incline with grace that seemed almost otherworldly. Each movement was precise, intentional, and I couldn't help but admire how effortlessly he carved through the snow, leaving a trail behind him that was as neat and orderly as his personality appeared to be. There was a magnetic pull to him, a beckoning that was hard to resist. I inhaled deeply, the cold air biting at my cheeks as I tried to focus on the mechanics of the snowplow turn, but my thoughts kept drifting back to Theo, lingering on the way he held himself, exuding both confidence and kindness.

My first attempt was, predictably, a mess. I leaned too far forward, the snow beneath me became a slippery trap, and before I knew it, I was tumbling unceremoniously into a soft mound. Laughter erupted around me, both from fellow skiers and from Theo, whose chuckles rang out like a warm melody amidst the crisp air. I could feel the heat rising in my cheeks as I brushed the snow from my pants, the embarrassment settling deep in my chest. But there was something about Theo's laughter that made the fall less painful, the sting of humiliation softened by the way he genuinely seemed to enjoy my clumsiness.

"Don't worry! It happens to everyone," he said, his voice a gentle balm against my frustration. He extended a hand, strong and reassuring, pulling me back to my feet. The moment our hands touched, an electric current surged through me, making my heart race as if it were training for a marathon. I had never felt such an immediate connection, a spark that ignited something deep within me, something I had thought extinguished after my last heartbreak.

As we continued the lesson, I found myself more attuned to him than to the technique. He explained the mechanics with patience, his brow slightly furrowed in concentration, as if he were sharing a sacred secret. I listened intently, hanging onto every word, even as the unspoken tension between us crackled like the snow underfoot. When he complimented my progress, saying, "You're getting better with every try," I felt a rush of warmth, a blend of pride and something softer that made me want to lean in closer. The urge was almost overwhelming, yet the specter of vulnerability loomed over me like a winter storm.

With each successive attempt, I felt the barriers I had so carefully constructed start to crack. The fear of falling—both literally and emotionally—was daunting, a dark shadow looming over my heart. I had spent so long nursing my wounds, bandaging them with the softest of dreams and the quietest of fears, but now, with every turn I perfected, I could feel my heart thawing. The slopes, once unforgiving and daunting, began to feel like a canvas for new beginnings, a place where I could rewrite my story.

The final run of the day arrived, and I stood at the precipice, my heart thumping with both excitement and trepidation. Theo positioned himself beside me, his presence a steadying force as we prepared to descend. "You've got this," he said, his voice low and sincere, and I could see the genuine belief in his eyes. It ignited a flicker of courage within me, urging me to take the leap, not just down the slope but into the uncharted territory of my own heart.

I pushed off, the rush of cold air enveloping me as I glided down the slope, feeling the freedom of the descent. For a moment, it was just me and the mountain, the world falling away, and all that existed was the rhythm of my breath and the exhilarating thrill of movement. But then, as I turned to glance back at Theo, that invisible tether between us pulled tighter, binding us in a moment that felt both fleeting and eternal. In that instant, I knew that the journey ahead would not just be about mastering the snowplow but about navigating the slippery slope of attraction that had taken root in my heart, daring me to embrace both the risks and the rewards of falling in love again.

The chill in the air was gradually giving way to the warmth of the setting sun, casting a golden hue across the snow, turning it into a canvas of dazzling diamonds. Each flake seemed to sparkle with promise, reflecting the vibrant energy of the moment. I steadied myself, heart pounding, as I made my way down the slope for what felt like the hundredth time that day. It was absurd how such a simple act—gliding through powdery snow—could evoke such a tempest of feelings. Each push off the snow, every awkward turn, held the weight of my budding attraction to Theo, a magnetic force that had begun to tether my heart to his.

As we took a break on the side of the slope, I caught a glimpse of him in profile. He was brushing the snow from his goggles, the late afternoon sun catching his tousled hair, making it shimmer like spun gold. In that moment, the world around me blurred, fading into a wash of white and blue, leaving only the vivid image of him in focus. I imagined what it would be like to reach out, to tuck a wayward strand behind his ear, to feel the warmth of his skin against my fingers. The thought was both exhilarating and terrifying, a kaleidoscope of emotions swirling inside me.

"Hey," he called out, breaking my reverie, "you okay?" His brow furrowed slightly, a mix of concern and curiosity dancing in his eyes. I nodded, a smile tugging at my lips, yet inside, I wrestled with the growing tension between us. Did he sense it too, or was it merely my overactive imagination, painting our interactions with hues of longing and desire? "I've just been thinking about how far you've come today," he continued, his voice brightening the chilly air. "You're a natural."

His words washed over me like warm cocoa on a frigid day, soothing yet stirring something deep within. It was more than just flattery; it was an acknowledgment of my effort, of my determination to break free from the shackles of self-doubt that had held me captive for too long. I had come to this mountain seeking adventure and escape, but I hadn't anticipated the exhilarating rush of connection with someone who seemed to see right through the walls I had built.

"Thanks," I replied, a teasing lilt creeping into my voice. "I'd like to think that falling over counts as practice." I gestured dramatically to the snowbank where I had unceremoniously landed a few runs prior, making him laugh. The sound echoed like music against the tranquil backdrop, pulling at the edges of my heart.

"True, but you know what they say: every great skier has a history of epic falls." He shot me a conspiratorial grin, and I felt the world shift, tilt slightly on its axis, as if the universe conspired to make this moment linger just a bit longer. The laughter faded, but the lingering warmth between us was palpable, thick enough to slice with a knife.

With the sun inching lower, casting elongated shadows over the slopes, Theo suggested we tackle one last run together. A part of me buzzed with excitement, while another part quaked with apprehension. I couldn't help but wonder what lay at the end of this descent. Would it be a swift glide down, exhilarating and freeing, or a spiraling plunge into uncharted emotional territory?

We positioned ourselves at the starting line, side by side, our breaths mingling in the cold air. I felt his shoulder brush against mine, a gentle reminder of his presence, and my heart raced anew. I could hear the whispers of the mountain around us, the crunch of snow under skis, the soft chatter of other skiers fading into the background. In that moment, it was just the two of us, suspended in a bubble of shared anticipation.

"On three?" he suggested, a playful glint in his eye. I nodded, forcing myself to breathe steadily. "One... two... three!"

We pushed off simultaneously, carving our way down the slope, the exhilaration surging through my veins like wildfire. The wind whipped against my face, stinging and refreshing, while the thrill of speed pulled a laugh from my lips. I could hear Theo's laughter mingling with mine, an infectious sound that fueled my own joy, echoing as we raced side by side.

As the slope steepened, I focused on maintaining my balance, letting instinct guide my movements. The world around me transformed into a blur of white, punctuated by patches of evergreen and the distant outline of the lodge nestled at the base of the mountain. I felt a surge of confidence as I navigated a particularly tricky turn, a sudden burst of elation coursing through me as I found my rhythm.

And then, just like that, I caught a glimpse of him out of the corner of my eye. Theo was right beside me, leaning into the turn with a grace that took my breath away. There was an effortless elegance in the way he skied, each movement fluid and confident, as if he was born to glide over the snow. It struck me then—this wasn't just about skiing; it was about connection, a palpable bond that intertwined our fates on this mountain.

As we approached the final stretch, I made the reckless decision to pick up speed, propelled by an intoxicating mix of adrenaline and something deeper—a desire to impress him. But as I swerved around a bend, I lost my footing, teetering dangerously close to the edge of control. Panic surged through me, but before I could fully comprehend what was happening, Theo was there, reaching out, his hand wrapping around my wrist with a firm grip that pulled me back from the brink.

"Whoa there!" His voice was a blend of concern and exhilaration, a cocktail that sent shivers down my spine. He steadied me, our eyes locking in that electrifying moment, the world around us fading into a stillness that made everything else seem trivial. Time hung suspended as I searched his gaze, seeing not just the thrill of the sport but a glimmer of something more—an invitation to explore the depths of this connection, to venture beyond the snow and into the landscape of our hearts.

"Thanks," I managed to breathe, my heart racing not just from the near mishap but from the raw intensity of the moment. We glided to a stop at the base of the slope, the buzz of the world flooding back in, yet I felt like we were suspended in our own universe, marked by that exhilarating brush of vulnerability. With each heartbeat, I sensed the weight of the unsaid, the uncharted path we stood upon—a path filled with promise, potential, and the enticing thrill of attraction that left me breathless.

The day unfolded like a pristine sheet of snow, unmarred and untouched, as I caught my breath from our near mishap at the bottom of the slope. The chill in the air had shifted to a gentle embrace, the sun now hanging low in the sky, casting long shadows that danced on the glistening surface. I felt a strange sense of euphoria swirling within me, a blend of adrenaline and something softer, something more profound that began to unravel my tightly held barriers. Theo stood beside me, still holding my wrist lightly, his eyes sparkling with a mixture of concern and unspoken curiosity.

As we both settled down, I couldn't shake the sensation of his warmth lingering on my skin, as if he had left a piece of himself behind. It was a moment suspended in time, a delicate balance between exhilaration and uncertainty, where the mountain seemed to fade away, leaving only us—a fleeting glimpse into what might be. I watched him shake the snow from his jacket, the subtle movements accentuating the strength in his arms, a reminder that here, in this majestic wilderness, there existed a profound vulnerability beneath the surface of our bravado.

"So, what's next?" Theo asked, a casual yet inviting tone threading through his words. I could see the flicker of excitement in his eyes, a glimmer that hinted at shared possibilities. My mind raced with thoughts that spun like the flurries of snow swirling around us. Should I play it cool? Dive deeper into the abyss of attraction? My heart whispered for the latter, urging me to embrace the moment rather than retreat into the safety of my doubts.

"Why don't we hit that hill over there?" I gestured toward a slightly steeper slope that loomed nearby, its pristine surface beckoning us like a siren's call. I could sense a hint of trepidation behind his confident facade, but he simply nodded, that familiar grin returning, igniting the warmth that had taken residence in my chest.

With every turn we took, I felt the world around us transforming—each twist and glide pulling us closer, the snow becoming a backdrop for the unspoken words hanging between us. We navigated the hill with a rhythm that felt almost choreographed, a dance of sorts that unraveled any remnants of self-doubt I had clung to. I let the snow beneath me fade into the background and focused instead on the connection blossoming in the open air.

As we reached the base, laughter erupted between us, a bright sound that rang out against the starkness of the mountain. "Okay, I'll admit it," I said, catching my breath, "I think I'm starting to enjoy this." The thrill of speed and the fluttering of my heart wove together like threads in a tapestry, crafting something new and beautiful.

"I knew you would," Theo replied, a teasing lilt in his voice that made me want to challenge him further. "It's like a drug, isn't it? The rush, the freedom, the chance to escape reality for a little while?"

I paused, the weight of his words sinking in deeper than I expected. Escape. The word resonated with me in ways I hadn't anticipated. It echoed the reason I had come to this mountain in the first place, seeking solace from a past riddled with heartbreak and disappointment. But now, as I stood here, sharing laughter and exhilaration with Theo, I realized that this escape was less about running away and more about finding myself—my passions, my joys, my courage to face vulnerability head-on.

"Yeah," I finally admitted, the corners of my mouth lifting in a genuine smile. "It's exhilarating, but I think you might be the best part." His gaze met mine, and for a brief moment, the world around us fell away again, the distance between our hearts collapsing under the weight of that connection.

The sun began its descent, casting a warm glow that melted the edges of the day, and with it came a bittersweet realization that our time together was limited. The thought sent a jolt through me, an urgent pang of desire to prolong this moment, to explore whatever spark had ignited between us. "You know," I started hesitantly, "I've been thinking that maybe we should celebrate this progress with something a little more... personal?"

Theo raised an eyebrow, intrigued. "Personal, huh? I'm intrigued."

A bold rush filled me, mixing with the fresh mountain air. "How about hot chocolate at the lodge? It's a little cliché, but... it sounds perfect right now." My voice wavered slightly, the request balancing on the edge of anticipation and fear. Would he see it as just another friendly gesture, or would he recognize the undercurrents of something more?

"Hot chocolate sounds great," he replied, a glimmer of understanding in his eyes, "but only if you promise to indulge in marshmallows."

"Deal," I laughed, the sound buoyant as we began our descent toward the lodge, our skis cutting through the snow with newfound ease. As we glided side by side, I felt a renewed sense of possibility in the air, an intoxicating mix of hope and nervousness that thrummed beneath the surface.

The lodge came into view, its rustic charm exuding warmth against the cold backdrop of the mountains. Wooden beams framed the entrance, adorned with twinkling lights that winked at us like stars captured in the embrace of the building. The scent of pine and cinnamon wafted from within, curling around us and drawing us closer to the inviting glow of the fireplace just inside.

Stepping inside, I was enveloped by a wave of warmth, the chatter of fellow skiers creating a lively backdrop to our budding intimacy. We settled at a cozy corner table, the flickering flames casting a soft glow across Theo's features, illuminating the playful glint in his eyes.

As we sipped our steaming mugs, I couldn't help but relish the sense of ease that washed over us. Conversations flowed easily, filled with laughter and teasing banter that felt both natural and thrilling. I watched him as he spoke, the way his hands animated his words, the way his laughter seemed to light up the room around us. I felt seen, not just as a skier but as someone capable of making genuine connections.

"Do you believe in fate?" he asked suddenly, leaning in slightly, the question catching me off guard.

"Fate?" I repeated, a playful smile forming on my lips. "Isn't that just a romantic notion to comfort the indecisive?"

He laughed, shaking his head. "Maybe, but what if it is real? What if this moment—us here, now—is part of something bigger?"

His gaze held mine, intense and searching, and I felt a shiver run down my spine at the weight of his words. There was an undeniable chemistry sparking between us, a connection that felt fated in its own right, and I found myself drawn to the idea, despite my instinct to tread carefully.

"I don't know," I mused, tapping my mug thoughtfully. "Maybe fate is just a fancy word for coincidence. But I do think that we're here, right now, and that's what matters."

Theo smiled, that disarming grin that made my heart flutter. "Exactly. Here and now. Let's make the most of it."

With the warmth of the fire crackling beside us and the world beyond the walls fading away, I knew that this just the beginning. The slopes had been a canvas for my rediscovery, but here, over hot chocolate and laughter, I felt the thrill of new beginnings unfurling before us. Each word, each shared smile, was a brushstroke on the masterpiece of our connection, a vivid reminder that sometimes, the greatest adventures lay not in the daring of the mountains but in the vulnerability of our hearts.

Chapter 4: Holiday Magic

The mountain, cloaked in a thick blanket of glistening snow, stood sentinel over our small town, its peaks brushing against the sky like the outstretched fingers of a frozen giant. Each day, the sun rose slowly over the ridge, casting a soft, golden light that shimmered across the icy landscape, transforming the mundane into a breathtaking canvas of white and silver. I stepped outside, the crisp air biting at my cheeks, invigorating my spirit as I inhaled the rich scent of pine and woodsmoke curling from the chimneys of nearby cabins.

The town was preparing for the annual holiday festival, a time when even the grumpiest of souls could be found wrapped in garlands of laughter and warmth. I ambled through the streets, festooned with strings of twinkling lights that danced in the night like fireflies caught in a net of frost. The buildings, draped in evergreen boughs, appeared almost magical, as if they had been plucked from a holiday postcard. Children dashed around with their cheeks flushed, their laughter blending harmoniously with the crisp sounds of the season.

Jessa, with her wild mane of curls and infectious laughter, was the embodiment of holiday spirit. She'd called me earlier, her voice bubbling with excitement, convincing me to join her and Theo for a night of ice skating at the outdoor rink. "Come on, it'll be fun! Besides, you need to confront that tension between you two," she had teased, her knowing tone making my heart race in an entirely different way. Theo had always been a source of intrigue for me, a magnet pulling me closer despite the swirl of uncertainty surrounding our connection.

The ice rink was nestled at the town's heart, illuminated by a canopy of lights that twinkled like stars fallen from the sky. As I approached, the sound of skates slicing through ice and the music drifting from the speakers filled the air, creating a symphony of joyful chaos. Jessa and Theo were already there, their silhouettes dancing against the shimmering backdrop. Jessa's laughter rang clear, slicing through the chill, while Theo stood beside her, a picture of casual confidence, his eyes catching the light in a way that made my breath hitch.

"Finally!" Jessa exclaimed, waving me over. I could feel the anticipation buzzing in the air as I joined them, my skates clapping against the ice with a sound that echoed my anxious heartbeat. "Are you ready for some fun?" she asked, her eyes sparkling with mischief.

"I'm more ready for a miracle," I replied, half-joking, as I tied my laces, feeling the rush of adrenaline course through me.

Theo grinned, his dark hair tousled by the wind, and there was a hint of something in his gaze—a challenge, perhaps. "Let's see if you can keep up."

With that, we took to the ice, and I let the chill beneath my skates propel me forward. The world melted away as I glided, weaving through the skaters, feeling the exhilaration fill my veins. But it wasn't just the skating that set my heart racing; it was the way Theo's eyes followed me, the way he seemed to be measuring every move, a silent dance unfolding between us.

As I circled back around, I caught Theo watching me intently, his gaze as warm as a cozy fire on a winter's night. I stumbled slightly, feeling the flush rise to my cheeks, but before I could compose myself, he skated toward me, effortlessly closing the distance. The world narrowed to just the two of us, the laughter of others fading into a distant hum.

"Need a hand?" he asked, his voice low, teasing, but with an undercurrent of sincerity that made my heart flutter.

"Only if you can keep me upright," I shot back, my own bravado surprising me.

With a playful smirk, he reached for my hand, pulling me closer until the heat of his body radiated against mine, dispelling the cold. The touch sent a jolt of electricity coursing through me, igniting a spark I thought had long been extinguished.

As we skated together, weaving through the other skaters, the world felt like a fleeting moment captured in time. Laughter bubbled between us as I awkwardly tried to keep pace with him, our hands clasped together, a lifeline amidst the chaos. I could sense the curiosity in his eyes, the way he studied my movements, and I felt myself leaning into that gaze, wanting to unravel the mystery that was Theo.

"Not bad for a beginner," he remarked, his tone light, but the way he held my gaze spoke of something deeper, a shared connection hovering just beneath the surface.

"Just don't tell anyone I fell," I laughed, my heart racing. The thrill of skating, combined with the warmth of his hand in mine, wrapped around me like a beloved sweater, comforting yet exciting.

With every lap around the rink, the distance between us shrank, until the laughter faded into an intimate silence, a moment suspended in the glow of the holiday lights. He leaned in slightly, the world around us blurring, and I could see the playfulness in his eyes turn serious for a heartbeat, a flicker of vulnerability that caught me off guard.

"Do you ever think about how fleeting moments like these are?" he asked, the question hanging in the air between us, heavy with implications.

I nodded, the warmth in my chest radiating outward, wrapping around the uncertainty that had kept me at arm's length for far too long. This moment, nestled in the embrace of the mountain and the soft snowfall, felt precious, like a secret I wanted to hold onto forever.

Maybe this holiday would be different. Maybe it would be the catalyst for something beyond just skills learned on the ice, something deeper, more enduring. As the laughter of the crowd enveloped us, I realized that amidst the holiday magic, I was beginning to believe that sparks could reignite, even in the chill of winter.

As the evening wore on, the air thickened with laughter and a cascade of memories waiting to unfold. The ice beneath our skates glistened like diamonds, each sparkle reflecting the energy swirling around us. The warmth of Theo's hand in mine felt like an anchor in this whirlwind of joy and excitement, a tether I didn't know I desperately needed. Jessa, ever the embodiment of joy, skated circles around us, her laughter bubbling like the warm apple cider being served at the nearby stall.

"What's next?" she called out, her eyes gleaming with the mischievousness of a kid on Christmas morning. "How about some hot chocolate? You two lovebirds look like you could use a warm-up!"

The teasing made me blush, and I could feel the heat creeping up my neck, but I didn't pull away from Theo. Instead, I glanced sideways, catching him smirking, a playful light dancing in his eyes. "Sure, hot chocolate sounds perfect," I replied, trying to sound casual, though my heart was racing at the thought of being alone with him, even if just for a moment.

As we skated to the edge of the rink, the world transformed into a blur of twinkling lights and shadows, my senses heightened by the thrill of proximity. The aroma of roasted chestnuts mingled with the sweet scent of peppermint, wrapping around us like an embrace as we left the ice. The nearby stalls, dressed in festive decorations, beckoned with promises of holiday treats, their owners animatedly chatting with townsfolk and visitors alike.

Theo and I drifted a little behind Jessa, and in that quiet moment, the chatter of the festival faded into a soft hum. "So, how long have you and Jessa been friends?" he asked, his voice low enough to feel intimate, as if we were sharing a secret amid the chaos.

"Since college," I replied, surprised by the sudden warmth that flooded my cheeks. "She has a way of making every moment an adventure, doesn't she?"

"Definitely. She has this infectious energy that just makes you want to join in," he said, nodding, his eyes flickering with admiration for her. "But I think she might underestimate you a bit. You've held your own on the ice tonight."

I laughed, a soft sound that felt foreign and free. "You should see me at karaoke. Now that's a different kind of challenge." The thought of me stumbling through a rendition of a pop ballad had us both chuckling. I could see it vividly: my off-key warbling met with Jessa's supportive cheers and Theo's bemused expression.

Just as I was about to respond, Jessa came bouncing back, her cheeks flushed from the cold and excitement. "I got us three cups! Get ready for the best hot chocolate you've ever had!" She handed us each a steaming cup, the rich aroma of chocolate wafting up, making my mouth water.

"Did you add the marshmallows?" Theo asked, and there was something undeniably charming about the way he raised an eyebrow, challenging her.

"Of course! Who drinks hot chocolate without marshmallows? That's just wrong," she scoffed, rolling her eyes playfully.

We wandered away from the rink, seeking a quieter spot to enjoy our drinks. The snow crunched beneath our boots as we moved toward a small clearing illuminated by lanterns. Here, the laughter of the crowd faded, replaced by the gentle whisper of the wind weaving through the trees. The atmosphere felt sacred, a pocket of tranquility amidst the bustling festival.

I took a sip, and the warmth spread through me like a cozy blanket. The sweetness danced on my tongue, and I closed my eyes for a brief moment, savoring the rich flavor. When I opened them again, I found Theo watching me, his gaze serious yet soft.

"Do you really enjoy this time of year?" he asked, the question surprising me. It was the kind of question that carried weight, inviting honesty.

I took a breath, letting the crisp air fill my lungs. "I do, but it's complicated. I love the lights, the joy, the sense of togetherness. But it also reminds me of things I've lost." I paused, contemplating my words, feeling vulnerable under his steady gaze. "It's like every twinkle reminds me of a memory that I can't quite grasp anymore."

"Yeah, I get that," he said quietly, a shadow crossing his face. "The holidays can bring up a lot. But they can also be about new beginnings."

His words hung in the air, threading between us like the soft glow of the lanterns. I was drawn to the way he spoke, his sincerity piercing through the usual festive bravado. This moment was intimate, fragile—a thread connecting two souls, both yearning for something deeper amidst the chaos of life.

As the conversation deepened, Jessa took a few steps away, claiming to check out a nearby stall, leaving Theo and me alone. The laughter and music from the festival faded into the background, and for a heartbeat, the world outside this bubble didn't exist. It was just us, standing together, the warmth of the hot chocolate cradled in my hands, my pulse quickening in the silence that enveloped us.

"Do you want to know a secret?" Theo asked, leaning in slightly, his breath warm against the chilly air.

"Always," I replied, my curiosity piqued.

"I think I'm falling for you," he said, the confession hanging in the air, fragile yet potent, like the first snowfall of winter.

The world tilted slightly, my heart pounding against my ribcage. It felt like the ground beneath us had shifted, and I was left reeling, grappling with the sudden clarity of his words.

"You...you can't just say that," I stammered, caught off guard. The weight of the moment pressed down on me, the beauty and terror mingling in my chest like a storm.

But instead of recoiling, he stepped closer, the heat of his body radiating against the cold. "Why not? It's true."

In the glow of the lanterns, illuminated by the magic of the season, everything felt possible. The tension that had simmered between us now erupted into something vibrant, hopeful, a spark igniting beneath the surface.

"Then maybe," I breathed, my voice barely above a whisper, "maybe I'm falling for you too."

The words slipped out, carrying the weight of my own truth, and in that moment, surrounded by the magic of the holiday, I felt the fragile threads of connection solidify into something more—a promise of warmth amidst the winter chill, the beginning of a new chapter shimmering with possibility.

The world around us pulsed with a magical energy, vibrant and alive, the air thick with anticipation. I felt as if we were caught in a snow globe, the bustling festival swirling around us in a blur of color and light while we remained anchored in our own moment. The tension that had crackled between Theo and me was now a warm glow, illuminating the space where unspoken words hung in the air like the delicate strands of a web, waiting for the slightest breath to set them free.

As the laughter of festival-goers echoed in the background, I couldn't help but steal glances at Theo. The soft light cast a halo around him, making his features glow with an ethereal charm. His expression shifted from playful to contemplative, as if he were weighing the gravity of the moment. I wanted to reach out and grasp the enormity of what was unfolding between us, but it felt delicate, like the first flakes of snow settling on the ground.

"So, what now?" I asked, letting the silence linger a moment longer than necessary, craving his response.

Theo shrugged, the corners of his mouth lifting into a grin that sent warmth rushing through me. "I suppose we could dive headfirst into the holiday festivities. Or," he paused, leaning closer, the scent of his cologne mingling with the crisp air, "we could just enjoy this moment. Together."

The word "together" hung in the air like an unspoken promise, and I nodded, a smile creeping across my face. We were enveloped in an atmosphere that felt limitless, like the horizon stretching far beyond the peaks of the mountains surrounding us. I could hear Jessa's laughter drifting from a nearby booth, where she had likely found another group of friends to charm.

"What about that booth over there?" I pointed toward a small stall adorned with glittering ornaments and handmade crafts. "I bet they have something delightful."

"Only if it's covered in chocolate," Theo replied, a mock-seriousness etched on his face, but I could see the lightheartedness dancing in his eyes.

We walked toward the booth, our hands brushing occasionally, igniting sparks with every touch. The vendor was a plump woman with rosy cheeks, her apron dusted with flour and sugar from her many treats. She greeted us with a wide smile, and I felt my own cheeks warm in response.

"What can I get for my favorite skaters?" she asked, her voice rich and welcoming.

"Chocolate-covered anything!" Theo declared, his enthusiasm contagious. I couldn't help but laugh as I scanned the array of goodies on display.

As I watched Theo interact with the vendor, I realized how effortlessly he brought joy to those around him. It was in the way he listened, his genuine interest turning a simple exchange into something personal. When she handed us each a chocolate-dipped pretzel, I noticed the way his eyes sparkled, the warmth of the season reflected in every glance.

We took our treats and drifted away from the booth, finding a cozy nook near a crackling fire pit where flames danced like fairies in the night. I sat on a wooden bench, the heat radiating from the fire enveloping me like a comforting blanket, while Theo settled beside me. The warmth of the fire mingled with the warmth building between us, creating an intoxicating blend that made it hard to think about anything else.

"I think you've officially corrupted my love for pretzels," I said, taking a bite and savoring the sweet, salty combination. "This is delicious."

Theo chuckled, taking a bite of his own, his eyes lighting up. "You're welcome. I pride myself on my impeccable taste." He leaned closer, his shoulder brushing against mine. "You know, I've been thinking..."

My breath caught, anticipation fluttering in my chest as I turned to face him. The flickering flames cast shadows across his face, highlighting the sincerity etched in his expression. "About what?"

"About how the holidays have a way of bringing people together." He paused, the flicker of the fire illuminating his features in a soft glow. "And how sometimes it takes a little nudge to make those connections."

"Are you suggesting we need a holiday miracle?" I teased, my heart racing at the unspoken depth of his words.

"Maybe not a miracle," he said, his gaze locked onto mine, "but a chance to explore what's right in front of us."

The air between us felt charged, every moment stretching into infinity as the reality of his words settled in. "What if this moment is a beginning, rather than an ending?" I ventured, emboldened by the atmosphere, the warmth of the fire and the taste of chocolate lingering sweetly on my tongue.

"I'd like that," he replied, the intensity of his gaze making my heart pound. "More than you know."

Just then, Jessa burst into our cozy space, her cheeks rosy and her arms full of holiday trinkets. "You two! You should see the line for the carousel!" she exclaimed, her excitement bubbling over. "We have to go ride it before they run out of tickets!"

"Do we have to?" I asked, my heart sinking slightly at the interruption. I wasn't ready to step away from this magical moment, the warmth of Theo beside me, the fire crackling softly in the background.

"Absolutely," she insisted, determination shining in her eyes. "Come on, it'll be fun! It's tradition!"

With a resigned chuckle, I stood, feeling the cool night air brush against my skin as I adjusted to the shift from intimate warmth to bustling excitement. Theo rose alongside me, and as we followed Jessa toward the carousel, I couldn't shake the feeling that this moment was merely the beginning of something profound.

The carousel, adorned with shimmering lights and painted horses, spun in mesmerizing circles, each ride filled with joyous screams and laughter. We stood in line, and I watched as Jessa chatted animatedly, her infectious energy drawing everyone in. The colorful carousel was a kaleidoscope of lights, music, and laughter—a perfect reflection of the holiday spirit.

As we climbed onto our chosen steeds—Theo beside me on a gleaming white horse—I felt the thrill of anticipation rise within me. The ride started, and we moved up and down in a gentle rhythm, the world around us blurring into a delightful whirl of color. Laughter erupted from Jessa as she playfully reached for Theo, pretending to hold onto him for dear life as the carousel spun faster.

In that moment, amidst the chaos, I caught Theo's gaze. It was electric, the way he looked at me, the connection deepening with every shared laugh and every tilt of our heads. It was a dance of hearts, a mingling of hopes that spun and swirled around us, just like the carousel itself.

As we spun, the world outside melted away, leaving only the warmth of shared moments. I could feel the pulse of life around us—the music, the laughter, the sweet anticipation of what was yet to come. The holidays held magic, but this, this was something uniquely ours, a memory forming like snowflakes in the air—delicate, beautiful, and breathtakingly real.

And for the first time in a long while, I believed in the possibility of magic, the kind that could spark between two souls ready to embrace what lay ahead, together.

Chapter 5: Breaking the Ice

The night wrapped around us like a velvet cloak, the moon's silvery glow illuminating the campsite where laughter danced on the breeze. Each crackle of the fire punctuated our stories, casting flickering shadows that wove in and out of the trees surrounding us. I sat on the cool earth, knees tucked beneath me, a fluffy marshmallow speared on a stick in hand, the sweet scent of it caramelizing over the flames. There was something about the way the firelight flickered, revealing the faces of those gathered—familiar and yet somehow transformed in this magical moment—that felt like a revelation. Theo, with his tousled hair and those eyes that sparkled with mischief, seemed more vulnerable than I had ever seen him.

As he spoke, his voice steady yet layered with uncharacteristic softness, I leaned in, the warmth of the fire against my skin contrasting with the chill of the autumn air. "You think it's easy, being up there?" he said, gesturing vaguely toward the heavens, where the stars twinkled like the flash of his usual bravado. "Always expected to know everything, to be perfect." He paused, as if weighing the gravity of his words. "Some days, I'm just faking it. The pressure—God, it's suffocating."

His confession hung between us like a shimmering thread, fragile yet strong. The fire crackled again, as if urging me to respond, to open up the vaults of my own heart. I felt a familiar flutter of hesitation, a twinge of fear, but there was something in his gaze, a sincerity that beckoned me to dive deeper. "You're not alone in that," I found myself saying, my voice a whisper against the backdrop of the night. "I know what it's like to feel like you're standing on a tightrope, afraid of the fall."

With that, I surrendered, allowing the words to spill forth like the molten chocolate I so desperately craved. I spoke of nights spent worrying about love, the gnawing fear that my heart would become a target for the arrows of betrayal once more. I shared my scars, the moments when trust slipped through my fingers like grains of sand, and I watched as Theo nodded, his expression shifting from playful banter to a shared understanding. It felt like a pact being formed between us, a delicate thread binding our vulnerabilities together under the vast expanse of the starlit sky.

As I looked around, I saw the others listening, entranced by our exchange. The laughter that had erupted just moments before faded, replaced by a palpable energy that enveloped us. I caught Ella's gaze, her bright eyes wide with empathy, and in that moment, I realized we were all yearning for connection, all aching to be seen. Theo's admission had unlocked something in me, like a key turning in a long-sealed door, and I was grateful for the warmth of the fire, for the way it illuminated the truths we often buried.

The more we shared, the more the distance between us shrank. With each laugh and each confession, I felt layers of my defenses peeling away, revealing a raw, tender part of myself that had been hidden for too long. Our laughter danced on the air, intertwining with the crackling of the flames. I could feel the weight of my past—the disappointments, the heartbreaks—beginning to lift, as if the fire were consuming my fears along with the logs, turning them into glowing embers.

A breeze swept through the clearing, rustling the leaves overhead and sending a shiver of anticipation down my spine. I could feel a connection forming, fragile yet exhilarating, as I caught Theo's eye across the flickering light. There was a softness there, a spark of something that made my heart race. My breath caught in my throat, and for a moment, time suspended, just us—two souls, tangled in a web of shared dreams and fears, tethered by the warmth of the fire and the truth in our confessions.

In that intimate cocoon of light and shadow, I dared to imagine what it might be like to take a chance on him. To step outside the walls I had built so carefully around my heart. What would it be to hold his hand, to share quiet moments wrapped in the warmth of his presence? The possibilities felt tantalizing, like the first sip of a fine wine, swirling with flavor and promise.

The night deepened, and with each breath, I felt the tension of uncertainty start to unravel. Theo's laughter rang out, deep and genuine, as he recounted a particularly embarrassing moment from his teaching days. I couldn't help but join in, the sound bubbling up from my core, filling the space between us with a lightness that was utterly refreshing. In those moments, my heart felt less like a fortress and more like an open garden, blooming with wildflowers of hope.

It was the kind of night that felt like a turning point, a moment suspended in time where everything shifted. As the flames flickered and danced, painting our faces in warm hues of orange and gold, I surrendered to the possibility of what lay ahead. The more we shared, the more I felt the past slip away, leaving room for something new, something bright and hopeful. I was on the precipice of something extraordinary, and the thought filled me with both excitement and fear. But under the vast sky, surrounded by kindred spirits, I couldn't help but wonder if maybe, just maybe, it was time to let the walls down and step into the light.

The fire continued to crackle, its warmth wrapping around us like a soft embrace, while the scent of toasted marshmallows wafted through the crisp night air. I relished the sweet, gooey texture of the marshmallow on my tongue, letting the sugary bliss melt away the remnants of doubt still lingering in the corners of my mind. There was an intoxicating mix of camaraderie and vulnerability that hung in the air, binding us together as we exchanged not just stories but pieces of our souls.

As the fire danced, I caught Theo glancing my way, a flicker of something unspoken passing between us. The shadows played tricks on my mind, drawing me deeper into the allure of his presence. His laughter was like music, rich and inviting, inviting me to lean closer, to unravel the layers of this connection we had stumbled upon. The light from the flames cast a warm glow on his features, highlighting the determination etched in his brow, the kindness in his gaze. It was a sight that tugged at my heartstrings, awakening a spark of hope I had long buried beneath layers of self-protection.

Ella leaned forward, her voice cutting through the playful banter, drawing our attention. "So, what's the most ridiculous thing you've ever done in the name of love?" she asked, her eyes glimmering with mischief. The question hung in the air, igniting a lively debate among us. I felt a rush of warmth flood my cheeks, the memory of my own embarrassing romantic escapade bubbling to the surface. The truth was, love had often felt like a series of misadventures—hilarious in retrospect, but excruciating in the moment.

I shared a story from college when I had concocted an elaborate scheme to impress a crush. "I pretended to be an expert in wine tasting," I admitted, laughter erupting from the group as they leaned in, hungry for the details. "But really, I had no clue what I was doing. I ended up spilling an entire glass of merlot all over my new white dress."

"Did you at least get the guy?" Theo asked, amusement dancing in his eyes.

"No," I replied, shaking my head with a chuckle. "He spent the entire evening trying to avoid the stains rather than talking to me. Clearly, I wasn't the vintage he was looking for."

Laughter erupted around the fire, filling the night with a warmth that rivaled the flames. It was liberating, shedding the heaviness of my past and inviting a sense of levity that had long been absent from my heart. The more we shared, the more I realized that our stories, laden with imperfections and blunders, were the very fabric of our humanity. It was the shared awkwardness, the blunders in the name of love, that made us relatable, made us real.

Theo's turn came next, and I leaned in, eager to hear the tale he would weave. "Alright, so there was this one time I tried to impress a girl by cooking dinner," he began, a wry smile forming on his lips. "Let's just say that my idea of gourmet involved frozen pizza and an excess of garlic bread. I managed to burn the garlic bread—like, completely charred—and when she arrived, I panicked and tried to hide it in the oven."

"What happened?" Ella pressed, her eyes wide with anticipation.

"The smoke alarm went off," he said, laughter bubbling up, "and she spent the next fifteen minutes waving a dish towel around, trying to fan the smoke away. It was like a scene from a bad rom-com. We ended up ordering takeout instead."

As his laughter faded into the cool night air, I couldn't help but admire how effortlessly he transformed a mishap into a moment of shared humor. It was in these exchanges, these little glimpses of ourselves, that I felt the walls I had built around my heart begin to crumble. The night became a sanctuary, where the usual boundaries faded away, allowing us to be raw and genuine.

The stars twinkled overhead, a canopy of glittering diamonds that felt like a witness to our unfolding connection. I found myself stealing glances at Theo, observing the way his laughter crinkled the corners of his eyes, the way he was entirely present in the moment, drawing everyone in. There was a magnetism about him that made it difficult to look away, and with every glance exchanged, I felt a connection deepening, a silent agreement forming without words.

As the fire continued to burn brightly, illuminating our faces in a warm glow, the conversation shifted to dreams and aspirations. "If you could do anything in the world, what would it be?" I asked, genuinely curious about the dreams that lived beneath the surface of the playful banter.

Theo took a moment, his expression thoughtful. "I think I'd want to open a little bookstore-café," he said, his voice rich with passion. "Somewhere cozy, where people can gather, share stories, and lose themselves in a good book. A place that feels like home."

I was captivated by his vision, picturing shelves lined with worn paperbacks, the aroma of freshly brewed coffee wafting through the air, and laughter echoing against the walls. "That sounds incredible," I said, a smile creeping onto my face. "And I can totally picture you running it. You'd have the best book recommendations."

"Only if you promise to help me," he teased, nudging my shoulder playfully. "We can create a book club that discusses all the ridiculous romantic adventures we've had."

"Deal," I replied, laughter bubbling up again, a sound that felt lighter, freer than it had in years. It was as if the burdens of expectation had lifted, allowing us to dream without the weight of judgment or fear.

As the fire began to wane, the world around us slowly transformed into a serene stillness, the crackle of embers now a soft whisper against the backdrop of a moonlit sky. With every moment that passed, I could feel my heart opening, expanding to welcome the possibility of something new. The laughter, the stories, the vulnerability—it all felt like a gentle reminder that we are never truly alone in our struggles. Underneath the vast expanse of the universe, we were just a group of souls searching for connection, for understanding, for a place to belong.

As the fire's glow began to dim, casting shadows that danced across the soft grass, a sudden gust of wind whispered through the trees, carrying with it the scent of pine and earth. It was a reminder that the world was still spinning, even as we clung to this precious moment, cocooned in our laughter and shared confessions. I could hear the distant sound of a river, its gentle babbling a soothing lullaby against the backdrop of our gathering. The night, once filled with uncertainty, now felt alive with possibilities, and I marveled at how quickly the fabric of our interactions had woven us into a tapestry of trust.

Ella nudged me gently, her mischievous smile breaking through the warm, intimate atmosphere. "Let's play a game!" she exclaimed, her enthusiasm infectious. "How about Two Truths and a Lie? It's the perfect way to learn even more about each other!" The suggestion hung in the air, a challenge beckoning us to peel back even more layers.

The prospect thrilled me. "Okay, I'm in!" I replied, my heart racing at the idea of exposing even more of myself while also teasing the others into revealing their secrets. As the group agreed, we formed a circle around the now low-burning fire, the glow flickering like the anticipation dancing in our eyes.

Ella went first, confidently rattling off her statements. "I've never broken a bone, I've gone skydiving, and I once accidentally dyed my hair green before a big presentation." The group erupted in laughter, dissecting each claim with playful skepticism. I could see the glimmer of joy in her eyes, the exhilaration of sharing her truths, and it was infectious.

As she revealed her lie, a vivid account of the unfortunate green hair incident, it became clear how each person in our circle was beginning to embrace vulnerability in their own way. Theo followed suit, sharing his truths with a combination of self-deprecation and charm. "I once lost a bet and had to sing 'I Will Survive' karaoke style in front of a crowd, I have a soft spot for romantic comedies, and I'm terrified of spiders."

The laughter that ensued after each revelation echoed into the night, merging with the whispering leaves above us. I felt the tension in my chest release with every shared laugh, every moment spent peering into one another's lives, feeling closer to each person around the fire.

Finally, it was my turn. I took a deep breath, summoning the courage that had buoyed me throughout the evening. "Okay, here goes: I once saved a puppy from a burning building, I can recite every line from The Princess Bride, and I've never ridden a bike."

The silence that followed was palpable, each person leaning in with curiosity. "The puppy one has to be true!" Ella exclaimed, her eyes wide with admiration.

"The bike one sounds more like a lie," Theo interjected, his brow raised in playful skepticism. "How can you have made it this far without riding a bike? It seems almost... un-American."

I chuckled, the warmth of their camaraderie soothing the remnants of my guarded nature. "The bike is the lie," I finally admitted, relishing their surprise. "I've had plenty of chances, but I always found it too intimidating, and my parents were terrible at teaching me."

Theo laughed, shaking his head. "Maybe we need to rectify that. Next time, we can have a bike lesson in the park!"

His casual suggestion sent a ripple of excitement through me, the prospect of shared adventures igniting a flame of anticipation within my heart. The night had shifted from simple laughter to the promise of new experiences, each revelation binding us closer together.

As we continued playing, the fire dwindled, glowing embers rising like fireflies into the night sky, scattering across the darkness. The moonlight poured down, illuminating the edges of our circle, casting long shadows that intertwined, just as our stories had. The air was thick with the scent of charred wood and toasted marshmallows, a reminder of the warmth we had created in this secluded corner of the world.

But as the game wound down, a quiet shift settled among us. A sense of unspoken understanding lingered in the air, the need for deeper truths starting to surface beneath the playful banter. Ella leaned forward, her voice dipping to a softer pitch. "So, what do we all really want?" she asked, her gaze shifting from face to face.

The question hung between us, pregnant with possibilities. I could feel my pulse quicken, the weight of it pressing against my chest. What did I want? I had been so focused on protecting my heart that I had almost forgotten to dream. It was as if the night had peeled away the layers of armor I had constructed, revealing the raw desires hidden beneath.

The group fell into a contemplative silence, the crackle of the remaining embers the only sound accompanying our thoughts. Theo's voice broke through the stillness, low and earnest. "I think I just want to feel like I'm making a difference. Like what I teach truly resonates with my students."

There was something profoundly beautiful in the vulnerability of his words, and I found myself nodding in agreement. It wasn't just about success for him; it was about connection, impact, and a desire to inspire.

Ella shared her own truth next, her dreams bursting forth like fireworks. "I want to open a bakery! A little place where people can come, relax, and just be happy over sweet treats. I want to spread joy one cupcake at a time!"

Her enthusiasm was infectious, and I could visualize the cozy café she dreamed of, filled with the scent of freshly baked goods and the sound of laughter spilling out onto the street.

Then, it was my turn, and I hesitated for a moment, caught in the vulnerability of the moment. "I think I want to feel free," I said, my voice steady but trembling. "Free to love, free to trust, free to explore the world without fear holding me back. I want to discover who I am outside the walls I've built."

A silence enveloped us, profound and filled with understanding. We were no longer just acquaintances sharing stories around a fire;

we had become a tapestry of souls, each thread interwoven with dreams and aspirations, fears and hopes.

As the fire's last embers glowed softly against the canvas of the night, I felt a profound sense of belonging settle within me. In that moment, under the watchful gaze of the stars, I allowed myself to breathe deeply, embracing the new beginnings that awaited. It was a beautiful reminder that life was not just about the past or the present, but about the intricate dance of connection that could light up the darkest nights and guide us into the dawn of something extraordinary.

Chapter 6: The Heart's Avalanche

Snow fell in thick, swirling sheets, transforming the once-familiar landscape into a mesmerizing winter wonderland. Each flake danced lazily through the air, blanketing the earth in a soft layer of white, muffling the world around us. The towering pines stood sentinel against the howling wind, their branches heavy with the weight of fresh snow. It was a scene out of a postcard, and I, with my bundled layers and vibrant red ski jacket, felt like I had been dropped into a fairy tale—albeit one that came with the grim prospect of being snowed in.

Jessa and I huddled together, our laughter mingling with the wind as we surveyed the conditions outside. The training sessions we had anticipated so eagerly had been dashed by this freak storm, leaving us both restless and itching for adventure. The resort's cozy lodge, with its roaring fireplace and hot cocoa, offered comfort, but it felt stifling after the excitement of our preparations. We needed something to shake off the cabin fever settling into our bones.

"Let's go out," I suggested, my breath visible in the frosty air, excitement bubbling beneath my skin. Jessa's eyes lit up, her enthusiasm matching my own.

"Are you crazy? It's a blizzard out there!" she laughed, pulling her wool hat tighter over her ears.

"Exactly! It's the perfect opportunity for a little wilderness escapade. What's the worst that could happen?" I shot back, grinning mischievously. With a nod of agreement, we decided to gather our gear and head into the unknown.

The three of us set off into the swirling snow, our laughter echoing against the mountainsides. Theo trailed behind us, the warmth of his presence a comforting reassurance. The tension that had simmered between us during the past few days was tangible, a silent current beneath our playful banter. I caught glimpses of him through the flurries, his dark hair dusted with snow, the way he smiled at us, and how his laughter rang out, deep and genuine, making my heart skip like a child's in a candy store.

We trudged through knee-deep snow, the world around us shifting with every gust of wind. The sun was an elusive memory, shrouded by thick clouds that hung low, but it didn't matter. There was something thrilling about being so alive amidst the ferocity of nature. Jessa and I took turns leading the way, our spirits soaring higher than the peaks surrounding us. As we navigated through the trees, our laughter broke through the stillness, a reminder that even the storm couldn't quell our spirits.

Eventually, we stumbled upon an unexpected sight—a cabin nestled against the mountainside, its worn wooden façade half-buried in snow. The door creaked ominously as we pushed it open, revealing a cozy, albeit dusty, interior. It felt like stepping into a forgotten world, a relic of the past adorned with snowshoes hanging on the wall and a stone fireplace that beckoned to be lit. A thick layer of dust coated the furniture, and old quilts lay piled high on the beds.

"Can you believe it? It's like something out of a movie!" I exclaimed, brushing a finger against the table's surface, leaving a trail in the dust. Jessa flopped onto an old couch, her laughter filling the room as Theo stepped inside, shaking off the snow like a dog after a bath.

"This place is amazing!" he declared, his eyes wide with wonder. I could see a flicker of excitement in his gaze, a shared thrill that resonated deeply within me. I was acutely aware of the warmth radiating between us, a current of unsaid words and lingering looks, igniting something I had only begun to recognize in myself.

With no cell service and the storm raging outside, we made ourselves comfortable, setting the fire ablaze and curling up on the couch. We pulled out our snacks—Jessa's famous homemade cookies and a thermos filled with hot chocolate. It felt like we were in our own little world, the storm outside a mere backdrop to our impromptu adventure.

As we settled in, laughter filled the space, echoing off the wooden walls. We played games, shared stories, and reveled in the warmth of each other's company. I felt lighter than I had in months, the burdens of my daily life drifting away like the snowflakes outside. Each moment felt suspended in time, a delicate balance of joy and anticipation.

But as the night deepened, an uninvited tension hung in the air, thick and electrifying. I caught Theo's gaze lingering on me more often than I dared to acknowledge, a warmth pooling in my chest that both thrilled and terrified me. Each glance felt like a question, unspoken yet palpable. I leaned closer, drawn in by an invisible force, heart racing as I fought against the urge to bridge that growing distance. Just as our worlds began to align, the sudden crash of thunder outside shattered the moment, making us all jump. The sound echoed ominously, reverberating through the cabin and reminding us of the storm's power.

"Maybe we should, um, keep the volume down," Jessa suggested, her eyes wide with a mix of fear and excitement. We shared a nervous laugh, but the moment lingered in the air between Theo and me like a fragile snowflake, ready to melt away at the slightest touch.

The storm raged outside, its howl a haunting lullaby, and we found ourselves bound by the whim of nature, drawn together in a way that felt both exhilarating and terrifying. As the fire crackled and the wind howled, I realized that sometimes, it takes a storm to reveal the heart's true desires, to strip away the layers of hesitation and fear, exposing what has long been buried beneath the surface. In that secluded cabin, with the snowstorm howling outside, we were all on the brink of something beautiful, even if we didn't quite know it yet.

The crackle of the fire danced with our laughter, a symphony of warmth against the biting cold outside. Each flicker of flame cast playful shadows on the cabin walls, transforming the dust and old wood into a living tapestry of our shared excitement. As Jessa recounted her latest skiing mishap, I leaned back against the couch, allowing myself to bask in the glow of our camaraderie. It felt like a cocoon, shielding us from the storm that raged just beyond the cabin's walls.

"Okay, but did you really think you could jump that ramp?" I teased, nudging Jessa playfully with my shoulder. Her face flushed with embarrassment, but she embraced it, laughing even harder.

"Hey! I nailed the landing—eventually!" she shot back, mock offense etched across her features. Theo chuckled beside me, and I caught a glimpse of his smile, the way it reached his eyes and crinkled the corners. It was a sight that sent a small thrill through me, awakening something I had buried deep within—a flutter of attraction I was still grappling to comprehend.

"Maybe next time you should stick to the bunny slopes," he added, raising an eyebrow in playful judgment.

"Just wait until I challenge you to a race!" Jessa exclaimed, her confidence shining through.

"Bring it on," he shot back, feigning bravado. The banter flowed easily, a balm against the tension that simmered beneath the surface, but I couldn't shake the feeling that our playful exchanges were the calm before the storm of emotions lurking just out of sight.

As we continued to chat, I found myself stealing glances at Theo when he wasn't looking. There was something magnetic about him, an energy that pulled me in and made my heart dance. The more time we spent together, the more I realized how deeply I craved his attention, how much I longed for the warmth of his gaze to linger on me just a moment longer.

Suddenly, the wind howled, shaking the cabin like a fragile leaf caught in a tempest. I jumped, the sound crashing into our laughter, a stark reminder of our reality. The fire crackled louder, the flames flickering erratically as if sensing our momentary unease. The cabin, once a sanctuary, felt like a fragile bubble, ready to burst at the slightest provocation.

"Should we check the windows? Make sure the storm isn't doing any damage?" I suggested, my voice barely masking the hint of worry creeping in. Theo nodded, his expression serious as he stood up and made his way to the window, pulling back the curtain.

Outside, the world had become an abstract painting of white and gray. Snow whipped violently through the air, obscuring the trees and swallowing the landscape whole. I watched him, his silhouette framed by the window, the soft glow of the fire casting a warm light around him. The way he held himself—confident yet grounded—made my heart flutter even more. I couldn't help but admire the ruggedness that made him so effortlessly captivating.

"It looks like it's only getting worse," he said, his voice low and steady. "We might be stuck here for a while."

"Great," I replied, trying to keep the fear from creeping into my tone. I didn't want to acknowledge the part of me that was secretly thrilled at the idea of spending more time with him, away from the distractions of the world outside. I could feel the weight of unspoken words pressing down on us, a silent acknowledgment that something significant was about to unfold.

"Let's make the best of it," Jessa chimed in, standing up and stretching her arms above her head. "Who's up for a game? We have cards!"

I laughed at her enthusiasm, thankful for the distraction. We settled into a makeshift game night, the cards a bridge over the fragile divide of our emotions. As we played, the laughter returned, lighter this time, but I could still feel the pull of Theo's gaze. Whenever our eyes met, the air thickened, crackling with an electric tension that was both exhilarating and terrifying.

At one point, Jessa excused herself to use the bathroom, leaving Theo and me alone in the dim light of the cabin. The moment she disappeared around the corner, I felt the atmosphere shift, a quiet intimacy settling around us. I swallowed hard, suddenly aware of every heartbeat, every breath, and every unspoken thought that hung between us.

"Are you okay?" he asked, his voice barely above a whisper, as if he could sense the whirlwind of emotions threatening to spill over.

"Yeah, just...this storm," I replied, my voice shaking slightly. I hated how vulnerable I felt in that moment, how easily he could read me. "It's a little scary."

"Yeah, it is. But I kind of like it." His gaze held mine, unwavering, and I could see the faintest hint of a smile tugging at his lips. "It makes everything feel more...alive, don't you think?"

I nodded, a smile creeping onto my face as warmth flooded my cheeks. "Definitely. Like we're part of some epic adventure."

"Exactly." He leaned closer, the distance between us closing, and my heart raced at the unexpected intimacy. "It's funny how we can find ourselves in places we never thought we'd be, isn't it?"

I bit my lip, my pulse quickening. "Yeah, but sometimes those places can surprise us in the best ways."

The moment hung between us, suspended in time as if the universe itself was holding its breath. I felt as if I were teetering on the edge of a precipice, teetering between the exhilarating thrill of possibility and the fear of falling. Just as I thought he might say something more, a loud crash echoed outside, a jarring reminder of the storm's power.

We both jumped, laughter bursting forth in nervous bursts, breaking the spell that had begun to envelop us. Jessa returned, oblivious to the tension that had simmered between us, and just like that, the moment slipped through my fingers like the snowflakes falling outside.

"Okay, who's ready to lose?" she challenged, brandishing the deck of cards with a mischievous grin.

The tension eased as we resumed our game, but beneath the laughter and friendly competition, I could still feel the echo of what had just transpired. The storm continued to rage outside, a wild tempest that mirrored the chaos within me. Each playful jab and lighthearted tease brought us closer together, yet a quiet voice in the back of my mind reminded me of the precarious balance we were walking.

As the night wore on, the storm outside raged unabated, but within the cozy cabin, we were cocooned in laughter and warmth, unaware that the real avalanche was only just beginning to unfold.

The night deepened around us, a blanket of silence settling in as we returned to our game, the previous tension dissipating into bursts of laughter. Jessa had taken on the role of the self-proclaimed dealer, shuffling the cards with a flourish that would've made a Vegas magician proud. As she handed out the cards, the cabin pulsed with life, the crackling fire illuminating our faces and casting warm shadows that danced across the walls.

"Alright, let's see who's going to dominate tonight," she proclaimed, her competitive spirit shining bright. I could sense her excitement, an infectious energy that propelled us into playful rivalries and banter, transforming the modest cabin into our own private arena. I glanced at Theo, whose eyes glimmered with mischief as he leaned closer, our shoulders brushing.

Each round unfolded like a comedic performance. Jessa, with her exaggerated reactions, would groan dramatically whenever I won, declaring it was pure luck rather than skill. I savored the victories, each one a small triumph, yet beneath the laughter, my thoughts often drifted back to Theo. He would throw me sideways glances when Jessa's attention was diverted, his eyes searching mine, igniting that familiar warmth within me. It was thrilling and terrifying, a tightrope walk on the edge of a precipice.

As the evening wore on, we began to trade stories—funny anecdotes from our childhoods, misadventures on the slopes, and aspirations that lay just beyond our grasp. The stories flowed easily, but it was in the silences between that I felt the gravity of our situation. With every shared laugh, with every unguarded moment, we were unwittingly weaving a tapestry of connection that was growing richer and more complex.

"I once tried to impress a girl by skiing backwards," Theo confessed, shaking his head at the memory. "Let's just say, it didn't end well. I ended up in a snowbank and she laughed so hard she almost fell over herself." His laughter echoed in the cabin, filling the space with warmth.

"Was she cute?" I asked, feigning nonchalance, but my heart raced at the thought of any girl vying for his attention.

"Very," he admitted, a hint of regret in his tone. "But I think she appreciated my commitment to the craft more than anything else."

"Oh, please, that's just a fancy way of saying you failed spectacularly!" Jessa teased, her eyes sparkling.

We erupted into laughter again, but beneath the surface, I felt a small pang of jealousy at the thought of him trying to impress someone else. It was a ludicrous notion, given that I barely knew him, yet the feeling stirred something raw and unsettling inside me.

As the game continued, we shifted to a round of charades, a decision that promised laughter but threatened to expose us to a different kind of vulnerability. Jessa was first to act, flailing her arms as she tried to mimic a skiing motion. Theo and I burst into laughter, struggling to decipher her exaggerated movements as she spun around the room like a whirlwind.

"Is it... skiing?" Theo guessed, barely able to contain his laughter.

"Bingo!" she yelled, triumphantly. "Next!"

When it was my turn, I felt a rush of adrenaline. I chose a dramatic scene, pantomiming a high-speed ski chase, complete with exaggerated facial expressions. I could hear Theo's laughter intertwining with my own, our eyes meeting in that deliciously electrifying way.

"Are you auditioning for a movie?" he quipped, leaning back as if to fully appreciate the performance.

I felt my cheeks flush, an embarrassing warmth creeping in as I exaggerated my gestures. "You know me, always looking for the next big break," I joked back, laughter bubbling up as I reveled in the moment, momentarily forgetting the storm outside and the swirling emotions within.

As the night deepened, the storm outside continued its relentless assault, but within the cabin, we created our own kind of magic. Time slipped away, and as the hours passed, our playful interactions began to give way to something more intimate. The air crackled with unspoken words, lingering touches, and fleeting glances that held the promise of something deeper.

Eventually, the cards were set aside, and we found ourselves nestled in front of the fire, the warmth enveloping us like a cherished memory. Jessa had succumbed to fatigue, her head resting against the arm of the couch, while Theo and I remained alert, caught in the magnetic pull between us.

"What's your biggest fear?" he asked, his voice low, almost conspiratorial.

I hesitated, the question hanging in the air like a fragile snowflake, one that could shatter with the wrong touch. "I guess... being ordinary. Just blending into the background, you know?"

He nodded thoughtfully, the firelight dancing in his eyes. "I get that. I think a lot of people share that fear. We all want to feel special, to leave a mark."

"What about you?" I probed, my curiosity piqued.

He took a deep breath, his expression growing serious. "I fear not living up to expectations. I've always been the one people look to, the one who's supposed to have it all figured out. But sometimes, I wonder if I'm just... faking it."

I sensed the vulnerability beneath his bravado, and it struck a chord within me. "You're not faking it, Theo. You're real. I see it in how you care for those around you."

He looked at me, a soft smile breaking through the weight of his earlier admission. "Thanks. That means more than you know."

Just then, another crash of thunder outside shook the cabin, sending a shiver through me. I instinctively leaned closer to him, drawn by an unspoken need for warmth and reassurance. The moment felt charged, and the boundaries we had been skirting began to blur.

"Do you ever think about what it would be like to just... let go?" I found myself asking, a whisper carried by the crackling flames.

"Let go?" He turned to me, curiosity igniting in his gaze. "What do you mean?"

"Just to stop worrying about what everyone thinks, to let yourself feel everything without fear," I replied, my voice barely above a murmur. "To embrace the wildness of life."

He studied me, and I could feel the intensity of his gaze as it roamed over my face, as if he were searching for something buried deep within me. "That sounds like an adventure," he finally said, a grin breaking across his face. "One I'm willing to take, especially if it's with you."

The air between us thickened, charged with the weight of possibility. I could feel the warmth radiating from him, pulling me closer, a gravity I couldn't resist. My heart raced as I leaned in, the distance narrowing until it felt like nothing could come between us.

Before I could process it, our lips met—softly at first, testing the waters, before everything around us faded away. The world outside melted into nothingness as we pulled each other closer, the kiss deepening into something electric, alive. The storm roared beyond the walls, but within that cabin, time stood still. It was a moment of surrender, a breaking of barriers that allowed our hearts to collide in an avalanche of emotion, burying everything else beneath the weight of our connection.

When we finally pulled apart, breathless and flushed, I realized that perhaps this unexpected storm had done more than trap us in a cabin; it had unleashed the very feelings we had both been too scared to acknowledge. And as the snow continued to fall, wrapping the world in a soft embrace, I knew we were on the brink of something transformative—together.

Chapter 7: Frozen Fears

The morning light broke through the cracks of the cabin, spilling golden rays onto the weathered floorboards, illuminating the dust motes dancing in the air. I blinked awake, still enveloped in the warmth of the heavy quilt, its soft fibers a stark contrast to the chill that seeped in from the frost-covered windows. The world outside was blanketed in an ethereal layer of snow, sparkling like a field of diamonds under the pale sun. It was beautiful, a winter wonderland that felt both magical and treacherous, much like the current state of my heart.

The warmth of the cabin felt foreign as I stretched out, expecting to see Theo curled up on the couch, his tousled hair cascading over his forehead like a dark wave. But the couch was empty, its fabric still pressed down where he had been sleeping. A strange sense of unease coiled in my stomach. Perhaps it was the chill of the morning air, or maybe it was something deeper—an instinct warning me that something was amiss.

I slipped out of bed, the cold hardwood floor biting at my bare feet. The cabin, once a haven, now felt constricting, as if its walls were closing in on me. I called out for Theo, my voice a fragile echo against the rustic timbers. Silence greeted me, stretching out into the vastness of the snow-laden woods beyond the cabin. My heart pounded louder with each unanswered call, the rhythmic thump mirroring the growing panic within me.

Dressed in layers, I pulled on my boots and ventured outside, the door creaking in protest as I pushed it open. A gust of frigid air hit me, sending shivers racing up my spine, but I pressed on. The landscape was breathtaking, the world transformed into a serene expanse of white. Pines stood tall, their branches heavy with the weight of fresh snow, and the only sound was the crunch of my footsteps as I ventured deeper into the woods.

With each step, my thoughts spiraled into darker places. What if something had happened to him? What if he'd gotten lost? I cursed the sudden surge of irrational thoughts, knowing full well how the wilderness could twist fear into a frenzy. As I wandered further from the safety of the cabin, the trees loomed around me like sentinels, their gnarled roots jutting out of the ground as if trying to grab hold of me. I shook off the paranoia, pushing through the underbrush, determined to find him.

After what felt like an eternity, I stumbled upon a clearing, and there, framed against the backdrop of towering pines, I saw him. Theo was crouched low, his breath rising in clouds of steam, surrounded by a whirlwind of snowflakes. He was trying to help Jessa construct a makeshift snow shelter, their laughter mingling with the soft whir of the wind. Relief washed over me in waves, but beneath it simmered confusion and frustration. Why had he left without saying anything?

"Hey!" I called, my voice breaking the serene stillness. They turned, and the sight of Theo's face illuminated by the playful sunlight brought a smile to my lips, but it faded as he met my gaze, a shadow flickering across his features.

"Where were you?" I demanded, my voice sharper than I intended, the worry morphing into irritation.

"I just needed some air," he replied, standing up slowly as if weighed down by more than just the snow.

"You scared me," I said, crossing my arms, suddenly feeling vulnerable and exposed beneath his piercing gaze. "You could have said something."

"I know," he sighed, running a hand through his hair, which was dusted with snowflakes. "I just... I had to think. Everything's been so intense between us, and I didn't know how to handle it."

His confession hung between us like the fragile icicles glistening in the trees. There was a vulnerability in his eyes, a depth that tugged at my heart. I wanted to wrap him in warmth, to reassure him that the connection we shared was something I longed for, not something to fear. But as I stood there, the fire crackling to life in my chest began to flicker with uncertainty.

"Intense?" I echoed, my heart racing. "Why does it scare you?"

He opened his mouth to respond but hesitated, the weight of unspoken words pressing down on him. I could feel the frigid air prickling against my skin, but it was nothing compared to the chill of uncertainty settling deep within me. This was the crux of our relationship—a tightrope walk between fear and exhilaration.

"We've been through so much together," he said finally, his voice steady yet laced with vulnerability. "And I guess I didn't expect to feel this way. It's exciting and terrifying at the same time."

Theo's honesty disarmed me, and I felt a flicker of understanding ignite within. I had been so consumed by my own fears that I hadn't paused to consider his. What if he felt the weight of my expectations? What if he, too, was standing on the precipice of uncertainty, staring into the abyss of possibility?

"I get it," I murmured, the words tumbling out, breaking the spell of tension. "I do. But running away doesn't help. We can face this together."

As I spoke, I reached for him, allowing my fingers to brush against his gloved hand. The touch sent a rush of warmth through me, melting away the snow of doubt that had begun to accumulate. He looked down at our hands, a spark of something unnameable igniting in his eyes. In that moment, I realized we were both navigating a labyrinth of fear and longing, each twist and turn drawing us closer to the center, where something beautiful awaited us.

"Let's build that shelter together," I suggested, a smile breaking through the tension. "We can face the storm, but we need to be a team."

With a hesitant smile, Theo nodded, and as we turned to join Jessa, I felt a weight lift from my shoulders. The warmth of connection swirled around us, a promise that even amidst the chill of uncertainty, we could forge a path forward—together.

The scent of woodsmoke curled around us, mingling with the fresh, crisp air as we gathered near the crackling fire, the orange glow illuminating the snow-dusted clearing. Jessa had crafted a makeshift bench from fallen logs, and we settled in, pulling our layers tighter against the biting cold. The warmth enveloped us, a contrast to the chilling uncertainty lingering between Theo and me. I watched as the flames danced, their flickering light reflecting the turmoil of emotions surging within me, each crackle punctuating the silence that stretched like a taut rope between us.

Jessa, always the spirited one, filled the air with stories that ebbed and flowed like the smoke, each tale more animated than the last. She spoke of past adventures, her laughter ringing out like silver bells, but even her effervescence couldn't entirely diffuse the weight in the atmosphere. Theo sat beside me, his expression a complex blend of contemplation and apprehension, the firelight casting shadows across his chiseled features. I stole glances at him, noticing how the flames flickered in his deep-set eyes, revealing layers of thoughts swirling behind that calm exterior.

"Did I ever tell you about the time I got lost hiking in Yosemite?" Jessa asked, her eyes sparkling with mischief. "I thought I was going to become bear food! But it turns out I just wandered a few miles off the path."

A smile tugged at the corners of my mouth, but the laughter felt forced, an awkward mask covering the tension that lingered between Theo and me. I could sense his internal struggle—this was a place of beauty and warmth, yet it was steeped in an emotional chill that left me restless. Jessa's stories painted vibrant pictures, but they felt distant, almost like echoes from a place I longed to escape.

After a particularly raucous tale about a near miss with a raccoon, Jessa glanced between us, her gaze sharp and insightful. "You two look like you're in a snow globe of confusion," she said, her voice light yet probing. "What's going on?"

I felt the heat rise in my cheeks, the warmth of the fire unable to dispel the sudden shyness that washed over me. Theo turned to me, his expression earnest, a silent plea for me to take the lead. I took a breath, the crisp air filling my lungs, grounding me in the moment. It was time to bridge the gap, to forge a connection amidst the flurry of emotions swirling like snowflakes in the wind.

"I think we're just figuring things out," I said, my voice steady despite the whirlwind inside me. "It's all... new."

"New can be scary," Jessa replied, her tone turning soft, almost reverent. "But it can also be exhilarating. Like a rollercoaster ride—terrifying and thrilling at the same time."

Theo's lips quirked up at the corners, but I could see the tension still coiling within him. The truth was, we were both on a precipice, peering down into the unknown, our feet firmly planted in a world that felt half-formed and hazy.

"You know, I've been reading this book about resilience," Jessa continued, her enthusiasm unwavering. "It talks about how vulnerability is the birthplace of creativity and change. Maybe being open to the unknown can lead to something incredible."

Her words struck a chord within me, resonating with the unvoiced fears and hopes I had been grappling with since our journey began. Theo's eyes flickered with understanding, and for a moment, the firelight cast a warm glow around us, wrapping us in an invisible cocoon of shared experiences.

"Jessa's right," Theo said, his voice low yet firm. "It's about embracing the fear, isn't it? We've both been carrying this weight, but it doesn't have to define us."

A spark of hope ignited within me. Maybe we didn't have to conquer our fears alone; perhaps we could forge a path together, each step illuminating the darkness that threatened to engulf us. I met his gaze, the connection we shared intensifying with each passing moment. It felt like a promise—a delicate thread weaving us closer together, even in the face of uncertainty.

As the evening wore on, the warmth of the fire began to seep into my bones, dispelling the chill lingering in my heart. Jessa's stories danced around us, lifting our spirits, and with each laugh, the weight of our fears felt lighter. We worked together, crafting the snow shelter, our movements synchronized as if we had choreographed the dance of construction.

The snow crunched beneath our boots, and with every handful we packed together, I felt the barriers between us begin to dissolve. The playful banter flowed naturally, creating an atmosphere charged with camaraderie, a safe space where our vulnerabilities could mingle with laughter.

With Jessa's guidance, we molded the snow into walls, shaping a refuge against the elements. It felt oddly symbolic—each block of snow representing the fears we were slowly chipping away, transforming the intangible into something tangible and real. I could see it in Theo's eyes as he focused, determination replacing the hesitance that had clouded his expression earlier.

"See?" I said, wiping the sweat from my brow, the cold air kissing my cheeks. "We make a pretty good team."

He looked up, a genuine smile breaking through the tension. "We do, don't we?"

As night fell, the stars burst forth in a dazzling display, twinkling above us like diamonds scattered across a velvet sky. It was a breathtaking sight, the kind of beauty that made the heart swell with longing and gratitude. I felt small yet significant, a mere speck in the vast universe, yet deeply connected to the people around me.

We finally stepped back to admire our handiwork: a sturdy snow shelter that stood proud against the landscape, its entrance welcoming and warm. I glanced over at Theo, whose face glowed under the starlight, each feature illuminated like a piece of art. In that moment, I understood that the fears that had threatened to tear us apart could instead be the very things that drew us closer.

"Let's call it our fortress of courage," I suggested playfully, nudging him with my shoulder.

"Fortress of courage," he echoed, a hint of laughter in his eyes. "I like that."

With that, I felt a shift within us, a delicate transition from fear to hope. And as we stood together under the vast expanse of stars, I realized that sometimes, it takes a leap into the unknown to discover the beauty of connection—a truth as profound as the glimmering night sky above us.

The night unfolded like a tapestry of dreams, the stars shimmering against the backdrop of an ink-black sky, as if the universe itself conspired to weave our fates together. I lay nestled in the warm embrace of our snow shelter, the fire crackling softly outside, sending tendrils of warmth into the icy air. Theo was beside me, the subtle rhythm of his breathing a soothing melody that lulled me into a tranquil state. I could still feel the spark of connection igniting between us, flaring with each shared glance and hesitant touch.

As I turned to face him, the flickering light revealed the contours of his face, framed by shadows and the glow of embers. I could see the remnants of our earlier conversation etched in his expression—an amalgamation of hope and uncertainty. "What are you thinking about?" I asked, my voice barely above a whisper, afraid to shatter the delicate moment we had crafted amidst the chaos.

He hesitated, his brow furrowing as he searched for the right words. "About how strange it is to feel so connected to someone in a place like this. It's like the snow is a barrier, yet it's also a bridge. Does that make sense?"

A smile broke across my face, the kind that felt like sunlight breaking through a storm cloud. "It makes perfect sense," I replied. "We're out here, isolated from everything familiar, yet somehow that makes the bond between us feel stronger."

Theo's gaze softened, and I sensed the walls around his heart starting to thaw. We were both discovering that vulnerability, while daunting, could be liberating. With the outside world cloaked in a blanket of snow, our little fortress became a sanctuary, a space where we could strip away the layers of fear that had previously held us captive.

Jessa's voice broke through the tranquility, her cheerful banter floating into our makeshift haven. "You two lovebirds better come out here and help me gather more firewood! We can't let this flame die, or I'll have to resort to my backwoods survival skills, and no one wants that!"

I chuckled, grateful for the warmth of her spirit that radiated even in the cold. Theo looked at me, amusement dancing in his eyes, and we exchanged a silent agreement before pushing ourselves up and stepping out into the frosty air. The night felt alive, the snow crunching underfoot as we moved toward the glow of the fire, the smell of woodsmoke mingling with the crisp scent of pine.

Jessa was tossing branches into the flames, the light illuminating her bright, determined face. "I was beginning to think I'd have to stage a rescue!" she teased, her laughter infectious. "What were you two doing, plotting your escape from the wilderness?"

"We were just discussing the intricacies of snowflakes and their emotional weight," I replied, unable to hide my grin.

"Ah, the emotional weight of snowflakes. Such a riveting topic!" she laughed, her voice brightening the cool night air. "Just make sure you're back for dinner. I've got a plan to turn this into a feast worthy of a winter cabin!"

As we gathered more firewood, I felt a sense of belonging blossom within me, a feeling that was as new as it was comforting. Working together, we fashioned a small pile of logs, our hands brushing occasionally in shared laughter and camaraderie. Each fleeting touch ignited something deep within, reminding me of how fragile yet powerful human connections can be.

The night wore on, and Jessa's culinary skills were nothing short of miraculous. She had managed to whip up a hearty stew using a combination of the supplies we'd packed and the wild herbs she'd foraged. The warmth of the meal filled our bellies and our hearts, fostering a sense of togetherness that eclipsed the cold outside. As we settled in around the fire, the shadows of the trees danced like specters in the night, their long fingers reaching out toward us as if curious about the stories we shared.

Between spoonfuls of steaming stew, I found myself captivated by the way Theo listened. He leaned in slightly, his eyes locked onto mine, a soft smile gracing his lips as I recounted the tales of my childhood. I spoke of snow days spent at home, building forts and engaging in epic snowball fights with my brothers, their laughter still echoing in my mind. The way Theo hung on every word made the past feel vibrant again, alive and breathing in the flickering firelight.

"I can't believe you grew up with brothers," he said, a playful glint in his eyes. "I'd always assumed you were a lone wolf. Now it all makes sense—the feisty spirit and relentless determination."

"Feisty, huh?" I teased, my voice dripping with mock indignation. "You'd better watch your back, or I might challenge you to a snowball duel."

"I accept!" he exclaimed, his competitive nature ignited. "But only if I get to be the one who throws the first one."

Laughter erupted around the fire, the warmth from our shared humor melding with the heat of the flames. As the night deepened, we sat close, sharing stories that danced around the shadows, weaving our pasts into a tapestry of understanding and friendship. In that moment, the world beyond our little haven faded, leaving only the three of us, connected by our shared experiences and the promise of tomorrow.

As the fire crackled and the stars twinkled above, I felt a profound sense of belonging. There was magic in the air, the kind that comes from being in the right place with the right people at the right time. The walls that had encased my heart began to crumble, and with them, the fear that had once loomed over me.

Theo turned to me, a contemplative look in his eyes. "Do you ever wonder what the future holds? For us, I mean."

The question hung in the air like a promise unspoken. I had been pondering that very thought, the weight of it filling my heart with both excitement and trepidation. "I do," I admitted, my voice steady yet tinged with vulnerability. "But I think what matters most is how we choose to face it. Together."

A warm smile broke across his face, illuminating the shadows that had lingered. "Together," he echoed, the word hanging between us, a bond forged in understanding and shared dreams.

As the night wore on, our laughter mingled with the crackle of the fire, and I realized that, amid the uncertainties of life, I had found something worth holding onto. Our connection, fragile yet resilient, was a thread weaving through the fabric of our experiences. Together, we would navigate the unknown, transforming the frozen fears of the past into the warm embrace of possibilities yet to unfold.

Chapter 8: The Leap of Faith

The mountain loomed large against the slate-gray sky, its peaks dusted with fresh powder that sparkled like diamonds in the fleeting sunlight. My breath mingled with the crisp air, forming soft clouds that drifted into the swirling breeze. There was an electric charge in the atmosphere, an exhilarating concoction of anticipation and fear that coursed through me like the adrenaline I'd soon need. The ski competition was a mere breath away, and I was caught in the thrilling limbo of what could be. With each beat of my heart, I felt the world shifting beneath my feet, a reality that was both intoxicating and terrifying.

The vast expanse of the mountain had become my second home, each slope and trail etched into my memory like a cherished story. From the cozy lodge, the scent of hot cocoa and pine clung to the air, wrapping around me like a warm embrace. The soft laughter and excited chatter of my fellow trainees created a vibrant symphony that echoed through the frosty air, but beneath the warmth of camaraderie, my heart drummed a different rhythm—one of doubt, courage, and longing. As I stepped outside, the chill nipped at my cheeks, turning them a rosy hue, but it was the warmth of Theo's presence that chased away the cold.

He had been my rock through the relentless training sessions, his patience a balm to my bruised ego. With tousled hair the color of chestnuts and eyes that sparkled like the mountain lake in summer, Theo had an effortless charm that drew me in. He was an enigma wrapped in layers of flannel and rugged denim, his laughter ringing clear like a bell on a quiet morning. Each moment spent together was a dance, a carefully choreographed routine of glances and subtle touches, and as I trained under his watchful gaze, I felt a connection that spiraled beyond the competition, deeper into the uncharted territory of my heart.

The slopes were my stage, and Theo was my guiding star. We spent countless hours carving our way through the snow, the sound of skis slicing through the pristine whiteness a melody that resonated in my bones. "You have to find your rhythm," he'd say, his voice firm yet tender, as we practiced on the gentle inclines. I would follow his lead, letting his energy fuel my determination, though a flicker of uncertainty often tugged at my spirit. Each run felt like a brushstroke on the canvas of my fear, a vivid depiction of the girl I wanted to become—a fearless competitor, a budding athlete, a woman willing to leap into the unknown.

As the last practice session arrived, I felt a swell of emotions battling within me. The air was thick with the scent of pine and adrenaline, and I was a tightly wound spring, ready to release. Theo approached me with an intensity that made my heart race. He took my hands in his, grounding me in the moment. "You're ready," he said, his eyes locking onto mine with an intensity that made the world around us fade away. I could feel the warmth radiating from his hands, a connection that was both electric and soothing. In that sacred space, surrounded by the mountains that held my fears and dreams, I let the whispers of his encouragement seep into my soul.

"Just trust yourself," he murmured, the sincerity in his voice wrapping around me like a soft blanket. With each word, I felt the weight of my insecurities begin to dissipate, replaced by a burgeoning sense of courage. It was a leap of faith—not just in the competition that lay ahead but in what could blossom between us. The thought of letting go of my fears, of launching myself into the unknown, became a mantra in my mind. I had to believe in myself as much as I believed in him.

The next morning, the sun broke through the clouds, painting the sky in hues of gold and azure. The air was electric with excitement as we gathered at the top of the slope, a gathering of hopeful competitors, each of us filled with dreams that danced in our eyes.

The moment was surreal, like standing at the edge of a precipice, the vast world below stretching out in both beauty and danger. I could hear the murmurs of my fellow trainees, their laughter mingling with the rush of the wind, but all I could focus on was the sound of my heart beating in tandem with the rhythm of the mountain.

As I prepared to make my descent, I closed my eyes for a fleeting moment, allowing the chaos to quiet into a steady pulse. I could almost feel Theo beside me, his presence a constant reminder that I was not alone. "You've got this," I whispered to myself, echoing the words he had instilled within me. With a deep breath, I opened my eyes, letting the vibrant world before me come into sharp focus. The slope stretched out like a wild ribbon, inviting me to take the plunge.

The countdown began, and the world narrowed into a singular point of focus—the slope, the snow, the exhilaration of the unknown. With one final breath, I pushed off, the rush of cold air enveloping me as I soared down the mountainside, the sound of the skis dancing over the snow resonating in my ears. Time slowed, each moment stretching into eternity as I felt the rush of adrenaline coursing through my veins. I was flying, untethered and free, embracing the leap of faith I had taken not just in the descent but in everything that had led me to this moment.

The world melted away as I glided down the slope, carving arcs through the fresh powder. The thrill surged through me like an electric current, each turn a testament to the countless hours spent under Theo's watchful eye. The mountain, once an intimidating giant, now felt like a friend, its curves welcoming me like an old companion. As I maneuvered through the soft, powdery snow, I was acutely aware of every sensation—the biting cold against my cheeks, the exhilaration bubbling in my chest, and the way the air rushed past, crisp and clean, filling my lungs with a new kind of freedom.

I felt alive. Each movement was fluid, a dance choreographed not by fear but by exhilaration. The sun bathed the landscape in golden light, illuminating the trees that lined the slope, their branches heavy with snow, glistening like diamonds in the early morning sun. I could hear the distant laughter of my fellow trainees mingling with the soft crunch of skis on snow, a melody that fueled my adrenaline. For a brief moment, I lost myself in the sheer joy of it all, forgetting the competition that loomed ahead.

With every turn, I felt more confident, more in tune with my body, a rhythmic harmony between skill and instinct. The beauty of the landscape enveloped me, the mountains standing like ancient sentinels, guardians of my newfound courage. I envisioned Theo at the finish line, his bright smile illuminating the crisp morning air, and I couldn't help but push myself harder, carving deeper into the snow, each run a promise to embrace what lay ahead.

But as I approached the base of the slope, my mind began to swirl with doubts, like dark clouds threatening to overshadow the brilliant sun. The cheers and shouts of the competitors echoed in my ears, and suddenly, the reality of the competition hit me like a gust of wind. What if I faltered? What if I failed? The thought gripped my heart, and my stomach twisted in a tight knot. I skidded to a halt, the ski tips digging into the snow, my breath hitching as anxiety clawed at my insides.

And then, there was Theo. He appeared beside me, a calming presence amidst the storm of my thoughts. "Hey," he said, his voice a gentle anchor, pulling me back from the edge of my spiraling fears. "You okay?"

I forced a smile, though it felt more like a mask than a reflection of how I truly felt. "Just... taking it all in," I replied, my voice steadying as I met his gaze. The warmth in his eyes sparked something deep within me, a flicker of resilience that I hadn't realized was there. "I'm ready. I really am."

He nodded, a small smile dancing on his lips, and in that moment, I saw not just my coach but my ally, a partner in this chaotic dance of competition and dreams. "You've worked hard for this. Trust yourself."

The simplicity of his words washed over me, calming the tempest within. I took a deep breath, letting the cool air fill my lungs, grounding me once more. "I will," I promised, the weight of his faith in me giving me the strength I didn't know I needed.

As we moved closer to the start line, the atmosphere buzzed with excitement, each competitor a vibrant thread in this tapestry of ambition and aspiration. The organizers called out names, each shout accompanied by a swell of applause that reverberated in my chest. I felt the rhythm of it all—the heartbeats of the crowd, the pulse of the mountain, the rush of the wind—melding into a symphony of anticipation.

When my name was announced, the world came alive with sound, a tidal wave of cheers crashing over me as I stepped into the spotlight. The snow glimmered underfoot, a beautiful expanse of white that mirrored the uncertainty swirling in my mind. Yet, there was a flicker of determination sparking within me, igniting a fire that threatened to consume my doubts. I was here for a reason, and it wasn't just to ski down a mountain; it was to reclaim my narrative, to embrace the adventure that life had laid before me.

As I positioned myself at the starting gate, I could hear Theo's voice cutting through the noise. "You've got this! Just remember what we practiced!" His unwavering belief wrapped around me like a shield, bolstering my resolve. I nodded, a gesture of gratitude mingling with my nerves, feeling the weight of his encouragement as I steadied myself for what lay ahead.

The countdown began, and the world narrowed into a singular focus—me, the slope, and the exhilarating plunge into the unknown. With each tick of the clock, I felt the rush of adrenaline surge through my veins, my heart pounding in time with the countdown. I released a breath I didn't know I was holding, letting go of everything that no longer served me. I was not just a competitor; I was a force of nature, ready to carve my own path down this majestic mountain.

With a final flick of my skis, I propelled myself forward, leaving the safety of the starting gate behind. The world exploded into motion, the wind whipping against my cheeks, the sound of the snow crunching beneath my feet a sweet symphony that urged me onward. I was flying, the mountains blurring around me in a cascade of white, each turn a testament to my growth, my strength, and the leap of faith I had taken.

In that exhilarating moment, I was no longer just me; I was the embodiment of possibility, a girl embracing the chaos and beauty of life with open arms. And as I carved my way down the slope, I knew that no matter what awaited me at the finish line, I had already won. The mountains whispered their approval, and the world opened up in front of me, an endless expanse of adventure just waiting to be embraced.

The slope unfurled beneath me like a crisp white carpet, a breathtaking expanse of fresh snow that beckoned me to dance. Each ski carved into the powder, leaving behind fleeting traces of my journey as I hurtled down with the confidence of someone who had finally shed the heavy cloak of doubt. The world around me melted into a blur of white and blue, the trees standing sentinel like proud guardians of my triumph. I was no longer just an athlete; I was a force of nature, embraced by the very essence of winter.

As I navigated the course, I could feel the energy of the crowd behind me, a distant yet palpable wave of encouragement. Friends and competitors alike were there, their cheers punctuating the cold air, weaving through my consciousness and intertwining with the rhythm of my breath. In that moment, the fear that had clawed at my insides faded into an echo of what once was. The mountain had transformed from an intimidating giant to a trusted ally, urging me onward with every turn.

But amidst the euphoria, flashes of doubt flickered in the corners of my mind. What if I stumbled? What if the leap of faith I had taken would end in a messy fall, embarrassing me in front of everyone, especially Theo? I shook my head, forcing those thoughts away. I had worked too hard, pushed too far to let insecurity sabotage my momentum now. With every carve, I channeled my energy, channeling not just my will to win but also the faith that Theo had instilled in me. His belief was like a tether, pulling me toward something greater.

As I approached the halfway point of the course, I caught a glimpse of him standing at the edge, his form framed against the backdrop of majestic mountains. The way he leaned forward, intent and hopeful, sent a surge of warmth coursing through me, battling the chill of the air. The world faded, and for a brief second, it was just the two of us suspended in that moment—his eyes meeting mine, igniting a spark that pulsed through the snow-covered landscape. It was a reminder that this was more than just a competition; it was a culmination of every lesson learned, every fear confronted, and every moment we had shared.

As I barreled down the slope, I recalled the countless days spent training with him. I remembered the way he would pull me up after a fall, his laughter ringing like a bell in the stillness of the mountain. He had been more than just a coach; he had become my confidant, my friend. I had opened up to him about fears that gnawed at me, allowing him to see the vulnerable pieces of me that I rarely shared. In those quiet moments, I had felt a connection bloom, fragile yet real, grounding me in a way I had never anticipated.

In the final stretch, the adrenaline surged through me like a wildfire, and I poured everything I had into that last run. I was a whirlwind of energy, bending low and twisting my body with practiced grace, embodying the spirit of the mountain itself. The finish line loomed ahead, an inviting ribbon of bright colors contrasting against the white canvas of snow. I could hear the crescendo of cheers rising from the crowd, a chorus that crescendoed into a wave of excitement. My heart raced, not with fear but with exhilaration.

Just as I crossed the finish line, I felt a jolt of triumph surge through me. I skidded to a stop, the momentum carrying me forward as I raised my arms in victory, the breathless laughter spilling from my lips in a joyous outburst. The applause enveloped me like a warm blanket, and I couldn't help but grin widely, my cheeks flushed with pride. I had done it. I had taken the leap and soared.

The atmosphere was electric as I looked around at the smiling faces of my fellow competitors. In that moment, it didn't matter who had finished ahead or behind; we were united by a shared experience, an unspoken bond formed through sweat and determination. The camaraderie felt like a living thing, breathing and vibrant, pulsating with energy as we celebrated our collective achievements.

And then, through the throng of excited faces, I spotted Theo pushing his way toward me, his expression a mix of pride and admiration. The world around us faded into a soft hum as he reached me, his eyes alight with an intensity that sent a thrill racing through my veins. "You were amazing!" he exclaimed, breathless from the excitement and the climb.

Before I could respond, he wrapped his arms around me, pulling me into an embrace that was as warm as the sun breaking through the winter clouds. I melted into him, the exhilaration of the competition mixing with the giddy rush of emotions that coursed through me. For a fleeting moment, the rest of the world faded away, leaving only us suspended in a cocoon of warmth and possibility.

"Thank you," I murmured against his shoulder, my voice muffled yet sincere. "I couldn't have done it without you."

He pulled back slightly, holding my gaze, and in that moment, the air between us crackled with unspoken words, a promise yet to be fulfilled. "You found the courage within you, and that's what matters most. I'm proud of you," he said, his voice steady and full of conviction.

As we stepped back, the noise of the crowd slowly returned, a jubilant celebration that surrounded us like a vibrant tapestry. The competition was over, but the adventure was only beginning. We shared stories and laughter with our fellow trainees, the spirit of victory lifting us higher than the peaks of the mountains that encircled us.

In the days that followed, we would reflect on this moment, this leap of faith, and how it had shifted something within me. I felt as though I had unlocked a new part of myself, a deeper understanding of who I was and what I was capable of. I was no longer just a girl standing at the edge of her fears; I was a woman who had embraced the uncertainty of life, ready to take on whatever came next.

With Theo by my side, I felt as though I could conquer the world—one slope, one leap, one moment at a time. The journey had just begun, and the possibilities stretched out before me, boundless and waiting to be explored.

Chapter 9: The Edge of Everything

The sun peeked over the jagged peaks, casting a golden hue across the pristine blanket of snow. It was competition day, and the air crackled with a vibrant energy, as though the mountain itself held its breath in anticipation. I could feel the electric pulse of excitement and nerves swirling around me, merging into a heady cocktail that made my heart race. The starting line was a chaotic symphony of laughter, chatter, and the rhythmic clanking of ski poles against boots, a stark contrast to the serene white landscape that enveloped us.

I stood there, shivering slightly in my bright red ski suit, a color that felt like a battle flag against the daunting mountain ahead. My fingers trembled slightly, whether from the chill or the exhilaration, I couldn't tell. The scent of fresh pine wafted through the crisp air, mingling with the sharp tang of winter. In the distance, I could hear the faint whoosh of skis slicing through the snow, a reminder of the competitors who had come before me, and the challenge that lay ahead. The slope seemed to loom larger, each ridge and curve whispering promises of both glory and disaster.

But amidst the chaos, my thoughts turned to Theo. I scanned the crowd, searching for his familiar silhouette against the sea of faces, my heart skipping a beat each time I thought I spotted him. He was my anchor, the one person who could turn my trepidation into courage with just a smile. When I finally caught sight of him, standing off to the side with his friends, my breath caught in my throat. He was leaning casually against a snow-covered tree, his dark hair tousled and his eyes sparkling with mischief. A wave of warmth flooded through me, igniting a fire in my chest that momentarily chased away the cold.

The starter's voice broke through my reverie, a sharp call that sent a shiver down my spine. I took a deep breath, the frosty air filling my lungs and solidifying my resolve. My heart pounded in rhythm with the countdown, a steady beat that drowned out the noise around me. One by one, competitors took their turn, launching themselves into the snow, gliding down the slope with grace and agility. I was next.

With a final glance at Theo, I pushed off, the world transforming into a blur of white and blue. My skis carved through the powder, the soft snow crunching beneath me, a crisp sound that echoed in my ears like applause. I felt the wind whip against my cheeks, a refreshing reminder of the chill that surrounded me, yet I was alive, exhilarated. Each turn was a dance with gravity, my body leaning into the slope as I navigated the twists and turns, adrenaline fueling my every move. I was in my element, my spirit soaring with each carve, each graceful leap.

But as I approached the first jump, I felt a flicker of doubt. Was I pushing myself too hard? The voice in my head was drowned out by the rush of excitement, urging me to keep going, to embrace the challenge. And just as I took off, a split-second miscalculation sent my world spiraling. My heart dropped as I felt the air leave my lungs, and suddenly, I was tumbling. The world spun in a dizzying whirl, snowflakes dancing around me like confetti at a parade.

Time slowed, each second stretching into infinity as I fell. Panic surged through me, but even in that moment, there was an odd clarity. I was free, unbound by the expectations that had weighed me down. And then, just as suddenly, I was caught. Strong arms wrapped around me, pulling me back from the brink. I gasped as I was yanked upright, my heart racing not from the fall, but from the warmth radiating from the body that held me.

Theo. His face was inches from mine, his expression a mix of concern and something deeper, something unspoken that flickered in his eyes. The world around us faded, the competition forgotten as I lost myself in that moment. I could feel the heat of his body, the steady rhythm of his breath, and for a heartbeat, time stood still.

"Are you okay?" His voice was a low murmur, tinged with worry, but I could hear the underlying current of something more, an urgency that set my heart racing anew.

"Yeah," I breathed, my voice shaky. "I think so."

He released me slowly, his hands lingering on my arms for just a moment longer than necessary, sending warmth coursing through my veins. The crowd around us faded back into focus, the competition coming back into view. But the stakes had shifted for me. It was no longer just about winning or losing; it was about facing the truth of what I felt for Theo, the undeniable connection that had been growing between us like the towering pines surrounding us.

Suddenly, the thrill of the competition felt insignificant compared to the revelation blossoming within me. I had to confront what lay ahead, a path that was fraught with uncertainty but also brimming with possibility. And as I looked into Theo's eyes, I realized that whatever the outcome of the competition, I was ready to embrace it all—the highs, the lows, and everything in between. The mountains had always called to me, but now, it was Theo's voice that resonated deeper, echoing in the chambers of my heart, guiding me toward a new adventure I never knew I craved.

The world resumed its frenetic pace as Theo stepped back, his hands slipping from my arms. A cacophony of voices surged around us, cheers and shouts rising and falling like the tides. Yet, amidst the jubilant clamor, a stillness settled within me. The adrenaline of the race was still coursing through my veins, but now it carried with it an unexpected warmth—a flicker of something profound that made me acutely aware of the space between us.

I could see him watching me, his brow slightly furrowed as if he were trying to decode the rush of emotions flitting across my face. For a brief moment, the chaos of the competition faded into the background, and all that mattered was the intensity of his gaze. It was a look I had longed to see, filled with an undeniable mix of concern and a yearning that made my heart flutter. I could hardly breathe, each inhale tinged with the reality of my racing thoughts.

I forced myself to break eye contact, shaking off the remnants of our shared moment as I rejoined the frantic energy of the day. Competitors hurried past me, some still buzzing with adrenaline, while others wore expressions of focused determination. The course ahead twisted like a serpent, a challenge waiting to be embraced. I could hear the distant roar of the crowd at the finish line, a sound that beckoned me to push forward. Yet, I hesitated, the weight of unspoken feelings and unsolved emotions holding me back.

My thoughts began to spiral, questioning everything—what would happen if I crossed that finish line? Would Theo be waiting, ready to celebrate, or would the moment dissolve into just another fleeting glance? As I stood there, heart racing and mind whirling, I felt a sense of urgency surge within me, compelling me to make a choice.

Gathering my resolve, I inhaled deeply, letting the crisp mountain air fill my lungs and clear the chaos in my mind. I had trained for this moment; I had prepared myself for every curve and jump. With each deep breath, I began to visualize the path ahead. My muscles tightened, and I felt the familiar rhythm of my heart syncing with the pulse of the mountain.

I pushed back the uncertainty and made my way to the starting line once more. As I readied myself, I locked eyes with Theo one last time. His encouraging nod sent a jolt of confidence through me. The world around us faded again, and it felt like it was just him and me in that moment, a silent pact forged in the chaos of competition.

When the starter's voice rang out again, I pushed off with a fierce determination, my skis slicing through the powdery snow like a knife. The crisp air stung my cheeks, but I embraced the chill, relishing the feel of the wind whipping past me as I accelerated down the slope. The path unfolded beneath me, each turn and jump igniting the fire within, reminding me why I loved this sport so fiercely.

But there was something different this time. It wasn't just the rush of adrenaline; it was the realization that I had to face my feelings for Theo head-on. Each turn of my skis mirrored my own internal struggle—how I danced around my emotions, always careful not to tumble into the depths of what we could become. And yet, here I was, plunging into the unknown, embracing the thrill of risk as I carved through the mountain.

As I approached the first jump, the familiar surge of anxiety bubbled up, but I tempered it with the thought of Theo. I launched into the air, feeling weightless for a brief moment before landing with a confident crunch in the snow. Each leap was a defiance of my fears, a proclamation that I would not shy away from the truth waiting to be uncovered.

The course narrowed as I raced down, the towering evergreens flanking me like guardians. I could hear the cheers from the crowd, a distant symphony of encouragement that urged me forward. My heart swelled as I envisioned crossing the finish line, and for the first time, I imagined Theo waiting for me, ready to wrap me in his arms, ready to share in the triumph of the moment.

As I approached the final stretch, I could see the finish line looming ahead, a bright banner flapping in the brisk mountain breeze. My legs burned, but I pushed through, feeling the exhilaration of the impending victory. And yet, amidst the excitement, doubt crept in, a whispering reminder of the fear that had haunted me. What if this moment was all there would ever be between us? What if my hopes crumbled like the snow beneath my skis?

But just as I began to lose focus, I caught sight of Theo again, his face illuminated with pride and support. His expression ignited something fierce within me, fueling my determination. With renewed vigor, I surged forward, my heart pounding not just from the race, but from the clarity dawning upon me. This was more than a competition; this was a chance to redefine everything, a moment that could alter the course of my life.

I crossed the finish line in a flurry of snow and laughter, the roar of the crowd crashing around me like waves. I could hardly comprehend the cheers, the jubilation of the moment. My knees buckled slightly as I came to a stop, breathless and exhilarated, feeling as though I had transcended the very mountain itself.

And then, amidst the whirlwind of emotion, I turned to find Theo rushing toward me, his arms outstretched, a radiant smile spreading across his face. It was in that instant, with the echoes of triumph still ringing in my ears, that I understood the true prize I had been competing for all along—the chance to embrace not just the thrill of the mountain, but the even more exhilarating leap into the unknown with Theo by my side.

The moment Theo enveloped me in his arms, the noise of the crowd faded into a distant murmur, as though I had been cocooned in a bubble of warmth and safety. I could feel the exhilarating rush of the competition fading away, replaced by an electric current that surged between us. As I looked up into his eyes, I saw not just the concern that had gripped him but also an unspoken promise—a connection that ran deeper than the mountain we stood upon.

"What a finish," he exclaimed, his breath coming out in frosty puffs, a testament to the crisp air that surrounded us. "You had me worried there for a second." His grin was infectious, brightening the gray day, and I couldn't help but smile back, my heart fluttering in my chest.

"Guess I like to keep you on your toes," I teased, feigning nonchalance while my stomach fluttered with something more than just the thrill of the race. I could feel the tension from moments before dissipating, and in its place, a sense of clarity emerged, solidifying the resolve that had been bubbling beneath the surface all along.

With the weight of my fears momentarily lifted, I glanced at the finish line, now a backdrop to the euphoria swirling around us. Competitors celebrated their victories and commiserated their defeats, and the air was thick with the scent of hot cocoa and grilled meats wafting from nearby food stalls. It was a festive atmosphere, a community bound by our shared love for the sport and the stories we carried, but all I could think about was what lay ahead for me and Theo.

"Come on, let's get some hot cocoa to celebrate," he said, pulling me along, his excitement palpable. As we maneuvered through the crowd, I felt a blend of nerves and exhilaration, as if I were stepping onto a precipice, poised to leap into something unknown yet thrilling.

We found a small, rustic stall adorned with twinkling lights that danced in the pale winter sun. The scent of rich chocolate enveloped us as we approached the window. A cheerful woman, her cheeks rosy from the cold, served steaming cups topped with whipped cream and a dusting of cocoa powder. I took a sip, the warmth spreading through me, melting away any remnants of anxiety that lingered in my mind.

"This is amazing," I murmured, savoring the rich flavors. I stole a glance at Theo, whose eyes sparkled with delight as he took a hearty sip of his own. There was a certain magic in the way he interacted with the world, as though he were finding joy in every small detail. The moment felt suspended in time, each laugh and every glance shared echoing with unvoiced feelings.

"Let's find a spot to sit," he suggested, scanning the area. We settled on a bench tucked beneath a sprawling oak, its branches laden with snow, casting a patchwork of shadows on the ground. The world around us blurred into a soft backdrop, leaving just the two of us in focus, the hum of celebration a distant echo.

"I still can't believe you caught me back there," I said, breaking the comfortable silence. "You really came out of nowhere."

He chuckled, his laughter rich and melodic. "Well, I couldn't just let you become a human snowball. That wouldn't be very heroic." His tone was light, teasing, but I sensed an undercurrent of sincerity beneath his words.

"Heroic? Please," I laughed, rolling my eyes. "I was the one who should have known better."

As we exchanged banter, a deeper realization washed over me, a wave that threatened to pull me under. Here we were, two souls connected by a shared experience, standing on the precipice of something new. I could feel the spark of attraction growing, morphing into something more substantial, something that beckoned to be explored.

"Do you ever think about what's next?" he asked suddenly, his gaze unwavering, as if he could peer directly into my thoughts. "After the competition, I mean."

The question hung in the air, heavy with significance. I opened my mouth to respond, but the words lodged in my throat. What was next for me? The uncertainty had always been a source of anxiety, a shadow that loomed over my dreams. "Honestly? I'm not sure," I admitted, the vulnerability of my answer surprising me.

"Maybe that's okay," Theo replied, his voice soothing. "I think sometimes it's good not to have everything figured out. There's freedom in that uncertainty."

His words struck a chord deep within me, resonating with the growing awareness that my life was a canvas, waiting for the brushstrokes of new experiences and connections. In that moment, the possibility of exploring my feelings for Theo became a part of that canvas, vibrant and full of promise.

As we spoke, the crowd around us ebbed and flowed like the tide, a living, breathing entity. Laughter mingled with the music drifting from nearby stalls, creating a symphony of celebration that mirrored the whirlwind of emotions within me. But amidst the joy of the day, I felt the gravity of my choices pressing down, the weight of every unsaid word lingering between us like a delicate thread, waiting for the right moment to be woven into something more substantial.

I looked at Theo, really looked at him, and I found in his expression a sense of understanding, an invitation to take that leap. "You know," I said softly, the words tumbling out before I could second-guess myself, "I think I've been afraid of what I might feel, what this could mean for us."

A flicker of surprise crossed his face, but it was quickly replaced by a knowing smile, the kind that made my heart skip a beat. "I get that. It's scary to put yourself out there, especially when you don't know how the other person feels."

I felt the heat rise to my cheeks, and the vulnerability of the moment enveloped us both. "But I want to know, Theo. I want to explore this. Us."

His eyes lit up, the excitement in them nearly palpable. "Really? You mean it?"

"Yes," I said, my heart racing. "I mean it."

The tension that had built between us released, and in its place, a new sense of possibility bloomed, vivid and alive. Just like the mountain we had conquered, it was daunting yet thrilling, a reminder that sometimes, the best experiences come from taking that leap into the unknown.

As we sat there, the chill of the air faded, replaced by the warmth of shared laughter and burgeoning hope. The world around us continued to celebrate the competition, but for me, the true victory was just beginning. With Theo by my side, I felt ready to embrace whatever lay ahead, ready to paint our story on the expansive canvas of life, each stroke imbued with the colors of love, adventure, and endless possibility.

Chapter 10: Echoes of Doubt

The moon hung high above the mountains, casting a silver sheen over the sprawling valley below, its light dancing across the jagged peaks like a whispered promise. I stood on the balcony, feeling the cool breeze wrap around me like an old, familiar scarf, each gust carrying the scent of pine and freshly turned earth. The sound of laughter and clinking glasses drifted through the open door behind me, a stark contrast to the turmoil brewing inside. The night had been filled with cheers and congratulations, but as I watched Theo from afar, the jubilation felt distant and hollow, overshadowed by the weight of my thoughts.

His laughter rang out, buoyant and free, a melody that seemed to echo through the crisp night air. I had always found solace in his presence, the way his smile lit up a room and how his confidence was magnetic, pulling everyone toward him. Yet, standing on the edge of this celebration, I felt like a ghost, lingering just out of reach. I remembered the warmth of his hand on my back as he helped me up after my fall, the genuine concern etched across his features. The memory was both a comfort and a torment, igniting the embers of something I had long tried to suppress.

My heart thudded in my chest, each beat a reminder of the words left unspoken, of the truth I feared would shatter this fragile moment. What if my feelings were unrequited? What if revealing my heart would sever the bond we had spent so long nurturing? The mountains loomed in the background, formidable and indifferent, their peaks standing tall against the night sky. I envied their steadfastness, their ability to endure the whims of nature, unyielding to the storms that would surely come. I wished for that kind of strength, for a moment of bravery that felt increasingly elusive.

As if summoned by my silent plea, Theo stepped out onto the balcony, the warmth of his presence a stark contrast to the chill in the air. He leaned against the railing beside me, the wooden slats rough beneath my fingers. For a moment, we stood side by side, gazing out at the moonlit expanse, the silence wrapping around us like a soft blanket. The stars twinkled above, indifferent to our turmoil, their brilliance a reminder of the vast universe beyond our small lives.

"Beautiful night, isn't it?" he finally said, his voice breaking the silence like the first rays of dawn slicing through the darkness.

"It is," I replied, my gaze still fixed on the mountains. "It almost feels like everything else fades away, doesn't it?"

He nodded, his expression contemplative, and I could see the shadows of his own thoughts flickering behind his eyes. "Sometimes I think we get so caught up in everything happening around us that we forget to just... be."

His words hung in the air, echoing my own internal struggle. In the throes of competition and camaraderie, I had lost sight of the essence of why I started this journey in the first place. It wasn't just about winning; it was about the joy of sharing moments with people who understood me, who saw the world through the same lens of passion and dreams.

"I feel like I've lost that a bit," I admitted, finally turning to meet his gaze. His eyes sparkled in the moonlight, deep pools of understanding and warmth that both soothed and stirred my heart. "After everything that happened, I'm not sure I know who I am anymore."

His brow furrowed slightly, concern creasing his forehead. "You're still you, you know. A fall doesn't define you. It's how you get back up that counts."

The sincerity in his voice ignited a flicker of hope within me, but doubt still clung to my thoughts like a stubborn mist. "But what if I can't get back up? What if I've already fallen too far?"

Theo shifted closer, his shoulder brushing against mine. "We all stumble, but that doesn't mean we can't rise stronger. I saw you out there, pushing yourself. You've come so far, even when you didn't believe it. That counts for something."

His words resonated with a truth I desperately needed to hear, but as I turned to face him, I caught a glimpse of vulnerability in his expression. It was fleeting, a crack in his armor that he quickly concealed, but it left me questioning. What was he feeling? Did he wrestle with his own doubts, the same way I did? It was a thought that sent my heart racing. Perhaps he, too, was seeking something more than just friendship.

"Thank you," I whispered, but the words felt inadequate. I wanted to convey so much more—to share the tumultuous whirlwind of emotions swirling within me, to explain how he had become a beacon in my darkness. But instead, I felt paralyzed by the fear of vulnerability.

The silence stretched between us again, thicker now, filled with the weight of our shared moments and the tension of uncharted territory. I took a deep breath, summoning every ounce of courage I could muster, yet the words that danced on the tip of my tongue refused to come forth. I could feel the barrier between us, as if an invisible wall had sprung up, one that I yearned to dismantle but was terrified to approach.

A sudden burst of laughter erupted from the gathering inside, breaking the momentary tension. Theo's gaze flickered back to the celebration, and for a heartbeat, I feared he would retreat, leaving me alone in this uncertain space. But then he turned back to me, a spark of determination igniting in his eyes.

"Do you want to go back in?" he asked, and I could hear the unspoken question beneath his words. Would we slip back into the safety of our friends, the comfortable banter that defined our relationship, or was this a pivotal moment where we could push beyond the boundaries we had established?

I hesitated, torn between the warmth of the crowd and the magnetic pull of the unknown that stood before me. The choice felt monumental, like standing at the edge of a cliff, with the abyss yawning below and the sky stretching infinitely above.

A cool breeze whispered through the trees, ruffling the leaves with a gentle sigh that seemed to echo my own inner turmoil. The laughter from inside faded, leaving a soft hum of distant conversations punctuated by the occasional clinking of glasses, but in this moment with Theo, everything else felt irrelevant. I could still sense the energy of the celebration, the warmth of camaraderie spilling into the night, but standing beside him, my heart raced as if we were the only two people in existence. The world beyond felt like a blur, hazy and indistinct, as I grappled with the moment's fragility.

His gaze lingered on the horizon, a thoughtful crease forming between his brows as he scanned the starlit sky. I marveled at how the moonlight illuminated his features, casting a soft glow that made him look almost ethereal. It was easy to forget the chaos of our lives in this suspended moment, the competition and the weight of expectations hanging in the air like a heavy fog.

"Sometimes I wish we could just freeze time," he murmured, almost to himself. "You know? Capture moments like this and hold onto them forever."

I turned my head slightly, intrigued by the vulnerability in his voice. "And what would we do with all that time?" I asked, a playful lilt in my tone, hoping to coax out a smile. "Stare at the mountains until we turn to stone?"

Theo chuckled, the sound warm and rich, a balm to my anxious heart. "Maybe. Or we could go on ridiculous adventures, chasing sunsets and diving into lakes. You know, the fun stuff."

His words hung in the air, buoyant and carefree, but beneath the levity lay an undercurrent of sincerity that tugged at my heart. I yearned to share that dream with him, to explore those sunsets hand in hand, but the shadows of doubt loomed ever larger, casting a pall over my thoughts. I wondered if he could sense my struggle, if the tension was palpable, or if I was simply overthinking every fleeting glance and brush of skin.

"What if time isn't the enemy?" I replied, trying to keep my voice light, though my heart was heavy. "What if it's the fear of what's to come? Maybe the adventures are too uncertain."

His gaze shifted to me, those deep, expressive eyes searching mine as if he could unearth the layers of uncertainty buried within. "But isn't uncertainty the essence of adventure? It's what makes it worthwhile," he countered, leaning slightly closer, our shoulders nearly touching. "The unpredictability, the thrill of not knowing where the road will lead. Isn't that what makes life exciting?"

"Or terrifying," I interjected, a smirk playing on my lips, but the tremor in my voice betrayed the truth lurking beneath.

"True," he admitted, a playful glint in his eyes. "But imagine the stories we'd have to tell. Like, remember that time we jumped into a lake in the middle of winter just to feel alive?"

The vivid imagery he conjured brought a smile to my face, but it felt like a fragile façade against the storm brewing inside me. The thrill of adventure he described resonated deep within my soul, but I still grappled with the constraints of my own hesitations.

"You make it sound so easy," I said softly, staring out at the darkness beyond. "But what if we jump in, and it's just... cold? What if we're not ready for it?"

Theo tilted his head, studying me with an intensity that made my heart race. "Then we learn to swim, right? Together. That's how it works. Life is full of unexpected depths. We just have to find our way through."

The sincerity in his voice struck a chord, reverberating through my chest. I longed to believe him, to embrace the notion that I could navigate the currents of life, but the fear still clung to me, a weight I couldn't quite shake off. I wanted to dive into the depths of whatever this connection was, to explore the untamed waters of my emotions, but uncertainty held me back like a heavy anchor.

"Can we really face everything together?" I asked, my voice barely above a whisper, daring to hope that he felt the same pull I did. "What if one of us gets lost along the way?"

He reached out, his fingers brushing against mine, igniting a spark that sent shivers racing up my arm. "Then we'll find each other. We're stronger together, remember? Whatever comes our way, I won't let you drift."

A warmth blossomed in my chest at his promise, but my heart wavered under the weight of my own insecurities. "I'm scared, Theo. Scared of what it means to open up, to be vulnerable."

His grip tightened slightly, grounding me in a way I hadn't expected. "We all have our fears. It's okay to be scared. But you don't have to face it alone. I'll be right here, cheering you on, no matter what."

His words washed over me, a gentle tide against the shore of my apprehensions. I wanted to believe him, wanted to grasp onto this moment and make it last. But the ghosts of doubt whispered incessantly in my mind, urging me to retreat, to hide from the truth that had been inching closer with every shared smile and lingering glance.

"What if it's not enough?" I finally blurted out, my voice trembling with the weight of my honesty. "What if I'm not enough?"

His eyes softened, and I could see the flicker of understanding in them. "You are more than enough, but it's not about that. It's about us. It's about sharing the journey, every messy, imperfect step of the way. You don't have to be perfect to be loved, you just have to be you."

In that moment, something shifted within me, a crack in the wall of uncertainty that had surrounded my heart for far too long. His words felt like a lifeline, and as the stars twinkled above, I realized

I stood on the precipice of something beautiful. With every breath, every heartbeat, the fear began to dissipate, replaced by the warmth of hope, the promise of possibility.

The mountains loomed large behind us, steadfast and unyielding, yet in the face of that daunting backdrop, I felt the thrill of adventure beckoning. Maybe it was time to embrace the unknown, to leap into the depths of our connection and discover where it might lead. As I looked into Theo's eyes, I saw not just a reflection of my own fears, but the glimmer of shared dreams waiting to be written, our stories intertwining like vines reaching for the sunlight.

The warmth of Theo's hand lingered on mine, a gentle reminder of the connection we had forged against the backdrop of uncertainties. The stars twinkled above us, indifferent yet mesmerizing, like tiny spectators to the drama unfolding on this little balcony in the mountains. With each passing moment, I felt the weight of silence shift, transforming from a heavy shroud into an intimate space where possibilities danced between us.

"Do you think we could be more than friends?" The words slipped out before I could rein them in, raw and unrefined, but they hung in the air, a fragile thread that tethered us to the moment.

Theo's breath hitched, the surprise flickering across his face like the flash of a shooting star. "You're serious?"

"Dead serious," I said, feeling a rush of adrenaline as vulnerability surged through me. The boldness of my admission invigorated me, yet I feared the implications of my words. The laughter inside had dwindled to a low murmur, as if even the party sensed the gravity of our conversation.

He turned to face me fully, his expression a mixture of excitement and apprehension. "I've thought about it," he confessed, his voice low, resonating in the quiet night. "But I didn't know if you felt the same way. I didn't want to risk what we already have."

His honesty was like a balm, soothing the jagged edges of my anxiety. "I don't want to lose you, either," I replied, my heart racing with every syllable. "But I can't keep pretending that I don't feel this pull between us. It's like a magnet, and the more I resist, the stronger it becomes."

A smile broke through the tension, a beacon of light that lit up his face. "Then why resist?"

In that moment, surrounded by the sprawling expanse of the night sky and the towering mountains, I realized the fear that had shackled me for so long was merely an illusion. It was time to embrace the thrill of the unknown, to forge a path that was uniquely ours. I took a step closer, drawn to him like the tide to the shore.

"I want to explore this," I said, my voice steady now, bolstered by a newfound determination. "To see where it can take us."

His eyes sparkled with a mixture of hope and mischief. "So, you're saying you want to be my partner in crime?"

"Absolutely," I grinned, feeling lighter, as if a weight had been lifted. "But I'm warning you—I may not be the easiest partner. I come with a whole suitcase of doubts."

"Bring it on," he replied, his laughter ringing like music against the backdrop of the stars. "Doubts can be navigated. We'll figure it out together, one step at a time."

The warmth radiating from him wrapped around me, dispelling the lingering chill of fear. I couldn't help but imagine the adventures we would embark on together, weaving through the tapestry of our lives as if we were creating a story only we could tell.

As we lingered on the balcony, the world inside faded further away, our laughter mingling with the crisp mountain air. With every shared glance and playful banter, I felt the walls around my heart crumble, the vulnerability morphing into an exhilarating freedom. It was a strange mix of intimacy and exhilaration, like standing at the edge of a cliff, looking down at the roaring waves below, knowing that the plunge could either invigorate or terrify.

"Let's make a pact," I suggested suddenly, the words bursting forth as my excitement bubbled over. "No matter what happens, we keep communicating. No holding back."

"Deal," he said, his smile widening, showcasing the boyish charm that had drawn me in from the very start. "We'll be open about everything—the good, the bad, the ridiculous. And if one of us starts to hesitate, we talk it out. No running away."

His sincerity resonated deeply within me, solidifying the bond that had begun to bloom. I nodded, feeling a rush of warmth, not just from the promise we made but from the realization that we were no longer standing on the precipice of uncertainty; we were diving headfirst into the beautiful chaos of possibility.

The night unfolded around us, rich with the sounds of nature—the rustle of leaves, the soft hoot of an owl echoing in the distance, and the whispering wind that carried with it the scent of damp earth and pine. I closed my eyes for a moment, allowing the sensory tapestry to envelop me, grounding me in the reality of this moment.

"Should we go back inside?" he asked, glancing over his shoulder at the party.

I hesitated, torn between the magnetic connection we were forging in the quiet and the vibrant energy swirling within the cabin. "Do you think they'll notice we're gone?"

"They might," he teased, his eyes glinting with mischief. "But let them wonder. We're writing our own story right now."

"Alright," I said, a playful grin breaking across my face. "Let's make our grand re-entrance."

With that, we turned toward the warmth spilling out from the cabin, hearts racing with the thrill of our newfound connection and the promise of what lay ahead. As we stepped inside, the laughter and music washed over us like a wave, pulling us back into the fold of our friends, but I felt a shift within myself. The air was electric with anticipation, each glance between us now imbued with a hidden language, a new understanding that simmered just below the surface.

The room was alive, filled with the joyful clamor of friends celebrating victories and sharing stories. But in that moment, I felt as if we were the only two people in the room, the world narrowing down to just Theo and me, our laughter mingling like a sweet melody amid the cacophony.

As the night wore on, we drifted through the crowd, our hands brushing occasionally, igniting sparks of warmth that sent shivers down my spine. Each shared glance and secret smile felt like a promise, a thread weaving us closer together. The party ebbed and flowed around us, but in our bubble of excitement, nothing else mattered.

Later, as we found ourselves standing under the fairy lights strung across the backyard, I felt a sense of clarity settle in my chest. I no longer questioned the path ahead; instead, I embraced the thrill of the unknown, buoyed by the knowledge that we were in this together. With each passing moment, I knew that whatever challenges lay ahead, we would face them side by side, navigating through the complexities of life and the depth of our emotions.

The mountains stood tall in the background, their presence a reminder of the journey we had begun and the adventures waiting just beyond the horizon. And as I looked into Theo's eyes, I saw not just a reflection of my own hopes but a partner ready to leap into the depths of possibility with me, daring to explore what lay beyond.

Chapter 11: Secrets of the Heart

A blanket of stars stretched across the clear night sky, their twinkling reflections shimmering on the snow like a scattered trail of diamonds. The air was crisp, infused with the scent of pine and the faint whisper of woodsmoke curling up from distant chimneys. My heart beat a little faster as I stepped outside, the powdery snow crunching softly under my boots, a soothing rhythm against the cacophony of my swirling thoughts. This place, with its soaring mountains and cozy cabins, had woven itself into the fabric of my being. The laughter of my newfound friends echoed in my ears, their faces illuminated by the warm glow of the lodge. Yet, an unease settled deep in my chest, a gnawing anxiety that accompanied the fading sunlight.

Jessa and Theo's conversation had rattled me to my core. The weight of their words hung in the air, almost palpable, each syllable striking like a bell tolling in a distant church. I had always seen Theo as a constant in this beautiful, chaotic existence we'd created together, a steady presence against the backdrop of towering trees and endless powder. His playful banter, the way he tucked his hands into the pockets of his flannel jacket, and the way he threw his head back to laugh, all felt like threads tying me to this place. The realization that he might walk away, leaving all of this behind, sent a shiver of dread down my spine.

As I moved closer to the lodge, my breath misting in the chilly air, I caught sight of him leaning against the railing, his silhouette framed by the twinkling lights strung overhead. My heart raced at the sight. There he was, so effortlessly handsome with his tousled hair and those deep, searching eyes that seemed to hold the secrets of the universe. I wanted to shout out to him, to let him know how much he meant to me, but the words caught in my throat like the cold air.

What was I supposed to say? "Hey, I heard you might be leaving, and that terrifies me"?

The thought made me wince. Instead, I took a deep breath, steeling myself for the conversation that felt inevitable. As I approached, the laughter and chatter from inside the lodge faded into a gentle hum, and all I could hear was the rush of the wind through the trees. It was just him and me now, in this fragile moment suspended between fear and desire.

"Hey," I said, my voice a little breathless, even to my own ears.

Theo turned, his eyes lighting up as they met mine, and the tension in my chest eased just a fraction. "Hey, there you are." He pushed himself off the railing, a smile breaking across his face that sent a warmth flooding through me. "I thought you'd be inside, warming up."

I shrugged, trying to play it cool despite the storm of emotions brewing inside. "Just needed some air, I guess. The snow is so beautiful tonight."

"Yeah, it really is," he agreed, his gaze drifting to the untouched blanket of white surrounding us. For a moment, we stood in silence, the kind that felt loaded with unspoken words. The sound of laughter from inside echoed softly, a reminder of the warmth and joy just beyond our little bubble.

"You're not thinking of leaving, are you?" I blurted out, the question spilling from my lips before I could catch it.

His eyes widened slightly, surprise flickering across his features. "Why would you think that?"

"Jessa mentioned something... about you having plans." I took a step closer, my heart thumping loudly in my chest. "I didn't realize you were planning to go."

He sighed, running a hand through his hair as he leaned against the railing once more, the wood cool against my fingers as I gripped it tightly. "It's complicated," he said slowly, his voice thoughtful, almost hesitant. "I've been here for a while, and I think it might be time for me to move on. I have some things I want to pursue back home."

A dull ache settled in my chest, like a heavy stone. "But this place... we've built something here, haven't we? I mean, it's not just the snow and the training, right?"

He turned to face me fully, the seriousness in his expression deepening. "Of course, it's not just that. I've loved my time here, but I can't ignore the pull of what's waiting for me back home. It's something I have to do."

"Does that mean you'll just... leave? Just like that?" The desperation in my voice surprised even me.

"I don't want to, but I feel like I have to." He leaned forward, his eyes searching mine. "It's hard to explain. There are things I need to take care of, and I can't ignore them any longer."

The wind whispered around us, carrying the distant sounds of music and laughter from the lodge, and for a moment, the world felt impossibly large and incredibly small at the same time. I wanted to reach out, to grasp his hand and pull him back from the edge of whatever decision he was contemplating. "You know you don't have to do this alone, right? We can figure it out together."

Theo hesitated, the weight of the moment pressing down on us like the thick snow blanketing the earth. "I appreciate that, I really do," he said softly, "but this is something I have to do for myself."

In that moment, the distance between us felt insurmountable, and a surge of emotion threatened to spill over. I wanted to argue, to convince him that there was more for him here than just snow and ski lifts. I wanted to show him the warmth of the friendships we had forged and the beauty in the moments we had yet to create. Instead, I stood there, heart in my throat, fighting against the impending sense of loss that loomed over us.

As the laughter from the lodge faded into the background, I realized that sometimes, love meant letting go, even when it felt like it would shatter you to do so.

The next morning, the sun rose with a reluctant brilliance, casting long shadows across the snow-draped terrain. The mountains stood sentinel, their peaks glowing pink and gold in the soft light, as if they were privy to some celestial secret. I sat on the edge of my bed, staring out at the dazzling display, my mind wrestling with thoughts that felt like a blizzard within. Each flicker of sunlight through the frosted window felt like a reminder of everything I was about to lose, and as I pulled on my ski gear, the weight of uncertainty pressed down on my shoulders like the heavy winter coat I struggled to fasten.

I stepped outside, and a chill kissed my cheeks, invigorating yet biting. The snow crunched beneath my boots, a crisp rhythm that seemed to echo the tumult within me. I took a deep breath, filling my lungs with the cold, fresh air that smelled of adventure and possibility. I moved toward the lift, my heart beating a nervous tempo, the excitement of the slopes mingling with the dread of the unknown. The lifts loomed ahead, a gateway to the heights where laughter and adrenaline mingled in a heady mix.

As I rode up, the landscape below unfurled like a beautiful tapestry. The sprawling pine forests whispered secrets in the wind, and the sunlight sparkled on the fresh powder, creating a dazzling sea of white. I thought of all the times Theo and I had conquered these slopes together, the playful shoves and the shared exhilaration, the thrill of racing down in a blur of snow and laughter. The thought of this being my last ride with him left a bittersweet taste on my tongue.

When I reached the summit, the view took my breath away. The expanse of white stretching into the horizon made me feel both insignificant and infinite. I stood for a moment, soaking it all in, and for the briefest of seconds, the troubles of my heart faded, replaced by the pure beauty of the world around me. But that fleeting sense of peace was quickly overshadowed by the gnawing anxiety that accompanied thoughts of Theo's departure. What if this moment, this blissful solitude, was the last memory I could share with him in this magical place?

I pushed off, carving through the snow, my body moving instinctively, but my mind was a tempest. Each turn felt like a distraction, a way to dodge the reality looming just behind me. I caught sight of him below, effortlessly weaving through the trees, a natural grace to his movements that made my heart skip. The way he navigated the slopes seemed to embody the freedom I longed for, yet it struck me then how tethered I felt to this moment, to him.

As I descended, I could see his dark jacket against the white landscape, a beacon pulling me closer. When I finally reached him, we collided into each other with a lighthearted shove, a familiar game of mock aggression that sparked a warmth within me. "Hey there, speed demon," I teased, trying to inject some levity into the heaviness that lingered in the air between us.

He grinned, his eyes bright and mischievous. "I could say the same to you! Thought I'd have to rescue you from the mountain. You were taking your sweet time up there."

"Just soaking in the view," I replied, matching his playful tone even as my heart ached. "Figured I might want to remember it, you know, before it's all gone."

His laughter echoed through the trees, but the lightness didn't reach his eyes. "You're not getting rid of me that easily," he said, but the way he said it was tinged with an undertone that made me doubt his words.

As we moved down the slope together, the wind whipping past us, I felt an urgency to voice the unspoken truth hanging between us. "I heard you and Jessa talking last night," I blurted out, barely catching my breath as we slowed at the edge of a glistening expanse of untouched snow.

Theo's expression shifted, a flicker of surprise followed by a guarded look. "Yeah, she might have mentioned some things. You know how it is... Just thinking about my options."

"Options?" I echoed, unable to hide the tremor in my voice. "Is leaving really one of them? I thought this place meant something to you."

"It does," he admitted, his tone growing serious as we turned to face each other. "But sometimes, the things that mean the most are also the hardest to hold onto. I can't ignore the pull of what's waiting for me back home."

"Are you sure that's what you really want?" My heart raced as I probed deeper, needing to understand the depth of his feelings. "You've built a life here, friends, memories... me."

His eyes softened, and for a moment, I thought I saw a flicker of uncertainty dance across his features. "I know," he said slowly. "And it's not easy for me either. But I need to chase my dreams, and sometimes that means making tough decisions."

The weight of his words settled heavily in the air between us, and I took a step closer, my heart thudding wildly. "What if I want you to stay?" I blurted out, the honesty spilling from my lips like the snowflakes swirling around us.

Theo took a deep breath, his gaze unwavering as he searched mine for something—maybe clarity, maybe hope. "I want you to be happy, but I also have to look out for myself."

"Can't you do both?" My voice trembled with desperation, and I reached out, brushing my fingers against his gloved hand. The contact sent a jolt of electricity between us, a reminder of the connection that thrummed beneath the surface. "This place, us... we could be a part of your dream too."

He looked down at our hands, a flicker of something unnameable passing between us, but he didn't pull away. "You have no idea how much I want that. But I also can't stay somewhere out of obligation."

Silence enveloped us, the quiet of the mountain wrapping around our unspoken fears like a fragile cocoon. My heart felt heavy, tethered to the possibility of losing him yet buoyed by the hope that maybe he could find a way to stay. The world around us seemed to fade away, leaving just the two of us standing on that snow-covered slope, tangled in our emotions, while the sun hung lazily overhead, casting long shadows that stretched like time itself.

In that moment, I realized that some choices were not just about what we leave behind but what we were willing to fight for in the face of uncertainty. The question lingered, suspended in the cold air, as our breaths mingled and the weight of our reality pressed heavily on both of us, demanding an answer neither of us was quite ready to give.

The air around us felt electric, charged with possibilities yet stifled by the weight of our unspoken fears. I could see the myriad emotions flickering across Theo's face—determination, uncertainty, a hint of regret—as he took a step back, leaving a chasm between us that felt impossible to bridge. The mountain stretched high above, its majestic peak a stark reminder of the choices looming before us. It felt as though the snow beneath us had become a mirror, reflecting the turmoil swirling in my heart, the chaos of what could be if only we could find the courage to confront it.

"Why does it have to be either/or?" I asked, my voice barely above a whisper, yet it felt as if I had shouted it into the vastness. "You could find a way to have both."

Theo rubbed the back of his neck, the gesture both familiar and disconcerting. "It's not that simple. Sometimes, leaving is the best way to grow, to explore what else is out there."

"But what if what's out there isn't as good as what you already have?" The words tumbled out before I could reign them in, a rush of desperation spilling forth. "You and I, we have something real here, and I don't want to lose that."

His gaze flickered to the slopes, the path we had traveled together, but I caught the sadness creeping into his eyes as he faced me once more. "It's not about what we have. It's about what I need to do for myself."

The weight of his declaration settled heavily in the pit of my stomach, and I felt an overwhelming urge to break the distance, to bridge the gap that had formed between us, both physically and emotionally. The cold air swirled around us, a reminder of the world outside our fragile bubble, and I took a step closer, my heart racing with the unspoken words that threatened to spill over.

"Then help me understand," I implored, my voice steady despite the tempest within. "Help me understand why you're willing to walk away."

His brow furrowed, and I could see the internal battle raging behind his carefully composed facade. "It's not just about walking away; it's about the opportunity to chase something bigger. I have a chance to work on a project back home that could really set me on a path I've always dreamed about."

The words hung in the air, heavy with promise yet edged with sorrow. "But what if that path leads you away from me?"

A flicker of hesitation crossed his face, and for a brief moment, I thought I had seen a crack in his resolve. "I don't want that," he admitted, his voice low, as if he were revealing a secret only meant for my ears. "But I can't ignore my ambitions either. They've been a part of me for so long."

In that moment, clarity surged through me like a swift current. I took a breath, filling my lungs with the cold mountain air, steeling myself for what I needed to say next. "You know, we're at a point in our lives where we have to decide what we truly want. You can chase your dreams, but can't we also find a way to support each other while doing it?"

His gaze softened, and the warmth of his presence enveloped me like the first rays of sunshine breaking through the clouds. "You really think we could make that work?"

"I do." My heart soared at the possibility, the fragile hope blooming within me like the first flowers of spring peeking through the snow. "This place is magical, but it's the people here who make it special. You don't have to give up everything to go after what you want."

A silence settled between us, and in that quiet, I could almost hear the distant echoes of laughter from the lodge—a reminder of the community we had built and the friendships we had forged. I reached out, closing the distance between us, and grasped his hand, grounding us in the moment. "We can figure this out together. I believe in us."

Theo's eyes searched mine, and for an eternity, we stood there, suspended in the beautiful uncertainty of it all. Finally, he exhaled, the tension in his shoulders easing as a reluctant smile crept onto his lips. "You really make it hard to walk away, you know that?"

"And you're making it hard to let go," I replied, my voice laced with a playful teasing that masked the raw vulnerability within.

"Maybe we should go inside," he suggested, his thumb brushing lightly over my knuckles, igniting a warmth that spread through me. "It's freezing out here."

I nodded, though I was reluctant to break the moment. We turned and began the descent, our laughter mingling with the wind, the sound bright against the backdrop of the mountain. As we made our way down, the path ahead seemed less daunting, illuminated by the light of shared dreams and newfound understanding.

The lodge loomed closer, its inviting warmth spilling out like a beacon against the starkness of the night. As we stepped inside, the scent of hot cocoa and cinnamon enveloped us, wrapping around us like a comforting embrace. The warmth seeped into my bones, easing the chill of the mountain air and filling me with a sense of belonging.

We found a cozy corner near the fireplace, the flames dancing and crackling, casting flickering shadows across the room. Friends gathered around, the vibrant chatter and laughter filling the space, a reminder of the life we had built here. I settled into the plush armchair, feeling the weight of the world lift slightly off my shoulders as Theo sank into the seat beside me.

"So," he said, his eyes sparkling with mischief, "what do you think about making a pact?"

"A pact?" I echoed, intrigued.

"Yeah. A promise to support each other no matter where life takes us." He leaned closer, the firelight flickering across his features, highlighting the earnestness in his expression. "We can chase our dreams and still hold on to what we have here. It doesn't have to be an either/or situation."

I felt a swell of warmth at his words, an affirmation of everything I had hoped for. "I like the sound of that."

"Then it's settled," he declared, a grin breaking across his face, infectious and bright. "We're partners in crime, and no mountain—or opportunity—will stand in our way."

Laughter erupted from the group around us, but the world around us faded as I focused on him, on the spark of something more that flickered between us. We may have been standing on the precipice of change, but together, we were forging a path that intertwined our dreams and our hearts, leaving behind the fear of what might come next.

As the fire crackled and the laughter swirled around us, I realized that sometimes the most beautiful things emerge from the most complicated of choices. In that warm glow, surrounded by the love of friends and the promise of a future yet to unfold, I felt a sense of peace wash over me. The journey ahead might be unpredictable, but it was a journey I was willing to take, hand in hand with the person who had unexpectedly become so integral to my heart.

And as I leaned into Theo, our fingers still intertwined, I knew that no matter where life led us, we would face it together, ready to carve our paths in the snow, leaving behind a trail of laughter, love, and uncharted possibilities.

Chapter 12: The Climb

The mountains loomed above us like ancient giants, their peaks piercing the crisp blue sky. Each breath filled my lungs with the earthy scent of pine and damp moss, invigorating my spirit with every step I took alongside Theo. The trail twisted and turned, revealing a vibrant tapestry of wildflowers that danced in the gentle morning breeze, their colors splashed across the landscape like brushstrokes on a canvas. I watched as bees buzzed lazily from blossom to blossom, their soft hum merging with the chirps of hidden birds. Nature's orchestra played a symphony, each note echoing the promise of the day.

Theo walked ahead, his tall figure moving gracefully over the uneven terrain. He was in his element, and I admired the way his dark hair caught the sunlight, forming a halo around his head. I could hear the subtle crunch of gravel beneath his boots, a rhythm that seemed to sync with the beating of my heart. Every now and then, he would glance back at me, his eyes sparkling with mischief, as if he was keeping a delightful secret just out of reach. It made me feel alive, a flutter of hope stirring in my chest that today might be the day I finally found the courage to say what had been simmering just below the surface.

As we climbed higher, the world below faded into a blur of greens and browns, a tapestry woven with threads of the ordinary life we were momentarily leaving behind. The air thinned, but it was not just the altitude that quickened my pulse. I felt as if I were shedding layers of myself with each step, discarding the doubts and fears that had burdened me for so long. With Theo by my side, the uncertainties felt manageable, like pebbles underfoot rather than boulders on my shoulders.

"The higher we go, the closer we are to the clouds," Theo said, a teasing lilt in his voice. I chuckled, envisioning ourselves floating among the cotton candy formations. "Maybe we can catch one and take it home," I shot back, the banter flowing effortlessly, just as it always did. It was moments like these that made my heart race—his laughter mingling with mine, creating a melody that felt uniquely ours.

As we approached a particularly steep incline, I focused my gaze ahead, allowing the scenery to envelop me. The mountains stood resolute, draped in their green cloaks, while a gentle breeze tousled the leaves overhead, whispering secrets of the ages. A stream gurgled nearby, its waters glinting like scattered diamonds in the sunlight, teasing the ear with promises of refreshment and renewal. I could almost imagine myself diving into its cool depths, letting it wash away the remnants of doubt that clung to me like fog.

But as we reached a rocky outcrop that jutted out over the valley below, my mind flickered to the confessions that danced on the tip of my tongue. I wanted to tell Theo everything—the way my heart skipped at his laughter, the warmth that bloomed in my chest when our hands brushed. This was the moment I had been waiting for, a sacred space carved out of time and earth, where everything felt possible.

"Let's take a break," Theo suggested, plopping down on a flat stone, the sunlight casting a warm glow over his features. I followed suit, my heart racing as I settled beside him. The view was breathtaking, a sprawling vista that unfolded like a storybook beneath us. The valley stretched out, a patchwork of farmland and wild thickets, dotted with clusters of trees that swayed like dancers in a grand performance. I could see the river winding its way through the landscape, glistening like a silver ribbon caught in the sun's embrace.

I inhaled deeply, the cool air filling my lungs, grounding me as I prepared to speak. "Theo, there's something I need to tell you," I began, my voice trembling slightly. But just as the words began to weave themselves into my mind, I shifted, my foot slipping on the edge of the rock. My heart dropped, a visceral panic surging through me as I lost my balance.

In an instant, Theo was there, his hand wrapping around mine with a firm grip that felt both electrifying and steady. Time slowed as I looked into his eyes, the shock mirrored there, but beneath it was a profound warmth that sent a spark of realization racing through me. He wasn't just my friend; he was the one I wanted, the one who made the world shimmer with possibility.

"Careful!" he said, concern lacing his voice. I nodded, breathless not just from the near-fall but from the intensity of the moment. Our hands remained clasped for a heartbeat longer, the contact igniting something deep within me—a realization that this was it. This was the moment that could change everything.

As I steadied myself, my heart pounded not just from the thrill of the hike but from the undeniable truth that had blossomed between us. The world around me faded, and in that brief, exhilarating encounter, I understood that I didn't just want to tell him how I felt—I needed to. The beauty of the mountains, the tranquility of the moment, and the safety of his grip enveloped me, and I knew I couldn't hold back any longer. Today was the day I would climb the mountain of my fears and finally reveal my heart.

His grip was like a lifeline, steadying me against the rocky precipice that felt more metaphorical than physical in that moment. My heart raced, not just from the scare but from the palpable energy swirling between us—a silent understanding that transcended words. The world, with its stunning views and breathtaking beauty, faded into a distant hum as I focused on the connection forged in the fragile space of that second. I could see the uncertainty flicker in Theo's eyes, mirrored by the way his brow furrowed slightly, and suddenly everything I wanted to say was drowned out by the thundering sound of my pulse.

"Are you okay?" His voice cut through the haze, warm and concerned, and I nodded, still entranced by the intensity of our shared moment. I took a breath, the air sharp and refreshing, filling me with resolve. This was it; this was my chance.

"I'm fine. I just..." I began, my voice trailing off as I searched for the right words. It felt monumental, as if I were standing at the edge of a cliff with everything below waiting to either catch me or let me fall. I had come here to confront my fears, but now, faced with the depth of my feelings, those fears seemed trivial compared to the possibility of opening my heart to him.

He tilted his head, curiosity glimmering in those deep brown eyes. "Just what?" he pressed gently, the sun casting a warm glow around us, illuminating the way the light danced in his hair. It was an innocent question, but the weight of it hung between us, pregnant with unspoken emotions.

"I just..." I hesitated, contemplating the sincerity that radiated from him. "I wanted to tell you that I care about you—like, really care. More than just friends." The admission tumbled out, raw and unpolished, yet filled with a truth that felt invigorating. It was as if the universe paused, holding its breath as the words settled in the air.

For a heartbeat, silence enveloped us, the chirping of birds and the rustling leaves fading into the background. I watched him process my confession, his expression shifting from surprise to something softer, more contemplative. I had seen him navigate through countless landscapes, both emotional and physical, but this terrain was new for both of us, and I could only hope he wouldn't shy away.

"Wow." The word slipped from his lips, carrying an undertone of awe that made my heart flutter. "I—wow." He ran a hand through his hair, a nervous gesture I'd come to recognize as his way of grappling with his thoughts. "I didn't know you felt that way."

"It's okay if you don't feel the same," I rushed to say, anxiety bubbling up inside me like an overboiling pot. "I just thought it was important to tell you. I've felt this way for a while, and I didn't want to hide it anymore." My voice trembled slightly, the vulnerability of it both exhilarating and terrifying. I was baring a part of my soul, and I had no idea how he would respond.

He took a moment, gaze drifting to the horizon where the mountains met the sky, painting a beautiful picture of blues and whites. "Honestly? I've been feeling something too," he finally admitted, his voice low and steady. "But I didn't know how to say it. I was scared it might ruin what we have."

Relief washed over me, mingling with a rush of adrenaline that surged through my veins. "So, you do feel something?" I pressed, daring to hope.

Theo turned back to me, a playful glint returning to his eyes. "I do, but I'm also terrified of losing our friendship if things go wrong." The honesty in his tone resonated, as if he were stripping away layers of pretense and showing me the raw man beneath. The shared laughter and adventures we had, all the moments that felt so significant, suddenly felt like the stepping stones leading us toward something deeper.

I shifted closer, emboldened by his admission. "What if we just took it slow? We can still be friends while figuring this out, right? We could just... see where it leads."

He smiled then, a radiant expression that lit up his features and warmed my heart. "I'd like that. I don't want to rush anything, but I also don't want to pretend these feelings aren't there."

The enormity of our conversation wrapped around us like a cozy blanket, shielding us from the cool breeze swirling about. I felt lighter, as if I had unclipped the safety harness that had held me too tightly for too long. This was the adventure I had been yearning for—one filled not just with breathtaking vistas but with the exhilarating possibility of exploring what lay between us.

As we sat on the rocky ledge, the wind tousling our hair, I realized I could feel the contours of my life shifting. We had climbed higher in more ways than one, our fears and hopes intertwining like the roots of the trees we had passed on our ascent. I caught his gaze again, and a smile crept across my lips, realizing that this was just the beginning of a new chapter, a shared journey that could lead us to places neither of us had dared to imagine.

With each passing moment, I felt a warmth grow in my chest, illuminating the path forward. "So," I ventured, keeping the tone light, "now that we've confessed, does this mean we get to plan our next adventure?"

His laughter rang out, bright and infectious, breaking the tension that had hung between us moments before. "Absolutely! I'm already thinking of where we should go next. Maybe somewhere with fewer rocks and more water?"

I nodded enthusiastically, my mind racing with ideas. "How about the lake? It's beautiful this time of year, and we could rent a canoe."

"Perfect. But let's make sure it's not on a cliff," he quipped, and we both laughed, the sound mingling with the rustling leaves around us.

In that moment, surrounded by the majesty of nature, I felt like I was floating—light as air and filled with a sense of possibility. The mountains had given me more than just breathtaking views; they had granted me clarity and the promise of something beautiful waiting just beyond the horizon. With Theo by my side, I felt ready to embrace whatever lay ahead, one step at a time.

The sun hung low in the sky, casting a warm golden hue across the rugged landscape, as if nature itself was celebrating our newfound honesty. We sat together on that rocky ledge, the world stretching endlessly beneath us, an unpainted canvas waiting for the brushstrokes of our shared experiences. The gentle breeze rustled through the trees, whispering secrets and possibilities, and I felt a sense of liberation as I breathed in the heady mixture of pine and earth.

"Let's take our time," Theo said softly, his eyes scanning the horizon where the mountains met the sky. "We don't have to rush into anything." The sincerity in his voice sent a flutter through my stomach, a delightful mix of anticipation and nerves. Here, in this moment, suspended between friendship and something deeper, everything felt right.

I leaned back slightly, feeling the sun warm my face, the pressure of the world slipping away like water through my fingers. It was a moment I wanted to capture, to etch into my memory as a reminder of our leap into the unknown. The mountains, sturdy and unyielding, stood sentinel over our conversation, their peaks dusted with the remnants of winter snow, glistening like scattered jewels against the blue sky. In that tranquility, it became increasingly clear that this was more than a hike; it was a pivotal shift in our lives, a chance to explore what had been simmering beneath the surface for too long.

"Should we take a picture?" I suggested, the idea bubbling up from a well of excitement. I pulled out my phone, eager to freeze this moment in time, to encapsulate the essence of the day—the beauty, the honesty, the promise.

"Absolutely! But only if you promise to smile." He shot me a grin that sent a thrill through me, as if I'd just been struck by lightning in the best way possible. I turned the camera around, positioning it to capture the breathtaking view behind us, but as I adjusted the angle, I caught a glimpse of our reflections—a pair of adventurers standing on the edge of the world, faces lit with joy and possibility.

"Ready? On the count of three!" I declared, my heart racing with excitement. "One, two..."

"Wait! I need a good pose!" he interrupted, feigning a dramatic stretch, which made me laugh.

"Alright, alright! You're such a dork." I chuckled, my laughter mingling with the crisp mountain air.

"Dork or not, I'm your dork now," he replied, the sincerity in his voice wrapping around me like a warm blanket. I felt a swell of affection, the kind that rooted itself deep within my chest, making me realize just how much this moment mattered.

"Okay, three!" I called, snapping the photo just as he threw his hands up in a mock superhero pose, the sun catching the glint in his eyes. I looked at the picture and smiled, capturing not just our faces but the essence of everything we had shared up to this point—the laughter, the challenges, and the beautiful uncertainty that lay ahead.

"Let's make a pact," I said, suddenly serious. "No matter what happens, we keep this friendship intact. Even if things get complicated."

"Deal," he replied without hesitation, and we sealed our promise with a fist bump, the childish gesture eliciting a burst of laughter that echoed across the valley.

The day wore on, and we explored the summit, pausing to marvel at the wildflowers that clung to the rocky soil, vibrant splashes of color against the backdrop of grays and greens. I found myself lost in the simple beauty of the moment, the weight of my worries dissipating like fog in the morning sun. Together, we foraged through patches of bluebells and bright yellow buttercups, our fingers brushing occasionally, sending electric sparks dancing along my skin.

As the sun began to dip, casting long shadows over the landscape, I felt an urge to sit down and simply absorb the world around us. We settled on a flat rock, our legs dangling over the edge as we shared stories of our childhoods. Theo recounted hilarious mishaps from camping trips with his family, while I shared tales of my adventurous spirit—how I once tried to climb a tree in our backyard, only to get stuck halfway up and require a dramatic rescue by my dad, who was wielding a garden hose as a makeshift lifeline.

"What about you?" I asked, glancing sideways at him. "What do you want to do with your life?"

He took a moment to ponder, a smile playing on his lips as he gazed into the distance. "I've always dreamed of traveling, of seeing the world. Maybe even documenting it in some way—through photography or writing."

The idea of him wandering the world, capturing its beauty and intricacies, filled me with a profound sense of admiration. "You'd be amazing at that. Your photos are already so vibrant and full of life."

Theo turned to me, his gaze steady and earnest. "Thanks. But what about you? What's your dream?"

My breath caught in my throat, and I hesitated. I had been so focused on us, on navigating this newfound territory of feelings, that I hadn't thought about my aspirations in some time. "I've always wanted to make a difference—maybe in education. To help others find their passion, just like I did."

"That's beautiful," he said, a soft smile illuminating his face. "You have a gift for inspiring people."

The sincerity in his words ignited a flame of determination within me. "Maybe we could travel together one day," I suggested, my voice thick with excitement. "Explore new places, meet new people. Imagine the adventures we could have!"

His laughter was infectious, a joyful sound that wrapped around us like a hug. "Count me in! But only if you promise to keep your feet on the ground and not climb any trees."

"I make no promises," I replied, giggling at the memory of my past escapades.

As the sun dipped lower in the sky, painting the world in warm hues of orange and pink, a comfortable silence settled between us. The evening chill began to creep in, and I instinctively moved closer to Theo, feeling the heat radiate from him as we shared the warmth of that moment.

"We should probably head back soon," he murmured, breaking the spell of stillness.

I nodded reluctantly, the thought of leaving this perfect sanctuary tugging at my heart. "Yeah, I guess so. But I don't want this day to end."

He looked at me, a playful glint in his eyes. "Then let's make it last a little longer. Let's take our time on the way down, maybe find a few more adventures along the way."

With a grin spreading across my face, I felt the thrill of possibility surge within me. We stood up, brushing off the dust from our clothes, and began our descent, taking our time to soak in every moment. As we walked, our conversation flowed seamlessly, each word a thread weaving us closer together.

With each step, I felt an undeniable connection blooming, like the wildflowers that adorned the mountainside. We were stepping into a new chapter of our lives, one that promised adventure, laughter, and maybe even love. The climb had been more than just a physical journey; it was a testament to our willingness to embrace the unknown, to face our fears, and to lean into the beautiful, messy reality of our hearts. And with Theo by my side, I felt ready to explore every winding path that lay ahead, armed with hope and a heart wide open to the possibilities.

Chapter 13: Unraveled Threads

The sunlight spilled across the small town of Maplewood like warm honey, illuminating the worn cobblestones that formed a path through its heart. I stood on the edge of the old park, the scent of freshly mown grass mixing with the faint aroma of blooming lilacs, as I watched him—Eli—his silhouette framed against the brilliant sky. The afternoon breeze whispered secrets through the trees, rustling the leaves in a symphony that felt almost alive. Yet despite the beauty surrounding us, an unshakeable heaviness settled over the scene, a tension that seemed to ripple through the air and press against my chest.

Eli's broad shoulders tensed as he turned away from the vibrant landscape, his eyes drawn toward the distant mountains, where shadows mingled with the fading light. He was caught in a world of his own, one I desperately wanted to pull him from, but how could I bridge the chasm that lay between us? I felt my heart beat a frantic rhythm, echoing the unspoken words swirling in my mind. My palms felt clammy against the fabric of my sundress, which fluttered gently in the breeze, a stark contrast to the tumult within me.

"I'm not the right person for you," he finally said, his voice barely more than a whisper, yet it struck me like a thunderclap. The words reverberated through my entire being, unraveling the threads of hope I had woven around us. I wanted to reach out, to grasp his hand and pull him back into the light, but the weight of his admission left me paralyzed. The space between us felt electric, charged with the unsaid, and I could almost hear my heart breaking like fragile glass.

"Why?" The word escaped my lips before I could stop it, fragile yet fierce, like a tiny bird daring to take flight in a storm. I took a hesitant step closer, desperate for an answer, for some glimmer of understanding to make sense of his retreat. His eyes met mine, and in that fleeting moment, I caught a glimpse of the storm raging inside him—fear, sorrow, and a longing so deep it nearly overwhelmed me.

"Because I'm a mess," he confessed, a bitter edge lacing his tone. "You don't know what I've been through." His gaze dropped to the ground, as if the weight of his past pressed him down, the very earth conspiring to keep him shackled. I wanted to scream at the injustice of it all, to shake him out of his self-imposed exile, but instead, I found myself taking a deep breath, forcing myself to remain calm amidst the chaos.

"Tell me, Eli," I urged, my voice gentle, coaxing him to peel back the layers of his pain. "I can't help you if I don't know what you're hiding." I could feel the warmth of the sun on my skin, the vibrant colors of the park fading into a soft blur as I focused solely on him. The world around us seemed to still, every sound dulled as I leaned in, willing him to open up.

He sighed heavily, the sound like the rustling of dry leaves in the autumn wind. "It's my family," he began, his voice thick with emotion. "We lost my sister in an accident a few years ago. I was supposed to protect her, and I failed." The admission hung between us like a specter, heavy and cold. I could see the memories flickering behind his eyes, shadows of a happier time that now felt like a distant dream.

I moved closer, feeling the pull of empathy draw me to him. "That's not your fault, Eli," I whispered, my heart aching for him. "You were a kid. You can't blame yourself for something that happened beyond your control." The sunlight danced around us, but it felt muted, as though the universe was holding its breath, waiting for him to let go of the burdens he carried.

His shoulders slumped, a picture of defeat. "I know that logically, but emotionally? It's a different story. I can't shake the guilt, the 'what ifs.'" His words poured out like a dam breaking, flooding the space between us with unfiltered pain. "I don't want to hurt you, too. It's better to keep my distance." The vulnerability in his voice pierced through the defenses I had built around my heart, and I felt the urge to reach out and envelop him in warmth and understanding.

"No," I insisted softly, a fierce determination igniting within me. "It's not better to isolate yourself. You need to let someone in, Eli. You can't carry this alone." I took a tentative step forward, extending my hand as if to bridge the gap between our worlds. The park around us thrummed with life—the laughter of children, the distant bark of a dog, the soft rustle of the wind through the trees. Yet all I could focus on was Eli, his turmoil a storm cloud casting shadows over my heart.

He stared at my outstretched hand, uncertainty etched on his face. It was a moment suspended in time, and I held my breath, praying he would take the leap. "I don't want to ruin this," he murmured, his voice thick with emotion. "What if I'm not worth it?"

The question landed like a weighty stone, and I felt an inexplicable urge to shake him until he understood the truth. "You are worth it, Eli. You deserve love and support just like anyone else," I declared, my voice steady even as my heart raced. "We all have our scars, but they don't define us. They're part of our story, part of what makes us human."

He finally looked up, meeting my gaze, and in that moment, I saw a flicker of hope ignite in the depths of his eyes. "You really believe that?" he asked, his voice barely above a whisper, as if fearing the answer would shatter the fragile connection we were building.

"I do," I affirmed, my heart swelling with a fierce affection for the man standing before me, grappling with his demons yet yearning for something more. "And I believe in you." I could feel the warmth of the sun on my face, a radiant embrace urging us both to step into the light, to unravel the tangled threads that bound us to our pasts.

As I stood there, my heart a jumble of confusion and determination, the world around us began to shift. The sun dipped lower, casting a warm golden hue over the park, and the shadows lengthened, mingling with the vibrant colors of the blooming flowers. I watched as Eli's shoulders sagged, the weight of his unshared burdens almost palpable. In that moment, I felt the urge to become his anchor, a lifeline in the tumultuous sea of his memories. The laughter of children echoed in the distance, a stark contrast to the silence that had enveloped us, and I found myself yearning to bridge that gap, to pull him into a brighter reality.

"Eli," I breathed, taking another step closer, my hand still outstretched. "I know it feels easier to shut everyone out, but that will only deepen the wounds. You don't have to face this alone." The sunlight glinted off his hair, highlighting the turmoil etched in his features, and I could feel the magnetism between us, a connection that defied logic yet felt undeniable.

He studied my hand for a heartbeat, the internal battle still raging in his eyes. The silence stretched, heavy with unsaid words, until finally, he closed the gap between us. Tentatively, he took my hand, his grip trembling as if he feared the weight of my belief in him. The warmth of his palm against mine sparked something deep within me, an electric charge that ignited my resolve.

"Why do you care so much?" he asked, his voice a mix of wonder and wariness. I felt the sincerity of his question seep into my bones, a challenge I was more than willing to embrace.

"Because I see you, Eli," I replied, my heart racing. "The real you, beneath all the pain and guilt. You're not defined by your past. You're more than what happened to you." A breeze stirred the air, carrying the sweet scent of lilacs and a hint of impending rain. I wanted him to feel the same hope blossoming within me, a fragile flower fighting for light amidst the shadows.

He let out a soft, mirthless laugh that sent a chill racing down my spine. "You make it sound so easy. Just move on, right?" The skepticism in his tone stung, yet I recognized it as part of his defense mechanism, a shield he wielded to protect himself from vulnerability.

"No, not easy. Necessary," I corrected gently. "It's a process, and it's messy, but it's worth it. You're worth it." I squeezed his hand, grounding him in that moment, allowing the silence to envelop us as we stood together in the fading light.

For the first time, I saw a flicker of hope in his expression, a hint of the boy he had been before tragedy had marked his life. It ignited a spark within me, a longing to help him rediscover the joy that had once radiated from his soul. But as quickly as it appeared, the shadow of doubt crept back into his eyes.

"I don't know how to let go," he confessed, his voice trembling. "What if I open up and it only makes things worse?"

"What if it doesn't?" I countered, my heart racing at the vulnerability I was inviting into our space. "What if you find peace, or even just a glimmer of happiness? You'll never know unless you try."

He met my gaze, and in that fleeting moment, I saw a kaleidoscope of emotions swirl within him: fear, desire, and a glimmer of hope that had long been buried. I could sense the fight within him, a longing to break free from the chains that bound him, yet a hesitation rooted in the fear of the unknown.

The sun sank lower on the horizon, bathing us in a soft orange glow. It felt like the universe itself was holding its breath, waiting for him to make a choice. I tightened my grip on his hand, willing him to take that leap of faith. "You don't have to share everything at once. Just start with something small. Maybe a memory or a moment that haunts you."

His brow furrowed as he considered my words, the tension in his shoulders easing ever so slightly. The moments ticked by, each second stretching into eternity as he wrestled with the decision. Finally, he nodded, a small, tentative movement that sent a wave of relief washing over me.

"Okay," he murmured, the vulnerability in his voice pulling at my heartstrings. "I'll try."

I smiled, feeling the warmth of connection bloom between us. "That's all I ask."

He took a deep breath, and I could see the wheels of his mind turning as he wrestled with the ghosts that had haunted him for so long. "It was my sister's birthday," he began, his voice shaking slightly. "We were supposed to go to the carnival, a tradition we'd kept since we were kids. But that day...it all fell apart."

The memories spilled from him like a broken dam, and I listened intently as he painted the vivid picture of that day—laughter, joy, and the vibrant colors of the carnival intertwined with the darkness of regret. The carnival lights flickered in his memory, the sound of laughter now tinged with a haunting echo of loss. I could feel his pain wrap around me like a heavy blanket, suffocating yet profoundly real.

"It was supposed to be a fun day," he continued, his voice quivering. "We'd planned everything—the rides, the games, the cotton candy. But instead, I got distracted for just a moment, and when I turned back..." His voice broke, and I could see the tears pooling in his eyes, a storm of emotion threatening to break free.

"I couldn't find her," he whispered, a wave of guilt washing over him. "I thought she was with her friends, and then...then I heard the sirens. I never got to say goodbye."

The confession hung heavy in the air, the weight of his loss settling around us like fog. I felt my heart ache for him, a pang of understanding blooming within me as I reached for the fragile pieces of his soul laid bare before me.

"You were a kid, Eli," I murmured, my voice steady yet gentle. "You did the best you could. You can't carry that guilt forever."

He looked up, searching my gaze for solace, and I saw the flicker of doubt mixed with a desperate need for validation. "But what if I let go of it? What if I forget her?"

The question struck me like a bolt of lightning, and I shook my head, determined to help him navigate this treacherous terrain. "Letting go doesn't mean forgetting. It means honoring her memory while freeing yourself from the pain that holds you back. You can carry her with you, Eli, in a way that brings you peace instead of sorrow."

The words hung in the air, a fragile bridge built between us, as Eli searched my face for the truth behind my words. I could see the battle within him, the desire to break free from his self-imposed prison clashing with the fear of losing a part of himself. And in that moment, I knew I would stand by him, ready to help him reclaim his life, one unraveling thread at a time.

The evening air wrapped around us like a velvet cloak, heavy with the scent of blooming jasmine and the faint traces of a lingering storm. Each word Eli spoke felt like a step deeper into the tangled web of his heart, and I was both terrified and exhilarated to navigate that intricate maze. The fading sunlight cast long shadows across the park, and with every flicker of twilight, I could sense the ghosts of his past beginning to shift uneasily, their presence still palpable yet somehow softened by the warmth of our connection.

"After she died, I became a shell of who I used to be," he continued, his voice steadying, yet I could still feel the tremor beneath the surface. "I pushed everyone away—friends, family. I thought if I kept them at arm's length, I wouldn't feel the sting of loss as sharply. But in doing that, I just ended up feeling more alone." His confession hung in the air, heavy and raw, and I felt the urgency to reach him, to extend a hand through the fog of his isolation.

"It makes sense," I replied softly, my heart aching for him. "It's a natural instinct to want to shield yourself from pain, but isolating yourself only amplifies it. You deserve to find joy again, to embrace the life that still exists around you." I took a step closer, the distance between us shrinking, a silent invitation for him to take that leap of faith. "You deserve to feel everything—both the good and the bad. That's what makes us human."

He looked down at our intertwined fingers, a flicker of uncertainty passing through his eyes. "But what if I can't?" The vulnerability in his voice felt like a raw nerve, exposed and trembling under the weight of his fears. "What if I try and fail? What if I hurt you in the process?"

"Then we'll face it together," I replied firmly, the words spilling out with a conviction that surprised even me. "I'd rather take that risk than let you suffer alone. You may think you're a mess, but I see potential, a spark that's waiting to be reignited. You are more than your past, Eli. You are a collection of moments, both beautiful and tragic, and I want to help you find the beauty again."

His eyes lifted to meet mine, and in that instant, I could see the walls begin to crack. A hint of something bright and hopeful flickered behind his gaze, like a candle flame daring to survive in a gusty wind. The sun dipped below the horizon, painting the sky with hues of purple and pink, an artist's palette spilling color across the canvas of the evening.

"I want to believe you," he admitted, his voice steadying. "But I don't know where to start. It feels overwhelming."

"Start with what you remember," I suggested, my heart racing with the prospect of pulling him from the depths of despair. "Think of a moment with your sister that makes you smile, a time when you felt happy. Share that with me."

His brow furrowed in concentration, and I could see the wheels turning in his mind. After a long pause, a small smile crept onto his face, illuminating the shadows in his eyes. "We used to sneak out at night to watch the stars. There was this spot by the lake where the world seemed to disappear, and it was just us, the water, and the sky. We'd make up constellations and pretend they were guiding us to our dreams."

The warmth of his memory radiated between us, wrapping around me like a cozy blanket. "That sounds magical," I breathed, caught in the vivid imagery he painted with his words. "What did you dream about?"

"Everything," he replied, his smile growing broader, the weight of the past lifting ever so slightly. "Traveling to far-off places, doing something that mattered. I wanted to be an astronaut, to explore the universe. She believed I could do anything."

The tenderness in his voice tugged at my heartstrings, and I couldn't help but smile back at him. "Then let's find a way to reclaim that dream," I urged, my spirit ignited by the possibility of what lay ahead. "What if we went stargazing again? Just you and me, by the lake. We can make new memories while honoring the old."

His eyes widened, a mix of surprise and intrigue painting his features. "You really would do that?"

"Absolutely," I affirmed, my heart soaring at the thought. "I want to see the world through your eyes, to help you rediscover that magic."

As the darkness enveloped us, the park transformed into a canvas of shadows, punctuated by the soft glow of street lamps flickering to life. Eli's expression shifted, and I sensed a renewed sense of hope beginning to take root within him.

"Okay," he said slowly, the corners of his mouth curling into a tentative smile. "I'll give it a shot. Let's go stargazing."

"Great!" I exclaimed, unable to contain my excitement. "We can pack some snacks—maybe some of those awful popcorn balls from the fair? You know, the ones with way too much sugar? I promise I won't judge you if you eat them."

He laughed, a sound that echoed through the evening air, and I felt the connection between us deepen. "Deal. But only if you promise to bring the thermos of hot chocolate I know you keep stashed in your cupboard."

We walked through the park, hand in hand, the stars beginning to twinkle above us like diamonds strewn across a velvet cloth. The laughter of children faded into the background, replaced by the gentle rustling of leaves, a symphony of nature that felt alive and vibrant, mirroring the emotions blossoming within us.

As we neared the lake, the moon cast a silvery path across the water, illuminating the ripples that danced beneath its glow. It felt like a secret world, untouched and waiting for us to explore. Eli hesitated for a moment, taking in the beauty before him, and I could see the tension in his shoulders start to ease.

"Is this where you used to come?" I asked, keeping my voice soft, not wanting to disrupt the moment.

"Yeah," he replied, his gaze fixed on the water, lost in memories. "This was our spot."

I squeezed his hand gently, a silent acknowledgment of the journey we were about to embark on together. "Then let's make it ours, too."

As we settled on the grassy bank, the familiar sound of the water lapping at the shore created a soothing rhythm. We stretched out beneath the stars, the blanket of darkness enveloping us in a cocoon of tranquility.

Eli leaned back, his eyes trained on the sky, and I watched as a shooting star streaked across the horizon, a fleeting reminder of dreams waiting to be grasped. "Look!" I exclaimed, my heart racing at the sight. "Make a wish!"

He turned to me, surprise flickering in his eyes. "What do I wish for?"

"Whatever your heart desires," I urged, my voice filled with hope. "A fresh start, healing, joy—whatever feels right."

He closed his eyes for a brief moment, and I held my breath, feeling the weight of his unspoken dreams settle between us. When he opened them again, a new light shone within, a flicker of possibility that made my heart swell.

"I wished to let go," he said quietly, his voice steady, infused with determination. "To find peace, to remember her but not be consumed by the pain. I want to reclaim my life."

The sincerity in his words ignited a fire within me, a shared resolve to face the future together, hand in hand. The stars twinkled overhead, shimmering like the hope that now filled the air between us, bright and unyielding, promising the beauty of what was yet to come.

Chapter 14: Finding Common Ground

The gravel crunched beneath my tires as I maneuvered the winding dirt road leading to Theo's childhood cabin, the rhythmic bumping matching the tumult of emotions in my chest. Tall pines lined the path like sentinels, their branches swaying in a gentle breeze, whispering secrets of the past. The sunlight filtered through the leaves, casting dappled shadows that danced on the ground, creating a patchwork of light and dark—a fitting metaphor for what lay ahead. With each turn of the wheel, anticipation thrummed through me, both for the promise of the day and the weight of what we were about to uncover.

The cabin emerged from the trees, its rustic charm unchanged by time. Weathered wood, a deep mahogany streaked with hints of gray, stood proudly against the encroaching wilderness. It looked as though it had grown from the very earth, a permanent fixture in the landscape that held countless stories within its walls. I parked the car and stepped outside, inhaling the crisp scent of pine and earth, a sharp contrast to the stale air of the city I had left behind. My heart fluttered at the sight of Theo, his silhouette framed by the cabin door. His expression was a blend of nostalgia and dread, his hands shoved deep into the pockets of his well-worn jeans, as if they could anchor him against the tide of memories crashing around us.

As I approached, I noticed the way his gaze flickered over the cabin, a storm brewing in those hazel eyes. "It's just how I remember it," he murmured, almost to himself, as though the cabin held its breath alongside him. I stepped closer, careful not to intrude on his moment, but I felt the weight of his grief in the air, thick and palpable. "Ready?" I asked softly, my voice barely rising above the whisper of the wind through the trees. He nodded, the movement slight yet definitive, and we crossed the threshold together.

Inside, the air was cool and musty, a blend of aged wood and timeworn memories. Sunlight streamed through the small, paned windows, illuminating dust motes swirling lazily in the golden light. The cabin felt like a time capsule, holding the essence of his childhood, preserved in an almost eerie stillness. We stepped into the living room, which boasted a fireplace lined with faded photographs. I could see the ghost of laughter in those frames: Theo as a bright-eyed child, his cheeks dusted with chocolate, his parents smiling proudly beside him. I fought the urge to reach out, to touch the images, knowing they were tethered to a sorrow that could drown the unprepared.

"Let's start here," I suggested, gesturing toward a weathered trunk that sat in the corner, its latch rusted but somehow still intact. The corners of Theo's mouth lifted in a wry smile, a flicker of warmth against the cold backdrop of grief. He knelt beside the trunk, and as he lifted the lid, the hinges creaked in protest, echoing the silent protests of his heart.

Inside lay a jumble of memories: old toys, tattered books, and remnants of a life once vibrant. A plush bear with one eye missing, its fur faded but still soft to the touch, caught my attention. "This guy looks like he's seen some adventures," I said, lifting it from the depths. Theo chuckled, a sound that broke through the heaviness, reminding me of the joy that once filled this space. "That was Sir Snuggles. I took him everywhere."

With each item we pulled from the trunk, the walls of sorrow seemed to loosen their grip, if only a fraction. We found a baseball cap adorned with the logo of Theo's favorite team, crumpled and sun-bleached, but undeniably still a relic of his childhood spirit. He held it in his hands, the corners of his lips twitching as he recounted stories of summer games, the laughter of friends echoing in the background, mingling with the sounds of the crackling grill. I could almost hear the clinking of bottles and the shouts of victory in the air, wrapping around us like a warm embrace.

As we sifted through the remnants, I encouraged him to share each story, to breathe life back into the memories that had grown dusty over time. It was as if the cabin itself was listening, leaning in with eager anticipation. I could see the shadows of his past softening, like clouds parting to reveal a sliver of blue sky. We laughed and cried in equal measure, our voices weaving through the air, stitching together the fabric of his history.

Then we unearthed a stack of old photographs, yellowed with age but bursting with life. I held one up, a snapshot of a family picnic, everyone beaming against a backdrop of lush greenery. "Look at that," I said, pointing to the pure joy radiating from his face. "You were a little charmer." Theo's gaze turned somber, the laughter fading into silence as he took the photo from my hands, his thumb brushing over the faces frozen in time. "That was the last time we were all together," he whispered, the weight of loss heavy on his tongue.

In that moment, I felt a surge of compassion for him, a fierce desire to help him heal. I reached out, placing my hand over his, grounding him. "You're not alone, Theo. You have me," I vowed, the sincerity of my words wrapping around us like a protective cocoon. As he met my gaze, I saw something shift within him—a flicker of hope igniting in those troubled eyes, pushing back against the shadows that had lingered for too long.

We continued to explore the cabin, transforming sorrow into something more profound, each shared memory illuminating the darkness. Laughter rang out, echoing off the walls, replacing the silence that had filled the space for far too long. Together, we crafted a new narrative, one woven with the threads of his past and the promise of tomorrow.

The sun dipped lower in the sky, casting a warm, golden hue across the cabin as we delved deeper into Theo's treasure trove of memories. Each photograph we examined seemed to breathe with life, their vivid moments suspended in time. I marveled at the way the past unfurled around us, a tapestry woven from laughter, tears, and the bittersweet taste of nostalgia. It was a fragile world we were reconstructing, but in those delicate threads lay the potential for healing.

Theo flipped through the stack of images, his fingers tracing the outlines of familiar faces, each one a chapter of a story that had shaped him. The room was filled with a quiet reverence as he shared anecdotes, his voice rising and falling like a gentle tide. There was a picture of a birthday party—balloons bobbing in the breeze, his younger self grinning as he clutched a slice of cake too big for his small hands. "I remember thinking I was the king of the world that day," he chuckled, the sound breaking the tension that had settled over us like a heavy blanket.

"You were," I replied, my smile broadening as I pictured him surrounded by friends, the air rich with the smell of frosting and excitement. "You had your own kingdom right here." The cabin, with its weathered walls and creaky floorboards, seemed to hum in agreement, a loyal witness to the joy that had once flourished within its confines.

We continued our excavation, and soon we unearthed a small, dusty journal tucked between a couple of aged books. Its leather cover was cracked but still held a certain charm, the kind that invited exploration. I held it up, my eyebrows raised in curiosity. "What's this?" I asked, feeling a spark of anticipation. Theo's expression shifted, a flicker of hesitation clouding his eyes.

"It's... it was my diary," he confessed, the words tumbling out with the weight of buried secrets. "I wrote in it when things got hard." I could see the reluctance etched on his face, but the vulnerability in his admission compelled me to encourage him. "Can we read it together?"

With a slight nod, he handed me the journal, and as I flipped through the pages, the scrawl of his younger self leaped to life. The entries were raw, the ink splattered with emotion—joy, confusion, and an underlying current of longing. One entry caught my eye, detailing a summer adventure where he and his friends had camped out under the stars, their laughter ringing out in the cool night air, the world at their feet.

"It sounds like you had some incredible adventures," I remarked, my heart swelling with admiration for the young boy who had sought solace in words. "You were fearless."

"Fearless is a strong word," Theo replied, a small grin breaking through his serious facade. "I was just a kid who didn't know what real fear was."

"But you faced your fears anyway, didn't you?" I pressed gently, eager to draw him out. The lines on his face softened, and he leaned back against the wall, his gaze distant as he pondered.

"Maybe. Back then, I thought I was invincible," he said, the hint of a smile lingering on his lips. "And then..." His voice trailed off, the weight of unspoken words lingering between us like an uninvited guest.

I felt an urge to bridge that gap, to show him that vulnerability was not a sign of weakness, but rather a testament to the strength it took to share one's pain. "What did you learn from all this?" I asked, gesturing to the journal, the photographs, and the cabin that cradled his past.

He took a deep breath, as if gathering the shards of his thoughts. "I learned that it's okay to feel lost sometimes. I learned that happiness is fleeting, but it's the moments that count. The people who share them with you..." His voice faltered, and I saw the shadows flicker back across his eyes.

The silence stretched between us, filled with the unspoken understanding that grief is an indelible part of love. In that stillness,

I recognized a reflection of my own heart, the scars that told tales of loss and survival. I wanted to reach out, to pull him into a comforting embrace, but I understood that he needed to process this at his own pace.

To lighten the atmosphere, I shifted our focus back to the trunk. "Let's see what else this treasure chest holds," I said, my tone playful. "There must be more than just serious journaling."

Theo chuckled softly, and the shadows began to recede. He leaned forward, rifling through the trunk with renewed vigor, and soon we uncovered a pile of art supplies: colored pencils, watercolors, and a half-finished canvas. "I used to paint," he admitted, the admission laced with a hint of embarrassment. "Not that I was any good, but it was a way to escape."

"Show me," I urged, excitement bubbling within me at the prospect of uncovering yet another layer of his past. I had always believed that art was a reflection of the soul, and I wanted to see what Theo's creations could reveal about him.

He hesitated, but then he shrugged, a reluctant smile creeping across his lips. "Okay, but don't judge too harshly. It was just a hobby."

As he rummaged through the supplies, I pulled out the canvas. It depicted a vibrant landscape—bold strokes of green and blue merging to form a rolling hillside, dotted with wildflowers dancing in a gentle breeze. The scene was alive with color, a stark contrast to the somber mood that had initially enveloped us.

"This is beautiful," I said, genuinely impressed. "You have a gift."

"Thanks, but it's nothing compared to real artists." He shrugged, but I could see the faint blush creeping up his cheeks, a spark of pride breaking through the layers of self-doubt he had wrapped around himself.

"Art isn't about comparison; it's about expression," I replied, and he met my gaze, the uncertainty flickering in his eyes. "It's about sharing a piece of yourself with the world."

As we explored the trunk further, we uncovered more remnants of his childhood—an old baseball glove, a stack of comic books, and a tiny, hand-painted figurine that resembled a superhero. "I made this in art class," he said, holding it up with a mix of nostalgia and embarrassment. "I thought I could create my own superhero."

"And did he save the world?" I asked, my curiosity piqued.

"He mostly just saved my sanity during math class," he laughed, a sound that echoed through the cabin, lighting up the dark corners. I watched him relax, the tension in his shoulders easing as laughter became a salve for his wounds.

Together, we breathed life into the cabin, turning a solemn task into a joyful rediscovery. The shadows still lingered, but they began to intertwine with threads of hope, reminding us that every story—no matter how painful—could lead to light.

The afternoon sun dipped lower in the sky, casting long shadows that crept like fingers across the cabin's wooden floor. Each beam of light illuminated the dust motes swirling in the air, creating a golden haze that felt almost magical—a fitting backdrop for the intimacy we had cultivated in our shared exploration of Theo's past. The laughter from moments before echoed softly in the corners, mingling with the weight of unspoken thoughts that still lingered between us.

Theo paused in his rummaging, his gaze drifting toward the window, where the vibrant greens of the forest met the blues of the sky, their colors blurring together in a perfect watercolor. "I used to sit there for hours," he said, pointing toward the spot where a worn-out armchair had once stood. "Just watching the world go by, dreaming about the future." His voice carried a tinge of melancholy, as if that future had slipped through his fingers like the grains of sand in an hourglass.

"Did you have any particular dreams?" I asked, my curiosity piqued. I wanted to peel back the layers of his heart, to see what aspirations lay buried beneath the pain.

His brow furrowed as he considered my question. "I wanted to be an artist—someone who could capture the beauty I saw in the world." He glanced at the canvas propped against the wall, a moment of vulnerability flashing in his eyes. "But then life happened."

"Life has a way of throwing curveballs," I said, my tone light to offset the heaviness of his admission. "But it doesn't mean those dreams are gone forever. Maybe they just need a little dusting off."

He laughed softly, a sound that warmed the air around us. "Dusting off is an understatement. It's more like they need a complete overhaul."

"Then let's give them a fresh start." The determination in my voice surprised even me, but I felt a surge of purpose—an urge to help him rediscover the artist within. "What if we make a day of it? A painting day, right here."

Theo raised an eyebrow, surprise flickering across his face. "You really want to?"

"Absolutely," I replied, my enthusiasm bubbling over. "Let's find those art supplies again and create something. It'll be like bringing this cabin back to life."

After a moment's hesitation, he nodded, a slow smile creeping across his lips, as if the idea had warmed him from the inside out. We dove back into the trunk, pulling out brushes and paints that had long been untouched. I noticed the spark of excitement in his eyes as he sifted through the materials, a glimmer of the boy who had once dreamed of filling blank canvases with color and life.

We set up an impromptu art station by the window, the late afternoon light streaming in to illuminate our workspace. The world outside was alive with the sounds of rustling leaves and the distant calls of birds, a symphony that accompanied our creative endeavor.

As we gathered our supplies, I felt an electric thrill, an anticipation of the beauty we were about to create together.

"Alright, what are we painting?" Theo asked, his playful tone igniting a spark of inspiration within me.

"Let's paint what this place feels like to us," I suggested, glancing around the cabin for inspiration. "Let's capture the essence of these memories."

With a nod of agreement, Theo began sketching the outline of the cabin, his movements hesitant but filled with determination. I chose a canvas to express the vibrant life that had once pulsed through these walls. As the colors swirled and blended beneath my brush, I felt the air shift, charged with an energy that resonated with our mutual desire to reconnect with our dreams.

We worked in companionable silence, the only sounds the rhythmic scratching of brushes against canvas and the occasional laughter that erupted as we playfully critiqued each other's work. I was amazed at how quickly Theo fell back into the flow of creation, the lines of worry easing from his forehead as he lost himself in the act of painting. The bright colors began to merge into a riotous explosion, a reflection of our shared joy and the catharsis that unfolded in those moments.

As the sun dipped lower, casting a warm amber glow throughout the cabin, I glanced over at Theo's canvas, and my breath caught in my throat. His painting captured not just the structure of the cabin, but the very essence of it—the warmth of the wood, the strength of its history, and the layers of emotion that clung to its walls like ivy. "This is incredible," I said, my voice barely above a whisper.

His cheeks flushed with pride, and he shrugged, trying to downplay the compliment. "It's just a sketch."

"Just a sketch? You've captured a piece of your soul," I insisted, the sincerity in my voice palpable. "You've brought this place back to life."

We continued to paint until the golden light turned to shades of pink and purple, the sky outside morphing into a breathtaking canvas of its own. The air cooled around us, but within the cabin, warmth radiated from our shared creativity, our laughter, and our budding connection.

Eventually, we took a break, stepping outside to breathe in the fresh evening air. The sun dipped below the horizon, casting long shadows that stretched like memories across the ground. I glanced at Theo, who stood with his arms crossed, gazing at the fading light. The contours of his face softened in the twilight, and for a moment, he looked peaceful—like a man finally allowing himself to feel the weight of the world lift, even if just for a little while.

"Thank you," he said, his voice low and sincere. "For this. I didn't realize how much I needed it."

"Thank you for sharing it with me," I replied, my heart swelling with a sense of purpose. "It's beautiful to see you reconnect with your passion."

As darkness fell, we returned to the cabin, where the flickering glow of a lantern cast gentle shadows on the walls. We placed our completed canvases side by side, a testament to the healing journey we had embarked on together. The room pulsed with the energy of transformation, a space that had once been steeped in sorrow now brightened by laughter, creativity, and the promise of hope.

In that intimate glow, I felt a connection deepen—a bond forged in shared experiences and vulnerable revelations. The weight of Theo's past lingered still, but now it was tempered with the understanding that he wasn't alone, that we could carry those burdens together.

As I looked at the paintings, I realized that we had created more than just art; we had woven new memories into the fabric of the cabin, laying down a foundation for healing that would echo long after we left. And in that moment, beneath the soft light and among the towering pines, I felt something shift within me too—a flicker of hope for both our futures, illuminated by the warmth of newfound friendship and the unyielding power of art.

Chapter 15: The Bonds We Forge

The cabin sat like a whispered secret nestled deep in the heart of the White Mountains, where the world around us transformed into a winter wonderland, blanketed in a serene layer of freshly fallen snow. Pine trees, laden with white, stretched towards the bruised twilight sky, their branches bowing under the weight of the ice crystals that clung to them like delicate jewels. Each breath I took formed a cloud of mist in the chilly air, and with each inhalation, I felt more alive, more aware of the soft crackle of the fire inside the cabin.

The flickering flames cast playful shadows that danced on the wooden walls, their warmth a stark contrast to the biting cold that surrounded us. My heart raced as I settled into the plush armchair, its fabric worn but welcoming, just like the atmosphere we had created in this refuge. The rustic cabin felt like a portal to a simpler time, where stories flowed freely, and laughter echoed through the pine-scented air. I could feel the emotional weight between us, an unspoken tension that thrummed like a living thing, pulsing in time with the steady beat of my heart.

He sat across from me, a glass of deep amber whiskey cradled in his hands, the liquid catching the firelight and shimmering like liquid gold. I watched him, mesmerized by the way his brow furrowed slightly as he prepared to delve into another story from his past. The lines on his face, etched by both laughter and heartache, drew me in, and I could almost hear the whispers of his memories dancing around us, begging to be shared. I could see it in the way his fingers drummed nervously against the glass, the unsteady rhythm betraying his calm facade. He was a tapestry of experiences, and I was eager to unravel the threads that bound him.

"The first time I ever skied," he began, his voice low and rich, like the whiskey he sipped, "I was about eight years old, and my dad thought it would be a great idea to take me to this little resort in New

Hampshire." He chuckled softly, a sound that made me lean closer, hanging on his every word. "Of course, I had no idea what I was getting into. I was terrified, but I didn't want to let him down."

As he painted the picture of a younger version of himself, clad in oversized ski gear that made him look more like a marshmallow than a boy, I could see the scene unfolding in my mind. The anticipation of that first ride up the slope, the crisp air biting at his cheeks, and the exhilaration of speeding down the hill—all those sensations mingled with the sweet, bittersweet nostalgia of childhood. "I fell—oh, did I fall," he continued, a smile creeping across his lips. "I ended up in a snowbank, and I remember looking up at the sky, wondering if I'd ever get the hang of it. But then my dad came over, helped me up, and we laughed until we couldn't breathe. That was the moment I realized that no matter how many times I fell, he would always be there to catch me."

His laughter faded into silence, and the weight of his words settled in the space between us. I could see the vulnerability glimmering in his eyes, a glimpse of the little boy who had longed for his father's approval. My heart swelled for him, each story he shared pulling me closer, creating an invisible tether that intertwined our souls.

"What about you?" he asked suddenly, his tone shifting as he leaned forward, eager to know me, to see beyond the surface. "What's your story?"

The question lingered in the air, heavy and expectant. I took a moment to gather my thoughts, considering the paths my life had taken and the memories that shaped me. "I grew up in a small town in Pennsylvania," I began, letting the warmth of nostalgia wash over me. "My parents ran a diner, a little place that was always buzzing with laughter and the smell of fresh pie. It was the kind of place where everyone knew each other, where secrets were shared over steaming cups of coffee." I paused, the image of my childhood washing over me like a comforting blanket.

"I remember one summer, my mom and I hosted pie-baking contests," I continued, a smile forming at the edges of my lips. "People would come from all over to enter, bringing their best recipes. The whole town would gather in our backyard, and it felt like the world was wrapped in a warm embrace. I would stand by my mom's side, watching her work her magic, her hands dancing over the dough as she shared stories about each pie. I learned that food could bring people together in the most beautiful ways."

As the words flowed from me, I felt the barrier between us start to dissolve, the warmth of shared experiences wrapping us in a cocoon of understanding. His eyes glinted with curiosity, urging me to go on. "But it wasn't all sweet," I admitted, the truth spilling out like a bitter aftertaste. "When I was fifteen, everything changed. My mom got sick, and the diner became a burden. The laughter faded, and the joy turned to worry."

His expression softened, the weight of empathy filling the space between us. I could see the reflection of my own struggle mirrored in his eyes, and the connection deepened, intertwining our stories like a braided rope.

"Sometimes," I whispered, my voice barely above a hush, "I wonder if we really ever heal from the things that scar us." The flickering fire crackled in agreement, sending a shower of sparks into the air as if echoing my sentiment.

With the weight of our shared vulnerabilities hanging in the air, I found myself leaning in closer, my heart racing at the magnetic pull between us. "You don't have to carry this alone," I urged, the words spilling from my lips in a fervent plea. In that moment, time slowed, and the world outside faded, leaving only the two of us bound by the fragility of our stories.

As he hesitated, the shadows of his past flickering in his eyes, I felt a spark of courage ignite within me. It was a risk, but in that stillness, with the warmth of the cabin surrounding us, I was willing to take it. Our lips brushed together, a tentative connection that ignited a flame, a spark of hope that felt like both home and danger intertwined.

The kiss lingered between us, electric and warm, a moment suspended in time as if the world outside had slipped away entirely. My breath mingled with his, and for a heartbeat, nothing else mattered. We were two souls unmoored in the vastness of the winter landscape, our hearts laying bare on the hardwood floor of that cozy cabin. I could feel the weight of his hesitation dissolve, replaced by an undeniable chemistry that thrummed in the air around us. I pulled back slightly, meeting his gaze, which was alive with emotions—curiosity, fear, and the flickering embers of hope.

"Wow," he breathed, the word almost lost in the crackling of the fire. "That was... unexpected."

Unexpected. The word echoed in my mind, resonating with a strange mixture of excitement and uncertainty. The very nature of our connection felt precarious, a fragile thread weaving between us, strengthened yet strained by the weight of our histories. In this cabin, surrounded by the scent of cedar and the warmth of the fire, I realized that we had forged a bond deeper than mere physical attraction. It was a connection anchored in vulnerability, a shared understanding of pain and longing.

I smiled, a gentle tug at the corners of my mouth, my heart racing anew as I brushed a strand of hair behind my ear. "Good unexpected or bad unexpected?"

"Definitely good," he replied, his voice low and sincere, the sincerity washing over me like the warmth of the fire. He leaned back, his posture relaxing, yet the intensity in his eyes remained. "But I have to admit, I'm not great at this. At all."

"What do you mean?" I asked, intrigued by his self-deprecating honesty.

"Emotions and feelings... they're a tangled mess for me," he confessed, a hint of vulnerability creeping into his tone. "I've always been more comfortable building walls than letting people in. But you... you make it feel different."

His admission hung in the air, thick with unspoken challenges and the promise of exploration. I nodded, recognizing the struggle in his words. "I get that. It's not easy to open up, especially when the past weighs so heavily on your shoulders. But maybe we can take it one step at a time? We don't have to rush into anything."

The tension in his shoulders eased slightly, and a smile broke across his face, transforming his features. It was a smile that spoke of gratitude and a hint of mischief, a willingness to embrace this new path we were carving together. "One step at a time sounds perfect," he agreed, his voice filled with a warmth that mirrored the crackling fire.

We spent the next hour lost in conversation, weaving our stories together like a tapestry, the threads intertwining in complex and beautiful patterns. He spoke of his love for the mountains, how they grounded him, reminding him of the strength he often felt he lacked. I shared tales of the little diner where I grew up, the way the scent of fresh-baked pie filled the air, and how those memories reminded me of home.

As he recounted adventures from his childhood—hiking the rugged trails, rock climbing, and even skiing with his father—his voice took on a vibrancy that drew me in. I could almost picture the young boy he once was, full of life and laughter, unafraid to embrace the world around him. Each story revealed another layer of his personality, exposing the fears that lingered beneath his charm, the insecurities that shaped him.

"I was always a bit of a daredevil," he admitted, a playful glint in his eye. "My friends called me crazy, but I never saw it that way. I just wanted to feel alive. But as I got older, I learned that sometimes, it's the risks we don't take that end up haunting us the most."

His words resonated with a depth of understanding that sent shivers down my spine. The fire crackled, sending sparks soaring into the darkened sky, mirroring the way my heart soared with every revelation. There was a raw honesty in our exchanges that felt sacred, as if we were peeling back the layers of our souls in a sacred dance of trust and vulnerability.

The wind howled outside, a haunting melody that seemed to echo our shared fears, but inside the cabin, we created our own sanctuary, one where laughter mingled with confessions, and the warmth of the fire wrapped us in its embrace. I felt an undeniable urge to protect this moment, to preserve the connection that had blossomed between us.

"What's the biggest risk you've ever taken?" I asked, my curiosity piqued.

He paused, considering my question, his brow furrowing in thought. "Probably moving to Colorado. I left everything behind—my family, my friends—chasing a dream that seemed so out of reach. I didn't know if I'd succeed, but I needed a change. I needed to find myself outside of everything that was familiar."

"I admire that," I replied, a warmth spreading through me. "It's brave to step into the unknown."

"It didn't feel brave at the time," he admitted with a chuckle, shaking his head as if to dismiss the thought. "I was scared out of my mind. I just wanted to escape what I felt was suffocating me. But sometimes, the best things come from the most terrifying choices."

His words hung in the air like an unspoken promise, a recognition that echoed through the fibers of my being. In that moment, I understood that we were not merely sharing stories; we were laying the foundation for something deeper, something that transcended our individual pasts and intertwined our futures.

As the night wore on, the fire flickered and waned, casting gentle shadows that danced against the walls. Outside, the snow continued to fall softly, blanketing the world in a serene hush. I glanced out the window, taking in the beauty of the winter landscape, the trees standing sentinel against the darkening sky.

In this sanctuary of warmth and trust, I felt a burgeoning hope, an unexpected excitement for what lay ahead. It was a hope intertwined with the realization that we were no longer just two individuals carrying the burdens of our pasts; we were beginning to forge a new path, hand in hand, through the uncertainties of tomorrow.

The kiss lingered like a gentle echo in the corners of my mind, each heartbeat sending ripples through the intimate space we had carved out within the cabin's warmth. The flickering flames danced, casting playful shadows that flickered across his face, illuminating the features that had, moments before, appeared so serious. The playful tension melted away, replaced by something deeper, more resonant. It was a shared understanding that we were both stepping into uncharted territory, a place where our pasts mingled with our hopes, creating an exhilarating cocktail of emotions.

I watched him take a deep breath, the weight of his thoughts hanging in the air like the soft snowfall outside. "You know," he said, breaking the silence, "I've been scared to trust anyone since... well, since I lost my dad." His voice was steady, but the vulnerability threaded through it made my heart ache. "He was my compass, the one who showed me how to navigate the world. After he passed, everything felt chaotic, like a storm that had swallowed up the map of my life."

I felt a pang of empathy pierce through me, a fierce desire to bridge the chasm of his grief. "I can only imagine how hard that must have been," I replied softly, my words hanging between us, a delicate thread binding our shared scars. "Grief can twist us, make us feel like we're spiraling through a blizzard with no way out."

He nodded, his gaze distant as if he were peering into the past, where memories swirled like the snowflakes outside. "It took me a long time to realize that holding on to pain doesn't keep us connected to the people we've lost. It just weighs us down." His voice was tinged with a hint of resolve, as if he were making peace with the ghosts that had haunted him for too long.

I could feel the urge to reach across the space between us, to take his hand and reassure him that it was okay to let go, that he didn't have to carry that weight alone anymore. But instead, I held my breath, savoring the moment, the warmth, and the spark that had ignited between us. "Maybe it's time for us to forge new connections, ones that honor the past but don't keep us shackled to it," I suggested, my heart pounding in my chest.

The fire crackled as he considered my words, his expression shifting from somber reflection to a burgeoning light of hope. "You make it sound so simple," he replied, a smile creeping across his lips, the corners of his mouth lifting as if the idea was as bright as the flames. "But you're right. We can't let our pasts define us. We have to choose to embrace the future."

"Exactly," I said, feeling a thrill of courage coursing through me. "And that future starts right here, right now." I motioned toward the snow-covered world outside, where the moonlight began to filter through the tall pines, illuminating the landscape in a soft, silver glow. "Look at that," I added, my voice rich with excitement. "It's like a blank canvas waiting for us to paint our stories on it."

He followed my gaze, and for a moment, silence enveloped us again. The beauty of the winter landscape stretched out before us, pristine and untouched. There was a magic in that moment, a promise of possibility. I felt a flutter of hope rise within me, intertwining with the warmth of our shared connection.

"Maybe we should take advantage of it," he said, his eyes gleaming with mischief. "What do you say we go outside and make our mark in the snow?"

"Are you suggesting we become children again?" I laughed, the sound ringing out like a silver bell. "I'm all in. But only if we can have a snowball fight afterward."

His grin widened, and suddenly, the cabin felt small, the world outside beckoning us with an irresistible allure. We scrambled to our feet, our hearts racing with the thrill of spontaneity. As we stepped through the door into the crisp night air, the cold nipped at our cheeks, invigorating and alive.

The snow crunched beneath our boots, the sound echoing in the stillness of the night, a playful invitation. I could feel my heart pounding with anticipation, and I couldn't help but glance sideways at him, his silhouette outlined against the shimmering backdrop of white. He looked impossibly handsome, a spark of mischief in his eyes that set my own heart alight.

We wandered into the open expanse, and I felt a giddy rush as I dropped to my knees, scooping up handfuls of snow. I quickly shaped the first snowball, packing it tight and firm. "You'd better be ready!" I called out, a laugh bubbling up from deep within me as I tossed the snowball at him, a burst of cold joy.

He ducked just in time, laughter spilling from his lips like a melody, infectious and bright. "Oh, you're going to pay for that!" he yelled, quickly forming his own counterattack. As he threw his snowball, it soared wide of its mark, and we both burst into laughter, the sound ringing out like a joyful anthem against the winter night.

We chased each other through the soft drifts, our playful war turning into a dance as we ducked behind trees and leaped over small mounds of snow. There was something liberating about shedding our pasts for just a moment, letting the purity of the snow and the thrill of the chase consume us. Each throw, each laughter shared, melted the ice that had formed around our hearts, leaving only warmth in its wake.

After what felt like an eternity of playful chaos, we collapsed into a snowbank, breathless and beaming, our cheeks flushed from the cold and laughter. "Okay, I think I've met my match," he admitted, lying back beside me, the snow framing his face like a halo of white.

"I think I've met someone worth taking risks for," I shot back, our eyes locking as the world around us blurred into insignificance. In that moment, the space between us vanished, replaced by an understanding that ran deeper than words.

I felt a sense of freedom wash over me, a realization that we had transformed our shared fears into something tangible—a bond forged in laughter and vulnerability. This was the beginning of something new, a connection rooted in authenticity that transcended our pasts.

As we lay there, staring up at the star-studded sky, the weight of our histories felt lighter, buoyed by the promise of tomorrow. There was a magic in the air, a vibrant energy that crackled between us like the flames of the fire we had left behind in the cabin. I knew, in that moment, that the journey ahead would not always be easy, but with him by my side, it would be worth every step. Together, we would navigate the wilderness of our hearts, embracing the adventure that awaited us with open arms, ready to paint our future against the backdrop of a world transformed by our shared stories.

Chapter 16: Underneath the Surface

The scent of saltwater mingled with the sweet, heady aroma of blooming jasmine as I stepped into the lavish resort lobby, the ornate chandeliers casting a warm, golden hue over everything. It was a space that buzzed with excitement and anticipation, the echoes of laughter bouncing off marble floors and textured walls adorned with local art. My fingers trailed across the smooth surface of the reception desk as I made my way through the throng, feeling the hum of energy around me. After the whirlwind of the training program, this celebration should have felt like an exhilarating triumph, but the weight of uncertainty hung heavily on my shoulders, a cloak of insecurity I couldn't shake.

The banquet hall was a marvel, adorned with rich, emerald drapes that seemed to catch the light, shimmering like the ocean waves outside. Tables were dressed in crisp, white linens, and the flickering candlelight cast dancing shadows, setting the stage for what should have been a night of joy. I paused for a moment at the entrance, feeling the fabric of my gown whisper against my skin. It was an enchanting blue that mirrored the ocean's depths, sparkling with each movement. I'd chosen it deliberately, wanting to project an image of strength and confidence, but the way my heart fluttered betrayed me.

And then I saw him.

Theo stood across the room, framed by a crowd of animated guests. His laughter rose above the rest, a bright, intoxicating sound that felt both familiar and foreign now, given the kiss we had shared not long ago. He was leaning in toward a girl whose smile dazzled like the summer sun, the two of them locked in a moment of shared delight. Her laughter rang out, rich and carefree, wrapping around him like a silken scarf. In an instant, the world around me began to fade, the vibrant colors dimming into a monochrome blur. My heart clenched painfully as the insecurities I thought I had buried surged back to the surface, crashing over me like an unrelenting tide.

What was I thinking? That a moment shared could transcend the intricate web of his social life? I felt like an interloper in my own narrative, a character brought in for a brief, dramatic flourish only to be relegated to the background once the real story resumed. As I stood there, the weight of doubt settled heavily in my stomach. Was I just a fleeting distraction in his life, or did he genuinely see a future that included me?

I forced myself to breathe, the rhythm a desperate attempt to steady the tumult inside me. The laughter, the music, the swirl of bodies—it all became overwhelming. I could feel the corners of my eyes prickling, the urge to retreat clawing at my insides. I had come here to celebrate our accomplishments, to embrace the growth we had shared in this vibrant little corner of the world, but instead, I felt like a ghost haunting the halls of a party I didn't belong to.

With each heartbeat, I grappled with the image of Theo and the girl, their shared joy pulling at the threads of my own happiness. Was it wrong to feel this way? To wish that he was looking at me like that instead? I recalled the moments we'd shared—the way his hand had brushed against mine, the way his eyes sparkled with mischief as he pulled me into that lingering kiss. I had felt seen and cherished, yet the reality of the banquet before me shattered that illusion, reminding me of the distance between our experiences.

Determined not to let my insecurities dictate the evening, I straightened my shoulders and took a step forward. Each step was a battle against the fear coiling inside me, but I reminded myself that I had overcome more challenging moments. As I walked into the hall, the fabric of my gown caught the light, glimmering like a beacon, a reminder that I was here, I was strong, and I deserved to celebrate my achievements.

Yet as I approached the bar, seeking a moment of solace in a cocktail, I could still feel the magnetic pull of Theo's laughter, drawing me in like a moth to a flame. I tried to focus on the murmurs of conversation around me, the clinking of glasses, and the clatter of forks against plates, but his presence was inescapable. I could almost feel the heat radiating from him, the warmth of his charm and the depth of his attention that I craved more than anything else.

Finally, I reached the bar, the cool surface of the polished wood grounding me in reality. I ordered a drink, a vibrant concoction of rum and pineapple juice, and took a moment to gather my thoughts. The bartender, a jovial man with a thick mustache, mixed the drink with a flourish, and I watched the colors blend together, marveling at the beauty of the moment, a small reminder that life was a series of layers, each one more intricate than the last.

As I raised the glass to my lips, the tangy sweetness danced on my tongue, refreshing and invigorating. I took a deep breath, inhaling the scents of citrus and sea salt, letting them wash over me like a gentle wave. I felt a flicker of determination ignite within, reminding me of the person I had become throughout this journey—someone who had the strength to face her fears, to confront the unknown.

And just as I was about to turn away from the bar, searching for a new distraction in the crowd, I caught Theo's gaze. It was electric, as if time had momentarily halted, leaving only the two of us suspended in a universe of our own making. My heart raced, a wild stallion breaking free from the confines of its stable. I was no longer just a participant in the banquet; I was a player in this intricate dance of emotion, a player determined to reclaim my place beside him.

His gaze anchored me in that moment, piercing through the cacophony of chatter and clinking glasses, igniting a spark of hope within my chest. For a heartbeat, the room around us faded into an indistinct blur, and all I could see was Theo's deep, inviting smile, the very one that had a way of unraveling my doubts with just a glance.

It was as if he had sensed my internal struggle, the confusion swirling beneath my exterior like a tempest waiting to break. The world had shrunk down to the two of us, suspended in a liminal space that promised possibilities.

I lifted my drink, taking a tentative sip, the sweet and tangy notes swirling through my senses. In that moment, the cocktail was not just a drink; it became a talisman of courage. I set my sights on him, determined to break the spell of uncertainty that clung to me. Gathering my resolve, I stepped away from the bar, moving through the sea of faces. The laughter and lively chatter of the banquet washed over me like gentle waves, yet all my attention remained fixated on Theo.

As I neared, I noticed the girl beside him, her presence as bright and enchanting as a summer sun. Her hair cascaded in soft, golden waves, framing a face alight with joy. For a brief second, an echo of jealousy gripped my heart, twisting it painfully. Was it her laughter that captivated him, or was it merely the thrill of the night? I forced myself to breathe, to push through the unsettling thoughts that threatened to overshadow my resolve. I could be confident; I could be enchanting in my own right.

"Hey!" I called out, my voice cutting through the din of celebration. Theo turned, his expression shifting from surprise to delight as he spotted me. The warmth of his gaze wrapped around me, sending a rush of adrenaline through my veins. He took a step closer, creating a bridge between us that felt electric.

"Wow, you look incredible," he said, his eyes wide with genuine admiration, and suddenly, the girl beside him faded into the background like a blurred painting in a gallery. His compliment was a balm to my anxieties, soothing the frayed edges of my heart.

"Thanks," I replied, trying to keep my voice steady, despite the butterflies fluttering wildly in my stomach. "You don't look too bad yourself." The banter came easily, a familiar rhythm in the melody of our interactions, rekindling the warmth that had sparked between us.

"Did you try the hors d'oeuvres?" he asked, gesturing toward a lavish spread laid out on a nearby table. "I swear they've perfected the art of tiny foods."

"I haven't yet, but you know how I feel about tiny things," I replied, a playful smile tugging at my lips. "They make me feel like a giant."

He chuckled, and the sound felt like home, wrapping around me and pushing away the lingering shadows of doubt. "I'm glad I'm not the only one who feels that way. It's like I'm eating appetizers that were made for ants."

The girl beside him, who had been momentarily overlooked, cleared her throat softly, her gaze darting between us. I could sense a flicker of discomfort in her demeanor, a silent question lingering in the air. Perhaps she hadn't anticipated this encounter, a rival unexpectedly appearing on the scene. It was a feeling I had become all too familiar with, the sensation of being a footnote in someone else's story, but I refused to allow that to happen tonight.

"Are you joining us for the dance?" Theo asked, his eyes sparkling with anticipation.

"Absolutely," I replied, my heart racing at the thought of twirling beneath the soft glow of the chandeliers. I had always loved to dance, to lose myself in the rhythm of music, to let go of inhibitions and simply be.

As we moved toward the center of the hall, the music enveloped us, a gentle blend of strings and piano that invited all to join in. The floor was alive with couples spinning and swaying, their laughter mingling with the melody. I felt the warmth of his hand wrap around mine, his touch igniting a rush of confidence that surged through me.

As we began to dance, our movements became a conversation, unspoken yet profoundly understood. With each step, I could feel the tension between us softening, the doubts melting away like ice under the sun. I had envisioned this moment a hundred times in my head, imagined how it would feel to glide across the dance floor with him, but reality exceeded my wildest dreams.

The way he held me, the rhythm of our bodies aligning perfectly, made me forget the girl, the uncertainties, the insecurities that had haunted me. I surrendered to the moment, allowing the music to weave its magic around us. We spun, twirled, and laughed, our bodies moving in sync as if we were two pieces of a larger puzzle finally clicking together.

"You're amazing at this," I said, my breath coming in quick bursts, laughter spilling from my lips as he expertly spun me, twirling me around the dance floor like a leaf caught in a playful autumn breeze.

He smiled, a cocky grin that made my heart race. "I had a good teacher," he replied, his gaze locking onto mine, and for a moment, the world around us disappeared entirely.

As the song shifted to something slower, he pulled me closer, the warmth of his body radiating against mine. Our faces were inches apart, and the air crackled with a mixture of desire and vulnerability. I could feel my heart pounding in my chest, a wild rhythm that matched the gentle thump of the music.

"Can I be honest?" he asked, his voice barely above a whisper, laced with sincerity.

"Always," I breathed, entranced by the intensity of his gaze.

"I've been thinking about our kiss. It made me realize something—I want more than just a fleeting moment with you. You're not a distraction; you're the main event."

The words hung in the air like a promise, wrapping around us like the gentle embrace of the night. For the first time that evening, my insecurities began to recede, eclipsed by the light of his declaration. In that dance, I felt seen, cherished, and above all, understood. We were no longer just two people caught in a whirlwind of uncertainty; we were something more, something real.

As the song faded into silence, the world around us came rushing back, but my heart felt lighter. I held his gaze, a smile breaking free across my face, an invitation to explore this newfound connection, ready to dive into whatever lay beneath the surface together.

The warmth of Theo's declaration lingered between us, shimmering like the glint of a distant star just before it fades into the vastness of the night. He stepped closer, his presence magnetic, as the fading notes of the song hung in the air, enveloping us in a cocoon of possibility. I had always believed in the magic of moments, but this one felt different, richer, as if it were imbued with all the hope I had kept bottled up for too long. The banquet hall buzzed with the energy of celebration, yet in that moment, it was just us, two souls tangled in the delicate dance of emotions.

As we pulled apart, the soft glow of the chandeliers cast a warm light on Theo's features, accentuating the sincerity in his eyes. I could still feel the echo of his words reverberating in my chest, pushing away the shadows of doubt that had threatened to overwhelm me. "So, what's next?" I asked, my voice steady despite the flutter of anticipation that danced in my belly. "Do we just waltz off into the sunset, or do you have something more extravagant planned?"

His laugh was rich, vibrant, a sound that tickled my senses and pulled me deeper into the moment. "Why not both?" he replied, a glimmer of mischief in his eyes. "But first, let's get some tiny foods. I'm starving."

The playful banter flowed between us like a current, rejuvenating and refreshing. We made our way toward the buffet table, and I felt a sense of lightness in my step, as if the weight of the world had lifted off my shoulders. The banquet spread was a feast for the eyes—a vibrant array of colors, textures, and aromas that wafted through the air, beckoning us closer. I could feel my stomach rumble in eager anticipation, the prospect of tiny bites almost as intoxicating as the dance we had just shared.

As we filled our plates with an assortment of canapés and delicacies, I caught sight of the girl from earlier, still hovering nearby with a group of friends. She cast a sideways glance in our direction, her expression a curious mix of confusion and something akin to disappointment. I dismissed it quickly, the moment I had with Theo fortifying my resolve. I had decided to embrace this new connection, to step into the light rather than retreat into shadows.

With plates piled high, we settled at a small table near the window, the evening light cascading in through the glass, illuminating our laughter. "So, tell me, what's your ideal first date?" he asked, leaning back slightly, an amused smile playing on his lips as he surveyed the small mountain of food between us.

"Oh, that's easy," I replied, enthusiasm bubbling forth. "A sunset picnic on the beach, complete with a spread of fancy cheeses and maybe a few embarrassing sandwiches."

"Embarrassing sandwiches?" he echoed, his brow raised in mock incredulity. "Now I need to know more."

I leaned forward, unable to contain my grin. "You know the ones—peanut butter and pickle or some bizarre combination only a child would love. It's all part of the charm."

"Now that's a culinary adventure I can get behind," he said, laughing as he plucked a tiny quiche from his plate. "How about we bring our own embarrassing sandwiches to the next banquet?"

My heart raced at the thought of us crafting our own adventures, creating moments that would stand out amid the swirl of ordinary life. "You're on," I declared, feeling the pulse of excitement course through me.

Just then, the host of the banquet stepped onto the stage, commanding the attention of the crowd. The atmosphere shifted as people began to quiet down, eager for the speeches and celebrations to commence. Theo and I exchanged a glance, an understanding passing between us—a shared anticipation for what was to come, for the culmination of our journey.

"Looks like the show is about to begin," he said, raising his glass in a toast. "To new beginnings."

"To new beginnings," I echoed, clinking my glass against his, the sound ringing with promise.

As the host spoke, I felt a shift within me, a realization dawning that this was more than just a celebration; it was a launching pad into uncharted territory, a chance to redefine who I was and what I wanted. The warmth of Theo's presence beside me solidified my courage, bolstering my confidence to embrace the unknown.

When the speeches concluded, a wave of applause erupted, followed by the rhythmic beat of music that coaxed everyone back onto the dance floor. The night was young, alive with potential, and I felt a magnetic pull toward the center of it all. As we joined the throng of moving bodies, the music enveloped us, vibrant and pulsating, an anthem of liberation.

With each song, I lost myself in the rhythm, the joyous energy igniting something deep within me. I twirled and swayed, feeling the weight of uncertainty fall away with every movement. Theo danced beside me, mirroring my steps, his laughter mingling with the melodies that filled the air. The worries that had haunted me earlier—of being just a fleeting moment in his life—evaporated, replaced by a sense of belonging that was both exhilarating and freeing.

As the night wore on, I could feel the connection between us deepening, a thread woven with shared laughter, stolen glances, and the whisper of promises yet to be spoken. We danced like no one was watching, as if the world outside had faded away. Each turn brought us closer together, a silent understanding blossoming in the space between our breaths.

Then came a slow song, a tender melody that wrapped around us like a gentle embrace. Theo stepped in closer, our bodies swaying softly to the rhythm, and I felt the warmth of his hands on my waist, a grounding presence amidst the swirling energy of the evening.

"You know," he murmured, his breath warm against my ear, "I've never met anyone like you. You're fierce and funny, and you make the mundane feel magical."

A flush of warmth crept up my cheeks, and I couldn't help but smile. "You're not so bad yourself," I replied, teasingly. "For a guy who likes embarrassing sandwiches."

He chuckled, the sound a melody unto itself, and pulled back just enough to meet my gaze. "I meant every word. I want to explore this—whatever this is—together."

In that moment, surrounded by the flickering candlelight and the soft murmur of celebration, I allowed myself to believe in possibilities. I leaned in, capturing his words like fireflies in a jar, not ready to let go of the magic we were creating together.

As we moved together under the dim lights, swaying to the music, I felt the weight of the world lift, the uncertainty that had haunted me replaced with an exhilarating sense of hope. This was my moment, our moment, and I was ready to dive headfirst into whatever came next.

Chapter 17: The Turning Tide

The air was thick with the mingling scents of rosemary and roasted lamb, wafting through the expansive ballroom of the historic Hotel Del Coronado, where golden chandeliers hung like ice crystals, reflecting a warm glow onto the sea of elegantly clad guests. Each table was adorned with crisp white linens, flickering candles, and blooms of vibrant dahlias, creating an atmosphere that felt both festive and suffocating. Laughter and clinking glasses mingled with a melancholic undertone, the kind that only arises when joy dances too closely with something unspoken—a heartbreak, a missed opportunity, or the ache of longing.

I caught glimpses of Theo, standing tall among a crowd of familiar faces. His laughter rang like a bell, drawing people in, and for a moment, I felt a twinge of pride at the way he navigated the social landscape with ease. Yet, as I watched him, surrounded by admirers, a bitter jealousy curled around my heart like smoke from a dying ember. I had always known that he was charismatic, but tonight, it felt like he was shining, and I was a shadow—a specter haunting the edges of my own story. Each smile exchanged between him and someone else felt like a knife twisting in my gut, a reminder of our tangled past that was now a tightrope walk of unspoken words and unshed tears.

I fought against the wave of emotions threatening to pull me under, determined not to drown in self-pity. Just as I felt my resolve wavering, Jessa appeared at my side, her presence a grounding force. She wore a gown the color of ripe blackberries, the fabric clinging to her in all the right places, her confidence radiating as brightly as the diamonds that sparkled around her neck. With a raised eyebrow, she studied me, her perceptive nature able to peel back my carefully crafted facade.

"Come on, spill," she said, her tone light but laced with genuine concern.

"It's just... I don't know, Jess. Watching him like this, I can't help but feel—"

"Like a fish out of water?" she interjected, tilting her head in understanding. "You're not just a fish, honey. You're a whole ocean. But it's okay to feel a little... lost sometimes."

Her words washed over me, and I exhaled slowly, feeling the weight of my emotions ease just a fraction. I had met Jessa during my first year in college, and our friendship had blossomed amidst late-night study sessions and shared dreams. She had a way of seeing through the cracks I tried so hard to hide, and in that moment, she was my anchor.

"You really think I'm strong?" I asked, a hint of disbelief creeping into my voice.

"Stronger than you realize. You've been through so much and still managed to find the light. You've faced challenges head-on, and now, you just need to talk to him."

The idea of confronting Theo sent a shiver down my spine, both exhilarating and terrifying. What if he didn't feel the same? What if he had moved on, leaving me to nurse my wounds in solitude? But standing there, fortified by Jessa's unwavering belief in me, I felt the stirrings of determination blossom.

"Okay," I whispered, my voice barely audible over the crescendo of laughter and conversation surrounding us. "I need to do this."

As the evening wore on, I excused myself, my heart racing as I navigated through the throng of guests, past the tables laden with untouched plates and half-empty glasses of wine. The chill of the night air hit me like a splash of cold water as I stepped onto the balcony, my breath visible in the crisp atmosphere. The vast expanse of snow-dusted mountains loomed in the distance, their peaks kissed by the moonlight, creating an otherworldly backdrop to my turbulent emotions.

There, leaning against the railing, was Theo, his silhouette stark against the glittering horizon. The moment I laid eyes on him, I felt the familiar pull of my heart—a magnet drawn to its counterpart. The moonlight traced the contours of his jaw, illuminating the warmth of his skin. He looked lost in thought, and for a fleeting second, I considered slipping away, letting him remain in his reverie while I tucked my feelings back into the depths of my heart.

But that hesitation faded as I took a deep breath, summoning the courage that felt like a long-forgotten friend. "Hey," I said, my voice breaking the tranquil silence, sounding softer than I intended.

He turned, surprise flickering in his eyes, quickly replaced by a warm smile that made the night feel less bitter. "Hey, I didn't expect to see you out here."

"Just needed some fresh air," I replied, stepping closer, the crisp breeze swirling around us like an uninvited guest.

Theo leaned back against the railing, his expression shifting from casual to something more serious. "You okay? You seemed a bit... off in there."

I paused, the weight of his concern crashing over me like a wave. Here was the man I had shared laughter and secrets with, the one who had become a part of my very fabric, and yet, I felt like a stranger navigating unfamiliar territory. The moonlight cast a silvery glow on his face, highlighting the warmth in his eyes that had always made me feel safe, yet right now, it fueled the tempest within me.

"I've been thinking about us," I started, the words tumbling out like loose marbles. "About everything we've been through."

His gaze sharpened, and I could see the flicker of understanding sparking within him. It was time to strip away the layers of confusion and let the truth spill forth.

As I stood there, the night air alive with the distant sounds of celebration, I felt the words teetering on the edge of my lips, anxious to break free. The chill from the balcony seeped into my bones, but it was nothing compared to the warmth of the moment, a gentle cocoon wrapping around us. Theo's eyes searched mine, and for a heartbeat, the world beyond the balcony—the glimmering lights of the hotel, the laughter of our friends—faded into insignificance. It was just us, suspended in a fragile bubble of possibility.

"I've been thinking about us," I repeated, my voice firmer this time, carrying the weight of all that had been left unsaid. The way he cocked his head to the side, a mix of curiosity and concern, sent a ripple of courage through me. "I miss what we had. I miss you."

The air grew still, the silence stretching like a taut string ready to snap. His expression shifted, and I could almost see the gears in his mind turning, processing my words, the implications hanging heavy between us like the promise of a storm. "I miss you too," he admitted softly, and that single phrase felt like a lighthouse beam cutting through the fog of uncertainty that had enveloped me for so long.

But I couldn't let the moment slide into comfortable nostalgia, even if the allure of our shared history whispered sweet nothings in my ear. I had to lay my heart bare, to expose the raw edges I had hidden for fear of being wounded again. "But it's not just about missing each other, Theo. We've been through so much, and I don't want to pretend that everything is fine when it isn't."

He straightened, a hint of tension sparking in his posture, and I could feel the shift in the air around us, electric and charged. "What do you mean?"

"The distance between us has felt insurmountable, like an ocean where once there was a stream. I can't help but wonder if we've let it become too wide." I paused, watching his brow furrow in contemplation, trying to gauge his reaction. "You've been so focused on your career and what's next, and I've been here, stuck in my own head, wrestling with insecurities. I don't want to be the obstacle in your life. I want to support you, but I also want to be a part of your journey, not just a footnote."

The silence was thick, almost tangible, as he absorbed my words. The moon hung low, illuminating his features with a silver sheen, and I was struck by how familiar yet foreign he felt in that moment. His eyes shimmered, a storm brewing within them, and I held my breath, waiting for the tempest to break.

"I didn't realize you felt that way," he finally replied, his voice laced with a mixture of surprise and something softer, more vulnerable. "I thought we were just... figuring things out, trying to navigate everything without getting too tangled in each other."

"Tangled," I echoed, the word rolling off my tongue like a bitter pill. "Is that all we've become? A knot waiting to unravel?"

"No," he said, shaking his head as if to dispel the notion. "I don't think of you that way. It's just... everything feels so chaotic right now. With work and family expectations, it's like I'm being pulled in a million directions. I didn't want to drag you into that mess."

The honesty in his voice struck a chord within me, resonating with my own fears. "But I want to be in that mess with you. I don't want to stand on the sidelines, watching your life unfold from afar."

Theo stepped closer, the space between us shrinking until it felt electric, charged with unspoken promises. "I don't want that either," he admitted, his eyes softening. "I guess I've been scared, too. Scared of what it all means and how it could change us. I didn't want to lose you, but I didn't know how to keep you close."

The vulnerability in his confession sent a thrill coursing through me, igniting a flicker of hope where once there had been only doubt. I stepped forward, closing the distance completely, our breaths mingling in the crisp night air. "Maybe it's time we stop being scared.

We can't let the fear dictate our choices, Theo. We owe it to ourselves to at least try."

The warmth of his gaze enveloped me, a comforting blanket against the chill, and I could feel the pull between us intensifying, an invisible thread tugging at my heart. "You're right," he said, a smile breaking through the shadows of uncertainty. "We've always been better together. Maybe it's time to rewrite the narrative."

His words hung in the air like a promise, and suddenly, the chaos of the banquet inside felt miles away. It was just us—two people standing at a crossroads, with the weight of the world pushing down on our shoulders, but the possibility of something beautiful lighting the way.

"What do you say we take it one step at a time?" I suggested, feeling a surge of excitement mingled with fear. "We can figure out what this looks like, together. No more pretending."

He nodded slowly, a smile tugging at his lips, and for the first time in what felt like ages, I saw a glimmer of the Theo I had fallen for. "I'd like that. More than you know."

As the last vestiges of daylight faded into the horizon, the stars began to sprinkle the sky, twinkling like scattered diamonds against a velvet backdrop. I felt a sense of calm wash over me, a sense that perhaps the tide was finally turning, carrying us closer to each other, to something more than just fleeting moments of connection.

I took a deep breath, allowing the crisp night air to fill my lungs, the promise of new beginnings swirling around us like a soft breeze. For the first time in a long while, I felt grounded, as if the chaos that had threatened to consume me was nothing more than a passing storm. Together, we could navigate the waves, buoyed by the strength of our shared history and the possibilities that lay ahead. The balcony was no longer a place of uncertainty; it had become our refuge, a sacred space where vulnerability could bloom and the weight of unspoken words could finally be lifted.

The tension between us hung in the air like the delicate chime of a distant bell, resonating with the promise of change. As we stood on that balcony, wrapped in our own world, I could feel the pulse of the night around us—the murmur of laughter from within, the clinking of glasses, and the faint strains of a string quartet serenading the evening. I had spent so long letting uncertainty cloud my heart, but now, it felt as if the fog was lifting, revealing a landscape full of possibilities.

Theo leaned against the railing, the moonlight casting a silvery glow across his face, highlighting the contours that made my heart flutter even now. "So, what does this mean for us?" he asked, his voice steady but laced with a hint of vulnerability that made my chest tighten.

I pondered his question, aware that the words I chose would weave the fabric of our future. "It means we embrace the chaos, Theo. We acknowledge our fears and our desires. We stop dancing around each other like we're on the edges of a cliff. If we want to be together, we have to leap."

He chuckled softly, the sound rich and warm, dissolving some of the tension lingering in the night air. "And if we jump and fall flat on our faces?"

"Then we pick ourselves up and try again," I countered, buoyed by the flicker of hope igniting within me. "I'd rather fall with you than soar alone."

His gaze held mine, a spark igniting between us that felt both electric and tender. "Okay, then let's jump," he said, his smile breaking through the tension like dawn breaking after a long night.

In that moment, we became more than just two people trying to navigate the complexities of our lives; we were partners in crime, united by shared dreams and aspirations. The thought sent a thrill racing through me, and I felt a warmth spreading from my core, wrapping around me like a soft blanket.

As the night wore on, we talked, really talked, peeling back the layers that had built up around us like walls. Theo shared his struggles at work—how the pressure of his job was like a vise tightening around him, making him feel as though he were constantly on the brink of drowning. I recounted my own journey, my battles with self-doubt and the suffocating fear that I wasn't enough. With each revelation, our bond deepened, threading through the complexities of our past and weaving a tapestry rich with understanding and compassion.

The hotel's warm glow flickered through the glass doors, and the laughter inside was a gentle reminder that life continued beyond our little sanctuary. The night air, once heavy with unspoken words, now shimmered with the lightness of possibilities. I caught sight of the stars, twinkling like tiny beacons of hope, and I felt a longing to embrace everything they represented—adventure, love, and the promise of a brighter tomorrow.

Theo broke our comfortable silence, his expression serious. "You know, I've always thought you were remarkable. You face challenges head-on, and it's one of the things I admire most about you."

His words wrapped around me, a comforting balm against the lingering insecurities that had plagued me for so long. "Thank you, but I wouldn't have made it this far without you, Theo. You've always pushed me to be better, to see beyond my own limitations."

The sincerity in his eyes stirred something within me, igniting the fire of determination. We had both been through storms, but we were here now, navigating the tempest together, ready to rewrite our story.

But as the hour grew late, and the laughter from the banquet began to dwindle into soft murmurs, reality loomed closer, and I felt a pang of apprehension. "What do we tell everyone?" I asked, the question hanging in the air like a cloud ready to burst.

"We tell them the truth," he replied, his confidence a reassuring anchor. "We tell them we're in this together, no matter the challenges ahead. We've spent too long hiding behind facades; it's time to embrace what we have."

His words resonated deep within me, striking a chord that made the decision feel less daunting. I nodded, feeling the weight of my fears lift just a little more. "Together," I echoed, the word tasting sweet on my tongue, a promise and a commitment.

As we stepped back inside, the warmth enveloped us like a gentle hug. The ballroom buzzed with energy, the air alive with laughter and joy, a stark contrast to the intimate cocoon we had just shared. Guests swirled around us like colorful ribbons, their happiness palpable. I could see Jessa across the room, her eyes sparkling as she engaged in animated conversation, and I felt a surge of gratitude for her unwavering support.

But my gaze flickered back to Theo, who stood beside me, radiating a kind of confidence that made my heart race. We exchanged a knowing glance, a silent agreement that we were ready to face whatever came next together.

I felt like a bird released from its cage, the exhilaration coursing through me as we navigated the room. Conversations ebbed and flowed around us, the clinking of glasses serving as a backdrop to our unfolding story. With every passing moment, I felt more alive, more connected to those around me and, most importantly, to Theo.

As we mingled, I caught snippets of conversations, the excitement swirling like confetti in the air. The banquet had been organized to celebrate local artists, and the vibrant pieces adorning the walls told stories of their creators—every brushstroke infused with passion, every hue a reflection of their experiences. I felt a kinship with these artists, each of us crafting our narratives, piecing together the fragments of our lives into something beautiful.

At one point, Theo leaned closer, his breath warm against my ear. "What do you think about all this? The art, the energy?"

I took a moment to absorb my surroundings, letting the vibrant colors and the lively atmosphere wash over me. "It's inspiring, isn't it? Everyone here is creating something that speaks to them, something real and raw. It's like they're putting their hearts on display."

"Exactly," he replied, his eyes sparkling with enthusiasm. "And I think we can do the same, with our own journey. We can create something beautiful out of all this chaos."

In that moment, I knew he was right. Our relationship was a canvas waiting to be painted, each brushstroke a reflection of our shared experiences, hopes, and fears. As we continued to mingle, I felt the weight of uncertainty lift. We were no longer tiptoeing around the complexities of our feelings; we were embracing them, ready to face whatever the world had in store for us.

With renewed determination, I grasped Theo's hand, our fingers entwining like threads of fate. Together, we stepped into the light, ready to paint our own masterpiece in the vibrant tapestry of life. The night sparkled with possibility, and for the first time in a long while, I felt like the architect of my own destiny. We were no longer just characters in a story; we were the authors of our future, pen poised to write a new chapter filled with love, laughter, and the kind of chaos that makes life worth living.

Chapter 18: Confrontation in the Moonlight

The moon hung high above the desert town, a luminous sentinel casting its silvery light over the cracked pavement and dusty streets. The air was crisp and invigorating, a stark contrast to the suffocating heat of the day that clung to the remnants of summer like a stubborn memory. I stepped out from the shadow of the diner, its neon sign buzzing softly, painting the world in hues of electric blue and pink. The distant sound of laughter and clinking glasses from within faded as I made my way toward the alley behind the building, my heart pounding like a persistent drumbeat.

Each step was a battle between hope and dread, the gravel crunching beneath my sneakers a reminder of my resolve. I felt a surge of adrenaline coursing through me, fueled by the possibility of finally breaking the silence that had stretched between us like a canyon too wide to cross. My mind was a whirlpool of thoughts—memories of laughter shared over coffee, stolen glances beneath the warm glow of street lamps, and whispered secrets that felt heavier than the stars overhead. But those beautiful moments were now tangled in a web of confusion and hurt, each thread pulling me closer to the confrontation I both craved and feared.

As I rounded the corner, I saw him standing there, silhouetted against the silvery glow of the moonlight. Theo leaned against the brick wall, his hands shoved deep into the pockets of his worn jeans, a posture that spoke volumes of the turmoil raging within him. The soft light highlighted the sharp angles of his jaw and the tousled waves of his dark hair, making him look both rugged and vulnerable. In that moment, he was everything I had ever wanted and everything I feared, wrapped up in the same imperfect package. I inhaled deeply, filling my lungs with the crisp night air, and stepped closer, feeling the chill seep into my bones.

"We need to talk," I said, my voice steady despite the trembling of my heart. The words hung between us, tangible and raw. Theo turned slowly, surprise flickering across his face, and in the depths of his warm brown eyes, I saw a flicker of recognition, a reflection of the chaos I felt inside. It was as if the very air crackled with unspoken words, secrets held too long and emotions straining against the constraints we had both imposed.

He pushed off the wall, stepping toward me, and I could see the tension in his shoulders. "I didn't want to hurt you," he replied, his voice thick with emotion, each word heavy with the weight of regret. "I thought keeping you at a distance would protect us both." His confession hung in the air, a revelation that shifted the ground beneath us. For a moment, the world faded away, leaving only the two of us wrapped in our own fragile universe.

I took a breath, the night air filling my lungs with determination. "But what about me?" I replied, the question escaping my lips like a breath I hadn't known I was holding. "What about what I want? You can't just decide what's best for both of us without asking." The words felt foreign on my tongue, yet they were laced with an urgency that demanded to be spoken. I had been silent too long, living in the shadows of his decisions, and now I was ready to step into the light, to reclaim my voice.

Theo's gaze dropped for a moment, and I could see the internal battle he was fighting. The flicker of uncertainty in his eyes was like a reflection of my own fears. "I didn't want to lose you," he admitted quietly, his voice barely above a whisper. "I thought that by pulling away, I could protect us from something that might hurt us both." The vulnerability in his confession sent a rush of warmth through me, the icy grip of anger thawing under the light of understanding.

In that moment, I realized that he was scared, just like me—scared of the pain that might come if we ventured into the unknown together. I stepped closer, closing the distance between us, our breaths mingling in the cool night air. The electric tension between us was palpable, a magnetism that pulled us together even as we grappled with the uncertainty that lay ahead. "You're not the only one who's scared, Theo," I said, my voice softer now, a soothing balm to the raw edges of our confrontation. "I'm terrified of what this could mean for us. But I can't let fear dictate my choices anymore." My heart raced as I held his gaze, searching for a flicker of hope within his stormy depths.

He reached out, his hand brushing against mine, the contact igniting a spark that surged through me. It was a simple gesture, yet it spoke volumes. "Then let's stop running," he proposed, his voice steady now, a newfound strength emanating from him. "Let's face whatever comes next together." I felt a smile break free, a moment of pure, unguarded joy. In that shared moment, we forged a pact, an unspoken agreement to leave the shadows of doubt behind and embrace whatever the universe had in store for us.

As the moon bathed us in its ethereal glow, the world around us transformed. The alley, once filled with the echoes of our hesitations, became a sanctuary, a space where we could shed the burdens of our past. Laughter danced in the air, mingling with the distant sounds of the town waking up to the night. The possibilities stretched before us like an uncharted path, inviting us to take the first steps into a new chapter, hand in hand.

I could feel the weight of uncertainty begin to lift, replaced by a fragile but undeniable hope. We stood together, two souls intertwined in the magic of the moonlit night, ready to face whatever awaited us beyond the horizon. With each passing moment, the fear that had once anchored me began to dissolve, replaced by the warmth of his presence and the promise of what we could build together. In that moment, I knew that whatever lay ahead—joy or heartache, triumph or struggle—we would face it as one.

The moonlight wrapped around us like a silken shroud, delicate yet intense, illuminating the raw edges of our emotions. In that quiet moment, I felt a pulse of something sacred between us, an unspoken acknowledgment that our hearts were no longer solitary entities. They danced in the fragile space between doubt and faith, teetering on the edge of something monumental.

Theo's hand lingered close to mine, fingers brushing together in a tentative connection that sent ripples of warmth through my chest. It felt surreal, like standing on the precipice of a cliff, gazing down into the unknown. Every heartbeat echoed in my ears, a metronome to our unsteady breaths. I longed to bridge the gap that had formed in our hearts, to pull him into the safety of my embrace, yet there was a delicate line between intimacy and fear.

"Let's walk," I suggested, the words tumbling from my lips as I turned to navigate the winding alleyway. The faint scent of jasmine lingered in the air, mingling with the distant hum of the town. Each step we took was a stitch, mending the fabric of our relationship with the hopes of tomorrow. We walked in silence, the moon following us like a watchful guardian, illuminating the cobblestone path ahead as if guiding us through the shadows of our past.

The alley opened up onto a small courtyard, framed by crumbling adobe walls that whispered secrets of times long forgotten. A rickety wooden bench sat beneath a gnarled tree, its branches stretched out like open arms. It was a place of respite, one that invited us to linger, to unburden our souls in the sacred stillness of the night. I settled onto the bench, the wood creaking beneath me, and gestured for Theo to join.

He hesitated for a moment, his brow furrowed in thought, but then he sat down beside me, the warmth radiating from his body enveloping me like a familiar blanket. The atmosphere buzzed with unspoken words, the weight of our feelings hanging in the air like the stars above, each one a fragment of our shared story.

"I don't want this to become another thing we regret," I finally said, my voice breaking the silence. The sincerity in my words pierced through the lingering tension, urging him to lay bare his thoughts. "I'm tired of pretending we're just friends." I felt the honesty of my own heart reflected in his gaze, a flicker of recognition sparking between us.

"I know," he replied softly, his eyes searching mine as if seeking a hidden truth. "I've been running from this, afraid of what it could mean for us. But it feels impossible to deny what we have." The admission lingered in the air, heavy with meaning, weaving a tapestry of hope amidst our fears.

A gentle breeze rustled the leaves above, creating a soft symphony that underscored the moment. I leaned closer, drawn to him like a moth to a flame, every instinct urging me to close the distance. "Then let's stop pretending," I said, my heart racing as I ventured into the uncharted territory of vulnerability. "Let's embrace whatever this is, together."

The silence that followed felt infinite, each second stretching like a taut string ready to snap. Finally, he turned to me, his expression a mixture of resolve and uncertainty. "You're right," he said, his voice steadying as if finding its footing on solid ground. "I don't want to lose you either."

In that moment, the air shifted, the tension dissolving like mist under the sun. I felt the warmth of a smile spread across my face, and Theo mirrored it, the corners of his mouth lifting in a way that made my heart flutter. It was as if we had both stepped into a new realm, where the boundaries of friendship blurred into something infinitely deeper.

Our laughter mingled with the night air, light and freeing, the burdens of our hesitations lifting one soft note at a time. The courtyard became a cocoon, sheltering us from the chaos of the world outside. It was a sanctuary where we could explore the uncharted landscape of our emotions without fear of judgment or consequence.

"What if we're making a mistake?" he pondered, his expression thoughtful, the hint of a smile still playing at the edges of his lips. "What if this doesn't work?"

I considered his words, the weight of uncertainty tugging at the corners of my mind. "But what if it does?" I countered, my voice brimming with the conviction of possibility. "What if we discover something beautiful together? Something worth fighting for?"

The night air crackled with the tension of unspoken desires, the echoes of our past colliding with the hopeful prospects of our future. I reached for his hand, intertwining our fingers, feeling the warmth of his skin against mine. It was a simple gesture, yet it felt monumental—an affirmation that we were ready to step into the unknown side by side.

His thumb brushed over the back of my hand, a tender caress that sent a jolt of electricity through me. "I want to take that chance," he said, his voice low and earnest, each word a promise etched in the air between us. "I want to see where this leads."

And just like that, the barriers we had built around ourselves began to crumble. The shadows of doubt dissipated, replaced by a light that flickered with the promise of new beginnings. We were no longer bound by the constraints of fear; we were free to explore the depths of our connection and the intricacies of our hearts.

In the moonlit courtyard, amidst the gentle rustling of leaves and the distant laughter of the night, we forged a new path. Together, we began to paint our story, one brushstroke at a time, creating a vibrant tapestry that would carry us through whatever lay ahead.

Our laughter blended with the whispering wind, and in that moment, I knew that we were ready to face the world as a united force, armed with the strength of our love and the courage to chase the unknown.

The laughter from the courtyard hung in the air like a cherished melody, lingering long after the last note faded. Theo and I remained side by side, fingers entwined, cocooned in the warmth of our newfound connection. The world around us pulsed with life, the distant chatter of late-night strollers and the soft murmur of the wind whispering secrets of old dreams. Each sound was a reminder that we were no longer just two souls navigating the tempest of uncertainty; we had begun to carve our own path through the darkness.

As we settled into this delicate dance of vulnerability, the sky transformed above us, shifting from its deep indigo to a twilight that shimmered with stars like confetti scattered across an expansive canvas. It was as if the universe itself was celebrating our decision, illuminating the shadows of our past while beckoning us forward into the light. The moon hung overhead like a benevolent guardian, casting a gentle glow that danced upon the cobblestones, urging us to embrace what lay ahead.

I leaned against the rough bark of the tree, its gnarled branches arching protectively overhead, and turned to Theo. The shadows played across his features, giving him an ethereal quality that made my heart race. "What now?" I asked, my voice barely above a whisper, filled with the wonder and fear of stepping into uncharted territory.

His gaze held mine, steady and unwavering, as if he were drawing strength from the very roots of the earth beneath us. "Now," he began, his voice firm yet gentle, "we let go of everything that held us back. We stop fearing what might happen and start embracing what is happening."

The weight of his words settled around us, a cloak woven from hope and possibility. I felt a surge of excitement, a tidal wave of optimism rushing through me. It was thrilling to think of the endless paths we could forge together, every twist and turn a chance to redefine ourselves beyond the constraints of our past mistakes. "And what does that look like for us?" I asked, my mind swirling with visions of our shared future.

A mischievous grin spread across his face, lighting up his features in a way that made my heart flutter. "Well, I'd say it starts with an adventure. Why not?" The spontaneity in his voice ignited a spark of joy within me. "Let's drive to the coast tomorrow. Just us, the open road, and whatever we can find along the way."

The prospect was intoxicating. A road trip—a classic escape. The thought of sandy beaches, crashing waves, and salt-kissed breezes filled my imagination, and I could already picture us laughing together, losing track of time as we explored tiny roadside diners and quirky gift shops that dotted the landscape. It was an invitation to step outside our fears and into a world brimming with possibilities. "You're serious?" I asked, unable to suppress the excitement bubbling within me.

"Absolutely," he replied, his eyes dancing with enthusiasm. "We've been stuck in our heads for too long. It's time to break free." The determination in his voice resonated with me, sending a thrill through my veins. I could feel the remnants of doubt slipping away, replaced by an exhilarating sense of adventure.

"Okay," I said, the word barely escaping my lips before a wave of adrenaline coursed through me. "Let's do it." A shared grin erupted between us, an unspoken promise of exploration that anchored us to this moment, a heartbeat away from a leap into the unknown.

As the night deepened, we lingered beneath the branches of the tree, sharing fragments of our lives, weaving our stories together with laughter and glances that held the weight of everything unspoken.

Each revelation felt like a brushstroke on the canvas of our relationship, building a vivid picture of who we were and who we could become. I shared stories of my childhood—how I had climbed trees taller than I was, searching for hidden worlds in the treetops, while he spoke of long nights spent fishing with his father beneath a sky illuminated by stars. Each memory we shared felt like a piece of a puzzle falling into place, revealing a future that sparkled with promise.

The moon hung higher now, a beacon in the night sky, and as the clock inched closer to midnight, I felt a soft chill in the air. Theo noticed and slid closer, wrapping an arm around my shoulders, an innocent gesture that sent my heart racing. The warmth of his body radiated through the fabric of my shirt, cocooning me in a blanket of safety and affection. I nestled closer, my head resting against his shoulder, the world around us fading into a soft blur as the focus shifted entirely to us.

"What if this is a mistake?" I murmured into the night, a tiny thread of apprehension tugging at my heartstrings. "What if we ruin everything?" The fear of jeopardizing the fragile bond we had just begun to forge loomed like a shadow over our connection.

Theo paused, his breath hitching slightly. "You know," he said slowly, "every great love story has its risks. But isn't it worth it to find out?" He turned to look at me, and I could see the sincerity etched in his features. "I'd rather take the chance than live in the 'what ifs' forever."

His words resonated deeply, echoing through the chambers of my heart. It was a reminder that love was not just a destination but a journey filled with bumps and detours that made the ride worthwhile. The anticipation of the unknown became a thrill rather than a fear, and in that moment, I felt myself surrendering to the adventure that lay ahead.

With newfound clarity, I looked into his eyes and saw my own reflection staring back—a mixture of hope and excitement, tempered by the undeniable weight of reality. "Then let's face whatever comes our way, together," I said, my voice steady now, resonating with conviction.

A smile broke across his face, one that seemed to illuminate the dark corners of the night. "Together," he echoed, sealing our unspoken pact with the power of our commitment.

As we sat there, the world around us faded away, replaced by the boundless expanse of what we could create together. We were no longer defined by the past but by the possibilities that lay ahead—a canvas waiting to be painted with laughter, tears, and the messy beauty of life lived fully.

With the moon as our witness and the stars as our guide, we surrendered to the moment, ready to embrace whatever the road might hold. The adventure had only just begun, and in the depths of my heart, I knew that I would follow him anywhere.

Chapter 19: Embracing the Unknown

The chill of the early morning air kissed my cheeks as I pulled on my woolen hat, its threads a comforting embrace against the biting wind. I stood at the foot of the majestic Rockies, their peaks dusted with a fine layer of powdery snow, sparkling like diamonds under the soft glow of dawn. Theo was beside me, a vibrant energy radiating from his every movement. His laughter, rich and full, cut through the silence of the crisp mountain morning, and I couldn't help but smile, the weight of the world lifting with each shared chuckle. Together, we were explorers ready to conquer the slopes, and with our hearts bared, we were about to dive into a day that promised to change everything.

The ski resort sprawled before us, a tapestry of vivid colors against the stark white backdrop of the mountains. Lodgepole pines stood like sentinels, their dark green needles contrasting sharply with the snow, while clusters of skiers and snowboarders wove their way through the maze of trails. The air was alive with the sounds of laughter, the rhythmic swoosh of skis gliding through fresh snow, and the distant chatter of friends enjoying the thrill of the mountains. I took a deep breath, the cold air filling my lungs, invigorating my spirit. This place felt like a playground, and I was more than ready to play.

As we strapped our boots into our skis, Theo's fingers brushed against mine, sending a warm jolt of electricity up my arm. It was a small gesture, but it echoed loudly in my heart. I looked at him, his blue eyes glinting with mischief, and in that moment, I knew we were more than friends embarking on an adventure; we were two souls unafraid to embrace the unknown together. I could feel the excitement bubbling within me, mingling with a hint of trepidation, but I pushed that aside. I was here to live, to experience, and to lose myself in the thrill of the moment.

With a shared nod, we pushed off together, carving through the soft snow as we soared down the slope. The adrenaline coursed through my veins like wildfire, a pulse that matched the rhythm of my heart. I leaned into the turns, the chill of the air rushing past me, invigorating and intoxicating. Theo was just ahead, and I chased him like a determined hound, every twist and turn a challenge, every descent a chance to close the distance between us.

As we navigated the slopes, the world transformed into a blur of white and blue. The sun, high in the sky, cast long shadows, and the mountains loomed like ancient guardians watching over our escapade. I could taste the cold on my lips and feel the snow crunch beneath my skis. Each bump sent bursts of exhilaration shooting through me, and I found myself laughing, my voice mingling with the howling wind. Theo, with his wild, untamed hair and contagious enthusiasm, became my compass, leading me deeper into this enchanting world.

We paused at the summit of a particularly challenging run, the landscape sprawling beneath us like a vast, white ocean. I looked out, my breath hitching as the beauty of it all sank in. "This is insane," I shouted over the wind, my heart racing not just from the physical exertion, but from the sheer joy that enveloped me. Theo turned to me, his grin infectious, and I felt an electric connection spark between us, the kind that whispered of shared secrets and endless possibilities.

"Are you ready to tackle the next one?" he called back, his eyes gleaming with the thrill of the unknown. I nodded, determination flooding through me. I wasn't just skiing; I was living, embracing every moment, every rush of air, every laugh shared.

The next descent was steep, a cascade of white inviting us to plunge into its depths. With a deep breath, I launched forward, carving my path through the fresh powder, the world around me fading into a serene silence, broken only by the rhythmic swish of my skis. The rush of the wind was exhilarating, a tangible reminder of my courage to leap into the unknown. Each turn was a dance, a playful conversation between me and the mountain, and I felt like a part of something larger, something wild and beautiful.

At the base, we met again, breathless and elated, the thrill of the run pulsing through us. We leaned against our poles, laughter echoing in the air, the bond between us solidifying with every shared experience. The sunlight glinted off Theo's cheeks, illuminating the happiness radiating from him. In that moment, I realized I wasn't just falling for the exhilaration of the slopes; I was falling for him too.

With each subsequent run, we pushed our limits, challenging one another, and laughing as we stumbled through missteps and falls, arms flailing like over-enthusiastic windmills. I felt alive, as if the mountains had awakened a part of me that had long been dormant, buried under layers of routine and self-doubt. I was no longer just Julia, the cautious planner; I was Julia, the adventurer, ready to embrace whatever came next.

As the day wore on and the sun dipped lower in the sky, painting the horizon with strokes of orange and purple, we gathered our gear, fatigue setting in but exhilaration still buzzing in our veins. With snowflakes dancing around us like confetti, we walked toward the lodge, laughter spilling from our lips, each step reinforcing the connection that had blossomed on those slopes. This was more than just a skiing trip; it was a celebration of life, of friendship, and of the daring leap into the great unknown that awaited us both.

The lodge was a sanctuary of warmth after our exhilarating day on the slopes, a cozy haven that contrasted starkly with the wildness outside. Thick beams of timber crisscrossed the ceiling, and the walls were adorned with rustic memorabilia—old skis, snowshoes, and sepia-toned photographs of skiers from a bygone era, their smiles frozen in time, echoing the laughter we had just shared. As we stepped inside, the aroma of rich hot chocolate wafted through the air, drawing us toward the large stone fireplace crackling invitingly in the corner.

I could feel the heat of the flames licking at my cheeks, a welcome relief from the chill that had settled into my bones. Theo and I found a small table near the window, overlooking the slopes where the shadows of skiers danced in the waning light. I sank into my chair, shedding the layers of winter gear like a snake shedding its skin, and reveled in the comfortable ache of my muscles, a testament to the day's adventures.

"Do you think we'll wake up tomorrow and decide to conquer the world?" I teased, stirring my hot chocolate, the marshmallows swirling like tiny clouds in a stormy sky. The thought made me chuckle, but there was an undercurrent of truth in my jest. With Theo by my side, I felt as though the world was ours to explore, the boundaries of my previous self steadily eroding.

"Only if the world is still standing," he replied, a grin playing at the corners of his mouth as he sipped from his steaming mug. His eyes sparkled with mischief, a hint of challenge that sent a thrill racing through me. "I'm thinking maybe a little night skiing tomorrow? Or we could take on that black diamond run that nearly scared the life out of you."

The memory of that steep slope sent a shiver of both fear and excitement down my spine. "You're trying to kill me, aren't you?" I laughed, the sound mingling with the soft chatter of other patrons. His laughter, deep and resonant, was a balm that soothed my nerves. It was the kind of laughter that made me feel safe, a promise that whatever came next, we would face it together.

After our drinks, we decided to explore the lodge. The atmosphere was festive, a delightful blend of laughter and the occasional clink of glasses, as families and friends gathered to share stories of their day. I marveled at the camaraderie enveloping the room, each group's laughter punctuating the air like joyful exclamations. The warmth of the gathering radiated through me, a stark contrast to the briskness outside.

"Let's go find that game room they mentioned at the front desk," I suggested, my curiosity piqued. Theo nodded, and together we made our way through the throng, weaving between tables adorned with half-empty plates of nachos and steaming bowls of chili, the tantalizing scents swirling around us.

As we entered the game room, the vibrant lights of the arcade machines flashed in a dizzying array of colors. A pool table stood at the center, its green felt inviting us to challenge each other. The air was thick with playful competition, the laughter echoing against the walls. I felt a rush of nostalgia, reminiscent of the weekends I spent at arcades with friends, and a bright grin spread across my face.

"Do you play?" I asked, gesturing toward the pool table, feeling an exhilarating flutter of excitement.

"Only if you promise to go easy on me," he replied with a playful wink. I picked up a cue stick, feeling its weight in my hands, and chalked the tip, pretending to study the layout of the table like a seasoned player. The moment felt electric, charged with a kind of energy that thrummed beneath the surface, teasing me with the promise of something more.

As we played, the friendly banter between us flowed effortlessly. I quickly realized that Theo was surprisingly adept at the game. Each time I missed a shot, he'd flash a smile, his teasing glances making me laugh even harder. "You're just trying to distract me," I accused playfully, feigning annoyance while failing miserably at hiding my own delight.

"Guilty as charged," he said, his voice low and conspiratorial, leaning closer. The warmth of his breath brushed against my cheek, igniting a warmth that spread through my entire being. I felt as though we were the only two people in the room, enveloped in our own bubble of shared laughter and friendly rivalry.

With each shot I took, each playful jab we exchanged, I felt my heart swell. This wasn't just about the game; it was about the effortless connection we were nurturing, each moment crafting the foundation for something beautiful. The sun slipped lower in the sky, casting golden rays that danced through the windows, illuminating the space in a soft, inviting glow.

After several rounds, we decided to take a break and grab some snacks from the nearby café. The barista, an older woman with a kind smile, served us plates of warm cookies and a pair of steaming lattes that we carried back to the game room. Settling into a corner booth, we relished the sweet, gooey treats, our laughter spilling freely as we swapped stories of childhood mischief and dreams yet to be realized.

"You know, I once tried to build a snow fort that was supposed to rival the White House," I confessed, leaning back in my seat. "I ended up with a glorified pile of snow and a sore back."

Theo threw his head back, laughter spilling out in waves. "You mean to tell me you weren't the reigning snow fort champion of your neighborhood? I'm shocked!"

"I know, right? It was a devastating loss," I retorted, my heart swelling with joy as we continued our playful banter. Each shared story and each chuckle layered our connection deeper, weaving an intricate tapestry of trust and understanding.

The night wore on, filled with laughter and shared secrets, and I found myself captivated by the man before me, his passion for life evident in every animated gesture and spark in his eyes. As I watched him speak, a sense of comfort washed over me, the kind that made me believe in the beauty of the unexpected.

In that little corner of the world, amidst the warmth of the lodge and the allure of the mountains outside, I felt a sense of belonging. It was a moment suspended in time, a slice of life that was perfect in its imperfection, and I knew that whatever came next, it would be an adventure worth embracing.

As the night deepened, the lodge hummed with energy, the atmosphere thick with camaraderie and warmth. Our laughter faded into the background noise of clinking glasses and chatter as the rustic wooden beams seemed to pulse with life. I glanced out the window at the velvet sky, peppered with stars that twinkled like diamonds scattered across black silk. It was a sight that made the heart swell with possibility, a reminder that there was so much more to explore beyond the confines of our small bubble.

"Want to venture outside?" Theo's voice cut through my reverie, playful curiosity glinting in his eyes. The suggestion was unexpected but thrilling, sending a jolt of excitement through me. I nodded enthusiastically, eager for another adventure, even as the warmth of the lodge wrapped around me like a familiar blanket.

We bundled back into our winter gear, laughter bubbling between us as we fought with zippers and scarves. The cold air hit us like a bucket of ice water when we stepped outside, but it was invigorating, breathing life into our spirits. The moon hung high, casting a silver glow over the snow-covered landscape, transforming the world into a magical wonderland.

As we made our way toward the slopes, the crunch of snow underfoot echoed in the stillness. The night was alive with the sounds of nature—the gentle rustle of pine branches swaying in the wind and the distant murmur of a stream, its waters flowing with a quiet determination. I felt a thrill run through me, a rush that came from being outside, away from the distractions of daily life, where it was just me and the wild.

"Let's try night skiing!" Theo suggested, his voice bursting with enthusiasm. My stomach flipped at the thought, a mix of exhilaration and apprehension swirling within me. Night skiing felt daring, like we were sneaking into a secret world that belonged to the brave. I hesitated for a moment, uncertainty tugging at me, but the spark in Theo's eyes ignited my courage.

"Okay, let's do it!" I replied, surprising myself with my boldness. With a shared grin, we grabbed our gear from the nearby shed and headed toward the lit slopes. The lights illuminated the trail, casting a warm glow that felt almost magical, like stepping into a scene from a fairy tale.

We began our descent, the snow glistening under the artificial lights. The familiar thrill surged through me as I leaned into the slope, the wind whipping past me, crisp and refreshing. Theo's laughter rang out beside me, buoyant and infectious, and I couldn't help but mirror his joy.

"Look at us!" he shouted, carving wide arcs in the snow. "We're practically pros!"

The confidence in his voice pushed me to ski harder, and as I glided down the slope, I felt a new freedom enveloping me. Each turn was a declaration, each acceleration a promise to embrace life fully, without reservation. I could hear my heart pounding in my chest, a steady drumbeat urging me forward, and with Theo beside me, I felt invincible.

After several exhilarating runs, we took a break, standing atop a small ridge overlooking the twinkling lights of the lodge below. The view was breathtaking—a sea of illumination against the vast, dark canvas of the night. I breathed in the cold, crisp air, the moment grounding me in the beauty of now.

"Can you believe how far we've come?" Theo asked, his voice softer now, filled with wonder. He glanced at me, his expression reflecting a mix of pride and intimacy, a connection that seemed to transcend words.

"I know, right? It feels like we're in a completely different world," I replied, meeting his gaze. There was a depth to his eyes, an intensity that made my heart race. In that moment, the distance between us felt palpable, charged with unspoken emotions and possibilities waiting to be uncovered.

With the air thick with anticipation, I turned my focus back to the slopes, eager to plunge into another run. The thrill was addictive, a sweet high that beckoned me to dive deeper into this adventure. As we sped down the hill together, laughter echoing through the night, I felt the boundaries of my world expanding, embracing the exhilarating uncertainty that came with it.

Eventually, we found ourselves back at the lodge, still buzzing from the adrenaline of the night. The atmosphere had shifted; it felt more intimate now, the laughter more melodic, the connections deeper. I settled into a plush armchair by the fireplace, the flickering flames casting a warm glow around us, wrapping us in a cocoon of comfort. Theo plopped down beside me, the heat of his body radiating against the chill that still clung to my skin.

"Tell me your dreams," he said, leaning forward, his elbows resting on his knees, curiosity dancing in his eyes. It was a simple request, but one that felt monumental. It beckoned me to dive deeper, to peel back the layers of who I was and share the most vulnerable parts of my soul.

I hesitated, the weight of my dreams suddenly feeling heavy and daunting. But as I met his gaze, the openness in his expression encouraged me to speak. "I've always wanted to travel the world," I confessed, the words flowing more easily than I expected. "To see places I've only read about, to experience different cultures and meet new people. It feels like there's so much more to life than what I've experienced so far."

Theo nodded, his expression thoughtful. "And what's stopping you?"

A small laugh escaped me, almost bitter in its honesty. "Fear, I guess. Fear of the unknown, of stepping out of my comfort zone. It's easier to stay in one place, to stick with what I know."

His gaze softened, and I could sense his understanding, the silent acknowledgment of the battles we all face. "But sometimes, the most beautiful things happen when we embrace that fear," he replied gently, a hint of determination coloring his words. "Like today. We pushed ourselves, and look how much fun we had!"

His words struck a chord deep within me, resonating like a bell tolling in the quiet night. Perhaps he was right. Perhaps it was time to shed the skin of my old self and embrace the thrilling uncertainty that life had to offer.

In that moment, something shifted. I felt lighter, as if a layer of doubt had been stripped away, revealing a glimmer of hope beneath. I turned to him, my heart racing, and saw the man before me not just as a friend, but as a partner in this journey of discovery.

"I want to see the world," I echoed, a newfound resolve tightening my grip on the possibilities that lay ahead. "And I want you to be a part of it."

Theo's eyes widened, surprise flickering across his face before it was replaced with a warm smile. "I'd like that," he said softly, the sincerity in his voice wrapping around me like a warm embrace.

The night wore on, but our conversation flowed effortlessly, weaving tales of adventure and dreams like a tapestry, each thread brightening the fabric of our budding relationship. I could sense that this was just the beginning—a spark igniting a fire that would light our way through the unknown.

As we finally stood to leave, the flickering flames in the hearth reflected the warmth blossoming between us. I knew we were stepping into uncharted territory, but I felt ready. With Theo by my side, the world awaited, bursting with color, excitement, and endless possibilities. The unknown was no longer a place of fear; it was a canvas waiting for us to paint our story upon it, and I was ready to embrace every bold stroke.

Chapter 20: The Melting Snow

The sun dripped through the pines, its golden rays spilling onto the forest floor like a warm embrace, inviting me deeper into the world around me. The air was fresh, crisp with the promise of new beginnings, and every breath felt like a rekindling of my spirit. With each step I took on that winding trail, the winter's grip on my heart began to thaw, mirroring the snow melting in the distant mountains. I was no longer just a bystander in my own life; I was a participant, my heart racing with the thrill of possibility.

Theo walked beside me, his presence as invigorating as the spring breeze. His laughter bounced off the trees, a melody that danced in perfect harmony with the symphony of nature. Every time he spoke, his eyes sparkled with enthusiasm, reflecting the azure sky above us. I could listen to him for hours, captivated by the way he articulated his dreams of carving through the powdery slopes as a top ski instructor. He painted vivid pictures with his words—flying down mountainsides, the adrenaline rushing through him as he helped others discover their own passions for the sport. It was infectious, igniting a warmth in my chest that felt foreign yet exhilarating.

"Do you think you'll ever compete?" I asked, my curiosity piqued. The notion of him racing against others made my heart flutter. There was something both thrilling and terrifying about the idea, like standing on the edge of a cliff, contemplating the leap.

He chuckled, running a hand through his unruly hair, a tousled mane that mirrored the wildness of the world around us. "Maybe someday," he replied, a hint of mischief glimmering in his gaze. "But for now, I just want to share the joy of skiing. It's not about the medals for me; it's about the smiles on my students' faces." His sincerity radiated through the air, wrapping around me like the gentle warmth of the sun.

We pressed on, our feet crunching against the remnants of snow that lingered like reluctant guests at a party. Each step felt like a declaration, a promise to ourselves that we were ready to embrace the life that lay before us. The vibrant colors of the wildflowers began to emerge, pushing through the earth, defying the lingering chill. I leaned down to inhale the sweet scent of blooming daisies, their delicate petals beckoning for attention. In that moment, surrounded by the beauty of the natural world, I felt alive.

With a sudden burst of energy, I grabbed Theo's hand, pulling him down the trail. The joy that erupted between us was palpable, a tangible force that propelled us forward. Our laughter echoed through the trees, intertwining with the whispers of the wind. As we raced, the world around us blurred, a kaleidoscope of colors and sounds that ignited a sense of freedom I had long forgotten. I could feel the exhilaration bubbling within me, a joy so profound that it chased away the shadows of my past.

The trail wound deeper into the woods, leading us to a clearing where the sun bathed the earth in a golden glow. I paused, my breath catching at the beauty before me. The vast expanse of the valley stretched out, dotted with patches of snow still clinging to the mountainsides, the remnants of winter battling against the surge of spring. It was a breathtaking vista that took my breath away.

"Wow," I whispered, my voice barely above a breath. "It's stunning."

Theo stepped closer, his shoulder brushing against mine as we both took in the sight. "This is one of my favorite spots," he said, his voice low and reverent, as if speaking too loudly might shatter the tranquility. "It reminds me that even after the harshest winters, beauty will always return."

His words settled in the air, a reminder of the resilience of life. In that moment, I realized how much I had learned from him. He was teaching me to embrace my journey, to recognize that healing, like the changing of seasons, took time and patience. I turned to face him, the sunlight illuminating his features, casting him in a golden hue that made my heart swell.

"Thank you," I said, my voice soft, filled with the sincerity I often struggled to express. "For everything. You've helped me more than you know."

His eyes searched mine, a moment of connection that felt electric. "We're in this together," he replied, his sincerity wrapping around me like a warm blanket. "And I'm just as grateful for you."

There was a softness in his gaze that made my heart skip a beat, a shared understanding that anchored us in that moment. The laughter faded, replaced by a silence thick with unspoken words, a realization of what we were building together—something beautiful and fragile.

I reached out, entwining my fingers with his, feeling the warmth of his palm against mine, grounding me in the present. The wind rustled through the trees, whispering secrets only we could hear, and I knew we were on the brink of something extraordinary. It wasn't just the beauty of the mountains that captivated me; it was the connection we were nurturing, each moment drawing us closer to a future I dared to hope for.

With the sun setting behind the mountains, casting long shadows over the landscape, we began our descent, the trail leading us back through the vibrant wildflowers. As we walked side by side, our hands still intertwined, I felt the remnants of my old self slowly melting away, replaced by a sense of hope that blossomed like the flowers around us. I was learning to embrace life again, and with Theo by my side, the journey ahead seemed filled with endless possibilities.

The sun hung low in the sky, casting a warm glow that danced across the landscape as we meandered through the blossoming wildflower trail. It felt as if the world around us was holding its breath, waiting for something profound to unfold. Theo's laughter, bright and unrestrained, filled the air, mingling with the rustle of leaves and the distant chirping of birds. Each sound echoed the vibrant energy that thrummed between us, wrapping around our hearts like a delicate thread binding our souls together.

As we reached the edge of a small pond, the water mirrored the cerulean sky above, a flawless canvas dotted with wisps of clouds. I paused to take in the scene, the beauty of it catching my breath like a fleeting moment of clarity. The wildflowers swayed gently in the breeze, their colors bold and unapologetic against the backdrop of greens and blues. I knelt beside the pond, the coolness of the earth grounding me, and dipped my fingers into the water, sending ripples that fractured the perfect reflection. It was an almost meditative moment, a reminder that even in nature, chaos could bring beauty.

"Hey, come look at this!" Theo called, his voice buoyant with excitement. I turned to find him crouched at the water's edge, his face illuminated with wonder as he pointed toward a family of ducks paddling gracefully across the pond. The ducklings bobbed along, fluffy and yellow, trailing after their mother like a line of tiny, sun-kissed clouds. Watching them, I felt a rush of warmth, a pang of longing for the simplicity of life in those moments.

"They're adorable!" I exclaimed, moving closer to him, our shoulders brushing lightly. He looked at me, his eyes bright with mischief, and before I could process what he was doing, he splashed a handful of water in my direction. The cool droplets hit my face, sending a shock of laughter bubbling up from deep within me. I retaliated, and soon we were caught in a playful water fight, splashing each other with abandon, our laughter mingling with the sweet sounds of nature.

Moments like these were treasures, little gems scattered throughout the everyday chaos of life. They shimmered in my memory, reminding me of the freedom I had almost forgotten, the joy that came with simply being present. In those moments, I felt a shift within myself, a gentle uncoiling of tension that had nestled in my shoulders for far too long. As the last remnants of winter melted away, so did the fears that had clung to me like shadows, darkening my spirit.

When our playful skirmish settled into laughter and gentle teasing, I noticed the way his gaze lingered on me, as if he were trying to memorize every detail of the moment. It made my heart flutter, a delightful weightlessness that sent shivers down my spine. I tucked a loose strand of hair behind my ear, suddenly acutely aware of how much I wanted to be close to him, to forge a connection that ran deeper than the laughter we shared.

"Let's sit for a while," I suggested, my voice softer now, tinged with a hint of vulnerability. We settled on the sun-warmed grass, the earth beneath us fragrant and alive. The sunlight dappled our skin, a gentle caress that felt both invigorating and calming. I turned to face him, our knees touching, and it struck me just how effortlessly our conversations flowed, as if we had known each other for lifetimes rather than a few fleeting weeks.

"What's your favorite thing about skiing?" I asked, genuinely curious about the passion that seemed to ignite a fire in his eyes. He leaned back on his hands, a thoughtful expression crossing his face as he considered my question.

"I think it's the freedom," he said, his voice low and sincere. "When you're out there on the mountain, it's just you and the snow. Everything else fades away—the worries, the noise, the chaos of life. It's pure bliss." His words painted vivid images in my mind, and I could almost feel the rush of wind against my face, the exhilaration of carving through untouched powder. "It's like flying, you know? Just you and the world."

"I can see that," I replied, feeling a thrill at the thought of that freedom. "It sounds magical."

"It is," he said, looking into my eyes with a warmth that made my heart race. "You should try it sometime. I'd love to teach you."

The invitation hung between us, laden with promise. The thought of skiing terrified me and thrilled me all at once. I imagined the sensation of gliding down a slope, the exhilaration coursing through my veins, mingling with the adrenaline of uncertainty. "I think I'd need a lot of practice," I admitted, a hint of shyness creeping into my voice. "What if I fall?"

"Falling is part of the journey," Theo said with a reassuring smile, his eyes sparkling with encouragement. "You get up, laugh about it, and try again. That's what makes it worth it."

His words echoed the lessons I had been learning throughout my own journey. Healing was not a straight path; it was filled with ups and downs, moments of vulnerability that could lead to growth if I let them. The way he spoke, with such conviction and warmth, made me feel safe, as if I were not merely surviving but truly living for the first time in a long while.

"I'd love that," I said, my voice barely above a whisper, the excitement bubbling just beneath the surface. Our gazes locked, and for a heartbeat, the world around us faded away, leaving just the two of us suspended in that perfect moment. It was a reminder that sometimes, the simplest invitations could lead to the most profound experiences.

As the sun dipped lower in the sky, casting long shadows across the pond, a comfortable silence enveloped us. I leaned back, letting the warmth of the earth seep into my skin, my heart full of hope. This was more than just a day in the mountains; it was a glimpse into a future where laughter replaced fear, and every shared moment felt like a promise—a promise of healing, of adventure, and perhaps, of love.

The sun began its slow descent, casting a warm, golden hue over the landscape, bathing everything in an ethereal glow. As we sat there, nestled in the embrace of nature, I felt an insatiable curiosity bubbling to the surface. I turned to Theo, eager to delve deeper into the tapestry of his life, a life that had somehow woven itself into mine.

"What was your first experience with skiing?" I asked, the question slipping from my lips like a well-placed note in a song. The way his face lit up at the inquiry was as illuminating as the setting sun behind him. He leaned forward, his elbows resting on his knees, and I could see the memories swirling in his eyes, vivid and alive.

"My dad took me for the first time when I was six," he began, a soft smile breaking through. "I was terrified, of course. The idea of sliding down a mountain felt like asking a toddler to leap from a skyscraper." His laughter mixed with mine, a symphony of shared understanding and camaraderie. "But once I was on the slopes, it was like nothing else mattered. I fell a hundred times, but each tumble was a lesson, a step toward the thrill of conquering the mountain."

I could picture him as a little boy, bundled in a bright orange snowsuit, his cheeks rosy from the cold, a fierce determination etched across his small face. "What about you? Have you ever tried it?" he inquired, tilting his head as if he could read my thoughts.

"No, but I've always wanted to. I grew up watching ski movies, dreaming of the slopes while bundled in blankets on my couch," I replied, my voice tinged with a hint of nostalgia. "It seemed like such a magical world, so far removed from my own."

"Then it's settled! You'll come with me next weekend. I promise I'll make it fun," he said, the enthusiasm in his voice buoyant and intoxicating. My heart raced at the thought, a delightful mixture of excitement and apprehension flooding my senses. The vision of skiing down those breathtaking slopes alongside him ignited something within me—a desire to break free from my past, to embrace the unknown.

As the sun dipped lower, painting the sky in strokes of pink and orange, I felt a new resolve solidifying in my chest. It was not just about skiing; it was about stepping into a world where fear didn't dictate my choices. With each passing day, Theo became more than just a friend; he was a catalyst for my transformation, a spark igniting the embers of my dormant spirit.

After a while, we reluctantly rose from our sunlit sanctuary, the golden hour fading into twilight. The trail beckoned us to continue our journey, and as we walked side by side, I noticed the small things—how the light caught the gold flecks in his eyes, the way his laughter blended with the gentle whispers of the wind, and how every shared glance felt charged with an unspoken promise.

As we entered a small grove, the trees arched overhead like old friends sharing secrets. I paused to catch my breath, the air thick with the scent of pine and blooming flowers. It was a momentary respite, but it felt monumental, the kind of stillness where everything seems possible. Theo noticed my pause and turned to me, a question flickering in his gaze.

"What's on your mind?" he asked, genuinely interested.

"I've been thinking about how much I've changed since I got here," I admitted, my voice barely above a whisper. "It feels like the mountains have a way of breaking down walls, revealing parts of me I thought were lost forever."

He nodded, his expression serious, as if he understood the weight of my words. "The mountains do that. They strip away the noise of the world, forcing you to confront what's inside. It's both terrifying and liberating."

The truth in his words resonated with me, and I took a deep breath, filling my lungs with the crisp, fragrant air. "I feel like I've been given a second chance to live," I confessed. "And it terrifies me. What if I fail? What if I stumble and can't get back up?"

"Then I'll be there to help you," he replied, his voice steady and reassuring. "You're not alone in this. We'll tackle it together, just like we did on the trail." His words wrapped around me like a warm blanket, and I couldn't help but smile, the fear that had been so relentless slowly starting to ebb away.

We continued our trek, the path illuminated by the soft glow of the moon rising overhead. The night was alive with sounds—the distant hoot of an owl, the rustle of leaves as creatures scurried through the underbrush. I felt a sense of belonging wash over me, an understanding that I had finally found a place where I could be unapologetically myself, a place where fear could coexist with hope.

As we neared the cabin where we had started our hike, Theo stopped, his gaze drifting toward the horizon where the last traces of daylight clung stubbornly to the sky. "You know, there's something magical about this time of day," he said, his voice softening. "It reminds me that every ending is just a new beginning waiting to unfold."

I pondered his words, feeling a swell of gratitude for the way he saw the world. "That's beautiful," I replied, my heart swelling with emotion. "I think I needed to hear that."

He turned to face me, the moonlight casting a silver sheen over his features. "You're stronger than you know," he said, his tone earnest. "And I can't wait to see where this journey takes you."

His gaze held mine, and in that moment, the world around us faded away, leaving just the two of us, bound by an understanding that transcended words. I could feel the warmth of his presence wrapping around me, igniting a flicker of courage deep within my soul. I knew then that I was ready to embrace whatever came next, to dive headfirst into the unknown, trusting that even in the darkest moments, there would always be a glimmer of light.

With that thought in mind, we stepped back toward the cabin, laughter spilling between us like the wildflowers blooming in the spring. Each shared moment felt like a promise—a commitment to face the fears that loomed ahead while nurturing the connection that had blossomed so effortlessly between us. As we reached the wooden door, I glanced back one last time at the trail, the mountains looming majestically against the night sky, a reminder that my journey was just beginning. The remnants of winter had melted away, leaving behind a landscape brimming with possibility, and I was ready to embrace it all.

Chapter 21: Past Shadows

Dinner simmered in the air, a mixture of garlic and herbs enveloping the cozy kitchen like a warm embrace. The soft glow of candlelight flickered against the walls, casting dancing shadows that mingled with the scent of fresh basil. I stirred the marinara sauce, letting the wooden spoon glide through the thick mixture, its vibrant red hue promising a taste that would linger long after the meal. The table was set for two, complete with mismatched plates that told stories of weekend flea markets and impulsive purchases. I always loved the way they clinked together, creating a melody of domestic bliss that resonated within the walls of our little apartment.

As I turned to glance out the window, the skyline of Chicago rose majestically, the skyscrapers a testament to dreams and ambitions. The city was alive, thrumming with a heartbeat that mirrored my own. Yet tonight, an underlying tension knotted in my stomach, whispering of an impending storm. I caught a glimpse of Theo as he stood by the fridge, a frown etched on his handsome face, his brow furrowed in deep thought. He had just received the call from his estranged father, and it hung between us like a thick fog, muffling our laughter and softening the warmth of our shared moments.

I set the spoon down and leaned against the counter, crossing my arms. "Hey, are you okay?" The question felt feeble against the weight of what he was grappling with, but it was all I could muster without feeling intrusive.

Theo turned slowly, the lines of tension deepening around his jaw. "Yeah, just... thinking." He sighed, and the sound was heavy, laden with a complexity I couldn't quite decipher. The air felt electric, thick with unspoken words, as if every flicker of candlelight dared him to express his turmoil.

"Thinking about the call?" I ventured, my voice barely above a whisper, as if saying it out loud would shatter the fragile moment we were in. He nodded, running a hand through his tousled hair, the kind of gesture that spoke of helplessness.

"I didn't expect to hear from him," he admitted, his voice cracking slightly. "After all these years, it feels surreal."

I took a step closer, the heat from the stove warming my skin. "You don't have to talk about it if you don't want to," I offered gently, although I felt the gnawing urge to dig deeper, to unearth the roots of his pain. "But I'm here if you need to. Whatever you decide."

Theo's eyes met mine, a flicker of vulnerability flashing across his features before it was swiftly replaced by a steely resolve. "I thought I'd buried that part of my life," he said, his words taut with emotion. "But it seems like it has a way of creeping back in when I least expect it."

I nodded, understanding that sometimes the past has a cruel habit of clawing its way back to the surface, no matter how much we try to bury it beneath layers of time and distance. I set the table, the clatter of forks and knives breaking the heavy silence, hoping that with every movement, I could coax him back to me, to the safe harbor we had built together.

As we sat down, the aroma of the meal wafted through the air, mingling with the palpable tension. I served him a generous portion of spaghetti, the strands twirling gracefully on the fork, a perfect metaphor for the complexities of our lives intertwined. He twirled his pasta absentmindedly, his eyes lost somewhere beyond the flickering candles, as if he were staring into the abyss of memories he had long tried to escape.

"Do you want to confront him?" I asked softly, testing the waters, wanting to gauge where he stood without pushing him into a corner.

He paused, the fork frozen mid-air, contemplating the question as if it were a riddle he was determined to solve. "I don't know," he finally confessed. "Part of me wants to, to finally get answers. But then there's this other part... the one that wants to keep that door closed. It's easier that way, isn't it?"

I understood the allure of avoidance, the comfort of keeping past wounds bandaged and hidden away. Yet, I also knew that true healing often lay in the heart of confrontation. "Easier isn't always better," I said softly, reaching across the table to squeeze his hand. "Facing the past might hurt, but it could also free you."

He looked down at our entwined fingers, the warmth of my touch grounding him. "I wish it were that simple."

"It rarely is," I replied, my heart swelling with affection for the man sitting across from me. His complexity was woven into the fabric of who he was, a beautiful tapestry of strengths and vulnerabilities. I wanted him to know that navigating the storm together was not just about weathering the turbulence but also about emerging stronger on the other side.

The conversation meandered like the Chicago River, flowing through tributaries of memories and fears, laughter and sorrow. We shared stories from our childhoods, the sound of our voices mingling like the comforting cadence of jazz drifting through the air from a nearby bar. I could see the flicker of hope in his eyes, the corners of his mouth turning upwards ever so slightly as he momentarily lost himself in the rhythm of our connection.

As the night deepened, I could feel the weight of the past settling like a blanket around us. We were two souls intertwined, navigating a path fraught with shadows but determined to illuminate each other's darkness. The city pulsed outside, unaware of the delicate dance we performed within the confines of our home. The challenge lay not just in confronting the past but also in embracing the love that flourished amidst uncertainty. And in that moment, as I watched

Theo wrestle with his emotions, I realized that love was not merely about the good moments; it was about standing together in the storm, hand in hand, ready to face whatever came next.

The next few days felt like a delicate dance, each step measured and careful, as if we were wading through a world of paper-thin ice. Theo was quieter than usual, lost in thought, his laughter often replaced by a faraway gaze that made my heart ache with longing for the man I knew was still there, just hidden beneath the weight of his past. I found myself cooking more elaborate meals, trying to coax him back to me with the familiar comfort of homemade spaghetti and garlic bread, the warmth of our kitchen a stark contrast to the coldness I sensed wrapping around his heart.

One evening, the wind howled outside, rattling the window panes and sending a chill through the room. The storm mirrored the turmoil brewing within us. I had settled onto the couch, cradling a mug of cocoa, its steam curling in the air like a gentle whisper. Theo walked in, his silhouette framed by the harsh light of the hallway, the shadows trailing behind him like a dark cloak.

"Hey," he said softly, taking a seat beside me. The cushions sank under his weight, and I instinctively leaned into him, craving the warmth of his presence. "What's this?" He glanced at the TV, where an old movie flickered, its black-and-white scenes playing out an age of innocence that felt a million miles away from our reality.

"Just something to take our minds off things," I replied, trying to keep my tone light, but the underlying tension still clung to us, refusing to let go.

He smiled faintly, his eyes softening for a moment as he watched the characters stumble through misunderstandings and reconciliations. I took a sip of cocoa, letting the rich sweetness wash over me, and turned to him, hoping to pry open the door to his heart just a little more. "Have you thought any more about what you want to do?"

The question hung in the air, heavy with unspoken emotions. He shifted, his gaze drifting toward the window, where rain pelted against the glass like a thousand tiny reminders of the storm outside. "I don't know," he murmured, his voice barely above a whisper. "Part of me wants to pretend it never happened. Just forget about it."

"And what would that change?" I pressed gently, trying to navigate the minefield of his thoughts. "You can't outrun your past, Theo. It's part of who you are."

He sighed, rubbing his temples as if to relieve the pressure building behind his eyes. "I know that," he replied, his tone laced with frustration. "But it's exhausting. I've spent so long trying to move on, and then this happens. It's like a ghost from my childhood just popped up out of nowhere."

I nestled closer, resting my head against his shoulder. "Sometimes confronting those ghosts can lead to closure. You have people who love you now, who want to support you."

His silence spoke volumes, and I felt the weight of his uncertainty pushing against the tenderness that had blossomed between us. I longed to help him see that confronting the shadows didn't mean facing them alone. It meant allowing the light of our shared moments to illuminate the darkest corners.

As the rain fell harder, the patter creating a soothing rhythm, I suggested we play a game we used to enjoy during our lighter days. "How about a round of our favorite trivia?" I offered, trying to coax a smile from him, though I could see the shadows still clouding his eyes.

To my surprise, a flicker of amusement danced across his face. "You think you can beat me this time?" he challenged, his tone playful yet edged with a vulnerability that made my heart flutter.

"Oh, please. I'm a trivia master. Just wait and see." I grinned, feeling the weight of tension lift, if only slightly.

We dug out the old trivia board game, the one that had seen us through lazy weekends and playful banter. I set it up, the colorful pieces gleaming in the soft light. With each question answered and each ridiculous fact revealed, the air around us lightened. Theo laughed, his genuine joy a rare treasure that made me want to bottle it up and carry it with me everywhere.

"Did you really just say that Napoleon was short because he was standing next to his guards?" he teased, chuckling as I feigned innocence, my expression completely grave. "That's not even a real trivia fact!"

"Don't knock my creativity," I shot back, laughter bubbling between us. The game unfolded, transforming our living room into a battlefield of wits, where the stakes were laughter and silliness rather than points. It was exhilarating to see him light up, his eyes sparkling as he quipped and bantered.

But as the night wore on, a quiet tension returned, threading itself through our lighthearted exchanges. Between rounds, I caught him staring into space, his brow furrowed. "What's going on in that head of yours?" I asked, suddenly serious.

He hesitated, his eyes narrowing as if he were weighing his thoughts. "What if I confront him, and it doesn't go the way I want?" The vulnerability in his voice broke my heart a little more, as if he were a ship stranded at sea, longing for the safety of the shore.

"Then we deal with it together," I said firmly, trying to anchor him with my conviction. "You don't have to face anything alone anymore. We've built something real. Let it be your strength."

He nodded slowly, as if considering my words. The storm outside raged on, but inside, the warmth of our shared laughter lingered, wrapping around us like a promise of resilience. As the trivia game continued, the shadows of doubt retreated just a little, replaced by the flicker of hope that maybe, just maybe, he could find the courage to confront the past without losing the light we had cultivated together.

That night, as I lay beside him, his hand entwined with mine, I understood that love was not merely the absence of darkness but the willingness to embrace it, to share the burdens and joys alike. And as sleep claimed me, I dreamed of brighter tomorrows, of a future where we would not only face the storms but dance in the rain together.

Morning light seeped through the window, casting golden streaks across the living room, revealing the remnants of our trivia night—the game board still sprawled across the table, cards scattered like forgotten dreams. I stretched, feeling the warmth of the sunlight on my skin, and turned to see Theo already awake, lost in thought as he gazed out at the city below. His expression was a blend of determination and trepidation, and it struck me that beneath the mundane rhythm of our everyday lives, a deeper battle raged.

"Good morning," I said softly, my voice still laced with sleep. He turned to me, and for a fleeting moment, I saw the shadows lift, replaced by a flicker of warmth in his gaze. "Did you sleep at all?"

"Not really," he admitted, running a hand through his tousled hair. "Just thinking about everything. About the call. About... everything."

I slid off the couch and padded over, the cool wooden floor grounding me as I took his hand in mine. "You know you don't have to make any decisions today, right?"

He nodded, yet I could sense the weight of expectation pressing down on him, an invisible chain he couldn't quite shake off. "I know, but it's hard to ignore. It feels like there's this ticking clock, and I have to decide before it runs out."

The clock on the wall seemed to mock us with its incessant ticking, each second a reminder of the urgency he felt. I pulled him gently to his feet, not wanting him to drown in his thoughts. "Let's take a walk. Fresh air always helps."

The bustling streets of Chicago welcomed us, alive with the morning hustle and the distant sound of street performers weaving melodies that danced through the air. As we strolled along the riverwalk, the sun glinted off the water, creating a shimmering pathway that felt almost magical. I reveled in the city's vibrancy, a stark contrast to the turmoil lurking within us.

"Look," I said, pointing toward a couple painting a mural on a nearby wall. The colors splashed vibrantly against the drab concrete, a beautiful reminder that creation often arises from chaos. "See how they're transforming that space? Sometimes confronting the ugly can lead to something beautiful."

Theo studied the mural, the lines and curves reflecting the artists' souls poured out for the world to see. "I get that," he murmured, his voice thoughtful. "But what if what I confront is just... ugly? What if it doesn't lead to anything good?"

"Then you'll deal with it," I replied, my heart steady. "Together."

We continued walking, the rhythm of our footsteps matching the beat of the city around us. I sensed a shift in him, a spark of determination igniting beneath the weight of uncertainty. As we approached a small café, I steered him inside, the rich aroma of freshly brewed coffee enveloping us like a warm hug. We ordered our usual—two lattes and a pastry to share—and found a small table by the window.

As we sat, I couldn't shake the feeling that the storm he was facing was not just external but an internal battle that had been brewing long before that phone call shattered the surface of our lives. "You know, it's okay to be afraid," I said, breaking the silence that threatened to stretch between us. "Facing your father is a big deal. It's okay if you're not sure what you want right now."

His brow furrowed as he stared at the latte art, the swirling patterns resembling the chaotic thoughts in his mind. "I just keep thinking about the last time I saw him. The way he looked at me, like I was nothing but a disappointment."

"I don't know what happened between you two, but he doesn't get to define who you are now," I urged, hoping to instill some belief in him. "You're so much more than that little boy he abandoned."

"I just wish it didn't hurt," he said, his voice thick with emotion. The vulnerability in his tone broke my heart a little more. "It feels like I'm stuck between wanting to know him and wanting to erase him from my life entirely."

"You're allowed to feel both," I said, reaching across the table to squeeze his hand. "You don't have to choose one over the other. You're allowed to feel the hurt and still want to reach out. That's what makes you human."

He smiled softly, and the warmth of his hand in mine ignited a flicker of hope within me. "Thanks for being here," he said, the weight of his gratitude settling comfortably between us. "I don't know what I'd do without you."

"Let's figure it out together, one step at a time."

As we finished our coffee, I could feel the energy shift. The heaviness that had clung to him like a shroud began to lift, replaced by a flicker of resolve. He looked out at the bustling street, and I could see him visualizing a path forward—one where he could confront his father without losing himself in the process.

Later that afternoon, as we strolled back, we stumbled upon a small gallery tucked away between two towering buildings, the white walls adorned with local artists' works. One piece caught my eye—an abstract representation of a storm, swirling dark clouds that collided with bursts of vibrant colors, a chaotic beauty that echoed our current lives.

"Look at that," I said, pointing to the piece. "It's like a reminder that storms can be beautiful, too."

Theo studied the artwork for a moment before nodding, his expression thoughtful. "It's messy, but there's something captivating about it. It's real."

"Exactly. Just like your journey. It's going to be messy and complicated, but that's what makes it authentic. You're allowed to be a masterpiece in progress."

We stood there, shoulder to shoulder, as other patrons drifted around us, oblivious to the quiet moment we were sharing. In that instant, I felt the unspoken bond of love wrapping around us, a shield against the uncertainty ahead.

As we left the gallery, the sun began its descent, painting the sky in hues of orange and pink, a stunning reminder that even the darkest moments can give way to beauty. Theo took a deep breath, and I could almost see him letting go of some of the weight he had carried. "I think I'm ready to reach out," he finally said, his voice steady.

"Whenever you're ready, I'll be right here," I promised, my heart swelling with pride for the man beside me, who was finally stepping into his own light.

That night, as we settled into the familiar comfort of our apartment, I felt a sense of peace envelop us, a fragile yet promising tranquility that whispered of hope. We curled up together, lost in our own world, and as I rested my head on his chest, I could hear the steady rhythm of his heartbeat—strong, resilient, and unwavering.

Tomorrow would bring its challenges, but for now, we had this moment. Together, we were ready to embrace the storm, ready to navigate whatever came next. And in that quiet assurance, I found solace, knowing that we were forging a path not just through shadows but into the light of a new beginning.

Chapter 22: A Fork in the Road

The air hung thick with the smell of freshly brewed coffee, a rich and inviting aroma that beckoned from the small, sun-drenched café nestled on the corner of Seventh and Main. It was one of those picturesque mornings when the world felt both intimate and sprawling, the kind of day that painted even the most mundane details in soft pastels. The sun streamed through the windows, casting playful shadows on the worn wooden floorboards, while the laughter of patrons created a warm tapestry of sound, punctuated by the gentle clinking of porcelain cups. I perched on the edge of a weathered chair, my heart thrumming a nervous rhythm that echoed the bustling energy around me.

I watched the world pass by through the café's window, a parade of colorful characters making their way through life, their hurried steps marking the passage of time that felt unbearably slow in that moment. Each face held a story, a snapshot of emotion—joy, sadness, anxiety. I clutched my steaming cup, the heat radiating through my palms like a lifeline. Outside, a little girl twirled in a sundress, her laughter bright and unfiltered, a reminder of innocence and carefree days, and it tugged at something deep within me. I could almost forget for a heartbeat that I was waiting for Theo, that we stood on the precipice of something heavy and unwieldy.

He had left to meet his father, a man cloaked in years of disappointment and silence. I tried to imagine what the conversation would be like, picturing Theo walking into that stark, sterile office building, the glass reflecting a version of himself that still bore the scars of childhood. My heart clenched at the thought of him standing there, facing the very person who had carved wounds deep into his spirit. The weight of anticipation settled like a stone in my stomach, a tangible reminder that life sometimes demands we confront our pasts.

Time drifted lazily as I continued to steal glances at the door, the large brass handle gleaming under the morning light. Each time it swung open, I held my breath, half-hoping to see Theo walk in, his usual carefree stride replaced by an aura of uncertainty. Finally, the door creaked, and my heart surged as I caught a glimpse of him. He stepped into the café, and the world outside seemed to dim, all focus shifting to the storm brewing within him.

His eyes found mine, a tempest of emotions swirling behind their stormy depths. As he approached, I could see that his normally buoyant spirit was encumbered by an invisible weight. I set my cup down, my pulse quickening as he slid into the chair opposite me, a crumpled piece of paper clenched tightly in his fist. The sunlight danced across his features, highlighting the lines etched by tension and turmoil.

"What happened?" I asked, my voice barely above a whisper, the world outside falling away.

He inhaled deeply, and I could see the struggle etched into his brow. "It was... intense." His voice cracked slightly, as if the mere act of speaking threatened to unleash the flood of emotions he had contained. "We talked about everything—about my childhood, about his expectations, about the silence that stretched for years."

A shudder passed through him, and my heart ached for the boy hidden beneath the man. I reached across the table, my fingers brushing against his, hoping to provide comfort through the simple act of touch. "You don't have to go through this alone, you know." My words wrapped around him like a warm blanket, an anchor in the chaotic storm of his feelings.

He nodded slowly, the corners of his mouth twitching upward momentarily. "I didn't know how much I needed to say all of that until it was out." He released the breath he had been holding, the tension in his shoulders easing ever so slightly.

"What did he say?" I prodded gently, not wanting to push him too hard but eager to understand the essence of their conversation.

Theo's gaze fell to the table, the crumpled paper twisting between his fingers like a fragile dream. "He... he apologized. I think he finally understood the impact of his absence. But I could feel the wall he built around himself—it was still there."

I watched as he wrestled with the memories, the ghosts of their strained relationship flickering behind his eyes. The café buzzed with life around us, but in that moment, we existed in a separate world, one filled with the echoes of unspoken words and a history that weighed heavily on both of us.

"Theo, healing takes time. You've carried this for so long; it's okay to feel conflicted," I said, trying to coax a smile from him, to light a spark of hope amidst the shadows.

He looked up, a mixture of gratitude and vulnerability reflected in his gaze. "It felt like a step, but I don't know if I can forgive him just yet."

I squeezed his hand, the warmth of my touch connecting us in an unspoken promise. "That's okay. You're allowed to take your time. Just remember, I'm right here."

The weight of the world seemed to ease ever so slightly as we sat together, two souls intertwined in the delicate fabric of trust and shared pain. Outside, the sun continued its journey across the sky, and the city buzzed with its relentless pace, but within the café, time felt like it had paused for us, offering a sanctuary where healing could begin.

The café around us hummed with life, but my attention was entirely absorbed by Theo, whose eyes seemed to dance between the realms of anguish and hope. As he spoke, the words tumbled out like leaves caught in a gust of wind, swirling around us in an unpredictable vortex of emotions. His fingers traced the rim of his cup absentmindedly, a subconscious gesture that mirrored the turmoil in his mind.

"I never thought I'd see the day when I would sit across from him and actually speak my mind," he confessed, a shadow of disbelief crossing his features. It was as if he had somehow stepped into a scene that belonged to someone else's life, a life where apologies and reconciliations flowed as freely as the coffee that filled our mugs.

I leaned in closer, the air between us thick with unspoken understanding. "What did you say?" I asked, my voice low, filled with reverence for the moment.

He took a deep breath, his gaze drifting to the window where a pair of elderly men played chess, their concentration etched into their weathered faces. "I told him how it felt—being left behind, watching him choose work over family. I felt like a ghost in my own life."

His words landed heavily between us, and I could feel the gravity of his truth pressing down on both of us. I wished I could reach out and smooth the wrinkles of his pain, but instead, I simply nodded, acknowledging the weight of his experience. The café was still bustling, yet we existed in a bubble, wrapped in the intensity of his revelation.

"What did he say?" I asked, intrigued by the nuances of their exchange.

A flicker of anger crossed his face, and he leaned back, running a hand through his tousled hair in frustration. "He tried to explain, to justify his choices like they somehow made it okay. It was infuriating—he didn't see me, not really. But at least he listened."

Theo's eyes sparkled with a mix of resentment and relief, revealing the complexity of feelings swirling within him. He continued, "I felt like I was finally making a case for myself. And then…" His voice trailed off, uncertainty creeping back in.

"Then?" I urged, eager to catch every word like a precious treasure.

"Then he looked at me—really looked—and for a brief moment, I saw the man I had wanted all those years ago," he said, a bittersweet smile creeping onto his lips. "He said he was proud of me, which… it felt like a balm to an old wound. But then he added that it was too late for us."

The disappointment in his voice resonated within me, and I squeezed his hand tighter, my thumb brushing over the back of his knuckles. "It doesn't have to be too late, Theo. Healing isn't linear. It can be messy, unpredictable. But every step you take matters."

He nodded slowly, his eyes distant as he processed my words. "Maybe. But I feel like we're on different paths now. He has his life, and I have mine. I don't know if we can meet in the middle."

The words hung in the air, heavy with the weight of unfulfilled expectations. A silence enveloped us, thick and suffocating, until the sound of the barista calling out orders broke through like a ray of sunshine. I watched the steam rise from the espresso machine, twisting and curling like the thoughts in my own mind.

"I think relationships evolve, Theo," I finally said, determined to illuminate the shadows looming over us. "Sometimes they reshape themselves into something new. Maybe your father needs time to adjust to the fact that you're not that little boy anymore."

He let out a soft chuckle, the sound a mix of disbelief and amusement. "You make it sound so easy. Just give him time, and he'll magically transform into the supportive father I've always wanted?"

"Not easy, no," I replied, my heart aching for him. "But possible. Healing is a dance—sometimes you lead, sometimes you follow. It's not always about forgiveness; it's about finding peace within yourself."

Theo's gaze turned thoughtful, as if my words were slowly seeping into the cracks of his heart. The café buzzed on, oblivious to our moment, while the sunlight poured in like liquid gold, bathing us in warmth. It struck me how, in the grand scheme of life, moments like these held the power to shift our realities, even if just for an instant.

"What about you?" he asked, his voice softer now. "Where do you find peace?"

I paused, surprised by the question. "I find it in the little things—watching the world wake up, like this café full of life, the laughter, the connections we forge. I find it in knowing that I'm here, right now, with you."

He smiled, and in that moment, the storm inside him seemed to settle, the tumultuous waves of uncertainty transforming into gentle ripples. "You have a way of making everything seem less daunting," he said, a spark of admiration lighting his eyes.

"It's not me, it's you," I replied with a wry smile. "You're the one taking the steps, putting in the work. You're stronger than you realize."

A comfortable silence fell over us again, this time infused with a sense of companionship and understanding. It was a quiet reassurance that, no matter how jagged the path ahead seemed, we would navigate it together. I could feel his gratitude hanging in the air, wrapping around us like a warm embrace.

As we sat there, time ebbed and flowed around us, the café remaining a hub of laughter and chatter, yet we were encapsulated in our cocoon of shared vulnerability. The world continued to whirl on outside, but for now, we had carved out our own small sanctuary amidst the chaos. It felt as if we were writing our own story, one filled with the ink of unresolved conflicts and hopeful beginnings, a narrative that promised growth and healing, no matter how long it took.

The atmosphere in the café transformed as the day wore on, each moment knitting together a tapestry of emotions, colors, and sounds. The vibrant clamor around us provided a comforting backdrop, wrapping us in the kind of warmth that felt both protective and invigorating. With the sunlight beginning to wane, it painted the walls in a golden hue, illuminating the dust particles dancing in the air, creating a soft glow that seemed to mirror the flicker of hope igniting within Theo.

As we lingered over our half-finished drinks, I noticed the tension in his posture gradually unraveling, the weight of unspoken truths shifting like a subtle breeze through the leaves. I took a moment to appreciate how the café had morphed into our safe haven, the smells of rich coffee and freshly baked pastries mingling with the aroma of possibility. I couldn't help but smile as I watched him, his face now a canvas of reflection, pondering not just the conversation he had just endured, but the myriad of paths laid out before him.

"Do you think he'll really change?" he asked, his voice thoughtful yet tinged with skepticism. "After all these years?"

I pondered the question, aware of the delicate nature of transformation. "Change is messy and rarely straightforward," I replied. "But people can surprise you. Sometimes, it takes the right catalyst—a conversation, a moment of clarity—before they realize how far they've drifted from what truly matters."

Theo nodded, a flicker of uncertainty dancing in his eyes. "I just wish I could see a clearer picture of what lies ahead. I mean, what if he can't change? What if this is just another round of empty promises?"

"It's okay to have doubts," I assured him, keeping my tone gentle. "But you have to focus on your own journey, too. What do you want from this? What does healing look like for you?"

He paused, his brow furrowing in contemplation. "I want to feel free of this burden, like I can finally breathe without carrying around the weight of his choices. But I also want a relationship—a real one."

His honesty struck me like a bolt of lightning, illuminating the depth of his desires amid the fog of hurt. I wanted to help him bridge that gap between hope and reality. "That's a powerful desire, Theo. You have the right to yearn for connection, but it's important to define that on your own terms. It starts with you finding your footing."

"Finding my footing," he echoed, as if trying to weave my words into the fabric of his understanding. "How do I do that?"

"Start small," I suggested. "What if you wrote down what you need from him? Not just the big things but the little moments that can build toward something meaningful. Maybe even share that with him."

His eyes brightened at the suggestion, a hint of excitement sparking in his gaze. "You think that would help?"

"Absolutely. It could be a way to open the door for real communication," I encouraged, feeling the atmosphere shift with each word. "It gives you a tangible starting point, a foundation to build upon, rather than just a nebulous wish."

The notion of taking control ignited something within him, and I watched as his determination began to take shape. "Okay," he said slowly, his voice steadying. "I can do that. I can lay it all out."

Outside, the city continued its rhythm, cars whisking by and pedestrians weaving through the streets. A couple strolled past, their laughter ringing out like a bell, a stark contrast to the weighty conversation unfolding between us. I felt a swell of gratitude for this moment, a reminder of how connections could blossom even in the most unexpected of circumstances.

"I'll help you," I offered, my heart swelling with a protective instinct. "We can brainstorm together. You don't have to face this alone."

Theo looked at me, his expression softening as the corners of his mouth turned up in a genuine smile. "You've really become my rock, you know that?"

"It's easy when you're someone worth rooting for," I quipped, the playful banter a welcome relief amidst the emotional depth.

With the sun dipping lower in the sky, we gradually shifted our conversation to lighter topics. We talked about our favorite childhood memories, and I shared my adventures in trying to bake with my grandmother, who had a penchant for flour explosions that left our kitchen looking like a snowy wonderland. Theo laughed, his eyes sparkling with delight, and I relished the warmth of his laughter echoing against the backdrop of the bustling café.

As the day faded into evening, the café's lights twinkled to life, casting a soft glow that made everything feel more intimate. The laughter and conversations melded into a comforting chorus, wrapping us in a shared experience that felt uniquely ours. In that moment, I realized how important it was to cherish the connections we form, to acknowledge the beauty in vulnerability, and to celebrate the small victories that marked our journeys.

Eventually, as the last remnants of sunlight slipped away, leaving a twilight glow in its wake, Theo leaned back in his chair, a contented sigh escaping his lips. "I think I'm ready to tackle this," he said, a sense of resolve seeping into his voice. "You've helped me see it differently."

I grinned, feeling a sense of accomplishment wash over me. "That's the power of perspective," I replied, my heart swelling with pride for him.

As we prepared to leave the café, I felt a shift within both of us—a turning point, perhaps. The uncertainty that had once loomed over us began to dissipate like the remnants of a storm, replaced by the promise of possibility. I walked alongside Theo, our hands brushing together as we stepped back into the vibrant world outside, ready to face whatever lay ahead.

The city buzzed with life, but as we stepped out into the night, it felt like the universe had shifted slightly in our favor. Together, we were embarking on a new chapter, armed with understanding and hope. The weight of the past had not disappeared, but it had transformed into a shared journey, and as we walked side by side, I couldn't help but feel that the road ahead, though uncertain, was one we were meant to travel together.

Chapter 23: The Beauty of Vulnerability

The warm summer evening air wrapped around us like a familiar embrace, thick with the scent of blooming jasmine and the distant hum of cicadas serenading the dusk. Nestled on the weathered porch of Theo's childhood home, a charming Victorian with peeling paint and a cracked front step, I felt the weight of the world ease from my shoulders. The porch creaked beneath us, a gentle reminder of the years it had witnessed—of laughter, of tears, of whispered secrets that danced through the spaces between the boards. Theo sat beside me, his shoulder brushing against mine, a touch that felt like an electric spark igniting something deep within.

As the sun dipped below the horizon, spilling hues of pink and gold across the sky, I caught glimpses of memories etched in the wood, echoes of a past I had yet to fully understand. This was the home that had cradled him through storms, the walls that had absorbed his fears and dreams, the very air laden with stories of who he had been and who he was becoming. I glanced sideways at him, catching the tail end of a smile as he plucked a wildflower from the railing, twirling it thoughtfully between his fingers. The shadows played across his features, revealing a boyhood vulnerability that lingered just beneath the surface of his strong facade.

"Do you remember the first time we met?" he asked, his voice low and inviting, drawing me into the depths of his memory. The soft light illuminated his eyes, making them shimmer like stars trapped in the depths of a stormy sea.

I chuckled, the sound mingling with the night's symphony. "You were covered in mud after that disastrous soccer game. I thought you were a wild creature from the woods, just trying to find your way home."

He laughed, a rich sound that filled the air, momentarily drowning out the cicadas. "And you were the girl who stood up for me, arguing with the coach about my unfair treatment. I had no idea who you were, but your passion drew me in."

I leaned back, letting the weight of his words settle within me. "Funny how we each saw something in the other that day, something worth fighting for."

In that moment, our playful banter transformed, shifting into something heavier, more profound. "I've always been good at fighting for others," he continued, his voice becoming more serious. "But I've struggled to fight for myself, for what I want. I've been so afraid of disappointing everyone that I didn't even know what it felt like to be honest about my own desires."

The honesty in his admission struck a chord deep within me. I felt an ache in my heart as I realized the gravity of his internal struggle, the burdens he had carried alone for too long. "You're not alone, Theo. I know what that feels like. The fear of being seen, of being vulnerable. It can feel suffocating."

The glow of the fairy lights above us flickered gently, casting a soft halo around our intimate conversation. It was as if the universe conspired to provide a sanctuary where we could shed our layers, exposing the fragile parts of ourselves we usually kept hidden. I took a deep breath, the scent of jasmine filling my lungs, and let my own truth spill forth like a long-held secret.

"There are days when I feel like an imposter," I confessed, my voice barely above a whisper. "Like I'm one step away from falling apart, and everyone will see the cracks. I worry that if they truly knew me, they'd turn away."

Theo turned to face me, his expression earnest and understanding. "But it's those cracks that make us human, isn't it? The fear, the self-doubt—it's all part of the package. I think I've spent so long trying to appear strong that I forgot how to just be... me."

His words hung in the air, heavy with meaning, wrapping around us like a warm blanket on a chilly night. It was in that shared vulnerability, that space where fears coalesced into a comforting bond, that I began to see him not just as the boy who wore bravado like armor but as a man grappling with his own insecurities. The weight of his past didn't diminish him; it made him more relatable, more real.

The night deepened, and the stars began to twinkle overhead, punctuating the inky sky with bursts of light that felt almost magical. "What if we let each other in, just a little more?" I proposed, my heart racing at the thought. "What if we explored this vulnerability together? It might be scary, but I think it could also be beautiful."

He considered my words, his brow furrowed in thought, before a small smile broke through. "I'd like that. I'd like that a lot."

As we sat there, the world outside fading away, I felt a profound intimacy blossom between us, nurtured by the openness we had dared to embrace. Each revelation we shared became a thread in the tapestry of our relationship, weaving a stronger bond crafted from honesty and understanding.

The fairy lights flickered above us, and for a moment, the hum of cicadas faded into the background, leaving only the rhythm of our breathing, synchronized as if we were two halves of a whole. I realized that true love wasn't merely about the dazzling highs; it was also about navigating the lows, the moments of doubt and fear, together.

In the fragile beauty of that summer night, I felt something shift within me, a lightness, a promise that we could walk this path hand in hand. The journey ahead was uncertain, but we were willing to face it together, unearthing the hidden treasures that lay in our vulnerabilities. Each scar, each fear, became a part of our shared story, and I couldn't help but believe that the best chapters were yet to come.

The following weeks unfurled like a delicate flower, each petal revealing a new facet of our shared existence. The initial flicker of vulnerability that had ignited between us grew, illuminating our evenings spent on the porch into vibrant tapestry moments of laughter, tears, and dreams interwoven in the soft summer air. With each passing day, we ventured further into the labyrinth of our souls, unearthing secrets buried beneath layers of expectation and fear. The gentle rustle of leaves above us and the warm glow of the fairy lights became our constant companions, bearing witness to the blossoming intimacy that enveloped us.

On one particularly sultry evening, the sky draped itself in hues of indigo, and the first stars punctuated the dusk like scattered diamonds. I found myself sipping a glass of homemade lemonade, the tartness refreshing against the balmy air. Theo sat opposite me, his fingers absently tracing the rim of his glass, a frown knitting his brows. The sweetness of the moment was overshadowed by an unspoken tension, a weight hanging in the air that begged to be acknowledged.

"What's on your mind?" I asked, tilting my head, allowing the strands of hair to fall loosely over my shoulder, hoping to coax the thoughts swirling behind his expressive eyes into the open.

He hesitated, his gaze shifting to the shadows that danced along the porch, and for a fleeting moment, I felt the flicker of his turmoil as acutely as the warmth of the summer night. "I've been thinking about my father," he finally admitted, his voice barely a whisper, almost lost to the night. "About how his expectations have woven themselves into my very being, shaping who I am and who I thought I should be."

A knot formed in my stomach as I realized the depths of his struggle. The father-son dynamic often bore the weight of unspoken demands and disappointments, a silent battle waged behind closed doors. "What do you want?" I prompted gently, feeling the gravity of his words settle between us.

His lips curled into a sardonic smile, tinged with bitterness. "I want to be free, but every time I think I'm breaking away, I feel his shadow creeping back in, reminding me of everything I'm not. It's like I'm caught in this perpetual cycle of trying to prove something to him, even though I know he doesn't deserve my energy."

The honesty in his words felt like a delicate unveiling of raw flesh, exposed to the elements. I reached across the table, my fingers brushing against his, a small gesture meant to ground him. "You're so much more than his expectations, Theo. You're not defined by him or anyone else. You're you, and that's enough."

He looked up at me, those dark eyes searching mine, and for a moment, I saw a flicker of hope amid the uncertainty. "But what if I don't even know who I am without those expectations?" he asked, a hint of desperation creeping into his voice. "What if I fail to find my own path?"

My heart ached for him, and I understood the paradox of trying to carve out one's identity while simultaneously breaking free from someone else's vision of who we should be. "Maybe that's the beauty of it," I suggested, my words coming with the weight of experience. "Finding your way isn't about the destination. It's about the journey, the exploration. You can take the time to discover what truly resonates with you."

The silence hung between us, thick yet comforting, as we let our thoughts meander through the tangled branches of our pasts. In that moment, I realized that vulnerability was not merely about shedding our defenses; it was also about empowering one another to face the uncertainties that lay ahead.

The night wore on, and the stars above began to twinkle with a brightness that mirrored the spark of revelation lighting up Theo's expression. "Maybe I've been too afraid to let go," he murmured, a dawning awareness illuminating his features. "Fear has always been my constant companion, and it's time I changed that."

A soft smile crept across my lips as I leaned back, sensing the shift within him. "Fear is a natural part of the process. It's what we do with that fear that matters. It can become a teacher rather than a cage."

His laughter danced on the night air, rich and warm. "You sound like a wise sage, but you're right. I want to embrace whatever comes next, even if it means facing discomfort. I don't want to be that boy who hides anymore."

I watched him with admiration, a sense of pride swelling within me. He was shedding layers, revealing a complexity I had always suspected existed beneath the surface. As the warm breeze rustled through the leaves, I felt the connection between us deepening, like roots entwining beneath the earth.

In the following days, we ventured out into the world, exploring local markets filled with vibrant colors and enticing aromas. Each encounter became a lesson in vulnerability and strength. We met artists and dreamers, the stories of their struggles and triumphs washing over us like waves on a shore. With every new face, Theo opened up more, his laughter ringing through the air, infectious and bright.

One afternoon, we found ourselves in a quaint bookstore, its shelves bursting with forgotten tales waiting to be discovered. The scent of old paper and leather-bound covers filled the air, inviting us into a sanctuary of words. As we roamed the aisles, I felt Theo's hand graze against mine, a silent acknowledgment of the magic swirling between us.

"What do you think makes a story truly resonate?" he asked, pulling a dusty tome from the shelf.

"The authenticity of the characters," I replied without hesitation. "When you can see their flaws, their struggles, and their growth, that's what makes them real. We're all a little broken in our own ways, and that's what connects us."

He regarded me thoughtfully, a spark igniting in his eyes. "Then maybe the stories we tell ourselves should be just as honest. No more hiding behind facades."

I grinned, exhilarated by the journey we were embarking upon together. With every conversation, every shared moment, we were crafting our own narrative, one rooted in vulnerability and acceptance. The fear that had once loomed over us like a dark cloud began to disperse, revealing a brighter horizon.

As the sun set behind the bookstore, casting a golden glow across the pavement, we stepped outside, the warmth of the day fading into a comfortable twilight. We lingered on the threshold, hesitant to part ways. "Let's make a promise," I proposed, my heart racing at the prospect. "A promise to always be honest with each other, to embrace our fears and celebrate our triumphs."

His smile radiated like the sun breaking through clouds. "I promise. No more hiding."

In that moment, the world around us faded, and all that existed was the bond we had forged through shared vulnerabilities. As we stood beneath the canopy of stars, I felt the weight of our journeys beginning to lift, allowing room for something extraordinary to blossom between us.

The days rolled into a rhythm, a harmonious blend of laughter, light, and lingering glances that spoke louder than words. Each morning, I awoke with a flutter of anticipation, the promise of the day blossoming like the vibrant flowers lining the path to Theo's house. It was as if the universe had conspired to fill every crevice of our lives with the sweetness of newfound freedom and exploration. The world outside our bubble beckoned, full of endless possibilities waiting to be uncovered.

One afternoon, we found ourselves in a bustling farmers' market, the air thick with the scent of ripe peaches and freshly baked bread. Stalls adorned with colorful produce and handcrafted goods beckoned passersby like sirens calling to sailors lost at sea. Children giggled and chased one another among the vibrant displays, their laughter weaving a thread of joy through the vibrant tapestry of the day.

"Let's make a meal together," Theo suggested, his eyes sparkling with mischief. "We'll start with whatever looks best here."

His enthusiasm was infectious. We wandered through the stalls, hand in hand, picking out ingredients as if we were artists curating our masterpiece. A bouquet of fragrant basil here, a plump heirloom tomato there, and a jar of golden honey that caught the afternoon sun, casting playful reflections on the weathered wooden tables. Each item felt like a piece of us, an expression of our blossoming connection.

With bags brimming, we returned to the kitchen in Theo's home, a cozy space filled with the aromas of previous culinary adventures. I pulled out a cutting board, and as I sliced the tomatoes, juice splattering playfully across the counter, I stole glances at Theo, who was bustling around, his energy infectious. There was something magical about cooking together, a dance of sorts, where we moved in sync, each action punctuated by laughter and shared stories.

"Did you ever think you'd be cooking with someone like me?" he teased, a playful smirk tugging at his lips as he tossed diced vegetables into a pan sizzling with olive oil.

"I always suspected you had a secret chef hidden beneath that brooding exterior," I quipped, returning his smirk. "But I didn't think I'd be the one to draw it out."

We shared a moment of lighthearted banter, the tension of our pasts melting away like butter on a warm skillet. I felt alive in a way I hadn't before—each slice of a vegetable, each stir of the pot, echoing the vulnerability we had embraced. In that shared space, our pasts began to dissolve, replaced by the warmth of the present moment.

As the meal simmered, the air filled with mouthwatering aromas, we settled onto the small patio outside, the twilight sky transitioning from shades of orange to deep indigo, sprinkled with stars. We ate under the glow of twinkling lights, the soft clink of forks against plates punctuating our conversation. It was a simple feast, yet it felt monumental—every bite a celebration of our progress.

"You know, this feels different," Theo said between bites, his eyes reflecting the flickering lights above us. "I've never shared a meal like this with anyone. It's like I'm uncovering a part of myself that was hidden for so long."

I smiled, my heart swelling with warmth. "It's the little things that mean the most, isn't it? The moments we once took for granted suddenly become milestones."

With every shared story over dinner, every laugh that danced into the cool night air, the walls we had once built around ourselves crumbled further. We were two people standing at the precipice of discovery, our vulnerabilities laid bare and embraced. We talked about dreams—mine of traveling the world, feeling the pulse of different cultures, and his of building a career that didn't hinge on anyone else's expectations.

The night deepened, and as the moon hung low in the sky, casting a silver glow on everything it touched, I felt the urge to share something raw and unfiltered. "I still carry the weight of expectations too," I confessed, my voice steady yet fragile. "In my family, success looked a certain way, and I've always felt like I was constantly falling short. It took me years to realize that what I want matters too."

Theo's gaze held mine, his expression softening with understanding. "I think we all have those voices in our heads, whispering what we should be. But that doesn't mean we have to listen."

His words resonated deeply, echoing in the chambers of my heart. I reached for his hand, our fingers intertwining, grounding us in that moment, in that space filled with shared vulnerability and authenticity.

As the night wore on, we gravitated closer, the energy between us crackling with an intensity that felt both electrifying and comforting. The world around us faded, and it was as if we were in our own universe, a bubble where expectations and fears dissolved into the night.

Eventually, our plates empty, we lingered in the stillness, the soft rustle of leaves above and the gentle hum of nighttime creatures creating a soothing symphony. I leaned back in my chair, sighing contentedly, and glanced over at Theo, who was staring at me with a mix of admiration and something deeper—an unspoken promise that lay just beneath the surface.

"What's next for us?" I asked, curiosity piquing my interest as I contemplated the future.

His smile widened, a glimmer of excitement lighting up his features. "We keep exploring. Each other, the world, ourselves. We have so much to uncover. I want to do it all, and I want to do it with you."

With those words, I felt a wave of certainty wash over me. It was a promise not just of adventures and laughter but of confronting the shadows we had carried for so long. Our connection had ignited something profound within us, a resolve to embrace the messy, beautiful journey ahead.

As the stars twinkled above, I realized that the beauty of our journey lay not only in the moments of joy but also in the courage to face the uncertainties. We were crafting a story together, rich with vulnerability, strength, and an unwavering bond.

With our hands still intertwined, I felt a thrill of anticipation for what lay ahead. We were no longer two separate souls navigating a tangled web of expectations; we were partners in discovery, and the world was ours to explore, one intimate moment at a time.

Chapter 24: A Weekend Getaway

The cabin emerged like a hidden treasure as we drove down the narrow, winding road, bordered by tall, whispering pines that swayed gently in the warm breeze. Their needles danced in the golden sunlight, casting dappled shadows on the gravel path, which crunched softly beneath the tires of my old Subaru. I could feel the anticipation bubbling within me, a joyous swell that mirrored the rippling water of Lake Serenity just beyond the trees. The moment we stepped out of the car, the scent of damp earth and pine needles filled my lungs, grounding me in the tranquility of this secluded paradise.

As I glanced over at Theo, his face lit up with a mixture of curiosity and delight, my heart fluttered. His dark hair tousled from the drive, he wore a soft, charcoal-gray sweater that brought out the warmth of his hazel eyes, which glimmered like jewels under the sun. He looked as if he belonged in this setting, each of his features carved with an authenticity that echoed the rugged beauty of the landscape around us. I couldn't help but smile, feeling the weight of the world slip away with each passing second. This was our escape, a chance to breathe and simply be—together.

We trudged up the few wooden steps leading to the cabin, its façade adorned with rustic charm—exposed logs, a moss-covered roof, and a porch swing that creaked invitingly. The door swung open with a gentle push, revealing a cozy interior warmed by the flickering glow of a fireplace. Soft, oversized sofas, upholstered in earthy tones, beckoned us to sink into their embrace, while the scent of cedar and pine wrapped around us like a comforting blanket. I tossed our bags onto the worn, wooden floor, their thud echoing in the stillness, as if signaling the start of our little adventure.

"Can you believe this place?" Theo exclaimed, stepping further inside and spinning around as if to take it all in at once. "It's like something out of a movie." His enthusiasm was infectious, and I couldn't suppress my laughter. I loved that he could find wonder in the simplest of things, that he could see the world through eyes untainted by cynicism. It reminded me of the reasons I'd grown so fond of him, the way he embraced life with open arms.

After settling in, we ventured outside, the sun now dipping lower on the horizon, casting a warm golden glow across the lake's surface. It shimmered like a million diamonds scattered across the water, each ripple reflecting the brilliance of the fading light. Theo and I walked hand in hand along the shore, our footsteps leaving ephemeral impressions in the damp sand. The air was rich with the scent of pine, mingling with the coolness of the evening breeze, sending shivers of excitement coursing through me. I felt alive, vibrant, and undeniably content in his presence.

We paused by a large rock jutting out from the water, its surface worn smooth by years of waves lapping against it. I perched myself on the edge, my legs dangling over the side, toes teasingly skimming the water's surface. Theo joined me, his laughter ringing out like music as he attempted to toss pebbles into the lake, each one splashing with a soft plop. I couldn't help but join in, our playful competition echoing through the serene landscape. It was moments like these that felt effortlessly precious, a blend of laughter, nature, and the simple joy of companionship.

As night descended, we returned to the cabin, where the fireplace crackled to life, sending warmth and light dancing across the room. The flickering flames cast shadows that waltzed along the walls, creating an intimate atmosphere. I set about preparing a simple dinner, chopping vegetables and sizzling them in a pan, while Theo fetched us glasses of red wine. The kitchen filled with the rich aroma of sautéed garlic and rosemary, a fragrant invitation that wrapped around us like the cabin's wooden beams.

Dinner was a delightful affair, punctuated by easy conversation and shared smiles. We talked about everything and nothing, our words flowing effortlessly as if we were old friends rediscovering one another. I watched Theo as he spoke, the way his hands animated his thoughts, his eyes lighting up with each passing moment. There was a sincerity in his laughter that tugged at something deep within me, and I found myself captivated by the ease with which he slipped into vulnerability, sharing stories that revealed the layers of his past.

After dinner, we migrated outside, where the night sky unfolded above us, an infinite canvas of stars that twinkled like diamonds scattered across velvet. We settled by the lake, the air cool and crisp against my skin, yet the warmth radiating from our connection kept the chill at bay. I wrapped a soft blanket around us, and Theo leaned in closer, our shoulders brushing as we both gazed up at the cosmos.

"Look at all those stars," he murmured, a hint of awe coloring his voice. "It's as if they're all whispering secrets."

I couldn't help but smile at his childlike wonder. "Maybe they are," I replied softly, "telling stories of all the things that have been and all that could be."

There, under the vast expanse of the universe, I felt a shift in the air, a palpable tension of hope and promise. Theo turned to me, his gaze serious yet tender, his breath visible in the cool night air. "I can see a future for us," he confessed, the sincerity in his words wrapping around my heart like a warm embrace. "One filled with love, laughter, and adventure."

In that moment, the world around us faded into a soft blur, leaving just us—two souls entangled in a delicate dance of possibility. I could feel my heart racing, a mix of fear and exhilaration coursing through me. We were standing at the precipice of something beautiful, and I was ready to leap.

The air was thick with possibility as we lingered by the lake, the soft murmurs of nature surrounding us like a comforting cocoon. I felt a delicate thrill at the edges of my consciousness, a whisper of something new taking root between us. Theo's confession hung in the air, both electrifying and terrifying, challenging me to open my heart just a little wider. The stars above twinkled in agreement, their distant glow a silent witness to our unfolding story.

In the days that followed, we plunged headfirst into the enchantment of our surroundings. Morning light spilled through the cabin's windows, casting warm golden beams that danced on the rustic wooden floors. I woke early, the sweet aroma of pine mingling with the earthy scent of dew-kissed grass, and found Theo still asleep, his chest rising and falling with the gentle rhythm of dreams. I tiptoed into the kitchen, my heart brimming with anticipation as I brewed a pot of coffee, the rich aroma filling the air like an embrace.

When I returned to the bedroom, I couldn't resist the urge to capture the moment. I slipped back under the covers, resting my head on his shoulder, the warmth of his body enveloping me. The stillness of the morning wrapped around us, an unspoken agreement that this was our sanctuary, free from the noise of the outside world. I gently brushed a lock of hair from his forehead, savoring the way his brow furrowed slightly before he stirred, blinking away the remnants of sleep.

"Good morning, sleepyhead," I murmured, unable to hide my smile.

His lips curled into a lazy grin, the kind that could ignite a thousand butterflies in my stomach. "What time is it?" he mumbled, his voice husky with sleep.

"Early enough for coffee and contemplation," I replied, holding up the steaming mug as an offering.

As he took a sip, a look of pure delight spread across his face. "You're a miracle worker," he said, his eyes sparkling with mischief. "What else have you got up your sleeve?"

With a playful smirk, I suggested a morning hike to explore the nearby trails. The thought of wandering through the towering pines, hand in hand with him, filled me with an exhilarating rush. We dressed quickly, slipping into comfortable clothes, and soon found ourselves surrounded by the beauty of the forest. The sounds of the wilderness enveloped us—the rustling of leaves, the distant call of a loon, and the whispering wind weaving through the branches above.

The trail led us along the lake's edge, where the sunlight danced upon the water, creating a sparkling pathway that seemed to invite us to follow. I felt the cool earth beneath my feet, grounding me as we walked side by side, the air crisp and invigorating. Theo's presence was magnetic; each shared glance, each brush of our shoulders, ignited a spark of connection that felt undeniable.

"Can you imagine living here?" I asked, my voice a soft reverie as I took in the breathtaking scenery. The landscape was painted with vibrant greens and the occasional burst of wildflowers, while the mountains loomed in the background, majestic and timeless.

"I could get used to this," he replied, his voice rich with contemplation. "It's like a reset button for the soul."

We paused at a viewpoint, the panorama unfurling before us like a living painting. The lake shimmered in the sunlight, a brilliant blue that beckoned us closer. I could see my reflection in the water, surrounded by the beauty of this moment, and I couldn't help but think how lucky I was to share it with him.

As we resumed our hike, the conversation flowed effortlessly, ranging from our childhood memories to our dreams for the future. I shared the story of how I once tried to build a treehouse in my backyard, only to discover halfway through that I had absolutely no idea what I was doing. He laughed, his deep chuckle reverberating through the trees.

"I think that's half the fun," he said. "The journey, not just the destination. Besides, who says treehouses have to be perfect?"

His words resonated deeply, echoing the sense of adventure that was slowly intertwining with my life. It was this very philosophy that drew me to him—a shared appreciation for the messy, imperfect journey that life often presented.

As we descended back toward the cabin, I felt a lightness in my chest, as if we had shed the weight of our worries along the way. The afternoon sun bathed everything in a golden hue, and the world felt expansive, filled with possibilities.

Once we returned, we decided to indulge in a lazy afternoon by the lake. Theo spread out a blanket, its plaid pattern a comforting touch against the soft grass, and we lay back, our fingers intertwined. The warmth of the sun enveloped us, creating a cocoon of warmth that invited us to surrender to the moment. I closed my eyes, letting the gentle lapping of the water and the distant calls of birds soothe my soul.

"Tell me a secret," Theo whispered after a comfortable silence enveloped us, his voice low and teasing.

I opened my eyes and turned to him, surprised yet delighted. "A secret? That's a tall order. You first."

He chuckled, shifting slightly to look at me fully, the sunlight highlighting the contours of his face. "Okay, I'll go first. I once tried to impress a girl by singing karaoke and ended up sounding like a cat in a blender."

I burst into laughter, picturing his bold attempt. "That's a good one! Did it work?"

"Let's just say it was a very short-lived romance," he replied, feigning a dramatic sigh.

"Your turn," he prompted, a playful gleam in his eye.

I hesitated for a moment, searching my thoughts for something equally amusing yet revealing. "Alright, here goes. I used to pretend to be a competitive swimmer in the summer, but I could barely dog paddle."

Theo's laughter erupted like the splash of a wave against the shore, filling the space between us with warmth. "That's amazing! I would have never guessed."

We exchanged secrets and stories, our laughter mingling with the sounds of nature, weaving a tapestry of connection that felt both sacred and exhilarating. In that moment, surrounded by the beauty of the lake and the towering pines, it became clear that we were embarking on a journey unlike any other, one that invited us to embrace the unpredictable and the imperfect—together.

The sun dipped low in the sky, casting a warm amber hue that mirrored the gold flecks in Theo's eyes. We lingered on the blanket, each moment stretching into the next, rich with laughter and teasing glances that felt like secret handshakes. The tranquility of Lake Serenity was infectious; it encouraged us to shed the remnants of our everyday lives, leaving behind only the simplicity of this shared experience.

As evening settled in, a light breeze rustled the leaves overhead, creating a soft symphony that accompanied the fading light. I shifted, resting my head on Theo's shoulder, feeling the solid warmth of his presence seep into me like the last rays of sunlight. There was something undeniably magical about the way the world transformed as the day surrendered to night. The lake took on a deep, indigo shade, mirroring the sky where stars began to punctuate the vastness, each one a twinkling promise of dreams yet to unfold.

"We should make a fire," Theo suggested, breaking the comfortable silence. His voice held a spark of excitement that made my heart race.

"Absolutely! But you know, I have no idea how to start one," I admitted, a sheepish grin spreading across my face.

"I've got this," he declared, a mischievous grin crossing his lips as he rose to his feet. "Consider me your firestarter."

As he gathered kindling and larger logs, I watched him, a quiet awe swelling within me. There was something undeniably captivating about his easy confidence, the way he moved with purpose and assurance. My heart fluttered at the realization that this was not merely a weekend getaway; it was a glimpse into a life we could share, a life filled with laughter, adventure, and perhaps even love.

The fire crackled to life with surprising ease, flames licking upward as Theo added more logs, their scent mingling with the fresh pine air. I settled back onto the blanket, pulling it closer around my shoulders as the warmth radiated from the fire, enveloping us in a cocoon of light and comfort. The flames danced like living beings, casting playful shadows on our faces and the surrounding trees.

"Okay, I have a question," I began, trying to sound nonchalant while my pulse quickened with anticipation. "If you could have any superpower, what would it be?"

Theo pondered this for a moment, his brow furrowing adorably as he looked into the flames. "Hmm... I'd probably choose teleportation. Think of all the places we could see in an instant."

"Teleportation?" I teased, "You're just trying to avoid traffic jams."

"Maybe! But also, imagine the adventures," he replied, his eyes sparkling with enthusiasm. "We could be standing on a beach in Hawaii one moment and at the top of the Eiffel Tower the next."

"That does sound tempting," I admitted, imagining us leaping from one breathtaking location to another, collecting memories like souvenirs. "But I think I'd choose the ability to talk to animals. Imagine all the secrets they must know!"

Theo chuckled, shaking his head in mock disbelief. "You would, wouldn't you? You'd end up starting a zoo and having deep conversations with a bunch of squirrels."

"Hey, they could have valuable life lessons!" I defended, laughter bubbling between us.

We continued to share silly hypotheticals, our voices mingling with the crackle of the fire and the rhythmic lapping of the water. The evening air, now slightly cooler, wrapped around us, but I felt warm all the way down to my toes.

As the stars twinkled brighter in the inky sky, Theo turned serious, his gaze focused on the fire as if he were searching for the right words. "You know," he began slowly, "being here with you... it feels like I've finally found where I belong."

My heart stuttered in my chest, caught between fear and elation. "I feel that too," I admitted softly, trying to keep my voice steady.

His eyes met mine, deep pools of sincerity that made my breath hitch. "I want to keep exploring this... whatever it is between us. I know we both have our pasts, our baggage, but I can't shake this feeling that it's worth it."

In that moment, the world faded away, leaving just the two of us under the vast, shimmering sky. My heart raced, each beat echoing the unspoken hopes that had been swirling within me. It felt as if time paused, the universe holding its breath in anticipation.

"What are you saying?" I asked, my voice barely a whisper, afraid to disturb the fragile magic surrounding us.

"I'm saying I want to be more than friends," he replied, the honesty in his tone sending butterflies fluttering through my stomach. "I want to see where this leads us."

A wave of warmth flooded through me, melting away the remnants of doubt and fear. "I want that too, Theo. I really do."

His smile was radiant, illuminating the space between us. "Then let's not waste another moment."

We moved closer, the warmth of the fire a backdrop to the electric connection crackling between us. When our lips finally met, it was as if the universe itself had conspired to create this moment—a perfect alignment of stars, hearts, and fate. The kiss was soft at first, tentative yet full of promise, and then it deepened, igniting a fire that rivaled the one flickering beside us.

As we pulled away, breathless and dazed, the world around us faded back into focus, the sound of the water lapping against the shore a gentle reminder that we were still anchored in reality. I looked at Theo, feeling an overwhelming rush of gratitude and excitement.

"Now what?" I asked, my heart racing with the possibilities.

"Now," he said with a grin, "we make the most of every moment we have here. Let's explore more of the lake tomorrow, try to catch some fish, and maybe even take a dip if the weather holds."

"And after that?" I pressed, unable to contain my curiosity about what the future might hold for us.

"After that, we make plans for all the adventures to come. But for now, let's just enjoy tonight."

With those words, we leaned back against the blanket, our hands still intertwined, the glow of the fire illuminating our faces. I looked up at the stars, each one a reminder of our dreams, our hopes, and the vast universe that seemed to echo our budding connection. In that moment, surrounded by the beauty of Lake Serenity, I felt an unwavering certainty that this was just the beginning—a chapter filled with laughter, love, and a future that sparkled with infinite possibilities.

Chapter 25: Uncharted Waters

The sun hung high in the cobalt sky, its rays piercing through the trees lining the edge of the lake, casting dappled patterns of light that danced on the surface. Each stroke of the paddle felt like a mini adventure, our voices echoing in the gentle ripples, blending seamlessly with the chorus of chirping birds and rustling leaves. As we pushed deeper into the heart of the lake, the world around us began to transform into a mosaic of vibrant colors—the emerald green of the pines, the golden glow of the wildflowers dotting the shoreline, and the crystal-clear water that shimmered like liquid glass beneath our canoe. It was a world I had only dreamed of, but here I was, in the midst of it, my heart swelling with joy.

Beside me, Jamie's laughter rang like music, infectious and bright. She had always been the adventurous one, the spark that ignited our escapades, and today was no different. Her sun-kissed hair whipped playfully in the breeze as she leaned over the side of the canoe, her fingers trailing through the cool water, creating small whirlpools that glimmered under the sun. The sight of her carefree spirit made me feel light, as if we were both weightless, floating on our shared dreams and laughter.

"Race you to that cove!" she declared, her eyes sparkling with mischief. Without waiting for my response, she dug her paddle into the water, propelling us forward. I chuckled, catching her enthusiasm, and joined her in the frantic rhythm, our synchronized strokes echoing the heartbeat of our adventure. As we neared the secluded cove, I could see the fringes of the shore framed by a lush tapestry of moss and wildflowers. It was a slice of paradise, untouched and inviting.

Once we beached the canoe, we scrambled onto the shore, our feet sinking into the soft, earthy carpet of moss, the rich scent of damp earth filling the air. I could feel the coolness of the ground seep through my shoes, grounding me in this idyllic moment. Jamie turned to me, her face lit with pure exhilaration, and for a moment, I forgot about everything else—the complexities of life, the challenges that loomed like shadows at the edges of my thoughts. Here, in this pocket of the world, we were untethered, free to explore the depths of our laughter and the nuances of our connection.

We ventured into the thicket, pushing through thick bushes and low-hanging branches, each step revealing new wonders. A flash of color caught my eye—a cardinal flitted from branch to branch, its bright red plumage a stark contrast against the verdant backdrop. Jamie and I stood mesmerized, our previous giggles dissolving into awed silence, momentarily lost in the beauty of nature's canvas.

"Look at that," she whispered, pointing toward a cluster of vibrant wildflowers swaying gently in the breeze. They were a mix of colors—pinks, yellows, and purples—each petal a brushstroke in this masterful painting. I knelt down to get a closer look, inhaling their sweet fragrance, which mingled with the fresh scent of pine. In this moment, I was overwhelmed with gratitude for the simplicity of being here, with her, amid nature's wonders.

But just as quickly as my heart soared, the sky began to change. The sun slipped behind a thick blanket of clouds, the bright blue replaced by ominous shades of gray. A gust of wind swept through the trees, rustling the leaves and stirring a hint of unease in my gut. I glanced at Jamie, who still wore a look of blissful ignorance, twirling in circles, her laughter resonating through the cove. I wished I could share in her lightness, but the weight of uncertainty hung over me like the gathering storm clouds.

"Hey, Jamie," I called, my voice slightly strained as I attempted to mask the sudden turmoil brewing inside me. "Maybe we should head back? The weather looks a bit—"

Before I could finish, a rumble of thunder echoed in the distance, reverberating through the air, mingling with the scent of approaching rain. Jamie stopped mid-spin, her face shifting from joy to concern as she looked up at the swirling sky.

"Wow, that escalated quickly," she said, a nervous laugh escaping her lips. Her eyes darted around the cove, searching for signs of an impending downpour. I could see the flicker of worry cross her features, and my heart twisted at the thought of her disappointment.

"Let's just enjoy a little longer," she insisted, her spirit unyielding. "We can wait it out here."

But as the wind picked up, whipping around us with an almost predatory force, my mind raced with thoughts of our relationship. I couldn't shake the feeling that this sudden change in weather mirrored the uncharted waters we had waded into together. With each passing moment, doubts began to creep in, shadowing the sunlight that had once bathed our afternoon in warmth.

Jamie picked a few wildflowers, their colors vibrant against the gray backdrop, her determination to seize the moment both admirable and heart-wrenching. The laughter and joy we had shared felt like a fragile glass ornament, and I feared the storm would shatter it, leaving us in shards, lost in the debris of unspoken worries.

As the first drops of rain began to fall, plopping against the leaves with a rhythm that echoed my racing heart, I felt the tug of reality. We were on a precipice, and as the skies opened up, drenching us in a downpour, I realized that we weren't just battling the elements; we were grappling with the future of our journey together.

The rain came down in sheets, drumming against the leaves and splattering on the ground like a thousand tiny percussionists in a chaotic symphony. The world around us transformed, vibrant greens now glistening under a sheen of water, each droplet dancing in the air like tiny prisms of light. I stood there, momentarily frozen, watching Jamie shake her head as if trying to dislodge the clouds hanging over us. She burst into laughter, her voice ringing out even louder than the rain, and for a heartbeat, the sound drowned out my spiraling thoughts.

"Come on!" she shouted, her eyes sparkling with mischief. "We can't let a little rain ruin our adventure!" With that, she took off, her bare feet splashing through puddles as she danced along the shoreline, embracing the downpour with a joy I both admired and envied. I hesitated, my heart caught between the exhilarating thrill of her spontaneity and the nagging worries tugging at the corners of my mind.

What if the storm was more than just the weather? What if this was a sign, a warning from the universe that our uncharted waters were about to take a turbulent turn? The very thought sent a shiver down my spine, and I instinctively glanced at the darkening horizon, where gray clouds mingled with deeper hues of impending twilight. I was losing my grip on the moment, and I knew it.

"Wait up!" I finally yelled, shaking off my anxieties like raindrops off my skin, and took off after her. The cold water splashed against my legs, invigorating me, grounding me in the present. Jamie spun around, her laughter trailing behind her like a stream of bright light breaking through the clouds. It was infectious; I couldn't help but join her, splashing and twirling in a mock ballet of our own creation. I felt a genuine smile break across my face, the kind that reaches all the way to your heart and refuses to leave.

Together, we found refuge under a sprawling oak tree, its gnarled branches offering some semblance of shelter from the rain. Panting from laughter, I leaned against the trunk, letting the coolness of the bark seep into my skin, while Jamie shook her hair like a drenched dog, droplets flying everywhere. We exchanged glances, her blue eyes sparkling as if they were lit from within.

"See? This isn't so bad!" she said, wiping her face with the back of her hand. "In fact, I think we look rather charming. Like a scene from a romantic comedy!" She flashed a grin, and I could hardly resist her exuberance. It was true; there was something undeniably freeing about being caught in the rain, about letting the world wash away, if only for a moment.

The rain softened, becoming a gentle patter, and I noticed how the air felt different—crisp and clean, carrying with it the heady scent of wet earth. It enveloped me, and for the first time that day, I felt the anxiety loosening its grip. Perhaps we were not so far adrift after all. Maybe this unplanned detour was just another part of our journey, an opportunity to navigate the murky waters that lay ahead together.

"Let's explore more!" I suggested, my voice brimming with newfound confidence. Jamie nodded enthusiastically, and we ventured back into the heart of the cove, where the world had transformed. The lush greenery sparkled, glistening like diamonds, and I felt a sense of wonder ripple through me. Each step felt like a discovery, a chance to unearth the layers of our surroundings and ourselves.

We wandered further into the cove, our laughter punctuating the air as we played hide-and-seek among the trees. I ducked behind a thick trunk, heart racing with anticipation, listening intently for her footsteps. Just when I thought I had the perfect hiding spot, she found me, leaping out from behind a bush with a triumphant squeal. We tumbled into a patch of wildflowers, their petals soft against our skin, their vibrant hues a sharp contrast to the gray sky.

In that moment, I realized how little I needed to worry. Sure, life was unpredictable, like the weather, but it was also beautiful, filled with spontaneous moments that stitched our lives together. Jamie brushed off her clothes, sending bits of grass and petals flying into the air, her laughter ringing out like music.

"Let's take a picture!" she exclaimed, pulling out her phone. I posed next to her, arms flung wide as if to embrace the storm. The rain danced around us, blurring the edges of our world, and in that fleeting moment captured in a digital snapshot, I felt invincible, untouchable by the worries that had plagued me just moments before.

As we caught our breath, Jamie's expression shifted. The lightness in her eyes dimmed slightly, replaced by something more pensive. "You okay?" she asked softly, her brow furrowing. It was a gentle inquiry, one that dug beneath the surface of my laughter, seeking the truth that lay hidden beneath the playful banter.

I hesitated, the weight of my unspoken fears settling between us like a thick fog. But just as quickly, I realized that I didn't want to spoil this moment with doubts. "Yeah, just thinking," I replied, trying to keep my tone light. "About how unpredictable life is. And how we're like this rain, unpredictable but beautiful, right?"

Her smile returned, though it was tinged with a hint of concern. "You know I'm here for you, right? No matter what storms come our way." Her sincerity wrapped around me like a warm blanket, and I couldn't help but feel a sense of comfort in her words.

"I know," I said, my heart swelling with gratitude. "It's just... sometimes I wonder if we're ready for what lies ahead." The clouds rolled back in, thickening the air with an almost palpable tension, and I wished I could shove my fears away, tuck them neatly into a box to deal with later.

Jamie stepped closer, her eyes searching mine. "We'll figure it out. Together," she said firmly, and I couldn't help but believe her.

As the rain continued to fall, washing away our worries with each droplet, I let myself lean into that promise, ready to navigate whatever uncharted waters lay ahead. With her by my side, I felt as if we could conquer any storm, one splash at a time.

The rain began to lighten, and with it came an enchanting quiet, the kind that cloaked the world in a serene hush. Jamie and I stood beneath the oak tree, the drops now a soft patter against the leaves above us, like nature's own symphony welcoming the calm after the chaos. I took a deep breath, inhaling the fresh, earthy scent that rose from the ground, revitalizing my senses. This was nature's way of cleansing, a reminder that even storms have a purpose.

As the last remnants of the rain fell around us, we took a step out from under our makeshift shelter, our feet squelching in the mud. The cove was transformed, shimmering under the gray sky, the water now reflecting the soft pastels of the clouds overhead. I watched as Jamie bent down to examine a particularly vibrant patch of flowers, their colors electrified by the rain.

"Look at these!" she exclaimed, plucking a small blossom and holding it up to the light. "They're like little jewels!" I couldn't help but smile, caught up in her infectious enthusiasm. She was like the sun breaking through the clouds, illuminating everything around her.

We ventured further, walking along the edge of the lake where the water lapped gently against the shore, each wave kissing the land like a lover reluctant to let go. Jamie began skipping stones, her arm moving with an effortless grace, and I was entranced by the way the stones danced across the water, each hop sending ripples outward, altering the stillness in their wake. It was mesmerizing, and I couldn't help but feel that our lives were akin to those stones—each decision, each moment, sending out ripples that shaped the course of our journey together.

As the last of the rain clouds drifted away, the sun broke through, casting a warm, golden light that filled the cove. I closed my eyes for a moment, letting the sun's rays wash over me, feeling as if the universe had orchestrated this perfect moment just for us. Jamie's laughter brought me back, and I turned to see her standing at the edge of the water, the sunlight creating a halo effect around her. She looked like a mythical creature, a siren calling me closer.

"Come on! Let's swim!" she shouted, her voice brimming with excitement. Before I could respond, she was already kicking off her shoes, her laughter echoing off the water. There was something wildly intoxicating about her spontaneity, a spark that ignited my own desire for adventure. I kicked off my shoes and followed suit, the cool water engulfing us as we dove in, each stroke pulling us deeper into the embrace of the lake.

We splashed and played, our laughter intertwining with the sounds of nature—the chirping birds and the rustling trees creating a harmonious backdrop to our joyous abandon. I lost track of time as we floated, the sun warming my skin and the water cradling my body. In those moments, I felt the weight of my worries lift, leaving only the pure, exhilarating joy of being alive.

After what felt like an eternity, we clambered out of the water, breathless and exhilarated, our skin glistening with droplets that sparkled like tiny diamonds. We sprawled on the warm grass, panting as we gazed up at the vast expanse of sky, now a brilliant blue, unmarred by any trace of the previous storm.

"I can't believe we did that," I said, my heart still racing. "You're crazy, you know that?" I shot her a teasing smile, and she playfully shoved my shoulder, the motion sending ripples of laughter between us.

"Crazy is what makes life worth living!" she replied, her voice filled with conviction. "Why stick to the ordinary when we can make memories like this?"

Her words struck a chord deep within me. It was true. Our lives had become a predictable rhythm, too focused on what lay ahead rather than savoring the moment we had right now. I turned to her, feeling a sudden surge of affection. "You make me want to embrace the chaos, you know that?"

She grinned, her eyes sparkling with mischief. "Good! Embrace it. Let's keep riding this wave of adventure!"

As we lay there, the sun bathing us in warmth, I felt a connection deepening, weaving an intricate tapestry of trust and affection between us. Yet beneath that trust lurked shadows, flickers of doubt creeping in at the edges of my consciousness. Could I truly allow myself to surrender to this feeling? To the uncharted waters of our relationship?

But before I could delve too deeply into my thoughts, Jamie stood up, brushing the grass off her damp legs. "Let's explore that little island!" she exclaimed, pointing toward a small landmass just a short paddle away, the trees atop it swaying gently in the breeze.

The thought of another adventure sent a thrill through me. I scrambled to my feet, my initial hesitations washed away by the sheer joy of being with her. "Lead the way!" I called, and we hurried back to the canoe, our excitement palpable as we climbed in, still damp from our earlier escapade.

The paddling felt different this time, the rhythm almost instinctual as we worked together, the water slicing cleanly beneath us. The closer we got to the island, the more curious I became. I imagined hidden treasures, secret nooks where dreams could take flight, just waiting for us to discover.

As we beached the canoe and stepped onto the soft, sandy shore, the sun cast a warm glow, transforming the small island into a slice of paradise. It was a wonderland of verdant greens and rich browns, trees bending over us like ancient guardians. The laughter of birds echoed above, and I felt a rush of exhilaration at the unknown adventures awaiting us.

We wandered through the thicket, Jamie leading the way with an unyielding sense of purpose, her laughter ringing through the trees. Every corner we turned revealed new wonders—a hidden grove of wildflowers here, a twisting vine there, each discovery fueling our sense of adventure.

At the center of the island, we stumbled upon a small clearing, a natural amphitheater surrounded by towering trees. Sunlight filtered through the leaves, creating a patchwork of shadows on the ground.

It felt sacred, a place untouched by time, and I could almost hear the whispers of those who had walked this path long before us.

"This is amazing!" Jamie breathed, spinning in a circle, arms outstretched, as if she could embrace the entire world. In that moment, I realized this was more than just a beautiful spot; it was a testament to the journey we were on together.

As I watched her, something clicked within me. This was our life—an unpredictable dance through the chaos, the beauty, and the uncharted waters. Here, surrounded by nature, with the sun warming our skin and the laughter of our hearts echoing in the trees, I felt ready to embrace the adventure, the storms, and everything in between.

With a newfound clarity, I stepped closer to her, my heart racing not just from the thrill of exploration but from the dawning realization that I was ready to take this leap. Ready to navigate the waves together, come what may, and to trust in the journey ahead. Whatever storms might brew on the horizon, I would face them hand in hand with her. The uncharted waters were no longer something to fear, but a canvas upon which we would paint our story—bold, vibrant, and utterly our own.

Chapter 26: Stormy Seas

The tempest surged with a fury that seemed almost personal, as if the sky had chosen this very moment to unleash its wrath. Dark, roiling clouds twisted and churned above, their ominous shades contrasting sharply with the vivid blue of the lake just moments before. Each gust of wind whipped the water into a frenzy, creating waves that crashed against the sides of our canoe, sending icy sprays of water cascading down our backs. I gripped the paddle tightly, my knuckles white with tension, my heart a frantic metronome as I tried to find some semblance of control in the chaos.

"Row harder!" Theo shouted, his voice barely cutting through the roar of the storm. I looked at him, drenched and wild-eyed, and for a fleeting moment, I wondered if it was the storm or the unresolved tension between us that truly frightened him. The wind whipped through his hair, making him look almost regal in his despair. But there was no time for philosophical musings; the canoe rocked violently, and I felt a jolt of panic rip through me as we crested another wave.

The world around us morphed into a whirlwind of sound and sensation—the thunder clapped like a drumroll announcing a catastrophe, the rain lashed against our faces like stinging needles. Each drop seemed to merge with the salt of my fear, and for a heartbeat, I could taste the bitterness of uncertainty. I fought to keep my focus, muscles straining against the resistance of the water, trying to find the rhythm in the discord. With each stroke, I felt the weight of our unspoken words, the heavy silence that hung between us like the storm itself.

We were surrounded by the thick scent of wet earth and the sharp tang of ozone, nature's own version of cologne, and I was acutely aware of every breath we took together, each one an echo of our shared history. I could almost hear the whispers of the moments that led us to this turbulent intersection—our laughter by the campfire, the sweetness of stolen glances, the weight of words we had left unsaid. It all crashed down around us now, threatening to drown us in its depths.

"Look, the shore!" I shouted, squinting through the sheets of rain that blurred my vision. Theo turned, his face lit momentarily by a flash of lightning, revealing the tension etched in his jaw. He nodded, his determination igniting something within me. We would fight against the storm, against whatever had kept us at arm's length for so long. With renewed vigor, I dug the paddle into the churning water, the rhythm now a steady pulse guiding us toward safety.

As we approached the shore, I felt a wave of relief wash over me, though it was quickly followed by an undercurrent of dread. We would be on solid ground soon, but would that ground be the refuge I yearned for, or merely the stage for the confrontation I dreaded? The waves crashed violently as we pulled closer, and with one final thrust of the paddle, we beached the canoe, the sound of wood scraping against sand a small victory amidst the turmoil.

We leapt from the canoe, our legs shaky beneath us, still buzzing with adrenaline. The storm continued to rage, but now we stood together under the shelter of a sprawling oak, its leaves shivering in the wind. We huddled close, the cool air prickling our skin, but it wasn't the chill that made me shiver; it was the storm brewing between us. Our breaths mingled in the air, a mingling of heat and vulnerability, and for a moment, time stood still, even as the world around us spun out of control.

I could see the storm reflected in Theo's eyes, a tempest of fear and vulnerability that mirrored my own. "Are you okay?" I asked, my voice softer now, stripped of its previous urgency. The vulnerability in his gaze made my heart ache, a deep, resonating thrum that demanded attention. I knew then that this was our moment to address the chaos that had silently crept between us like a thief in the night.

"I'm..." he began, his voice trailing off as he searched for words, perhaps battling the demons that clawed at his mind. The storm overhead raged on, but it felt like a mere backdrop to the storm unfolding in our hearts. "I don't know, honestly."

The admission hung in the air, thick and palpable. It was as if the storm had torn down the barriers we had built, exposing our raw, unfiltered selves to one another. My chest tightened as I took a step closer, the distance between us shrinking with each heartbeat. "We've faced worse than this," I said, my voice steady despite the tempest swirling around us. "Together, we can figure it out."

He looked at me then, really looked, as if he were searching for the pieces of himself that I held. The rain continued to pelt down, each drop a reminder of the chaos outside, but here, under the shelter of the oak, we created our own world—a fragile sanctuary amid the storm. I reached out, fingers brushing against his, a tentative gesture that seemed to spark a flicker of hope between us.

The moment felt electric, charged with possibility and uncertainty, and I could feel the weight of everything we hadn't said, the hopes and fears we'd tucked away in the corners of our hearts. Would we allow this storm to tear us apart, or would we emerge from it stronger, forged in the fires of our trials? The choice hung heavy in the air, but for the first time, I felt ready to face whatever lay ahead.

The rain continued its relentless assault, a symphony of droplets drumming against the leaves overhead. Each impact felt like a metronome, counting down the moments until we had to face the storm that raged not only outside but within the sanctuary of our hearts. The air was thick with moisture and uncertainty, the scent of wet earth rising to meet us, and I was struck by the realization that the world around us had transformed into a chaotic masterpiece.

Each gust of wind seemed to howl with secrets yet untold, echoing the questions that hung between us like an uninvited guest.

I turned my gaze to Theo, his features half obscured by the downpour, but his eyes still shone with a raw honesty that I found captivating. "What do you fear the most?" I asked, my voice barely above a whisper, yet it felt as loud as thunder in the storm. His brow furrowed, a mixture of surprise and contemplation crossing his face, and I wondered if my question had cut deeper than intended. I took a step closer, letting the rain drench me further, as if the cold water could wash away the barriers we had built.

He hesitated, glancing down at the ground, where puddles reflected the turbulent skies. "I guess... I fear being seen," he said finally, his voice soft but steady. "Not just by you, but by anyone. I've built these walls, you know? It's easier to keep people at a distance than to let them see the mess that is me."

His confession struck a chord deep within me, resonating like a note plucked from an unseen instrument. I thought of the countless moments we had shared, of the laughter that felt as if it could bridge any divide, yet here we stood, marooned on an island of unspoken words. "But you're not a mess," I replied, my conviction rising. "You're real. And real is messy sometimes. It's part of what makes you... you."

He looked up then, and in that brief moment, the storm above us seemed to pause, waiting with bated breath. The rain dripped from his lashes like tears held back too long, and I could see the battle raging behind his eyes. "It's easier to pretend," he admitted, vulnerability spilling from him like the rain cascading off the branches. "Easier to wear a mask and show the world what it wants to see. But with you, it's different. I don't want to hide. Not anymore."

The weight of his words hung between us, fragile yet powerful. I felt a rush of warmth spreading through me, igniting a flicker of hope. "Then don't hide," I urged, stepping even closer, emboldened by the honesty swirling around us like the storm itself. "Let me see you. All of you."

His breath caught, and for a heartbeat, the world fell silent. In that silence, I felt a shift, a subtle realignment of the universe that whispered of possibilities. The rain, which had once felt like a ferocious beast, transformed into a soothing balm, washing over us and softening the edges of our fear. We stood there, the pulse of the storm synchronizing with the rhythm of our hearts, and I sensed the promise of something new.

"Okay," he said, his voice barely audible over the soft hiss of the rain. "But you have to promise to be patient with me. This isn't easy for me."

"I'll be here," I replied without hesitation, and as I said it, I believed it. There was something grounding about our exchange, a tethering of souls amidst the chaos. With each heartbeat, I felt the bonds of fear unraveling, exposing the raw fabric of who we were.

As if responding to our newfound honesty, the wind shifted, carrying with it a cool breeze that brushed against my skin, invigorating and alive. I closed my eyes for a moment, relishing the sensations—the sound of rain, the scent of wet earth, the warmth radiating from Theo's body just inches away. I could feel the pulse of life thrumming through the storm, beckoning us to embrace the wildness of our emotions.

"Tell me something about you that I don't know," I prompted, eager to peel back another layer of his carefully constructed facade.

Theo's eyes sparkled with a hint of mischief, even as the storm raged around us. "Alright, but you have to promise to share something too. Fair's fair, right?"

A smile tugged at my lips, the tension easing just a fraction. "Deal. You go first."

He took a deep breath, his gaze drifting to the horizon, where the dark clouds seemed to meld into the water. "I once tried to learn how to surf," he admitted, a chuckle escaping his lips. "Needless to say, I didn't get very far. I ended up taking a tumble and inhaling a lot of seawater instead."

The image of him, tall and determined, struggling against the waves, sent a delightful warmth through me. "I can picture that. You with your long limbs flailing around like a windmill," I teased, laughter bubbling up in the air between us.

He laughed, the sound a balm against the backdrop of the storm. "Yeah, it wasn't my proudest moment. But I did discover that I love the ocean, even if it doesn't always love me back."

"Maybe the ocean just has a thing for drama," I countered, my heart swelling at the unexpected lightness that had entered our exchange. "It sounds like you two are kindred spirits."

"Maybe so," he mused, glancing back at me, the corner of his mouth curling up. "But now it's your turn. Something I don't know."

I hesitated, the weight of his gaze urging me to dig deep. "Alright, here goes. I was terrified of the dark as a kid," I confessed, a slight flush creeping into my cheeks. "I used to sleep with a nightlight until I was twelve. And sometimes, I still do if I'm feeling anxious."

His expression softened, genuine curiosity lighting his features. "I get that. There's something unnerving about not knowing what's lurking in the shadows."

"Yes!" I exclaimed, my relief palpable. "Exactly! It's like your imagination just runs wild."

"Maybe that's why we're drawn to the storm," he replied thoughtfully. "It's a reminder that chaos can be beautiful, even if it's frightening."

The rain began to ease, a gentle patter now, and I could see glimpses of blue peeking through the clouds above. It felt like a metaphor for us, a promise that even in the darkest moments, light could break through if we were willing to face the storm together. I took a deep breath, the air infused with the smell of damp earth and something else—something bright, hopeful, and filled with possibility.

In that moment, beneath the sheltering oak, with rain-soaked clothes clinging to our skin and laughter mingling with the last roars of thunder, we stood on the precipice of something new and extraordinary. The tempest might have raged outside, but inside, we were beginning to find our calm amidst the chaos.

The clouds began to part, revealing patches of sky that transformed from slate gray to a soft, hopeful blue. A light breeze danced through the air, teasing the droplets of rain from our hair and clothes, leaving us shivering yet exhilarated. I could feel the tension between us easing, the warmth of Theo's presence a steady anchor in the aftermath of the storm. We stood under the oak, its gnarled branches swaying like wise old arms embracing us, and I was struck by the beauty of the moment—a blend of chaos and calm, vulnerability and strength.

"I used to come here a lot as a kid," I murmured, allowing myself to be swept up in nostalgia. "My grandparents had a little cabin not far from here. I spent summers chasing fireflies and pretending I was some kind of woodland fairy. I'd collect acorns and make little necklaces out of them."

Theo turned to me, his eyes brightening with intrigue. "Really? You? A woodland fairy?" His laughter was warm, wrapping around me like a cozy blanket. "I can't quite picture it."

"Oh, I was quite the sight," I replied, feigning a regal stance, arms akimbo. "Crowned with wildflowers, decked out in my finest leaves and twigs. I was basically the ruler of the forest."

He chuckled again, shaking his head in disbelief, and I felt the warmth of shared laughter ignite a spark of something deeper within us. "I'd like to see pictures of that," he challenged, a playful glint in his eyes.

"Not a chance!" I shot back, laughing. "Those photos are hidden in a vault, never to see the light of day again."

The moment hung between us, a delicate tapestry woven with threads of laughter and memories. And yet, beneath the lightness, the weight of our shared truths lingered, like the storm clouds that had just dissipated. I sensed Theo shifting, a movement of energy that hinted at more beneath the surface.

"Do you still feel like that fairy?" he asked, the playful tone dropping to a whisper, as if we were sharing a secret only the trees could hear. "Or has the world turned you into something else?"

I paused, searching for the right words. "Sometimes, I forget," I admitted. "Life has a way of burying those dreams beneath responsibilities and expectations. But every now and then, when I'm near the water, I remember. I feel like that girl again."

His gaze softened, and in that moment, I realized he understood. He too had been shaped by his own storms, yet here we were, emerging into the light, willing to shed our pasts. "You're still that girl," he said gently, his sincerity washing over me like the after-rain freshness. "You just need to believe it."

Before I could respond, the air shifted again, and the clouds above began to darken once more, rolling in like an unexpected guest. "We should find some shelter," I suggested, scanning the area for a nearby trail or path. "I'd prefer not to get caught in another downpour."

He nodded, and together we stepped away from the oak, the ground slick and squishy beneath our feet. As we walked, the vibrant hues of the forest enveloped us, each leaf glistening with rainwater, the scent of pine mingling with the earthy smell of damp soil. I could hear the soft rustle of branches and the distant call of birds, their songs punctuating the tension still lingering between us.

We found a narrow trail, winding deeper into the woods, framed by tall pines that swayed gently in the breeze. The landscape around us felt alive, pulsing with a vibrant energy that echoed my own heartbeat. "This place is magical," I said, glancing at Theo, who seemed entranced by the beauty surrounding us.

"Maybe we'll discover a hidden fairy realm," he teased, raising an eyebrow. "You can reign supreme while I stand guard."

I laughed, my heart soaring. "Only if you promise to wear a crown made of twigs and leaves."

As we ventured further down the path, the atmosphere began to shift. The sunlight filtered through the trees in a golden haze, casting dappled shadows that danced on the forest floor. I could feel the weight of our earlier conversation lingering, yet it no longer felt burdensome. It was an invitation to explore the depths of our connection.

"I think about how easy it is to hide," Theo mused, his voice contemplative. "I mean, it's almost a reflex. You're taught to keep your vulnerabilities tucked away, to put on a brave face."

I nodded, feeling the resonance of his words. "It's like armor, isn't it? But it gets heavy, carrying all that around."

"Exactly," he said, a small smile breaking through his somber expression. "I never realized how exhausting it was until now."

The trail curved sharply, leading us to a clearing where sunlight pooled like liquid gold. In the center stood a moss-covered stone, ancient and wise, a silent witness to the world's changes. We approached it, our footsteps silent on the soft ground.

"Do you think this stone has seen things?" I asked, running my fingers over its cool surface. "Like the storms that raged above and the calm that followed?"

Theo stepped closer, his shoulder brushing against mine. "Probably. It's a reminder that everything is temporary. The storms, the sunshine, even us."

I turned to him, surprised by the depth of his insight. "You're not just a pretty face," I teased, but the words came out softer than I intended, laced with sincerity.

He chuckled, the sound light and airy, and for a moment, the weight of our earlier exchanges felt lifted. "I do have my moments of wisdom, you know."

"Clearly," I replied, a grin spreading across my face. "But seriously, I think it's beautiful how we can share these moments, how they bring us closer."

"Yes," he said, his voice lowering to a husky whisper. "It's like peeling back layers, revealing what's underneath."

I met his gaze, and the world around us faded into a blur. The trees, the sky, the damp earth—it all melted away until it was just us, standing there, hearts exposed and raw. There was something electric in the air, a magnetism that pulled us closer, and I felt an undeniable urge to bridge the gap that had lingered between us for so long.

In that moment, surrounded by the remnants of a storm and the promise of sunlight, I took a step forward, closing the distance. "I want to be here with you, Theo," I confessed, my voice steady but my heart racing. "Through the storms and the calm."

He searched my eyes, and I held my breath, willing him to see the truth behind my words. Finally, a slow smile spread across his face, radiant and genuine, and I felt a wave of warmth wash over me. "I want that too," he said, stepping closer, the space between us evaporating like the morning mist.

The world resumed around us—the gentle rustle of leaves, the distant call of a bird, the soft crunch of fallen twigs beneath our feet—but all I could feel was the connection igniting between us. The storm had revealed our true selves, stripped away the armor, and now we stood bare and vulnerable, ready to face whatever came next.

As the sunlight broke through the clouds, illuminating the clearing with its warmth, I knew we were on the precipice of something profound. The path ahead would be filled with challenges, but together, we would navigate the tempest, hand in hand, hearts entwined, and emerge into the light, unafraid of the storms that life might bring.

Chapter 27: Calm After the Storm

The storm had receded, leaving in its wake a breathtaking clarity, as if the world had been washed anew, each blade of grass glistening like emeralds under the sun's tender caress. I drew in a deep breath, letting the crisp, cool air fill my lungs, invigorating me like a splash of cold water on a hot summer day. The lake before us shimmered with an iridescent glow, each ripple reflecting the azure sky as if the heavens themselves were kissing the surface. I sat cross-legged on the sun-warmed stones at the water's edge, the rough texture grounding me to this moment of stillness.

Theo sat beside me, his silhouette strong against the soft backdrop of nature's masterpiece. His hair, tousled by the wind, framed his face in a way that made my heart skip—a blend of mischief and sincerity. He had a way of looking at the world that made everything seem possible, even when the storms raged. The remnants of the storm hung in the air, a muted reminder of the chaos that had just passed. Yet, here we were, cocooned in a serene sanctuary, where time felt suspended, like a note held long after the music had stopped.

Turning toward him, I saw shadows dance in his eyes, a mix of vulnerability and strength that drew me in. "We can't ignore the storms in our lives," I murmured, the words spilling from my lips as if I had been holding them back for too long. "They shape who we are, but they also give us the chance to grow." I hesitated, searching for the right way to express the tumult of emotions swirling within me. "Every drop of rain, every gust of wind—it's all part of this intricate tapestry of living."

Theo remained silent, his gaze fixed on the horizon where the sky kissed the water, the deep blues blending seamlessly into soft pastel hues. The unspoken words hung between us, heavy yet comforting, like the warmth of a well-worn blanket on a cold night. The quietude was almost palpable, each rustle of leaves and distant call of a loon punctuating our shared solitude.

It felt like we were in our own universe, removed from the world's noise. The storm had left behind not just physical debris but emotional fragments that needed mending. As the lake mirrored the sky's tumultuous emotions, I pondered how easily we could slip back into the chaos, retreating into our shells rather than confronting the vulnerabilities that lay exposed.

"Do you remember the last time it stormed like this?" I asked, nudging him lightly with my shoulder, trying to coax him from his reverie. He turned to me, a small smile creeping across his face, the warmth of it melting the frost that lingered in the air between us.

"Yeah," he said, his voice a gentle rumble, "I was afraid we'd lose the old oak tree by the park."

I chuckled, recalling the image of the gnarled tree, its roots sprawling like ancient fingers gripping the earth. "It stood its ground, though, didn't it? Like us."

"Exactly." His smile widened, eyes lighting up as he recalled the resilience we had both witnessed. "It's funny how something so strong can weather so much."

Our laughter drifted across the lake, mingling with the sounds of nature, weaving a bond between us that felt unbreakable. It was moments like these, in the aftermath of turmoil, that I understood the beauty of vulnerability—how it could connect two souls in ways that mere words often failed to capture.

As I watched the sun begin its descent, painting the sky in hues of orange and pink, I felt a stirring in my chest—a longing to bridge the gap between us. "You know," I ventured, my heart racing, "I used to think that storms were just things to endure. But now..." I trailed off, the weight of my confession pressing against my ribcage.

"But now?" he encouraged, leaning closer, the intensity of his gaze locking onto mine.

"But now, I think they're necessary," I said, my voice steady, despite the tempest of emotions swirling within me. "They strip us bare, exposing our true selves. And in the eye of the storm, we find clarity."

Theo's expression shifted, the shadows deepening as he absorbed my words. "You think that's true?" he asked, his brow furrowing slightly as if wrestling with his thoughts. "Even the hard parts? The moments we'd rather forget?"

I nodded, the memory of my own storms rushing back—those moments when I felt lost in the waves, battling fears that threatened to consume me. "Especially those moments. They teach us the most about who we are. They help us understand our strengths and our limits."

"Is that how you see it?" He seemed genuinely intrigued, a flicker of something deeper passing between us. "I've always thought of storms as just... well, storms."

"Maybe it's time to see them differently," I suggested, my heart racing with the possibility of our connection deepening. "What if we embraced them? Allowed ourselves to be vulnerable, knowing that the sun will shine again?"

The corners of his mouth curled upward, a smile breaking through the shadows as he looked at me. "You have a way of turning a storm into a lesson, don't you?"

"It's a gift and a curse," I replied, mirroring his grin, though I felt a weight in my chest as the gravity of my words sank in. "But it's one I wouldn't trade for anything."

In that moment, as the last rays of sunlight dipped below the horizon, painting the world in twilight hues, I realized that love was not merely about the radiant days basked in sunlight but also about standing firm together in the rain, embracing the tempests as they came, and finding beauty in the chaos.

The world around us seemed to hold its breath, the remnants of the storm still hanging in the air like whispered secrets. The sun dipped lower, casting golden rays that danced upon the water's surface, creating ripples that sparkled like scattered diamonds. I could hardly take my eyes off Theo, his profile silhouetted against the light. The way he squinted at the horizon, lost in thought, revealed layers of complexity that I longed to unravel. I wanted to reach out, to grasp his hand, but uncertainty tightened around me like a storm cloud, thick and heavy.

"It's beautiful," I said, breaking the silence, my voice barely above a whisper. The sound of the water lapping at the shore seemed to echo my thoughts, mirroring the soft pull of my heart toward him. "I don't think I've ever really appreciated moments like this until now."

Theo turned his head, his eyes locking onto mine, and in that instant, the air shifted. "What do you mean?" he asked, a genuine curiosity flickering in his gaze.

I hesitated, searching for the right words to articulate the profound shift I felt within myself. "I guess I mean that we often get caught up in the noise, the chaos of our lives," I replied, my fingers absently tracing the cool stones beneath me. "It takes something like a storm to remind us to pause and breathe, to really see what's around us."

He nodded slowly, absorbing my words. "You're right. Sometimes it's like we're running a race, and we forget to stop and enjoy the scenery."

The corners of my mouth curled upward as I regarded him, a glimmer of hope igniting within me. "Exactly. Maybe we need these storms to force us to slow down, to reconnect with ourselves and each other."

The gentle breeze ruffled his hair, causing a few strands to fall across his forehead. It was an endearing sight, and I felt my heart swell. Moments like this—the quiet exchanges, the shared understanding—were what I craved.

"Speaking of storms," he said, shifting slightly, "what's been brewing inside you? You said you were feeling things more deeply."

I sighed, my gaze drifting to the shimmering lake as I contemplated his question. "It's just..." I paused, the words tangling in my throat. "I think I've spent so much time building walls to protect myself that I've forgotten how to let people in."

His expression softened, and I saw the flicker of empathy in his eyes. "You're not alone in that. I think we all have our defenses."

"I've always believed that vulnerability is a weakness," I admitted, feeling the weight of my confession settle between us. "But now I'm starting to see it differently. There's strength in being open, in allowing ourselves to be seen, even when it's scary."

Theo leaned back on his hands, his body relaxed but his eyes intensely focused on me. "It's scary, but it's also freeing," he replied thoughtfully. "Like shedding a heavy coat in spring, finally feeling the warmth of the sun on your skin."

A soft laugh escaped me, and I met his gaze with newfound intensity. "You have a way of making things sound poetic."

"It's a talent," he said with a playful grin, the teasing glint in his eyes making my stomach flutter. "But seriously, you're onto something. When we allow ourselves to be vulnerable, we're opening the door to deeper connections."

I nodded, feeling the truth of his words resonate within me. "And it's those connections that matter most, right? In the end, it's not about how many people we know but the depth of those relationships."

The silence that followed was charged with unspoken possibilities, the kind that crackled in the air, promising new beginnings. I felt as if we were on the precipice of something significant, a threshold that could lead us into unexplored territory.

Just then, a flock of ducks glided across the water, their soft quacking punctuating the serenity. I watched them with a mix of amusement and admiration. They seemed so carefree, effortlessly navigating the lake, undeterred by the chaos that had preceded their arrival. "Look at them," I remarked, pointing. "They're so in sync with each other. It's like they trust that they'll find their way."

"Maybe that's what we need to do," Theo suggested, his voice soft yet resolute. "Trust that we'll find our way through the storms together."

The weight of his words settled over me like a warm blanket. I wanted to believe that—needed to. "Together," I echoed, the word tasting sweet on my tongue. "That sounds nice."

A comfortable silence enveloped us, the kind that felt like a shared secret, a bond being forged amidst the fading daylight. The sky above us transformed into a canvas of deep oranges and purples, as if nature itself was applauding our newfound understanding.

As the sun dipped lower, I felt an unexpected urge to share more. "You know, I used to think that being strong meant never needing anyone. I prided myself on my independence."

Theo's expression shifted to one of understanding, and I continued, "But I've learned that true strength lies in vulnerability. In allowing someone to see your flaws and still choosing to stand by their side."

"I couldn't agree more," he said, his voice laced with sincerity. "Being strong doesn't mean going it alone. It means having the courage to share your burdens."

I studied his face, the sincerity etched in his features sparking a flicker of hope in my heart. "Do you think we can be that for each other?"

His gaze held mine, a promise lingering in the air between us. "I'd like to think so."

The world around us seemed to hush, as if nature itself was leaning in to listen. My heart raced, not from fear, but from the exhilarating possibility of what lay ahead. The promise of storms weathered together, of hands held tightly amidst the chaos, ignited a fire within me.

As the last remnants of daylight faded, I felt a sense of peace washing over me. The chaos of the world was still out there, but here, in this moment, everything felt right. Together, we were beginning to uncover the beauty hidden beneath the surface, learning to navigate the waters of vulnerability with each other as our guiding stars.

The sun dipped further beneath the horizon, casting an ethereal glow that transformed the landscape into a realm of shadow and light. As twilight deepened, fireflies began to twinkle, their dance mimicking the flicker of hope blooming within me. Each pulse of light seemed to echo the connection I felt with Theo, an unspoken agreement that we were on the brink of something extraordinary. I could sense the weight of our past burdens slowly dissipating, carried away by the gentle breeze that whispered secrets through the trees.

The sounds of the evening wrapped around us, a comforting blanket of chirping crickets and distant rustles, creating a symphony of serenity. I leaned back, letting the warmth of the stones seep into my skin, feeling grounded in this moment as if the earth itself was holding me close. "You ever think about where life takes us?" I asked, the words spilling forth like the water lapping at the shore.

He turned to me, his brow furrowing in contemplation. "All the time. It's like we're on this winding road, and sometimes you can't see where it leads. All you can do is hope it's the right path."

"Hope and maybe a little faith," I added, the irony of the statement hanging in the air. I had spent so long clinging to my own ideas of control that faith felt like a foreign concept, but here, sitting beside him, it began to resonate.

The colors in the sky deepened, morphing from warm pastels to rich indigos, the first stars twinkling into existence like scattered diamonds in an endless sea. I shifted, resting my chin on my knees, the coolness of the stones a stark contrast to the warmth radiating from my heart. "It's funny," I mused, "how a storm can clear the air but also leave you feeling vulnerable."

"Vulnerability isn't weakness, though," he countered, his tone firm yet gentle, a guiding light in the encroaching darkness. "It's an invitation to connect, to let someone see you in your rawest form."

His words washed over me, igniting a flame of understanding. "I've always been the one to put up walls, to stay on the safe side of things. But lately, it feels like those walls are crumbling, and I don't know if I should let them fall or start rebuilding."

"Maybe you don't have to choose," Theo suggested, his voice steady and warm. "What if you let some walls down while keeping others? It's okay to protect yourself, but it's also okay to allow someone in."

I met his gaze, the intensity of his expression stirring something deep within me. "You make it sound so easy."

"It's not," he admitted, a hint of vulnerability creeping into his voice. "But it's worth it. Finding someone who will stand beside you, through the storms and the sunshine—there's nothing better."

As the shadows deepened, I felt the weight of his words settle into my bones. The world around us transformed, and it struck me how much had changed in just a few hours. The storm that had raged earlier had not just stripped away the chaos; it had opened a door to clarity, revealing hidden truths that longed to surface.

The lake, once tumultuous and churning, now lay still, mirroring the calmness that was seeping into my heart. "You know, I used to think that love was just about the grand gestures—the fireworks, the passionate moments. But maybe it's the quiet times like this that matter more," I said, my voice barely above a whisper.

Theo nodded, his gaze softening as he absorbed my words. "The quiet moments are the ones where we really get to know each other. It's not about the show; it's about the connection."

We sat in silence for a while, the air thick with unspoken thoughts, the silence pregnant with possibility. I could feel the cool breeze caressing my skin, stirring the hair on my neck and sending a shiver of excitement down my spine. "What if we allow ourselves to be seen?" I ventured, my heart racing at the thought. "What if we lean into the vulnerability together?"

The corners of his mouth turned up, a smile breaking through the intensity. "I'd like that. It's scary, but it could be beautiful."

"Together?" I asked, locking my gaze onto his.

"Always."

A sense of peace settled over me, filling the spaces that had once been occupied by doubt and fear. I felt lighter, as if the storm had washed away not just the chaos but also the burdens I had been carrying for too long. The connection between us had grown, weaving a tapestry of trust that I had never fully embraced before.

As the stars began to dot the sky like a celestial map, I took a deep breath, savoring the coolness of the evening air. "What's next for us, then?"

Theo tilted his head, contemplating. "I think we take it one day at a time. No pressure, just openness. Let's see where this leads."

The simplicity of his words struck a chord within me, resonating with the truth I had been seeking. I felt an urge to laugh, to dance in the shadows of uncertainty that had once paralyzed me. "One day at a time," I echoed, a smile breaking free. "I can handle that."

And just like that, the weight of the future, the expectation, and the fear began to lift. The moment felt fragile, yet full of promise, a delicate balance of hope and vulnerability. I could feel the universe shifting around us, aligning our paths in ways I had never anticipated.

As the evening deepened, I realized that this was more than a moment; it was the beginning of a journey. The storms had not just passed; they had cleared a path for something beautiful to bloom. The possibilities stretched out before us like the night sky, infinite and inviting.

I turned to Theo, his eyes reflecting the starlight, and for the first time, I felt an undeniable sense of belonging. Together, we were embarking on an adventure—not just through the storms, but through the vibrant, messy, beautiful chaos of life.

And as I nestled closer to him, feeling the warmth radiating from his body, I understood that love wasn't just a fleeting moment or a grand gesture. It was the quiet resolve to weather the storms together, to embrace the uncertainty, and to find beauty in the journey, one day at a time.

Chapter 28: Building Bridges

The sun dipped low on the horizon, casting a golden hue over the snow-capped peaks that stood sentinel over our little town of Evergreen, Colorado. I pushed open the door to my apartment, the familiar creak of the hinges greeting me like an old friend. The scent of pine wafted in from the nearby trees, mingling with the faint aroma of fresh coffee that lingered from earlier in the day. Each step inside was a gentle reminder of the comforting chaos of my life—ski gear strewn across the living room, ski lift tickets stuck haphazardly to the fridge, and the cozy throw blanket crumpled on the couch where I often sprawled after long days on the slopes.

As the warmth of the indoors enveloped me, I sank into the couch, a plush sanctuary against the world outside. The fading light painted the walls with soft pastels, and the flicker of the fireplace began to dance in the corner. I pulled out my phone, scrolling through photos from the season. Each picture told a story—a moment frozen in time: the exhilaration of racing down the slopes, the laughter shared with friends, the breathtaking sunrises that spilled over the mountains like melted butter on warm toast. But alongside those joyful memories, a quiet anxiety began to bubble up within me.

The end of the ski season loomed like a dark cloud threatening rain. What would I do once the lifts stopped turning? Teaching had ignited something in me, a spark I had never anticipated. Yet, the thought of returning to the predictable grind of an office job was suffocating. I wanted to chase the thrill, to seize the day, but how could I balance my newfound love for teaching with the demands of adult life? Just then, a soft knock interrupted my reverie.

It was Theo, his tall frame filling the doorway, snowflakes clinging to his tousled hair. He grinned at me, and my heart did a little flip. There was something about him that felt like home, something that made the world outside fade away. He strolled in, shedding his jacket and boots with an easy grace, as if he belonged here, in my cozy chaos. "Thought you might want some company," he said, his voice warm and inviting.

"Always," I replied, unable to suppress a smile. The weight of my worries lightened in his presence. As we settled into our familiar routine, sharing a steaming mug of hot cocoa—rich, thick, and topped with a swirl of whipped cream—our conversation flowed effortlessly, weaving between the mundane and the extraordinary. I found solace in the way he leaned forward, eyes alight with enthusiasm as he spoke of his own dreams.

"The ski season's ending, but that doesn't mean our passion has to," he said, his tone a mixture of excitement and resolve. "What if we started our own ski school? Just imagine it—a place where we could share what we love with others." The idea hung in the air, charged with possibility, like the first hint of spring after a long winter.

My heart raced at the thought, and a spark of hope ignited within me. "You mean, like, a real ski school?" I asked, barely able to contain my disbelief. "We could teach kids, families—everyone! It could be something special." The more I considered it, the clearer the vision became, painting our future in vibrant strokes. I could see the snow-dusted slopes filled with eager students, laughter echoing in the crisp mountain air as we guided them through their first turns.

"Absolutely," Theo said, his eyes gleaming with determination. "We could blend our teaching styles, make it fun and accessible. We could create a community."

I leaned back, envisioning a world where we could shape the futures of budding skiers, where we could share our passion with others while nurturing our own dreams. It felt like a bridge spanning the uncertain chasm between what was and what could be. The thought thrilled me, igniting a fire in my belly. "What would we call it?" I mused, my mind racing.

"How about 'Evergreen Ski Academy'?" Theo suggested, his voice imbued with the confidence that I wished I felt. "It's got a nice ring to it, don't you think?"

The name rolled off my tongue, sweet and satisfying. "It's perfect. It feels like home," I agreed, the excitement bubbling over. The more we discussed the idea, the more tangible it became—filled with plans for lessons tailored to all skill levels, safety protocols that prioritized fun without fear, and the unique atmosphere that only a small-town ski school could offer.

As the night wore on, we scribbled notes on a napkin, sketching out ideas and laughing at our own enthusiasm. We talked late into the evening, the flames in the fireplace crackling as if cheering us on. Each suggestion and each laugh built a solid foundation, and with every passing moment, I felt the weight of my uncertainties begin to lift.

Somewhere in the back of my mind, the ghosts of self-doubt lingered, whispering that it might be too much, too soon. But with Theo beside me, the fears felt less daunting. His belief in this dream sparked a resilience within me, urging me to imagine the possibility of a life where passion and purpose intertwined seamlessly.

The stars outside twinkled like a million tiny lights, reflecting the dreams that had begun to take shape in the cozy glow of my apartment. We were building something together, a bridge toward a shared future, and it felt like the most exhilarating journey of all.

The next morning unfolded like a scene from a cherished memory, the sunlight spilling through the window and pooling on the hardwood floor. I awoke to the sound of birds chirping outside, their melodies a joyful reminder of life bustling beyond my walls. The sweet scent of brewed coffee beckoned from the kitchen, a warm invitation that coaxed me out of the blankets' embrace. As I shuffled towards the aroma, I could already picture Theo leaning against the counter, mug in hand, his easy smile brightening the space around him.

And there he was, clad in his favorite flannel shirt, the colors vibrant against the pale walls, as he expertly frothed milk for his morning coffee. The kitchen felt alive, infused with laughter and the warmth of our shared dreams. I wrapped my fingers around a steaming mug, feeling the heat seep into my palms and rise to greet my face. "Good morning, sunshine," he said, eyes sparkling with mischief. "Ready to conquer the world of ski schools today?"

"Ready as I'll ever be," I replied, taking a sip and savoring the creamy sweetness. The taste was as comforting as the conversation that flowed easily between us, bouncing from the technicalities of our budding business to the dreams of what our future might hold. The world felt full of possibilities, vibrant like the colors of a sunset melting into the horizon.

We dove into the logistics, sketching out plans on a worn notebook that had seen better days. It was filled with doodles and half-formed ideas, a chaotic tapestry of our hopes and aspirations. "We need to think about instructors," Theo suggested, his brow furrowing in concentration. "We'll want people who can share our vision, who understand what it means to teach with passion."

I nodded, imagining a crew of enthusiastic instructors, each bringing their unique flair and energy to the slopes. "We could host workshops for them," I proposed, my excitement bubbling over. "Train them in our methods, make sure everyone's on the same page. I want it to feel like a community."

He leaned in closer, a glint of admiration dancing in his eyes. "Exactly! And we can have themed days for the students—like 'Freestyle Fridays' or 'Family Fun Weekends.' We'll make it an experience, not just lessons."

Ideas flowed like a river, each thought sharpening our vision, enhancing the image of Evergreen Ski Academy in our minds. As we planned, the world outside transformed, the mountains standing proud against the clear blue sky. They were our backdrop, solid and unwavering, reminding me of the grounding reality of this dream.

A few hours later, with plans taking shape, we decided to take a break and stretch our legs. The snow had turned into a soft, slushy mess, the kind that made the world feel new and playful. We grabbed our jackets and headed out, laughter spilling into the crisp air as we made our way to the nearby trails.

The path crunched underfoot, each step a reminder of winter's tenacity, even as spring whispered promises of warmer days ahead. The trees, heavy with melting snow, looked like they were shedding their winter coats, their branches reaching out in eager anticipation. I breathed in deeply, the scent of damp earth mingling with the sweetness of pine.

Theo walked beside me, hands shoved deep into his pockets, his presence a comforting weight. We wandered, exchanging stories and playful banter, our voices carrying over the whispers of nature. Each moment felt suspended in time, a sweet escape from the looming responsibilities of adulthood. It was during these simple interactions that I felt most alive, the thrill of potential igniting a fire in my heart.

As we reached a clearing, we paused, gazing out over the valley that spread before us like a patchwork quilt of greens and browns. The sky above was a brilliant blue, an artist's palette that inspired a sense of wonder. "This is what we're fighting for," Theo said quietly, his voice almost reverent. "This beauty, this freedom. We want to share it."

I turned to him, the intensity of his gaze igniting a spark within me. "We're not just building a ski school," I replied, my heart racing. "We're creating a community, a place where people can come together, learn, and grow. It's about more than just skiing."

His smile widened, the kind that melted away any remaining doubt. "Exactly. It's about connections, experiences, and memories.

We'll teach skills that go beyond the slopes—confidence, teamwork, and resilience."

We lingered in that moment, the air thick with promise and possibility. The challenges of running a business felt like distant clouds, obscured by the warmth of our shared dreams. We had a vision, a purpose that gave meaning to the risk we were willing to take.

As we made our way back, the conversation shifted to our next steps. "We should look into permits and local regulations," Theo suggested, his tone practical, yet laced with excitement. "We want everything to be legit from the start."

"Right," I agreed, enthusiasm bubbling over. "And we can start reaching out to local schools, see if they'd be interested in field trips or group lessons. We need to build our network now."

With every new idea, our excitement grew, feeding off each other's energy like a bonfire. The world ahead felt brighter, painted with the vibrant colors of hope and ambition. The thought of our ski school was no longer a distant dream but a burgeoning reality, one that we were shaping together.

That night, as the stars blinked awake in the velvet sky, I reflected on the day. Our laughter and ideas floated through my mind like fireflies in the dark, illuminating the path ahead. I felt a sense of purpose settling deep within me, a quiet reassurance that this was just the beginning. With Theo by my side, we were ready to build something extraordinary—a bridge to a future where passion and possibility would intertwine, creating a life that was undeniably our own.

The weeks that followed our exhilarating brainstorm transformed into a flurry of activity, each day a new puzzle piece in the grand picture of Evergreen Ski Academy. The scent of fresh paint and wood shavings filled the air as we spent hours at the local community center, where our makeshift office quickly became a hub of creativity and ambition. I found myself immersed in a world where spreadsheets and scheduling met adrenaline and snowflakes, each detail bringing us closer to our dream.

Our first order of business was securing a location. We envisioned a cozy lodge where families could gather, a place alive with the chatter of excited children and the soothing crackle of a fireplace. One Saturday afternoon, we huddled in Theo's car, bundled in layers against the chilly breeze, scanning the landscape for a suitable site. The mountains loomed majestically in the distance, their snowy peaks glistening in the sunlight, as if beckoning us to claim our spot among them.

"There! That one," Theo exclaimed, pointing to a charming log cabin nestled at the foot of a gentle slope. Its rustic charm, complete with weathered wood and inviting porch swings, seemed to whisper promises of warmth and community. As we parked, a gust of wind whipped through the trees, sending a shower of soft snowflakes fluttering around us like confetti celebrating our bold endeavor.

Stepping inside, we were greeted by a rich tapestry of natural wood and inviting warmth. The large windows framed views of the mountain that felt like an artist's canvas. It was a blank slate begging for our vision. We stood there, side by side, as if the space held the very essence of our hopes. "This is it," I breathed, barely able to contain my excitement. "I can already see the lessons happening right here."

Theo grinned, his enthusiasm infectious. "Imagine families gathering here for lessons, sipping hot chocolate while they wait. We could create a little café vibe—maybe serve homemade pastries."

The more we envisioned, the more alive the space became in our minds. We pictured bulletin boards filled with photos of smiling students, their beaming faces capturing the joy of skiing for the first time. The thought of creating a safe haven for skiers of all ages, where fear melted away like snow in the sun, sent a thrill racing through me.

With our dream location identified, the next step was navigating the labyrinth of permits and regulations that lay ahead. It felt daunting, a mountain of paperwork to scale, but we tackled it together, transforming an intimidating task into an adventure. I learned quickly that my knack for organization came in handy, with color-coded folders and detailed timelines littering the tables, each marking a milestone on our path to establishing the academy.

Amidst the chaos of planning, we began to spread the word about our vision, drawing interest from locals eager for something new in their community. We attended town meetings, where we passionately pitched our concept, explaining how our school would foster not just skiing skills but a sense of belonging and adventure. "We want this to be a place where families can come together, where friendships are forged on the slopes," I declared one evening, my voice steady despite the butterflies in my stomach.

To my delight, the response was overwhelmingly positive. Word began to spread like wildfire, with neighbors sharing our vision and rallying around us. Even the local ski shop offered to collaborate, helping us find gear for our future students.

As we moved closer to launching, the excitement reached a fever pitch. One crisp Saturday morning, I awoke to find a fresh blanket of snow adorning the landscape, transforming Evergreen into a winter wonderland. It was as if nature herself was celebrating our journey. I bundled up and headed to the slopes, eager to embrace the invigorating chill.

The snow crunched beneath my boots as I navigated the familiar trails, the quiet beauty of the mountains reminding me of why I had fallen in love with skiing in the first place. The crisp air filled my lungs with each exhilarating breath, and I couldn't help but imagine our future students carving their paths on these very slopes. I could almost hear their laughter echoing through the trees.

That afternoon, we gathered with a few local skiers, sharing our vision and inviting them to participate in the first trial lessons. Their excitement mirrored my own as we gathered at the lodge, a small group with an enormous dream. Each participant brought a unique energy, creating a tapestry of camaraderie and eagerness.

Theo stood at the forefront, exuding confidence as he demonstrated basic techniques, his voice rising above the chatter like a rallying cry. I joined him, enthusiasm bubbling over as I guided a young girl who clutched her ski poles tightly, her eyes wide with a mixture of fear and exhilaration. "Just breathe," I encouraged, kneeling beside her. "You're stronger than you think. Feel the snow beneath you; let it support you."

With each lesson, I watched as fears dissolved into laughter, hesitations melted into courage. The joy of teaching filled my heart, amplifying my resolve. This was what we had dreamed of—a community of learners, each person unlocking their potential with each turn down the mountain.

As the sun dipped below the horizon, painting the sky in hues of orange and pink, we gathered outside the lodge, basking in the glow of our shared accomplishment. We toasted with mugs of steaming hot cocoa, the sweet warmth spreading through us like the joy of shared success. "To Evergreen Ski Academy," Theo declared, raising his mug, his eyes shining with a mix of mischief and pride. "May it be the start of something extraordinary."

The night was alive with laughter, the promise of tomorrow hanging in the air like the sparkling stars above. It was a celebration not just of our efforts but of the connections we had forged—between friends, between dreams, and between the slopes and our hearts. In that moment, I felt an unwavering certainty that we were building more than a ski school; we were constructing a bridge to a vibrant community filled with adventure, laughter, and an unquenchable thirst for life.

Chapter 29: An Unexpected Surprise

Wandering through the cluttered aisles of the antique shop, I inhaled the mingled scents of dust and varnish, an olfactory tapestry woven over decades. The walls, lined with shelves of faded knick-knacks, echoed stories of lives long gone. Each trinket was a whisper from the past, begging to be noticed, yet I found myself drawn to an unassuming corner where a half-torn velvet curtain swayed gently, as if it held secrets of its own.

As I pushed aside the curtain, I discovered a treasure trove of forgotten relics. Old typewriters with keys like blackened teeth, tarnished silver frames holding memories in faded photographs, and ornate jewelry boxes that creaked like old bones. It felt as if I had stepped into a different era, a sanctuary for lost memories waiting to be reclaimed. I caressed a delicate locket, imagining the secrets it once held, but my fingers soon found their way to a dusty box perched on a high shelf, almost as if it were trying to hide from the world.

I hoisted myself up, the wooden step creaking beneath my weight, and when I opened the box, a collection of photographs lay nestled within. They were black and white, aged with time but bursting with life. My heart fluttered as I flipped through them, each image revealing moments frozen in time, capturing laughter, tears, and the simple joys of life. Then, one photograph caught my eye—a breathtaking ski resort nestled amidst snow-draped mountains, a scene that seemed to pulse with warmth and camaraderie despite the chill of winter.

The resort's vibrant ski slopes gleamed in the sunlight, the glint of snow contrasting beautifully with the evergreen trees dotting the landscape. A group of people, bundled in colorful winter attire, laughed as they tumbled into fluffy snowdrifts, their joy palpable even in two dimensions. I could almost hear the echoes of their laughter and the whoosh of skis carving through the powder. There was something about this image that tugged at my heartstrings, igniting a longing for the warmth of connection and the thrill of adventure.

I purchased the photograph with a sudden surge of urgency, my fingers brushing against the cool cash register as I paid the shopkeeper. With it cradled in my arms, I made my way to the coffee shop next door, eager to show Theo what I had found. The bell above the door chimed, announcing my entrance into the cozy café, where the aroma of roasted coffee beans mingled with the sweet scent of pastries.

Seated at a small wooden table, I unfolded the photograph, my heart racing with anticipation. Theo, with his tousled dark hair and those impossibly warm brown eyes that seemed to read my soul, leaned forward, curiosity dancing on his features. As he studied the image, a flicker of recognition passed over his face, followed by a shadow that clouded his expression.

"This place," he began slowly, his voice tinged with nostalgia, "this is where my family used to come every winter." The words hung in the air, heavy with unspoken memories. I felt my heart drop as I watched the light in his eyes dim, replaced by a distant gaze that seemed to reach into a painful past.

"We spent our happiest moments here," he continued, his tone growing wistful, the corners of his mouth turning down. "Skiing down those slopes, laughing around the fire at night, my parents... they were so alive then."

The photograph now felt like a bridge between our lives, a shared connection that tethered us together in ways I had never anticipated. The joy of his memories clashed violently with the sorrow that swept over him, and I wished desperately to ease the ache of loss that was etched into his every word.

"Before the accident," he added, the finality of his statement sending a chill through the warm café. I reached out, placing my hand over his, feeling the warmth of his skin against mine.

"I'm so sorry, Theo," I whispered, my heart breaking for the pain that lingered in his memories. I could almost see the past unfolding before me, a tapestry of moments both beautiful and tragic. It was as if the photograph had unlocked a door to a world I had never known, revealing the fragments of his childhood and the family that had shaped him.

"Thanks," he murmured, a soft smile breaking through the shadows. "It's just... I didn't expect this. I've always wanted to take you there." The idea danced between us, a flicker of hope emerging from the sorrow. I could see his wheels turning, the hope rekindling a spark of adventure.

"Let's go," I said impulsively, feeling a surge of excitement. "Let's find that place together." His eyes widened with surprise, and for a moment, the café faded away, leaving only the two of us enveloped in possibilities. The weight of our pasts, both light and heavy, seemed to shift, allowing space for something new to blossom between us.

As he considered my proposal, a smile broke across his face, lighting up his features. "I'd love that."

In that moment, the air felt electric with unspoken promises and the thrill of adventure. Our lives, once shaped by sorrow, were now intertwining in a way that felt fresh and alive. With each heartbeat, I realized how much I longed for him, for us, and for the life we could build together amidst the echoes of our pasts.

The days following our discovery drifted like the first flakes of winter, slow and deliberate, each one layering new experiences over the foundation of our shared past. The anticipation of visiting the ski resort shimmered in the air around us, transforming mundane moments into something imbued with a sense of possibility. Every time I caught Theo's eye, a flicker of excitement passed between us, and my heart would skip in rhythm with the anticipation building within me.

Our evenings became filled with planning, discussions of packing lists and routes, accompanied by the soundtrack of our laughter and playful banter. I found myself reveling in the mundane—deciding which boots would be warm enough for snow, what snacks to stash in our bags, and how many layers I would need to prevent the icy tendrils of winter from seeping through. Each decision, however trivial, felt monumental as it weaved together our lives, stitching us closer like the knitted scarves we had draped around our necks that uncharacteristically chilly autumn.

On the eve of our departure, the atmosphere in my small apartment was charged with an infectious energy. I was a whirlwind of motion, running through my last-minute checklist. As I rummaged through my closet, I unearthed my long-forgotten ski gear, its fabric stiff with neglect. Memories of previous trips flooded my mind—gliding down the mountainside, wind whipping through my hair, laughter echoing through the crisp air as friends fell into snowdrifts. I could almost hear the distant sound of clinking mugs and cheerful chatter from the lodge, where the fireplace crackled and people gathered, warmth radiating from both the flames and the camaraderie.

"Do you have everything?" Theo's voice broke through my reverie, grounding me in the moment. He leaned against the doorframe, arms crossed, a smirk playing on his lips as he watched me flit about like a caffeinated squirrel. His presence filled the room with warmth, even as the autumn chill seeped in through the cracked window.

"Of course! Just a few last touches," I replied, spinning around to face him, my arms full of mismatched socks and hand-knit mittens. The sight made me laugh—a chaotic array of colors that barely matched, yet somehow seemed to express the vibrancy of the adventure ahead.

"Right. Because everyone needs six pairs of socks for a weekend trip." He raised an eyebrow, the playful glint in his eyes undeniable.

"You can never be too prepared," I shot back, sticking my tongue out in mock defiance, the absurdity of my predicament not lost on either of us.

In that moment, the nerves that had been knotting my stomach all day began to unravel. With each quip, the weight of our pasts, the tragedy that had woven itself into the fabric of Theo's memories, seemed to lift slightly. It felt as if we were standing on the precipice of something beautiful, like the first rays of dawn chasing away the shadows of night.

We set out early the next morning, the world outside bathed in a soft, golden glow that hinted at the promise of a new adventure. The drive was filled with a blend of music and conversation, the kind that stretched comfortably over miles like a well-loved blanket. We took turns picking songs, the air thick with nostalgia as we reminisced about our favorite tunes from high school, belting out lyrics that were half-remembered but felt as if they were etched into our very beings.

The landscape shifted as we climbed higher into the mountains, the trees transforming from sturdy pines to delicate spruces, their branches heavy with a fresh coat of snow. It felt surreal, as if we had entered a postcard, every turn unveiling another breathtaking view. I found myself glued to the window, my breath catching at the beauty unfolding around us—the sun glistening off the untouched snow, casting diamonds over the terrain that seemed to stretch endlessly before us.

As we approached the resort, a giddy excitement swirled within me. It was everything I had imagined and more—an expansive lodge nestled against the mountainside, its wooden beams and stone façade exuding a rustic charm that felt like a warm embrace. The gentle hum of laughter and conversation floated through the air, wrapping around us as we stepped inside.

"Welcome to my childhood," Theo murmured, his voice barely audible over the lively chatter. I could see the memories flicker across his face—scenes painted in vibrant colors that only he could perceive. I wanted to reach out, to bridge the gap between his past and our present, to help him weave the two together into something beautiful.

The scent of pine mingled with the rich aroma of hot chocolate, pulling us deeper into the lodge. We made our way to the main area, where a roaring fireplace danced at the center, surrounded by plush seating that invited relaxation. Theo's face lit up as he spotted an old-fashioned ski lift poster hanging on the wall. "I remember this!" he exclaimed, pointing animatedly. "We used to argue over who got to choose the slope each day."

"I can't wait to see your skills," I teased, nudging him playfully.

We spent the afternoon exploring the resort, sipping cocoa and laughing over tales of mishaps and triumphs on the slopes. Each story seemed to weave a tighter bond between us, stitching together fragments of our lives into a tapestry rich with shared experiences.

Later, as evening descended and the sky transformed into a canvas of deep purples and blues, we settled in front of the fire, the warmth of the flames enveloping us. Theo's gaze drifted to the photograph we had found, resting on the table between us, its faded edges glowing softly in the flickering light.

"I can't believe we're here," he said, his voice laced with wonder. "It feels like a dream."

I smiled, my heart swelling with affection for the man beside me, for the moments we were creating together. In that instant, I understood that this was more than just a trip to a ski resort; it was a journey into the heart of who we were, an exploration of the roads we had traveled, and the paths we were yet to forge together.

As the embers crackled and popped in the fireplace, casting playful shadows on the walls of the lodge, I felt a sense of belonging settle over me, like a warm blanket pulled tight against the cold outside. The atmosphere was electric with the laughter of other guests and the melodic chatter that filled the air, punctuated by the clinking of mugs and the unmistakable aroma of something delicious wafting from the kitchen. I could hardly believe how quickly we had transformed from two people navigating the murky waters of our pasts to this—two adventurers stepping into a shared future that felt impossibly bright.

"Ready to hit the slopes tomorrow?" Theo's voice broke through my reverie, his eyes dancing with mischief. The challenge hung between us like a ripe fruit, ready to be plucked.

"Absolutely!" I replied, my excitement bubbling over. I could already envision the rush of cold air against my face, the exhilaration of racing down the mountain, and the thrill of laughter echoing against the serene backdrop of snow-capped peaks.

Theo leaned closer, his warmth radiating against the chill in the air. "You know, I might have a few tricks up my sleeve," he teased, his lips curving into a knowing smile that sent butterflies fluttering in my stomach. I had a feeling he was remembering some childhood exploits on those very slopes, and I couldn't help but wonder what kind of skier he had been.

"Tricks? I'll be the judge of that," I replied, throwing a playful wink in his direction. The banter felt effortless, weaving us closer together as the night deepened and the fire flickered low.

As the hours slipped by, we shared stories of our childhoods—his filled with ski vacations and familial warmth, mine with spontaneous road trips and impromptu camping adventures that left my parents exasperated but ultimately proud of my adventurous spirit. It was incredible how each story unspooled threads of our lives, creating a tapestry that was uniquely ours.

The evening wore on, the room gradually emptying until only a few scattered guests remained, and our laughter became a gentle hum in the quiet. In the soft glow of the firelight, Theo's expression shifted, his gaze momentarily distant, as if he was traversing the landscape of memories that had brought him to this moment.

"Do you ever think about what could have been?" he asked, his voice barely above a whisper.

I studied him, searching for the right words. "I think about it a lot, actually," I confessed, my heart racing at the vulnerability we had both laid bare. "But I also believe that what's ahead of us can be just as beautiful, if not more so. Sometimes the past is just a stepping stone to something greater."

He nodded, a flicker of understanding in his eyes. "I like that. It feels... hopeful."

With that simple exchange, we sealed an unspoken pact between us, a commitment to embrace whatever lay ahead with open hearts and eager spirits.

The next morning, the sun rose like a golden coin tossed into the sky, illuminating the snow-covered landscape in hues of pink and orange. It was breathtaking, as if the world had been dipped in a painter's palette. We gathered our gear, the thrill of adventure coursing through our veins.

Outside, the air was crisp and invigorating, each breath feeling like a promise of new experiences. We made our way to the slopes, the crunch of snow beneath our boots a delightful prelude to the day ahead. As we reached the lift, the towering mountains loomed above us, majestic and imposing, yet welcoming, inviting us to conquer their heights.

"I'll race you to the top!" Theo shouted, already bounding toward the lift as if the mountains themselves were calling to him.

"Hey, no fair! You have longer legs!" I called after him, laughing as I hurried to catch up.

The ride up the lift was an exhilarating experience, the wind whipping through our hair as we ascended higher. I stole glances at Theo, the way his eyes sparkled with anticipation, the way his laughter rang out like a bell against the silence of the snow-draped mountains. In that moment, I realized just how much I adored him—not just for the adventures we shared, but for the way he seemed to embrace life with a childlike wonder that was utterly infectious.

When we reached the summit, I took a deep breath, the panoramic view taking my breath away. It was a postcard scene, the world unfolding in front of us like a magical dream. I couldn't help but feel small yet alive, a tiny speck in this vast, beautiful world.

"Ready?" Theo's voice pulled me from my reverie.

"Ready!" I shouted, my heart racing as we strapped our skis on, anticipation crackling in the air like static electricity.

The moment I pushed off the edge, the world blurred around me—the rush of cold air, the sharp sound of skis slicing through snow, the exhilaration coursing through my veins. I could hear Theo laughing behind me, the sound invigorating and encouraging. As I sped down the slope, I felt free, my spirit soaring higher than the mountains themselves.

We zigzagged down the trail, the world around us a blur of white and blue. I felt like I was flying, every turn igniting a spark of joy that brightened my heart. Each time I glanced back, I could see Theo effortlessly maneuvering through the snow, his laughter echoing like a melody that kept me moving forward.

As we reached the bottom, breathless and exhilarated, we came to a stop beside each other, hearts pounding in rhythm. "That was amazing!" I exclaimed, a wide grin splitting my face.

"Not too shabby for a beginner!" he teased, nudging me playfully.

We took a break, sipping steaming mugs of cocoa at a quaint little chalet nestled at the base of the slopes. The sun hung low in the sky, casting a golden glow over the mountains and bathing everything in a warm light. I watched as Theo animatedly recounted his most embarrassing moments on the slopes, his gestures large and exaggerated, each story punctuated by fits of laughter that made my heart swell.

"Okay, but my turn!" I interjected, eager to share my own stories of ski mishaps, clumsy falls, and near-misses that had turned into lasting memories.

As we exchanged tales, something shifted between us, the air charged with unspoken feelings and possibilities. Every laugh, every shared glance, ignited a spark of connection that was undeniable. With each story, we peeled back the layers of ourselves, revealing our vulnerabilities and dreams, intertwining our lives even further.

The day wore on, and as the sun dipped below the horizon, painting the sky in hues of purple and gold, I felt an overwhelming sense of gratitude. The past might have shaped us, but it was the present that held the promise of what we could become. Together, we were creating a future bright with hope, one where laughter and adventure intertwined with the love that was quietly blossoming between us, like the first flowers pushing through the winter snow, determined to thrive.

Milton Keynes UK
Ingram Content Group UK Ltd.
UKHW041834121024
449535UK00001B/68